AND THE GIRL
NEXT DOOR

ALIX JAMES

Cover Design by GetCovers.com
Cover Image Licensed by Period Images
Background image licensed by Shutterstock

Blog and Website: https://alixjames.com/
Newsletter: https://subscribepage.io/alix-james
Book Bub: https://www.bookbub.com/authors/alix-james
Facebook: https://www.facebook.com/ShortSweetNovellas
Twitter: https://twitter.com/N_Clarkston
Amazon: https://www.amazon.com/stores/Alix-James/author/B07Z1BWFF3
Austen Variations: http://austenvariations.com/

For all my Author friends! You keep me inspired.

CONTENTS

PROLOGUE

Pemberley, Derbyshire
1804

"With all due respect, Mr. Darcy, what you propose could create.. difficulties."

Mr. Edward Gardiner scanned the document presented him by the gentleman once more, his quill hovering over one line in particular. He removed his spectacles and looked across the desk at its owner—a man in his early fifties with greying temples and a grave expression. "*A single power loom can replace as many as a hundred skilled weavers and be operated by a handful of unskilled laborers.*' Sir, that is..."

Mr. Darcy sat back in his chair. "It will displease the weaver's guild. Yes, I know. But there is no help for progress, Gardiner. What I want to know is the financial outlay."

"Well." Gardiner shook his head and replaced his spectacles to look over the proposal once more. "Your idea is intriguing. You have already secured the backing of other suppliers?"

Mr. Darcy nodded. "Pemberley's flocks alone produce enough wool to meet approximately a quarter the initial demand, according to my figures, and my brother-in-law, Lord Matlock, can produce twice as much. It will be no trouble securing the wool. So, you see, Gardiner, I can build a woolen mill here on the river, provide a steady income for fifty or sixty families and a secure future for Pemberley, or I can sit back and watch another do it. One who, I might add, may have fewer scruples than I."

Mr. Gardiner nodded slowly as he touched his quill over each line. "It appears you are right. I see nothing wrong with your estimates, but I would like to take this to a friend in London to have him examine it for anything we might have overlooked."

Mr. Darcy stood from his desk, signaling the end of the interview. "Of course, Gardiner. You have always advised me well in matters of business, and I expect no different on this occasion."

Mr. Gardiner folded the leather portfolio and held his breath. "On that matter, sir, I must confess—I am giving up my position." He met the gentleman's eyes, then looked down again. "I was married last year, sir."

"Yes, I recall. One of our local beauties... Miss Fairbanks, was it not? Lovely girl."

"Indeed." Gardiner's face glowed with pleasure. "With my marriage came certain... advantages. I have been operating a small import business on the side for some years, and now I shall be able to expand and purchase my own warehouse."

Mr. Darcy's stern features softened. "It could not happen to a more deserving man. I am pleased for you, Gardiner. But I do hope you can refer another financial adviser to me... Ah, Fitzwilliam. Just a moment, Gardiner."

Mr. Darcy stepped from around his desk and extended a hand toward the door. "Did you send for them?"

Gardiner turned to see a young man of probably twenty, equal in height to the senior Darcy but lacking the father's commanding presence and ease. Lanky and thin, with a face that looked fresh from the schoolroom, the youth glanced at Gardiner before inclining his head to his father. "Yes, Father. They are in the blue drawing room."

"Very good." Darcy looked back to Gardiner, his expression growing somber. "I do not believe I have ever introduced you to my son and heir, Fitzwilliam. Fitzwilliam, this is Mr. Gardiner from London."

The young man required no further introduction. He bowed immediately. "Mr. Gardiner."

"Sir." Gardiner bowed in reply. "Well, Mr. Darcy. I shall be on my way, then, and I—"

"Sir, if I may impose on you, there is one other matter which, I am afraid, is more pressing even than the business for which I summoned you." Darcy gave his son a nod, dismissing the young man, and closed the door.

"Oh? Then I hope I can be of service."

"So do I." Darcy sighed heavily. "I have a ward—a young lady who has been in my care since she was little more than a babe. She is now a rather precocious thirteen."

"I did not know that, sir. Perhaps that is the young lady I saw at archery in the gardens when I arrived? She appeared to be besting her companion—I believe it was your younger son?"

Darcy gave a thin smile. "Yes, Elizabeth Smith. She and my son George are... close."

"I see, sir." Then, his stomach lurched when he realized what the name "Smith" probably meant. "Oh. I *see*. You, ah... you have a problem, then, do you?"

Darcy's features settled into a scowl. "You would not be the first to assume *that*, but I assure you, that is not the difficulty. She is not my natural daughter, though some claim to see a resemblance. And I am exceedingly fond of her—so much so that I have put off doing what must be done for far too long. However, her presence here is becoming more and more... problematic."

"What are you asking, sir?"

Darcy sighed and gestured for Gardiner to follow him. They walked through the long corridors, passing a dozen of Pemberley's servants and as many doors on the way. Finally, they stopped before an opened pair of double doors, and Darcy paused. "I doubt they will even notice us."

Gardiner looked into the room and saw a youth of approximately fifteen or sixteen lounging on a thick Persian rug and laughing as his companion, the young lady, aimed a grape at his mouth with a catapult made of a spoon and a spool of thread. "You missed, Lizzy!" he crowed. "I win the bet, so it's my turn to pi—" He broke off with a series of coughs.

The girl, Elizabeth, shot to her feet, whooping and twirling around. "I got you that time! Don't you know to close your mouth instead of bragging, George? Now, *I* get to pick what we do this afternoon, and I want to play chess."

"Chess?" The lad flopped back on the floor with a dramatic sigh. "On a sunny afternoon? I wanted to ride around the lake."

"You know I can't keep up with you on horseback. You'll get on that fast hunter of yours and scare the wits out of me. But I do love watching you squirm when I make you sit still at the chess table. A deal's a deal, and you lost, George."

Mr. Darcy softly drew the doors closed and turned to Gardiner. "They are inseparable, that pair."

Gardiner felt a squeeze in his chest. "And you cannot let the situation become a permanent one, is that the trouble?"

Darcy tilted his head with raised brows and beckoned Gardiner back to his study. Once inside, he drew out a thick portfolio from his desk. "You have guessed the situation rightly. Had she been born on the right side of the blanket, nothing would make me prouder than to accept Elizabeth as my daughter-in-law. She is clever, cheerful, of good character, and would make an able partner for even the most discerning of men. She also has a trust in her name that will see her established wherever she marries, but it cannot be in... certain circles."

"I am afraid I do not understand, sir."

Darcy opened the portfolio and laid it on the desk. "Her origin is known to only two people—her natural parent and me, and it must remain that way. However, as Elizabeth matures, the family resemblance is becoming too striking to ignore. If she were seen, discovered, introduced to the wrong people, it could be ruinous for more than just her. Do you understand, Gardiner?"

He shook his head. "I suppose, but what am *I* to do on the occasion?"

"You have advised me for years. I know you to be a man of unimpeachable character, and what's more, your... your status in society would protect her from discovery."

"You want *me* to become her guardian?"

Darcy raised his brows. "I would make it worth your while."

"Well... sir, it is not a matter of the money. I can hardly offer such a young lady a good home just now. I am always gone, and my wife, while she would adore a daughter, is... ah..."

"I see. If Mrs. Gardiner is already *enceinte* and cannot often count on your assistance, it is a deal to ask."

"Just a moment..." Gardiner held up a finger. "How old did you say she was?"

"Thirteen in April."

"I do have four nieces in Hertfordshire. One is fourteen and too often alone, for her three younger sisters do not share her interests and disposition. It might prove profitable for Jane to have such a girl as Elizabeth come to live with them."

"Is the situation an honorable one?"

"In every way. My brother-in-law, Thomas Bennet, is a gentleman. An idle one, but he is a kind man who... egad, he would like nothing more than to sharpen the young lady's skills at chess. I think the family might suit her, sir. And if you are prepared to... ah... assist..."

"I will add something to the dowries of Bennet's other daughters if he can provide a kind and loving home for Elizabeth. I cannot see any harm befall her, Gardiner."

"If Bennet does take her in, I will still view her well-being as my personal responsibility," he vowed.

Darcy nodded wearily. "Good. For there is another concern." He placed a hand over his heart and heaved a low sigh. "My doctor fears that one more bad spell such as I had last winter could turn very grave indeed. I cannot lay this responsibility on Fitzwilliam. He does not know the truth, nor does he have the heart to do what I must to protect them all... Pray, Gardiner, will you look after her? I must have your word."

Edward Gardiner cast an eye over the documents Darcy had spread before him, but he never read the contents. He just swallowed and nodded. "I will look after her like a father, sir. Or..." he chuckled. "At least a very protective uncle."

ONE

Darcy
Derbyshire, 1811

"**D**ARCY, YOU MUST UNDERSTAND. I do wish to support you in this matter, but it is delicate."

My uncle, the earl of Matlock, paced my study with his hands clasped behind his back. "The laborers have employed violence to reach their ends. One cannot lightly endorse that."

I laced my fingers together on the desk. "Indeed, but would any have heeded them otherwise? They've no other method of redress. I do not condone violence at the mill any more than you do, but I do believe men such as we have a duty to see fair laws enacted. I would not have Parliament descending upon my door in ten years' time, demanding untenable measures simply because we did not act sooner and more rationally."

"What do you intend to do? Tear out the power looms? Or pay them all a hundred times what they're worth?"

"I did not say I had a solution. My father had that mill built on the river with the hope of providing work to families. He saw this great shift coming long before it did—families forced from the farms to the cities where there is dismal housing, poor availability of food. He was hoping that a mill in the country could prevent some of those youths from having to remove to Manchester."

"Aye, and he did not account for the trouble of getting enough labor to keep it running."

"He did. But he was thinking of a time in the future, when the population will be more abundant here. Of building something bigger than just the woolen mill."

Matlock scoffed, shaking his head as he wandered to the window to peer out. "Preposterous, Darcy. What would you do, try to house and employ an entire town?"

I lifted my shoulders. "If needs be. He saw that as a possible end."

"But why? I never understood this. Oh, I supported him, as I support you, but Pemberley is not hard up for money. You have your rents and your investments. Managing this alone is enough to keep a man occupied, so I know you are not bored. Why would you trouble yourself with the business?"

I pulled back from my desk and rose to my feet, crossing the room to look out the same window. "Left to my own devices, I doubt I would have. But my father started this, and I mean to see it carried through."

"Your father started a great many things," Matlock reminded me. "Do you intend to do that with all of them?"

I crossed my arms and raised my brow. "You are speaking of something specific, I believe?"

My uncle snorted. "Do I need to? But perhaps, yes, I will choose something specific. What of George? Do you truly intend to permit him to sail to America and cultivate tobacco?"

I chortled and shook my head. "George has not sufficient ambition for such an endeavor. He only said that to gain attention, and so far, it has worked. He has a dozen investors already, willing to back him, and he never even intends to sail."

"Then, why, Darcy? Why would he breed interest in something he has not the inclination to carry through?"

"Because he is George." I sighed and slowly paced the floor, measuring my footsteps by the loops and whorls in the rug design. "He has been like that since he was a child, and yet, no one has ever checked him. He could say he meant to plant a city on the moon or toss it all aside to become a wandering cynic, and still, he would find people to pledge him their help. It is simply his way."

"It is a mercy he is at least a man of good principle, else he would be a dangerous rogue, indeed."

I stopped before the portrait my father had left hanging on the wall of his study—a likeness captured some fifteen years earlier, of three children and a spaniel dog—and let go a deep sigh. "You think he has good principles, do you?" I mused softly.

My uncle turned to follow me. "I never heard otherwise. Has he done something to disgrace the Darcy name?"

A frown grew on my face, and I shook my head slowly. "It is not so much that he has disgraced his name... more that he has done nothing to honor it." I turned around. "I will own the truth—I am becoming concerned about his utter lack of direction. First, he meant to study the law, then for the church, then he meant to purchase a commission and serve alongside Richard. Yet, he has done none of these but has, in fact, developed a rather unhealthy obsession with racehorses. The only accomplishment he can name is that he has more friends than he can even recall."

"Not friends of any distinction," Matlock pointed out. "Dandies and fops, every one of them."

"Not all. He is rather close friends with some young viscounts."

"As I said. Dandies. Men who have too much wealth and not enough to do."

"You are sounding rather like my father." I chuckled as I wandered to the astrolabe, my eyes flicking over the polished brass lines. It was beautiful—a masterpiece of quality and engineering. But I had no earthly use for the thing. And sadly, it was rather like my brother—splendid and impressive to look upon, but absolutely worthless.

"If I sound like George Darcy, Senior, it is perhaps because I admired his character. We looked up to him, every one of us. He managed to produce one son after his own likeness, but the second? A wastrel and a cad who will spend his inheritance before he has even found a wife."

I fingered a wheel on the astrolabe, my brow furrowed, then turned back to my uncle. "On that point, I mean to carry my way. I have informed him that he must find some suitable employment for himself before the end of the year. I will not suffer him to become a drunk and a gamester. I care not what it is, so long as it forces him to act like a man of three and twenty and not a youth of three and ten."

"And how do you mean to force him to do that? He is of age now, and you do not control his inheritance."

I crossed my arms. "I have my means. Perhaps you would rather not know them."

Matlock studied me with a quizzical look. Then he shook his head. "Indeed. Perhaps not. Well, Darcy, what do you wish me to do about this letter you are writing? I can present it to a few undersecretaries, perhaps garner some support for your way of thinking..."

"Lord Belmont."

His jaw dropped. "You... what?"

"You heard me. I would present my findings and opinions directly to the man who has the power to do something. Is he not head of the committee?"

"Well... yes, but... Belmont! I might as well ask for an audience with His Highness."

"That would do as well, I suppose."

"You are serious!"

"I am asking. You can refuse, and so can he. But nothing is to be gained without venturing the attempt."

Matlock frowned, his mouth working into an unhappy scowl. "Very well. Draft your letter, and I will do all in my power to see it presented to Lord Belmont."

"Thank you, Uncle."

Elizabeth
London

"L IZZY, DID YOU SEE this ribbon? Is it not perfectly divine? How well it would look with my eyes! Johnny Lucas did say I looked ravishing in green."

I paused and turned back to look at the length of ribbon Kitty was showing me. "Oh, indeed. You ought to ask Uncle if he can get you an entire bolt of this. I think I have seen nothing to rival its effects against your complexion. Why, it makes your eyes almost a different color!"

"You see?" Kitty crowed to Lydia. "I told you that dull red was nothing to this. I'm going to Uncle right now." An instant later, the sisters were scrambling against one another, elbowing each other as they ran down the aisle to find Uncle Gardiner.

"You shouldn't encourage them, Lizzy," Jane admonished me. "You know Uncle's generosity, and he will not like to disappoint them."

"And yet, disappoint them he shall, for I happen to know the price on that ribbon. He gave them a strict allowance this time, and they have already exceeded it."

Jane looped her arm through mine, and we wandered to the end of the aisle. "Well, I have no such ambitions," she said. "A bit of lace to make over my ball gown. You recall how Lydia stepped on the hem? I tried saving it, but it is utterly ruined. What are you going to get today?"

"Hmm. I think just a little muslin for a new chemise. Nothing elaborate or very costly."

"And yet, you were given the highest allowance of us all," Jane said, nudging my elbow with a smile.

"Only because I have never spent all of what he offered. I believe he keeps a rolling tally of how far under budget my purchases always are."

Jane giggled. "Or perhaps because you're his favorite."

"Stuff and nonsense. He feels responsible for me, but he needn't. I am quite well enough, and I would not wish him to think he has some special obligation to me that he does not have for the rest of you."

Jane lifted her shoulders, and we continued to wander through Uncle Gardiner's warehouse without much conversation. He was not really *my* uncle—more of a guardian, but he had invited me to call him such, and at the time, I was feeling particularly adrift and cast out. Someone who offered the kinship of his family, and who was so kind through that terrible time, became to me the dearest man alive. So, yes, I called him my uncle.

Just as I called Jane my sister, though it was merely a term of affection. And Papa, and .. and Mama... all of them, really. In seven years, they had become family to me, so much so that it was difficult to recall a time when I did not even know them.

When I did think of the "time before," as I called it in my mind, it seemed a nebulous dream. A ghostly memory, the sort where one has to verify the remembered "facts" with others, to determine how much of it was true and how much fancy. The one thing I could recall with absolute clarity was George.

But that was not a happy thought, though it should have been. For years, I wrote letters to Pemberley, and for the first six months, I received swift replies. Then, nothing. It was as if I no longer existed. But I am a stubborn creature, and I would not permit myself to be ignored, and so I kept writing.

It was two years before Papa finally sat me down over a chess board and forced me to recognize the truth—George Darcy had no intention of writing back. He was a wealthy young man, probably away at Eton or Cambridge, and whatever else had come his way, I was one thing that no longer lay in his path.

I would never see him again.

"Lizzy, what do you think of this one?" Jane released my arm and reached for a fine length of lace, fingering it to test the quality. If there was one thing Mama had taught us all, it was how to determine quality—or, rather, how to make our pin money stretch the farthest while still retaining the *appearance* of quality.

I curled my hand under the length, rolling my fingers through it, and shook my head. "Very poor. I am surprised Uncle even keeps such a sample in stock."

"Not all garments require the highest quality," Jane reminded me. "Should I be expectant and demanding that every gown of mine have the very best lace?"

"No, but we are not looking for lace for your night dresses, but your ball gown. Jane, I fear you will not be demanding and expectant *enough*, and not merely in matters of lace."

She scoffed lightly and shook her head. "Are you talking about my cousin Collins again? Honestly, Lizzy, it is as if you had already met the man and knew him to be a cad. Perhaps he is handsome and of good character."

"Yes," I murmured absently as my eyes roved the shelves. "And perhaps you will discover a silver spoon in the haystack."

"I think you mean a 'needle in the haystack.'"

I stopped and plucked a roll of lace from a higher shelf. "No. I meant it as I said it. Because if you want to find something special, you have to look in the right places. *This* is the lace you should buy—from the *top* shelf, not the bottom."

Jane fingered it dubiously, her eyebrows lifting ever-so-slightly in admiration. "Trust you, Lizzy, to turn a mere shopping outing into a metaphor for men."

I lifted my shoulders. "Shopping for lace, shopping for men— 'tis all the same, really. Know your means and do not settle until you find the best one you can afford."

Jane shook her head and dropped the lace into a little basket Aunt had given us to carry our purchases. "If I did not know you better, Lizzy, I would say those words smack of bitterness."

"Bitter? Why, no, not in the least. I am merely a realist. We cannot always have the very best."

She tucked her arm inside mine and hugged it, drawing me close as we continued walking. "Or perhaps one person's 'best' is not another's. Perhaps the 'very best' man for you is still out there searching until he finds Elizabeth Bennet of Hertfordshire."

I rolled my eyes and chuckled at her. "I am become too much of a cynic to believe in fate or star-crossed loves. If such a thing existed, I know already the man who would inevitably cross my path at just the right moment for us to meet our destiny, but it will never be so. Therefore, I will bide my time and look to my means, and perhaps one day I will happen upon a balding gentleman in his forties, ready for his second marriage. And if I am very lucky, perhaps he will not have bad breath and eight unruly children."

Jane scoffed. "You do yourself too little credit, Lizzy. But come, let us show these to Aunt Gardiner and see if Lydia and Kitty have left any tea for us."

I bounced into a playful curtsey. "After you, milady."

Two

Darcy

"Fitzwilliam! There you are. Egad, man, it is eight in the evening, and here you are in your study. Do you ever stop working?"

I lifted my eyes from the crop estimates my steward had presented me earlier in the day and sat back in my chair. "Do you ever start?"

My younger brother sauntered toward me, shaking his finger with a knowing grin. "Oh, testy this evening, are we? Very well, perhaps I shall not introduce my friend to you. He is waiting in the drawing room, but I can just as easily send him away."

I dipped my quill in the inkpot and made a note beside one line, then cleaned the quill and put it away. I was meticulous and not fast—mostly because it drove George mad to watch me moving so slowly.

"Good heavens, man. It is a bloody good thing you employ men to do the hard work around here, or nothing would ever get done."

I raised my brow as I put my ink away. "Yes, what a mercy I have a man to cut wood and another to muck out the stables. It leaves me all that time to sit at my desk."

"Are you coming?" he demanded. "Because Bingley is going to drink all my Scotch while I am away."

"*My* Scotch," I corrected. "And I told Huxley you were not to serve my best spirits to your guests any longer."

"Oh-ho-ho!" He wagged a knowing finger at me. "It just so happens I *did* buy this bottle. It was when we were in Edinburgh on holiday. Got a bloody good price, too."

"Language, George," I admonished. I wasn't sure why I bothered. It never did George any material good, and it made me sound like a tired old codger trying to parent a full-grown man. I rose from my desk and straightened my jacket. "Very well, let me to this Bingley fellow you insist on me meeting."

George's face blossomed. "About jolly time. Gad's teeth, Fitzwilliam, you have ink on your fingers like some common clerk."

"I do not." But I twitched, just to make sure... I had, after all, been writing all evening.

"Got you!" George laughed. "Come, brother, you must smile a little when you meet my friend. He is not used to bold and commanding figures such as yours. You will frighten him off."

I shot my brother a sideways glance. "If he is a friend of *yours*, perhaps he deserves to be frightened off."

"Ah, very good. I see your sense of humor has returned. I say, Fitzwilliam, you are become rather dusty, spending all your days in the study. It will do you good to meet my friend."

I sighed. "Very well. How did you meet this one? Did he pay your gambling debts at the racetrack? Or did you meet him in Town while trying to decide which gold watch fob to purchase?"

"Neither. He is a very respectable chap I met in school."

"Oh, so you do remember the place? That is encouraging."

"I remember a fat lot of rules, but with some sport mixed in for good measure. You will like Bingley—he's not like Howard or Bixby. Son of a steel mill tycoon who—"

"I thought you said he was respectable."

"He can carry on a real conversation, which is more than I can say for *some* men of my acquaintance. Come, Fitz. Smile a bit. Here we are."

I fidgeted with my fingers as the footman opened the door. There were many things I would rather do than meet another of George's friends. Shaving my eyeball or going for a dip in the icy North Atlantic seemed intriguing. I spared my brother a glance as he waltzed into the room and made his presentation with a flourish.

"Fitzwilliam Darcy, my friend Charles Bingley of Sheffield. Bingley? My brother."

Bingley was a pleasant enough chap, I daresay. He did look perfectly respectable, and he lacked the overly polished look I had come to expect of George's friends, which I thought promising. He did not smell as if he had bathed in milk and champagne, and I even detected a few hairs on his buckskin breeches from my pointer, Wellington. That meant he must have petted my dog, and any man willing—and able—to win Wellington's approval could not be all bad. I smiled tightly and inclined my head. "A pleasure, Mr. Bingley."

"The pleasure is all mine."

"Join us for a round, will you?" George beckoned, reaching for a glass. "Bingley has just returned from America, have you not, Bingley?"

"Oh, indeed? Were you there on business or pleasure?" I let George pour my glass and took a sip. And nearly gagged. So *that* was why George said he got a good price on the bottle. It might as well be turpentine. I swallowed, but the ghastly stuff burned all the way down and rumbled about my innards like a firebrand.

"Business," Bingley answered. "An ironworks in Pennsylvania—the fellow paid me a preposterous sum to look over his smelting process and help him make some refinements. My family's mill..." He blinked and broke off, clearing his throat. "Well. That is probably of no interest to you."

"Quite the contrary," I assured him. "But will you excuse me for a moment?" I rang the bell for Huxley, and when he appeared, I went to the door to speak in a low voice. "Bring us a proper bottle of Scotch, will you?"

"Yes, sir."

Huxley disappeared, and I returned to George and Bingley. "Forgive me. You were saying something about your steel mill?"

Bingley's face flushed. "Well, I... I suppose it might not seem very genteel to you. My father raised me as a gentleman, but he also desired that I should understand the steel industry. Our mill, in particular, has perfected a process that yields high-quality cutlery."

"Cutlery?"

Bingley shifted his feet, glanced at his glass, then George, and finally back at me. "Ahem... ah, yes. More, eh... economical than silver, do you see?"

"Yes, quite. Ah, here is Huxley." I went to the sideboard as my butler presented my best aged Campbelltown. "Thank you, Huxley. Yes, a fresh glass if you please." I glanced over my shoulder at George and Bingley, both trying not to look like they were watching me. I sighed. "And two more fresh glasses."

Rather shortly, we were all suited with full glasses of my best Scotch, and I pretended not to notice the smug look on my brother's face. Once again, he had charmed me out of a bottle. But I was rather more interested in listening to what Bingley had to say than scowling at George.

The chap was clever. Rather too modest, and I wondered how George had stumbled into his acquaintance, but I found him no punishment to speak with for a quarter-hour. Perhaps George had accidentally found a friend who could speak of something more serious than hunting hounds and racehorses.

Elizabeth

WE WERE ALL WEDGED around Uncle Gardiner's dining table, a scene reminiscent of a crowded market stall rather than a family dinner. I sat, half-listening to Kitty and Lydia's animated chatter about their day's conquests in Uncle Gardiner's warehouse and half-wondering if it were possible to die of boredom induced by excessive talk of ribbons and hats.

Jane was the picture of polite interest, but I knew her well enough to catch the glimmer of amusement in her eyes. Unfortunately, it was not Lydia and Kitty who were the subjects of her amusement, but me, with the way my eyes were rolling and my head kept bobbing as I tried to keep from nodding off. Uncle Gardiner was pouring out what looked like his third glass of wine—a wise man, fortifying himself for the evening ahead.

"Oh, Mama, the ribbons!" Kitty squealed, nearly knocking over her water glass in her excitement. "Such colors! You would have thought we were in Paris! I'd no idea Uncle had so many new types of trim!"

"And the fabrics, Mama!" Lydia chimed in. "I found this silk that would make even a duchess green with envy! I told Lizzy it would look perfectly dashing on her, but she would not purchase any, so I took all of it."

I couldn't help but chuckle. "I do hope the duchesses of London can sleep tonight, knowing the Bennet sisters are on the loose."

Mama was nearly trembling with excitement. "Mr. Bennet, did you hear? My good brother has been so kind. Why, each of the girls has new fabric to make winter gowns—for you know they are grown so tall, most especially my Lydia—*and* he gave them each an allowance to find lace and ribbons! Our girls are always the belles of Meryton, you know, but now, even Mrs. Long will be forced to admit there is nothing to my girls."

Papa, who had been trying to hide behind his newspaper, peered over with a look of feigned horror. "My dear, if you insist on discussing ribbons and lace any further, I may have to seek refuge in the library with a more sedate companion, like Gibbon's 'Decline and Fall of the Roman Empire.'"

I smirked. "I am sure Gibbon's empire declined due to a severe shortage of ribbons, Papa."

"No, as I recall correctly, one of the chief reasons for Rome's decline was overspending." Papa shot a significant glance at Mama before sipping his wine.

"I thought it was due to invasions," Uncle Gardiner mused, scratching his chin. "The Huns and the Goths, was it not?"

Papa cleared his throat. "Ah, and speaking of invasion, I had a most interesting rumor before we left Longbourn. It seems that Meryton has been deemed a likely town to house winter training for the militia. Open fields, not far from London, you see."

Mama's mouth dropped in a gasp, but then she stiffened and shook her head. "Oh, Mr. Bennet, how you tease me! You see, do you, what I put up with?" she lamented to Aunt Gardiner. "He is forever trying to get a rise out of me, but I say, I will not have it! No, indeed, I shall not be baited into excitement over something six months away that no one can even tell for certain. Everyone knows I am the model of patience, and he is trying to upset me."

"Indeed, my dear, for I like nothing better than to hear and see you in a perpetual state of agitation." Papa sipped his wine, raised his brows, and saluted my uncle with his glass. "An excellent vintage."

"You approve?" Uncle Gardiner asked. "I only just had it brought in from a little winery in Kent. It is nothing to the French wines, of course, but more than passable. The weather is favorable for growing, and the distance easy, which saves a great deal on the cost, of course."

"Yes, you see, Brother, that is precisely what I have been saying!" Mama lamented. "The weather *is* fine, and it is an easy journey. I have been telling him he ought to take us sea bathing, but will he listen?"

"My dear, you mistake my refusal to go to Kent for failure to listen. Be assured, I have, indeed, heard you. I simply choose not to exert myself to the journey." He sipped a little more wine. "And expose myself to ridicule," he mumbled under his breath.

"What, ridicule! Only if you do *not* take us. Mr. Bennet, your daughters' health! Sea bathing is essential this year to withstand the heat and bring the blush to their cheeks. Why, all the fine young ladies partake. Think of our complexions."

"I daresay their complexions already spark envy, my dear. Shall we risk a county-wide scandal?"

Ignoring him, Mama turned to Aunt Gardiner. "Sister, you see the benefits, do you not? A change of air! There is nothing to it. Why, you ought to come with us."

Aunt Gardiner held up a hand, shaking her head. "I am afraid I cannot. We are off to Lambton next week, actually."

"Lambton?" My head snapped up, and my heart fluttered against my ribs. I had not heard the name of that dear town in years, and I gazed at her as if she had just cracked my soul open.

Aunt and Uncle both glanced at me, then shared a look. "Yes, Lizzy. I had a letter from my sister Helen. She married Mr. Westing of Farthingdale three years ago, and she is in need of some... assistance." She glanced at Uncle again. "We intend to travel on Wednesday. Your uncle shall return directly, but I may remain until autumn."

I swallowed. "And... and where is Farthingdale, exactly?"

She thinned her lips and sighed. "About three miles from Lambton, just north of the old Turnditch Road."

My stomach twisted, and my breath caught. "That is not far from Pemberley."

"Elizabeth," Uncle warned. He said no more, but the shake of his head was enough to still the words of denial I saw simmering on Aunt's lips. She did not wish to say them any more than he did, but they appeared to be unanimous in their opinion. I should not be asking about Derbyshire, or Lambton, or Pemberley.

"Come, come, Lizzy, you look as if you would ask to go along," Papa scoffed. "What of all the officers I just mentioned? Should you not prefer to set your cap somewhat closer to home?"

I bristled. "I am not thinking of 'setting my cap' for anyone. It is only that I have not seen the Peaks district since I was almost too young to remember it, and perhaps I could be of some help, Aunt. Did you not say your sister had a young daughter already?"

She hesitated. "Anne Rose is two, but she already has a nurse."

My shoulders sagged. "Please, Aunt?"

"It is not a holiday, Elizabeth," Uncle Gardiner added. "There will be precious little time for pleasure and no entertainment for you."

"Entertainment! I offered to help, Aunt. Surely, there is *something* I can do. And if we brought Jane as well," I offered archly, "you needn't be at any pains to exert yourself for my amusement. We know how to make ourselves useful and discreet, do we not, Jane?"

Jane's eyes widened, and she sat back in her chair. "Oh, Lizzy, I do not know. To invite myself, I cannot..." She shook her head.

Aunt sighed and gave Uncle a long look. "To be quite truthful, Helen did say that Anne Rose's nurse wished to travel to see her mother—apparently, she is ill. Helen agreed, so long as the nurse returned before the new baby arrived. I suppose..." She leveled a cautious look at me, her mouth quirked into a frown. "You two *could* be very helpful if Helen agrees. My dear?"

Uncle Gardiner wiped his mouth and raised a brow at me. "Lizzy, you may well find things... very different to what you recall. Things are never quite the same as we remember in our childhood."

I leaned forward with a grin. "Uncle, I am counting on it."

He sighed and frowned, then turned to Mama and Papa. "Well?"

Papa shook his head. "If they prefer the rocks and trees of Derbyshire to the officers of Meryton, what am I to do on the occasion?"

Mama gasped and swatted at him with her handkerchief. "How you tease me! Mr. Bennet, did you not hear the name 'Farthingdale?' Why, with such a fine name, surely there will be good company and perhaps even single gentlemen in the area. And if not, they will be home well in time to meet these officers you claim are coming to Hertfordshire."

I sat back in my chair and smiled at Aunt. She rolled her eyes and shook her head. "Very well, Lizzy, you have got your wish. I will write to my sister."

THREE

Darcy

"WHAT OF THE WHEAT? Was there much damage from the storm in April?" I traced a finger down the column of figures before me, the morning light casting a stern glow across the papers.

Mr. Daniels, my steward, leaned forward and pointed to a note he had scribed along the edge. "It was still early, and the crops recovered well, so the damage appears to have been minimal. And the barley yields are promising this year, Mr. Darcy," he said, pointing to another column of numbers.

"Very well," I murmured, my mind half on the harvest, half elsewhere. "Keep an eye on the western fields. Last year's drought hit them hard."

Before Daniels could respond, the door burst open, and in strode George. "Fitzwilliam! Buried in figures and frowning again, I see."

I looked up, barely concealing my annoyance. "Some of us have responsibilities, George."

He lounged against the doorframe, shaking his head with a knowing tsk. "And you manage them so well, dear brother. Why should I add to your burdens?"

I sighed, my frustration with his indolence a familiar ache. "It wouldn't hurt you to try."

"Numbers, numbers, numbers. Don't you ever tire of them?"

"It is called management, George. You should try it sometime."

George laughed, his carefree demeanor untouched by my barbs. "Why bother when I have such a proficient elder brother?"

I scowled at him, but what good would it do? I turned back to Daniels, attempting to refocus on the task at hand. "The sheep flocks, Daniels. Have the shearers completed the task this season? What of the newly weaned lambs?"

"Yes, Mr. Darcy, and the numbers are looking better than last year," Daniels began. "The fleeces are—" but George pushed himself off the doorframe and sauntered over.

"Sheep, always sheep. Darcy, when will you admit that your true love is a flock of woolly creatures?"

I shot him a withering glance. "Pemberley is, first and foremost, a farm that depends on its flocks. Our tenants are all farmers. The mill's output depends on them. Or would you have us ignore the very source of our livelihood?"

George strolled over, peering at the ledger as if it were a curious artifact from a foreign land. "Oh, I'm sure it's all very important. Counting sheep, watching grass grow…"

Daniels shifted uncomfortably. I could sense his eagerness to finish our discussion and escape George's jests. "The wool quality is excellent this year, sir. It should fetch a good price."

"Ah, the art of turning grass into gold," George began to wander around the room, idly inspecting the various objects on my shelves. "You are an alchemist, brother."

I tried to ignore him, refocusing on Daniels. "Ensure the highest quality batches are sent to the mill. I want to see if we can increase the thread count without affecting the durability."

George suddenly seemed to take an interest. "Quality? Durability? That sounds exactly like what Bingley was prattling on about earlier. Egad, I am surrounded by it."

I paused, my pen hovering over the ledger. "Bingley?" My interest was piqued despite myself. "What exactly did he say?"

George gave a casual shrug. "Something about innovations in steel production. Far above my understanding, but it seemed to excite him greatly. Chap ought to find a hobby. That is precisely why I invited him to stay the month, you know. I told him some sport would do him good. He claims to be a proficient archer, and I mean to teach him to fish. And I only just learned that he has never played cricket! The very idea!"

"You invited him for an entire month?" I set my pen down, the numbers and figures before me suddenly less interesting than they had been a moment ago.

George wandered to the window. "Of course. Why, you do not think I am less than a proper host, do you?"I growled. "You might have mentioned it before."

"And you would have put pin to it. But now that he is here, and you do not disapprove of him, I say it is a happy circumstance. Bingley has some diversion, and I..." He tossed a paperweight in the air and caught it... "I found something to take your attention off me. He is an interesting fellow, is he not?"

I raised a brow. "Bingley is a more valuable friend than most of the brash young bucks to whom you have introduced me. In fact, I was rather intrigued by some of the innovations he was describing last night at dinner."

As if on cue, Bingley's voice echoed from the hallway. "Darcy, are you in?"

George grinned. "Speak of the devil. Perhaps now you can hear about these innovations firsthand, brother."

I closed the ledger with a decisive snap, then stood and buttoned my jacket. "We shall continue this later, Daniels. Will you have a sample of this year's fleece brought round? Thank you."

Bingley stepped into the room, his face lighting up as he spotted George. "Ah, George, did you ask him yet?"

I looked from one to the other, wondering what fresh mischief my brother had concocted. "Ask me what, exactly?"

George rolled his eyes and shot his friend a sigh of mock exasperation. "Bingley here came to me with a matter of great importance. Alas, it was quite beyond my humble capacities. I advised him to consult you, the fount of all wisdom."

Bingley, now looking slightly embarrassed under my inquiring gaze, cleared his throat. "Well, Darcy, I've been giving some thought to... ah, branching out a bit. I'm considering leasing or even purchasing an estate."

"An estate?" I repeated. "And what prompts this ambition?"

Bingley's expression turned earnest. "It was my father's fondest wish to see me settled as a gentleman of property. And, well, it would greatly add to my sisters' happiness. I am hoping to secure something by the end of the year."

I leaned back, assessing him. This was a side of Bingley I hadn't anticipated. "Your father's wish, you say? That is a commendable reason. And thinking of your sisters' well-being shows thoughtfulness. What sort of advice do you seek?"

"Everything, I am afraid. I know not where to begin, but I was hoping you might guide me. I had a letter from my youngest sister only this morning, and she is all eagerness for me to be about the business, but I've not yet found a competent adviser."

"It would be my pleasure. You see, George? Not everyone is indolent. Some desire to better themselves and become useful to their families."

George, who had been lounging by the window, straightened up. "You are perfectly convinced that I lack all ambition."

"I would be delighted if you proved me wrong."

He grinned. "Then prepare yourself to be delighted, for while you are sprouting roots behind your desk, I have been making rather illustrious connections abroad."

"And what would that be? Another tale of your adventures in Town? Or have you bought another racehorse?"

"You wouldn't understand. 'Tis a matter of the heart, brother. You said I should contribute something to my own upkeep, and so I have. I have captured the fancy of the loveliest creature on earth."

I couldn't help but scoff. "Your romantic escapades hardly qualify as contributions, George."

"You might be surprised, brother. But go on, discuss your mills and cogs. I shall not bore you with tales of the heart."

I crossed my arms. "Oh, consider me most diverted. Let me guess. She wears too much rouge and can be found on Drury Lane."

"No, no." George waved his hand dismissively. "Nothing of the sort. I've been... well, I've been courting a young lady. A very *respectable* young lady, I might add."

"'Courting,' George? I think 'seducing' is the word you are looking for."

"I am quite serious, brother," he replied, a hint of defensiveness creeping into his voice. "I know I've given you little reason to think so, but I *am* capable of genuine affection."

Bingley watched us, a slight smile on his lips. "I have met her, Darcy. She is quite a catch, I must say."

I regarded George with a newfound curiosity mixed with a healthy dose of skepticism. "And if I were to ask the young lady's name?"

He buffed his fingernails on his jacket and inspected them. "You might be pleased. I cannot say, really. Sometimes, I've no idea what would please you."

I narrowed my eyes and cleared the last papers from my desk. "Humor me."

He shrugged. "Lady Lucilla, daughter of Lord Belmont."

My desk drawer slammed closed when my hand twitched. I froze, then glanced carefully up at him. He was jesting again, and I would not be taken in this time. So, I played along, waiting for whatever prank he meant to deploy. "Lady Lucilla, is it? I heard she was courted by Viscount Eddington, with a betrothal expected any day. You must have charmed the lady until she cannot think straight."

"There you have it. I rescued her from Eddington and his staggeringly dull friends when I was at Ascot in April. The twenty-second, if you must know, at half past three in the afternoon, just before the eighth race went to the post."

I stared at him. "There, you have tipped your hand. You never recall anything with such precision, so what are you after this time?"

"Nothing! Bingley, am I not telling the truth? I introduced him to her in Town a fortnight ago, and she avowed all the details I just told you."

"On my honor, the lady recited it precisely as he has said," Bingley concurred. "And I might say she added one or two embellishments regarding what George said to her about..." Bingley broke off suddenly, and I caught a faint shake of George's head.

"About?" I prodded.

"About which horse she ought to be cheering for," George supplied quickly. "And she was so taken with my advice that she gave me leave to call on her and her mother the next afternoon."

I surveyed him dryly. "Her mother is not the worry. It is Lord Belmont who ought to concern you. I cannot think he would lightly approve of his only daughter being courted by the second son of a mere country squire. Particularly one with a—forgive me, George—a reputation such as yours."

"Would you believe he fancies me?"

I went to the sideboard and poured some brandy, offering a glass to Bingley. "No."

"You see, Bingley? I told you he would not believe me. Very well, have it your way, brother. I shall tell Lord Belmont that you did not care to meet him next week when he brings his family on a tour of Matlock and Dovedale." He flicked a bit of imaginary dust from his sleeve and strolled toward the door.

I spun around, the brandy sloshing slightly in my glass. "Lord Belmont is coming to Derbyshire?"

George kept walking. "Oh, yes. They are expected to break their journey in Duffield on Tuesday next, and from there, I believe they meant to journey on as the ladies felt comfortable—a month in the Peaks, at least. Lady Belmont said she most particularly desired to tour Matlock and Pemberley, as she heard there was nothing to the natural beauty of the grounds. There you have it." He shrugged and walked out the door.

I blinked, my brandy utterly forgotten. "What the devil?" I breathed.

"I will say," Bingley mused, "the lady does appear to be quite taken with George."

My head snapped around. "What? She does?"

Bingley lifted a shoulder in a helpless gesture. "Perhaps I am no fit judge. I have courted very little myself, and I find, more often than not, I ascribe more feeling than is truly present, but it did appear to me that she was fond of him. She blushed a great deal and touched her hair whenever he spoke to her, and once, I saw her permit him to touch her hand. Is that affection or merely gentle manners from a noble young lady?"

"It is astonishing, that is what. Do you know who she... or rather, who Lord Belmont is?"

He shook his head innocently. "Should I? I mean, of course, apart from their rather impressive names?"

I cleared my throat and tossed back a larger gulp of brandy than good manners permitted. "He is no mere earl or viscount. He is The Most Honourable The Marquess of Belmont. Highly favored by Prince George, powerful in the House of Lords. Whatever land in Berkshire is not owned by the crown belongs to Belmont... well... almost." I was pacing the floor by now, worrying my empty glass between my fingers and frowning at the carpet. "And he has been one of the primary voices in Parliament regarding factory regulation."

"Oh." Bingley's voice sounded pale, and when I glanced back at him, his face matched. "I say... he is rather an important fellow, then, is he not?"

"For more reasons than one. Bingley, if George truly has got himself mixed up with Lady Lucilla, he is farther over his head than he knows. Lord Belmont would be a fool to permit George to court his daughter. If she marries anything less than an earl—or a future earl, at the minimum, it would be nearly scandalous."

"But if she did...?" Bingley posited.

"If she did..." I blew out a sigh. "Either it would be everything I could wish for—a chance to speak to Belmont directly regarding my concerns for the new laws being proposed—or I would suspect Belmont is using George for something." I twisted my glass in my hands, and a wry thought came to me. "I suppose, either way, George has finally found a way to make himself useful to *someone*."

FOUR

Elizabeth

T HE MORNING WE DEPARTED for Lambton dawned bright and clear, as if the weather itself approved of our excursion. I stood before my small trunk, meticulously packing, each item a silent testament to the anticipation bubbling within me. Jane watched me with a bemused smile.

"Lizzy, do remember we are going to assist Aunt Gardiner, not attend a season in London," she teased, folding a shawl with her usual precision.

"I am well aware, Jane," I replied, tucking a book into a side pocket. "But one never knows what adventures might find us, even in Lambton. Why, we might go out walking, or Aunt's sister may receive callers... best to be prepared, right?"

"Have you seen Mr. Westing's estate? What is it like?"

I folded my gowns and thought for a moment. "I do not recall Farthingdale, but it must be close to Pemberley. From what I understand, the estate itself is about the size of Longbourn or perhaps a little smaller. But Lambton is decidedly smaller than Meryton, so if you were entertaining thoughts of meeting handsome gentlemen..."

"Lizzy, you know that is not why I agreed to come. I wanted to help, nothing more. But I do confess that I could not pass up a chance to see the place where you and Aunt grew up. From the way you both talk, there is no place in the world as lovely as the Peaks."

"There is not." I tucked a pair of stockings into the crevice between two gowns and straightened. Another pair of boots would be good, but I had not brought my sturdy and worn walking boots from Longbourn. My flimsy town boots would have to do. Besides, it was not as if...

Not as if I would be running through the hills and dales like a girl of thirteen again. My mind wandered back to the days spent at Pemberley. To George Darcy, with his laughing blue eyes and a smile that could stop a girl's heart.

How we used to race through the halls, our footsteps ringing out like the joyous toll of a bell. How vividly I remembered the games we played, hiding in secret nooks, the thrill of being discovered mixed with the delight of concealment. George, with his mischievous grin and boundless energy, was always the ringleader, and I, ever willing to follow in whatever adventure he concocted.

Did he remember me with the same fondness, or had time erased those carefree days from his memory?

The thought of my childhood friendship–more than a friendship, because I had loved George with my whole heart—still left a bittersweet pang in my chest. In the quiet moments, I sometimes found myself longing to recapture that sense of freedom and friendship, to ask him if he ever missed it too. But the years had stretched between us, a widening chasm filled with silence and unspoken questions. I folded the last of my gowns, tucking away the nostalgia with it, wondering if our paths would ever cross again.

It was not impossible. As I had told Jane, Lambton was small. Derbyshire, while sprawling, was rather intimately connected. If there were a picnic or some sport or entertainment to be had, or neighbors welcoming a new child or hosting guests from out of town, George Darcy would know of it. He could not help it.

Then again, perhaps he was not even in Derbyshire this summer. He could be... he could be anywhere. In the army or tucked safely away at some far-flush parish as the rector or... or even married.

I clenched my teeth and closed my trunk. Best not to let my imagination spin on what I did not know.

Five days in a carriage is usually sheer torment for me. Jane is different—she can while away the dullest of hours simply by staring out of a window and letting her soul rest. But I am cut from a wry and off-grain cloth—the seconds, I suppose. I never can stand to sit idle, and I cannot abide the tingling of ideas and energy, all threatening to burst through my skin at the slightest breath of wind on my cheeks. This journey, however, proved that I can, in fact, sit still for five days. If it is *home*, that will greet me when the carriage door opens on that last day.

"I wonder if Pemberley is as majestic as I remember," I mused aloud during a lull in the conversation.

Uncle Gardiner turned the page of his book. I caught the edge of his glance, but he dropped his eyes again to his book before he spoke. "Places change, Lizzy, as do people. Best not to set your heart on past memories."

"Yes," I sighed. "I suppose." But there was no help for it.

The tame and rolling hills had given way to spiraling rocks and mountains broken by verdant fields. Aunt Gardiner kept us amused by stories of her youth and her sister, Helen Westing, née Fairbanks. But I could not join in sharing my own memories, for they were far too precious and fragile. Instead, my mind wandered, landing on George Darcy, Senior–Father, I used to call him. The man who used to bring me gifts and mend my hurts and sing to me when I had a nightmare.

The man who had sent me away. With no word of explanation, no warning... The man who had simply gazed back at my forlorn tears that last day, closing the door of his study when I begged not to be torn away. What had I done? I had pleaded to know, and he never replied.

I could still picture him sitting in his study, a fortress of efficiency and goodness around which everything at Pemberley always revolved. What truths were nestled in those quiet corners? His words were always measured, his advice sound, but on the matter of my eviction from my home, there was nothing to be said. But one thing I knew; the man I called Father was never wrong. So, the fault must have been mine.

Would he welcome me now, I wondered, with the same fatherly affection, or would I see a flicker of something else, some hidden reason dancing in his gaze? The thought of confronting him, of demanding answers, sent a thrill of both fear and excitement through me.

Did I dare? How could I not? I was no longer a child to be sent away, and I no longer resented... all of it. The Bennets were my family now, and I was happy. I had a good life. But he owed me an answer, and perhaps one day, I would have it.

But not today. Today, we rolled through Lambton and took a turn off the main road that would have taken us west to Pemberley. Instead, we drove north for another half hour. Farthingdale was, indeed, smaller than Longbourn but built on a rambling slope and set in such a way that it looked longer upon its face, giving the house an appearance of size that was rather misleading.

As we stepped down from the carriage, Mr. Westing met us at the door.

"Gardiner!" he greeted our uncle with an outstretched hand. "And Madeline, my dear. Helen will be overjoyed to see you."

Aunt let him kiss her hand, and then she turned to present us. "Robert, these are the nieces I wrote to you about. Miss Jane Bennet and Miss Elizabeth."

Mr. Westing bowed to us. "Welcome, and may I express my deepest gratitude? For certainly, you may have had your choice of amusements this summer, and you came here to help your aunt. I fear my poor Helen may have to lay more on our dear Madeline here than she had hoped, so your arrival is a true blessing in these trying times."

"How is Helen?" Aunt asked. "Not overexerting herself, I trust?"

"Ordered to keep to her bed, I am afraid," Mr. Westing replied. "The doctor was here two days ago, and he said she was not resting enough. Poor thing is going mad, confined to her room and wondering about the management of the house and our little Anne Rose. She will be overjoyed to see you."

Without a moment's hesitation, Aunt hurried inside and up the stairs. Mr. Westing turned to Jane and me, his demeanor still warm but tinged with the fatigue of a worried husband. "Please, come in. Sarah will see to the ladies, and Gardiner, I fancy a drink in my library would not go amiss?"

The interior was cozy and peaceful—a world away from the grandeur of Pemberley or the loving chaos of Longbourn. Jane and I turned round, our gazes crossing as we both surveyed the house. Yes, we could pass a very pleasant month or two here.

The maid led Jane and me up the narrow steps of Farthingdale, then opened the uppermost door at the top of the staircase. The attic room, nestled under the eaves of the house, was quaint and simple. Twin beds with patchwork quilts sat under a sloping ceiling, and a small window offered a view of the stretching fields.

As she checked the window shutter and straightened the quilts, she turned to us apologetically. "Miss Bennet, Miss Elizabeth, I am sorry we cannot offer more suitable accommodation. Mrs. Westing regrets she has but one guest room, which your aunt and uncle are using."

Jane's smile was reassuring as she glanced around. "This is quite comfortable, thank you. We don't need much."

The maid nodded and set down a basin of water and some fresh linens on a small table. "Mrs. Westing asked me to tell you that tea will be served in the drawing room shortly."

"That sounds lovely, thank you," I replied, placing my small bag on one of the beds. The room, though small, had a cozy charm, and the prospect of tea was a welcome one after our journey.

After the maid left, Jane made use of the basin to freshen her face. As I waited for my turn, I wandered over to the small window, peering out at the landscape bathed in the soft light of the afternoon. The fields stretched out to the west, a lush expanse of green that bordered the edge of memory and longing. Under my breath, almost without thinking, I murmured, "*Pemberley...*"

"What's Pemberley like, Lizzy?" Jane's gentle voice caught me off guard. I hadn't realized she heard my quiet musing.

I turned, a flush of embarrassment warming my cheeks. Jane's curious eyes were upon me, filled with a mix of interest and sisterly concern. I moved slowly, sinking onto the edge of the bed, feeling the weight of her question. Pemberley, with all its grandeur and shadows of the past—how could I encapsulate it in mere words?

I paused, gathering my thoughts, searching for the right way to describe a place that was so much more than just a grand estate—a place interwoven with my earliest joys and deepest questions. My gaze drifted back to the window.

"I am sure I could not do it justice. Then again, if I were to describe it as I feel it in my heart, as I remember it, I would lead you to think it is better than heaven itself, and the reality would surely disappoint."

Jane folded her shawl and laid it on the bed. "Well, what do you remember most about it?"

Most? That was easy. George—forever and always, my best friend and the boy I'd given my heart to when I was just a girl. Then there was Father, with his deep voice and stern looks that were always warmed by affection. And Fitzwilliam, too. I was never as close to him as to George, but he had been a good sort of a "brother" to me. Always ready to rescue me from whatever scrapes George got me into, but always so serious that we never had a good laugh about it later.

But to Jane, I said only, "The grounds are the most beautiful in all the world, I think. There is a lake we used to swim in when we were very young. Well... I never did, being a girl. Father thought it was not proper for me to swim with the boys, but George and Fitzwilliam..." I cleared my throat and lifted my shoulders. "There is no formal garden like there is at Netherfield, but there is a maze of rose hedges, a wilderness behind the house, and a folly... I suppose you would like that the best. It is on a slope, and you can see the entire valley from there. In fact, if our eyes were sharper, we could see it from this window."

Jane had a strange look on her face–staring at me oddly. But she covered it with a smile and came to sit beside me. "You miss them still."

I lifted my shoulders and fiddled with the lace on the edge of my sleeve. "I suppose I always will."

"Perhaps not."

I looked up. "What do you mean?"

She chuckled and took my hand. "As you said, one never knows what adventures may find us."

FIVE

Darcy

"**F**ITZWILLIAM, TO WHAT DO I owe this unexpected pleasure?" Lord Matlock inquired as he invited me into his study.

I took the seat he offered and shook my head when he gestured to the sideboard. I had not come to share drinks and bandy gossip. "It is about George," I began, cutting straight to the heart of the matter. "He claims to be courting Lady Lucilla, Lord Belmont's only daughter. More than that—Belmont is bringing his entire family on a tour of Derbyshire. They ought to be arriving in Duffield today, and according to George, they wish to tour both our homes."

Lord Matlock's eyebrows shot up. "Indeed? That is most surprising, yet... not entirely unwelcome news."

"Not unwelcome?" I leaned forward. "What could George possibly offer Lady Lucilla? She's the daughter of one of the most influential men in England." The idea was ludicrous—George, whose most significant achievement to date had been an uncanny ability to avoid any form of meaningful labor, and a Marquess's daughter. "Lord Belmont's son-in-law will be expected to be one of the most powerful men in the kingdom. She could marry a duke, for pity's sake."

'Yes. She could." Matlock began to pace, a thoughtful expression playing across his features. "Belmont, for all his stature and wealth, is an exceedingly indulgent parent. He adores his daughter, and he is getting on. It may be that he has mellowed some in his dotage and is permitting her some leeway in the choosing of her husband. She cannot inherit any title beyond her honorific, and she certainly has no need for money."

"Dotage! Preposterous. Belmont is as hale as you or I. But even if he were not, his son, the Earl of Winston, could profit substantially if his sister were to marry well. He would not limit his legacy so."

"'Tis said that Belmont himself married for love. Well... the first time, poor wretch. His second marriage was more to his family's liking."

I narrowed my eyes. "What happened to his first wife?"

My uncle folded his hands on his desk. "Died in childbirth, they say, and the child who was to be the heir died with her. Egad, you ought to know this story. Half of the *ton* would have known all about it, and it was much the same as with your mother."

"I know very little of my mother's friends," I murmured.

"I did not mean to imply they were friends. In fact, I cannot say whether Anne even knew Lady Belmont. But, be that as it may, I say there can be no harm and only good from encouraging George's suit of the lady. Belmont may even permit him to declare himself."

"I cannot credit it," I countered, struggling to keep my tone level. The thought of George, with his haphazard approach to life, winning the favor of a marquess was more than a little far-fetched. "Indulgence is hardly a reason to believe he'd permit his daughter to be courted by someone like George."

The corner of Matlock's mouth quirked in a wry smile as if he found my disbelief amusing. "Fitzwilliam, you do not appreciate the unpredictable nature of affection. And let us not forget, George has a certain... charm."

I couldn't suppress a snort. George's charm, indeed. The same charm that had convinced half of Derbyshire's mothers he was eager for a match with their daughters, only to leave them bewildered when he inevitably lost interest. "Charm is hardly a suitable foundation for a courtship with a lady of Lady Lucilla's standing."

Matlock stopped pacing and faced me, his expression serious. "Perhaps, but we mustn't underestimate the value of a good match, even if it seems unlikely. Encourage this, Fitzwilliam. It could be beneficial. You said yourself the lad needed direction and purpose."

I frowned. "Encouraging George in this seems... reckless. Belmont's favor is not something to be toyed with."

"Perhaps," Matlock conceded, "but consider this: supporting George in this endeavor could also open doors for you. Belmont's visit to Derbyshire is an opportunity—not just for George, but for Pemberley."

His words gave me pause. The potential advantages were undeniable, yet the risks loomed large. Could George's whimsical pursuit of affection be the key to greater opportunities, or would it lead to unforeseen complications? Winning Belmont's favor could be remarkably advantageous for me, but not like this. Not using his daughter and my brother as the hook and line. George was the only other Darcy. He was my brother, my responsibility, and I would not see him fall to ruin.

"What if he *is* serious about her?" I wondered aloud. "I know it seems almost farcical, but he was speaking of her in a way I have never heard from him before." I met my uncle's gaze. "If he truly is... serious... what happens to him when Belmont inevitably puts a stop to his designs? Or worse, what if Belmont is simply toying with him for... I cannot know what."

"And just what could his reason be for something like that?" Matlock shook his head. "No, Belmont is not an evil man. Well! No more so than any other man with so much power. He hasn't the time to amuse himself with your brother. Either he tolerates George's attentions to Lady Lucilla because, up to now, George has not distinguished himself as a serious contender, or because he means to permit something more permanent. Either way, there is no harm in letting George have his way in this."

"And then what? Let him propose marriage? Be publicly humiliated when her father sends him packing?"

"Might do the lad some good to be humbled a little." My uncle poured me a drink from his decanter, whether I wanted it or not, and gave it to me. "Your skepticism is warranted, Fitzwilliam, but think of the future. This could be good for George, and beneficial for your interests. Do all you can to make Belmont's visit to Derbyshire a memorable one."

As I left Matlock's estate, his advice echoed in my mind. The drive back to Pemberley was filled with contemplation. Could I, in good conscience, encourage George in this pursuit? And what of my own interests in the matter? I kneaded my eyes with my fingers and sighed.

George was going to prove my undoing someday. I was sure of it.

Elizabeth

T WO DAYS HAD PASSED at Farthingdale, and they unfolded with the serene predictability of country life. Aunt Gardiner was nearly constantly at her sister's side, so she had authorized Jane and me to take over the management of the house, to a point. We consulted with the maid, helped with Anne Rose, and dabbled in a bit of cooking—for the estate was not large enough to keep a permanent cook, but Mr. Westing had hired a girl from the village to help during his wife's indisposition.

However, today promised something different. Mr. Westing, eager to show us the beauty of his corner of Derbyshire, had proposed a tour of Black Rocks. Jane and I, along with Uncle Gardiner, climbed into the carriage with a picnic basket. I clasped Jane's hand and could hardly contain a squeal of delight.

"Have you seen them before?" Jane asked.

"Oh, many times. We all used to come here before Fitzwilliam went away to school. After that, George and I came back once, but it was not the same without Fitzwilliam."

Jane looked at me quizzically. "But I thought you said George was the adventurer and his elder brother was dull."

"Not when it came to the rocks. George was afraid of heights, but Fitzwilliam used to climb to the top of the tallest rocks and tell us all that he could see from up there." I laughed. "And he used to tell tales of knights charging over the cliffs and dales in battle to thrill us—claiming they were things he had read in his schoolbooks. Now that I think of it, I fancy he made most of them up, but he was always so serious in other matters that we believed every word. Oh! And now I shan't speak anymore. Just let me drink all this in."

Jane chuckled and fell quiet beside me. The path to Black Rocks wound through lush fields, gradually giving way to a more rugged landscape. Towering rock formations loomed above us, their dark silhouettes stark against the soft blue of the sky. The beauty of the place was almost overwhelming, with the wildness of nature on such a grand display.

"Oh, Lizzy, you were right!" Jane exclaimed, her eyes wide with wonder as we approached the craggy cliffs. "It's magnificent!"

I couldn't help but agree. The majesty of the rocks, formed by centuries of wind and weather, stood as silent sentinels to the passage of time. "It's like something from another world," I mused aloud, my gaze following the jagged lines of the rocks as they pierced the sky.

Mr. Westing had the carriage stop as he pointed to the sharp ridge a little way off. "They say the view from the top is quite spectacular, but I should not wish to tire the ladies."

"Oh, we are accustomed to walking," Jane replied quickly. "I know Lizzy would not miss it."

I glanced down at my boots, tilting my foot to examine the thin sole and fine leather. Well... "No." I lifted my head and smiled widely. "I wouldn't miss it."

"LIZZY, I DO HOPE the cobbler can help. I feel it was my suggestion that led us to climb those rocks."

The door jingled as I opened it. "Nonsense, Jane. It was an adventure. I would wear out a hundred pairs of boots for the pleasure of seeing that view," I replied as we approached the counter. It was a funny business, walking while the heel of my boot was flopping loosely, but I managed not to fall again. "Besides, I know Mr. Watson, the cobbler. He was always friendly—he used to give us candies when we came to town with Mr. Darcy on errands. I am sure he will be quite helpful."

But Mr. Watson was not immediately visible. I leaned over the counter and stood on my toes, trying to see behind the corner that led to his workbench. "Mr. Watson?" No answer. I called him again, with the same effect. At last, I picked up a little brass bell from the counter and gave it a ring.

We heard a muffled curse and a chair squeaking, and the cobbler emerged with a look of perfect indifference. "What can I do for you ladies?" No preamble, no genuflection. Just a blunt question.

"Good afternoon, Mr. Watson!" I beamed. "It is so good to see you again."

His cheek twitched, and then his gaze swept me up and down. "It is, then?"

"Ah, perhaps you do not remember me. It has been some years, after all. I am Elizabeth Bennet—well, you knew me as Elizabeth Smith."

He blinked.

"I... used to live at Pemberley? We came here quite often with Mr. Darcy."

Something flickered in his eyes, but it was not recognition. "As you say, madam."

I sighed. "Well, I was out climbing earlier today, and I damaged my boot. I was hoping you could repair it."

He shrugged and began to turn away. "Leave it on the counter and come back in two days."

I started to follow him. "You see, that is just the trouble. I haven't another pair with me, and I was hoping..."

He sighed heavily and turned around. "Let us see it, then."

I lifted my skirts just enough to show him the flopping heel from my damaged boot. "Is it a very difficult repair?"

He gestured with his hand, as if expecting me to just hand him my foot. I grimaced and leaned on Jane's shoulder to untie the laces, then hopped on my good boot to pull it off and give it to him.

He examined the boot, then glanced at me, his brows knitting slightly. "You said your name was Smith?"

"Yes, it was."

He harrumphed. "Never heard of you."

"I suppose it does not matter. Can you fix my boot today?"

He turned the boot in his hands, inspecting the damage. "Will take a while. You'll need to wait. Don't have a retiring room for ladies here."

"That bench by the window will do well enough, I imagine."

Jane leaned close to my ear. "Are you sure we should impose on him, Lizzy? We could always send for another pair from Mrs. Westing for now. I think her feet and yours are close to the same size."

"Nonsense, Jane. We are here now, and I'm sure Mr. Watson will do a splendid job. Besides, this gives us a chance to reminisce about old..." I sighed. The cobbler had gone back to his workbench, taking my boot and any hope of conversation with him. "Well, I suppose we may as well amuse ourselves by looking out the window. I will tell you all I remember about the people passing."

Jane chuckled and gave me her arm so I could hop to the bench. "Nothing like a good bit of gossip, is there, Lizzy?"

Six

Darcy

T HE BUSTLE OF LAMBTON'S market day surrounded me as I made my way down the high street. Vendors cried their wares, housewives examined vegetables, and farmers led their livestock through the throng. I nodded in acknowledgment to the familiar faces I passed while keeping a vigilant watch for any signs of the visitors I awaited.

The impending arrival of Lord Belmont and his family at the Lion's Head Inn necessitated a level of preparation befitting their status. Ensuring their accommodations were up to standard was not typically within my purview, but the importance of this visit to Pemberley—and, by extension, to George—could not be overstated.

I stepped into the Lion's Head Inn, where I was greeted by the innkeeper with a deferential nod. "Mr. Darcy, sir! What an honor. Will you be requiring rooms today?"

"Not today. I've come to inquire about a party arriving shortly—the Marquess of Belmont and his family. I understand they are to lodge here during their stay."

"Why, yes, sir!" His chest puffed up importantly. "The Marchioness herself wrote last week engaging my very best rooms. They are expected by this very afternoon."

"So soon? That is excellent. Lord and Lady Belmont must want for nothing during their stay. I have given orders for some of the best from my cellars to be delivered for their comfort. Please place any... additional expenses to secure their convenience on my account." Belmont might boast ten times my wealth, but I would gladly bear the expense to pave the way for George's courtship.

"That is exceedingly generous, Mr. Darcy. Thank you."

"Not at all. I imagine Lord Matlock will invite Lord Belmont to stay at Matlock Estate once they have been introduced. Should he accept the invitation, I will be sure your establishment loses nothing by it. Am I understood?"

"Quite, sir."

"Very good. Give my respects to your wife, and will you send a message to Pemberley the moment Belmont arrives?"

The innkeeper agreed, profusely thanking me as I took my leave. One task complete. Now, on to Watson's shop—my boots ought to be ready for collection. Most of my acquaintances had their boots made in London, but my father had discovered Watson's talent some twenty years ago and even paid for him to refine his skills under a master in Town. Since then, he had crafted every pair of boots I had ever owned. It lent him distinction, and it pleased me to keep my custom close to home.

Ordinarily, I would have sent Daniels or Huxley to collect them, but I was a mere two doors away, and I preferred to look sharp when the formidable introduction to Lord Belmont took place. My present boots, though polished to a shine, were looking somewhat the worse for wear.

The merry jingle of the doorbell announced my entry. Ah, there was old Watson, emerging from the back workroom. But before I could greet him, a whisper from the corner caught my attention.

Two young ladies sat on the bench beneath the window, heads together, casting the occasional furtive glance in my direction. One I could not see clearly, but the other...

My heart gave an odd flutter. Something about her profile stirred a memory I could not grasp. Had we been introduced? Attended some society ball together? Surely, I would remember a face so pleasing.

And yet, she seemed intent on avoiding my gaze. Every glance I stole was met with reddening cheeks and downcast eyes as she whispered to her companion. She even gave her bonnet a faint tug, covering what little I could see of her face. Bloody unusual.

"Ah, Mr. Darcy." Watson emerged from his workroom, carrying my new boots as if they were a babe in arms. "All ready, sir, and I think you will agree, this is the finest pair I have ever made for you. Please, sir, inspect them and see for yourself."

I took them awkwardly, attempting to focus on Watson's prattling about the quality of the leather, the skill of his stitching. But my eyes wandered again and again to the ladies by the window. Who was she? The question nagged at me. Something about the arch of her neck, the mahogany curls peeking from beneath her bonnet... so familiar, and yet...

"Top grain leather, and I made the heel just slightly wider, as you requested. And, sir, if you notice, the inner lining is doe skin—soft as a dove, sir."

"Yes, thank you, these are quite satisfactory," I managed to interrupt. I reached for my coin purse to pay him.

The hushed whispers continued from the corner. My neck began to prickle as if I were the subject of discussion. Well, I probably was.

It was not as if that were unusual, and there was little else for them to be looking at in the shop.

"Will there be anything else today, Mr. Darcy?" Watson inquired.

"What? Oh, no. No, nothing else." I fumbled the coins onto the counter, anxious to escape the shop.

As Watson placed my boots in a padded box and carried them out to my carriage, I risked one last glance toward the whispering ladies. And this time, my eyes met a pair of fine, dark eyes looking directly at me.

My breath caught in my throat. Those eyes... yes, I knew them. Knew that intelligent glimmer, the arch of her brows. But from where? It was maddening, like reading a book in a language just beyond comprehension.

The lady's lips parted, her cheeks blooming crimson once more. She quickly dropped her gaze with a nervous half-smile. Evidently, she recognized me as well.

But before I could speak, she turned away hastily, looping her arm through her companion's. "I do hope Mr. Watson is almost finished with my boot. Uncle will be growing impatient, and Aunt will be missing us for tea."

I pushed out of the door in bewilderment, the sound of hooves and carriages rattling on the cobbles outside. Watson had passed off my boots to the coachman and now stared at me expectantly.

"Er, yes. Good day to you, Watson. I've left you something extra for your trouble."

"Thank you, Mr. Darcy. Always a pleasure to serve anyone at Pemberley."

"Indeed." I started to mount my carriage but paused. "Watson, those ladies in the shop. Was one of them... barefoot?"

He shrugged. "Broke her heel out walking and said she had nothing else to wear. But she said a great deal, sir, and I cannot think half of it is true. Putting on airs and so on. Begging your pardon, sir."

I narrowed my eyes. "Indeed. Thank you, Watson."

Who was she? All the ride home, the question echoed through my mind. I sifted through faded memories of boyhood mates, sisters of my friends, distant relatives, and acquaintances from long-ago balls. But the match eluded me. As the carriage passed beneath Pemberley's ancient oak, I glanced up at the vista of meadow and stream that had been my childhood playground. And there, in a long-forgotten pocket of memory, the answer struck me like a brick.

A trio of laughing children, skirts and trousers muddied... one boy with a near-constant grin, towheaded and mischievous. A taller boy, lanky and serious even then. And a girl...

My breath caught, then stopped entirely. *The girl.* Chestnut curls escaping her braid, hands planted defiantly on her hips. Challenging the boys to races, to climbing trees, her dark eyes flashing.

"*Lizzy...*" Her name escaped me in a whisper.

Could it truly be her? Here, now? How different she looked now, and yet, how perfectly familiar. The lively glimmer in her eyes remained unchanged.

But... why had she been there today? Where had she come from, and why had she never contacted us? Unease mingled with my astonishment. Did she mean to call at Pemberley?

No. Impossible! Why, if it truly had been Elizabeth Smith, she would have greeted me. She would never have permitted me to walk away without... well, without doing something very impertinent. Like leaping from the bench to embrace me around the neck. No, surely, it had to be another lady.

But I had not seen Elizabeth Smith in over seven years, and in all that time, no lady had ever called to mind the girl I'd once known. And nobody had ever told me why she had been suddenly carried off to live heaven-only-knew-where.

The carriage pulled into the drive, and I gazed up at the imposing facade of the house, its windows winking at me in the afternoon sun. Somewhere within were the answers to the riddle of her disappearance all those years ago. Concealed in the ledgers and letters in Father's study, if I had but the courage... and the time... to look.

But with Lord Belmont's imminent arrival, I could not consider it at present. I tucked away the disquieting questions about the mysterious lady for another day. There were more pressing matters that required my attention now.

Still, I could not resist one backward glance over my shoulder toward Lambton as I mounted the steps.

Elizabeth

M Y EYES FOLLOWED MR. Darcy's retreating form until he disappeared into the crowded Lambton street. I pressed a hand to my racing heart, willing it to slow. What must he think of my foolish behavior, refusing even to meet his gaze? But the shock of seeing him again so unexpectedly had stolen both my courage and my manners.

"Lizzy!" Jane tugged at my arm. "Why did you not greet Mr. Darcy properly? He clearly recognized you."

"Hush, Jane!" I pulled her back down onto the bench, glancing nervously toward the counter where Mr. Watson worked, oblivious to our whispered exchange.

"I still cannot believe it was him," I murmured. "He is so.. . changed." My mind conjured the image of the tall, imposing figure who had just departed. So unlike the skinny, awkward boy of my memories, who was usually too shy to speak to anyone unless compelled by duty. The man I'd just seen looked like he was used to authority and decisiveness.

"He recognized you, did he not?" Jane pressed.

"I think so, but..." I twisted my handkerchief, shame creeping into my cheeks. What must he think of me now? "Well, probably not. Everything is different, Jane. I felt utterly unprepared. My gown is dirty and six years out of date, I have only one boot on, and there stood Fitzwilliam, looking as grand as a duke!"

"Oh, Lizzy." Jane shook her head, a gentle smile playing about her lips. "Still such particular friends with him after all this time, are you?"

I swatted her arm with my handkerchief, eliciting a giggle. Trust sweet Jane to find amusement in my discomposure. "It was not Fitzwilliam who was my particular friend. He was so much older than George and I were. By the time I was old enough to remember much of him at all, he was away most of the year at school. I could not presume..."

"Lizzy, you used to be one of his family. Just as much as you are now a part of ours. Surely, you could have spoken to him."

"It has been seven years!" I protested. "He was like an elder brother to me once. But now..." I pictured the formidable man who bore the name Master Darcy. Would the laughing, shy youth I once knew still linger behind those intelligent eyes? Or had he hardened into a stranger? My heart squeezed at the thought.

"At least we know they are arrived in Derbyshire for the summer," Jane commented. "Although I confess surprise to hear him called merely 'Mr.' Darcy. Is his father...?"

A knot formed in the pit of my stomach, my own unspoken fear taking shape. *Surely not*, I counseled myself. Fate could not be so cruel as to steal him away without even a farewell. Although...had I not suffered that very cruelty when they sent me from Pemberley all those years ago?

"Lizzy?" Jane's voice broke my reverie. "Do you think Mr. Darcy's father has passed?"

I shook my head firmly, as much to convince myself as her. "I cannot believe it. Although..." I hesitated, hating to give voice to the possibility that had lurked at the edges of my perception ever since we came to Lambton. "Although I have heard no word of him in the village gossip. Only a passing reference to 'Mr. Darcy' overseeing the estate, the same as ever."

Jane smoothed her skirt pensively. "Indeed. But as I said, I think Mr. Darcy recognized you. Surely you will call on the family?"

"If he had recognized me, he would have said something."

"Perhaps he was not certain, but he truly did have a strange look on his face when he saw you. I say you should take your card by. What need is there to stand on ceremony with old friends?"

"Perhaps..." I twisted my handkerchief again, my mind spinning faster than the carriage wheels carrying Mr. Darcy back to Pemberley. What would I say if I faced him again? Demand answers about why I had been so callously cast out and forgotten? Pour out seven years of buried anger and heartache? Or simply pretend the past had never happened?

"Lizzy?" Jane prodded gently. "If they were such dear friends once, should you not call?"

"I... I shall have to consider it carefully." I stood abruptly. "Let us see if my boot is repaired."

Jane's eyes followed me with curiosity, but she let the matter drop as I hurried to the counter.

Soon, we were equipped again for walking, my freshly mended boot once more securely on my foot. As Watson counted my coins, my eyes were continually drawn to the door through which the mysterious "new" Mr. Darcy had vanished.

What was I afraid of? As a girl, never would I have permitted awkwardness or pride to keep me from the company I craved. Surely, beneath the expensive clothes and imposing stature, some glimmer of my old friend Fitzwilliam remained?

But it was not Fitzwilliam who made my heart sing, still after all this time. It was not Fitzwilliam whose merry voice and blue eyes had never left my imagination for more than a day.

George himself was another matter. Had it been *he* in that shop, I've no doubt I would have leapt up and made him spin me in a dizzy loop until we both collapsed from laughter, like in the old days. Had it been George, he would not have stared at me with that question in his eyes like he was trying to place me...

No, I pushed that tender string of thought aside. This was not the moment to unravel old wounds. I had found the elder Darcy brother again after years of aching curiosity, and that was... well, that was something. Was that not an opportunity to be seized before it slipped through my fingers once more?

Jane and I stepped back out into the bustling high street. My eyes instinctively sought out a particular carriage, but neither the vehicle nor its occupant were anywhere in view. I wondered if Mr. Darcy was even now arriving at the stately house on the hill, so beloved in my memory. Would he speak of encountering me? Wonder at my behavior? Or had the fleeting meeting already faded from his thoughts?

"Lizzy!" My uncle's voice called out, followed swiftly by his figure exiting the inn. "There you are. Let us away home, for I am certain your aunt and Mrs. Westing are eager for our return."

Jane greeted my uncle warmly as he helped her into the carriage. But while she chatted brightly over the excellent views and glorious day we had enjoyed, my thoughts drifted once more to Pemberley. To the past, to the future...and to Mr. Darcy. One of them, anyway.

SEVEN

Darcy

I TUGGED AT MY cravat, the starched linen suddenly feeling restrictive. Or perhaps it was the company that had me on edge. I stood in Matlock's front hall awaiting the arrival of our eminent guests—Lord and Lady Belmont, along with their son, Lord Winston, and their daughter, Lady Lucilla.

My uncle emerged from his study, an uncharacteristically anxious look marring his usually stoic features. "Are they come yet?"

"The carriages have just entered the drive," I replied. Before I could inquire further, a commotion at the entrance announced the newcomers.

I straightened my shoulders and schooled my features into impassivity. But inwardly, curiosity and uncertainty warred within me. Soon, I would stand face to face with one of the most influential men in England—and the father of the young lady my scatterbrained brother had suddenly professed to love.

Two footmen hurried forth to assist the descending visitors. First came a tall, distinguished gentleman I took to be Lord Belmont himself. His keen eyes surveyed his surroundings, taking in every detail. I felt rather like a specimen pinned on display as his shrewd gaze passed over me.

Lady Belmont emerged next, leaning heavily on her husband's arm. She was still a handsome woman, though time had lent some softness to her features. She walked gingerly, a woman accustomed more to carriages than her own two feet.

And then, with a lyrical laugh that I could have picked out of a crowded ballroom, came Lady Lucilla on her brother's arm. George sprang forward, eagerness propelling his long limbs into an ungainly scramble down the steps. He greeted Winston as if they were old friends—perhaps they were—and then, his eyes were all for Lady Lucilla.

"My lord, my lady, welcome to Matlock." My uncle bowed graciously over Lady Belmont's extended hand before turning to make the remainder of the introductions. As Belmont presented Lady Lucilla, I could not help but note the heightened color in her cheeks or the shy smile that hovered uncertainly until her gaze lit on George. Interesting...

Soon, we had all been conveyed within to partake of refreshments before the tour of the house and grounds began. As Matlock led Lord Belmont and his son, Lord Winston, to his study for cigars, I found myself observing my brother and the object of his infatuation. They made a rather mismatched couple—Lady Lucilla was petite, polished, and somewhat reserved, while George loomed over her, energy and enthusiasm pouring off him unchecked.

Yet she did not seem to mind his exuberance. Indeed, her reserve appeared to thaw whenever he spoke to her. She smiled readily, her pretty green eyes remaining fixed on his face in a most particular way. And though George lacked all subtlety, the affection in his looks toward her could not be mistaken.

I sipped my wine, watching in quiet astonishment. Never would I have imagined my directionless brother capable of wooing a lady such as Lady Lucilla. Still less likely was her returning his regard with equal ardor. It was baffling, and yet... Could George have found purpose at last in his pursuit of love?

"Come, Darcy, bring your glass." My uncle stood in the doorway, beckoning. With a final curious glance at the young couple, I followed to join the other gentlemen, jerking my chin to summon George to follow me. But he merely gave me a shake of his head in return. Somehow, he had persuaded the countess to permit him to remain with the ladies as they took their tea.

That was no way to begin, if he meant to impress Lord Belmont. I sighed and simply followed my uncle. George could pave his own path to ruin.

Cigars and fresh glasses awaited us in the hazy confines of the study. His Lordship relaxed in an armchair, keen eyes following me as I entered. He wasted no time. "So, you are the elder Mr. Darcy I have heard of."

I froze momentarily. Had he been discussing me with George? I dipped my head. "Fitzwilliam Darcy, sir, at your service."

"Hmm, just so." He drew slowly on his cigar as if considering how much to swallow. "Perhaps you did not know, but I met your father once."

I raised my brows. "No, I did not."

His Lordship waved a hand through the haze of his cigar smoke. "It was merely an introduction in passing. We spoke for less than ten minutes, but he impressed me as a man of quality."

"That he was, my lord. I thank you for remembering him well."

"Indeed. And what think you of this fanciful attachment between your brother and my daughter, Mr. Darcy?"

The question took me off guard. I had expected more banter and posturing, not such a direct query so soon. Carefully, I lowered myself onto the vacant chair across from his Lordship. "If the attachment brings them joy, then I can only wish them happiness. Although..." I hesitated, unsure whether complete candor would help or harm my brother. Lord Belmont raised one sardonic eyebrow at my unfinished sentence.

"Although you doubt young George's constancy," he finished bluntly. "No need to hesitate, Mr. Darcy. I am well aware of his reputation, and Winston knows him well. Women of a certain bluestocking ilk warned Lady Lucilla most fervently against him."

I shot an uneasy glance at my uncle. He studiously inspected his cigar, but I could detect amusement twitching his mouth.

"My brother would admit that he... sowed a few wild oats," I replied cautiously. "He has not always been the most constant of men. But his affection for your daughter has lent him more gravity of purpose than I have seen before."

Lord Belmont let loose a barking laugh. "Gravity of purpose? By God, from everything I hear, any woman under fifty is in danger from George's wild purposes. Still..." He leaned back, regarding me through half-lidded eyes. "My daughter sees something worthy in him. Who am I to argue? At her age, I stormed across Europe on a headstrong quest for love and glory. Both overrated, to my regret."

I stared. Was one of the most powerful men in England truly implying his acceptance of George as a suitor for Lady Lucilla? Before I could assemble a reply, Lord Belmont had already turned the subject elsewhere.

"Winston tells me your property in Derbyshire is extensive, spanning the river valley."

"Indeed, the estate has been in my family for several generations."
I swiftly composed myself to discuss crops, acreage, and architecture—safer topics, despite the ever-present wariness that His Lordship was assessing *me* as much as my land.

"And your father built a woolen mill on the River Dale?" He tapped his cigar. "Has that been a successful venture?"

I shifted uneasily. "My father did not build it with profits in mind. At least, not as his chief objective. While it is true that the mill is profitable, his aim was to provide a better return to the local farmers for their wool and the prospect of work for those who might otherwise have been drawn away to the cities."

His eyes narrowed, and he studied me over his glass—bold and rather challenging. Surely, he meant to intimidate me, but I did not intimidate lightly.

"I read your letter. You have some intriguing notions, Darcy. Radical—why, one might almost think you were on the side of the Luddites from the way you speak."

"Far from it. But I do have some sympathy for their cause. I only propose a reasoned approach so that future violent strikes might be avoided, and so—"

"Yes, yes. We will speak of it some other time. Perhaps I will call on you at Pemberley during my stay in Derbyshire?"

I swallowed. "My lord, you would be most welcome. Your entire party, as a matter of fact. My brother and I would be pleased to host your party for dinner while you remain in the area."

"No more pleased than I would be to accept, but last I heard, Darcy, you were yet a bachelor yourself."

How could I have been so stupid? It was not as if I did not know the proper protocol. It was my eagerness to be useful to George... which was laughable, for when had he ever reciprocated? I pasted a quick smile on my face. "Alas, you are correct. Pemberley has no hostess—and sadly, I've no means to remedy that before your departure."

"Another time, Darcy. Lord Matlock has graciously extended his hospitality, and I am certain that Lady Belmont prefers the comforts here to the inn—no disrespect to that establishment. I understand that 'someone' took pains to ensure we would be most comfortable there."

I inclined my head. "You can be at no loss to understand my reasons."

"Indeed not. It shows a steadiness of character and a gentleman so young, so I presume you also foresaw a possible alteration to our plans. In fact, I have already sent my carriage to return with our trunks. Surely, we will see you here at Matlock on occasion."

"I am confident that George could not be kept away."

The conversation meandered, but my thoughts kept returning to George and Lady Lucilla as we enjoyed the cigars and brandy. I watched His Lordship closely for any indication of his true feelings, but his face remained inscrutable. If anything, he seemed to regard his headstrong daughter's choice with a sort of resigned amusement. Was he toying with George?

As the visit shifted from a mere afternoon call to an impromptu dinner party, Lord and Lady Belmont took their leave to refresh themselves before dinner. George escorted Lady Lucilla into the garden with an irrepressible smile, their heads already bowed together in intimate conversation. I watched them go, marveling at this sudden shift of fortune.

"Well, Darcy." Lord Matlock regarded me with deep satisfaction, as if he had somehow orchestrated the entire improbable affair. "I told you not to stand in your brother's way, did I not?"

"So, you did." I turned to stare out the window where George's tall frame was just visible over the hedge, his laughter mingling with Lady Lucilla's softer tones.

"Just look at them, mooning over one another as if they stand a chance." Matlock shook his head. "Well, young love must run its course, I suppose."

I glanced sideways at him. "You believe this is merely a passing fancy, then?"

He scoffed. "Hardly a realistic match, is it? Oh, let them dream for now. Belmont seems amused more than anything. Though if it gets serious…" He trailed off ominously.

I nodded, expecting no less. The future likely carried either painful disillusionment or outright disaster for George's romantic aspirations. And yet… perhaps even the briefest taste of love's ideal was worth the price.

If nothing else, it had brought some much-needed direction to my wayward brother's existence. For that alone, I would not interfere but simply let matters take their course, however unlikely the fairytale ending. After all, happiness and wisdom were often born of adversity. And where affairs of the heart were concerned, certainty remained elusive.

Elizabeth

"T

HERE NOW, MISS ANNE, don't you look so very smart today?" I secured the satin bow under the little girl's plump chin as she squirmed in my lap.

"Such a good idea of yours to take Anne Rose out for some air, girls," Aunt Gardiner said approvingly from the doorway of the house. "My sister is doing much better today. The tonic from the apothecary has helped her headaches. But still, she is not to be getting out of bed overmuch, and I am certain she appreciates you keeping little Annie entertained."

"We are happy to help in any way," Jane replied earnestly. Anne Rose clapped her hands and gazed around excitedly from under her ruffled bonnet. "The change of scenery will do her good, and I am looking forward to seeing more of the country, myself."

Aunt bade us a good afternoon, and I gently guided the pony drawing Mrs. Westing's phaeton along the road leading out of Farthingdale. We trekked for over an hour in the carriage, our progress leisurely to accommodate Anne's demands to stop whenever she wanted. All was pastoral tranquility until the pony suddenly pricked up its ears. I followed its gaze to a cluster of buildings nestled by the twisting river ahead.

A pang stabbed my heart as I surveyed the oh-so-familiar hills, rising to touch the drifting clouds. Change of scenery, indeed. My soul felt as if a vital piece of myself had been restored upon returning to these beloved dales and valleys. I drank in the glories of the Peaks with eyes that remembered them well from girlhood adventures under a different name.

I pulled gently on the reins. "Why, that must be the woolen mill Mr. Darcy built," I exclaimed. "It was but half-done when Mr. Darcy... that is, when last I saw it."

"Shall we stop a moment? I should like to admire it. I have never seen a mill so close. Look at that great water wheel!"

As we drew nearer, the reason for the pony's alertness became apparent. Shouts echoed from within the nearest work building, followed swiftly by the door banging open. A thick-necked man stumbled out, propelled forcefully from behind. He wheeled to face his assailant—a grim-looking overseer with outrage etched in the lines around his mouth.

"I'll have no lollygagging or smoking pipes on my watch!" The overseer's bark carried clearly across the yard. He emphasized his point with a sharp jab of his finger. "You were warned, now off with you!"

"Here now, you can't go tossing a man out his place for naught but lighting his pipe," the worker blustered. His protestation was met with a swift kick to the backside. With a stream of curses, the disgruntled laborer snatched up a stone from the riverbank and hurled it forcefully. Glass shattered, an angry counterpart to the overseer's answering shout.

Jane's alarmed gaze flew to the closed door, now sporting a gaping hole at waist height. "Oh! Surely, he will not..." She clasped her niece's little shoulders, concern furrowing her brow.

I swiftly gathered the reins, my unease growing as more men boiled out of the doorway in pursuit of their banished companion. "Come, let us be off quickly."

I clucked to the pony, and the merry little creature hurried on, carrying us away from the scene at the mill. But still, the angry shouts and calls of "Bring him back!" rang clearly in the summer air. My pulse beat faster until we topped the hill, and the golden fields of wheat rose to hide the vista of seething discontent behind stone walls.

A fragile silence enfolded us, broken only by the creak of the phaeton and Anne's happy babble. I risked a sideways glance at Jane as she bit her lip anxiously. "So much anger and resentment," she finally murmured. "But surely one man's careless mistake does not merit dismissal?"

"The mill is built mostly of wood, Jane. I remember Father... that is, Mr. Darcy, talking about it when he was building it. A fire would be the most dangerous thing in the world. He used stone where he could, and I think I remember him saying something about iron beams, but the roof and the walls and floors would be like dry tinder. And if the flame were hot enough, even wool would ignite like cotton." I glanced over my shoulder, back toward the mill. "Did you see, it was not merely the overseer chasing that man away? No one else wants to risk a fire."

"They would turn out one of their own?"

I shrugged. "If needs be, I suppose they would. But I think it is oftener the case that the workers are allied against the overseer. And the mill in general. I remember it was not popular when it was first built because of the power loom. I wonder if that has changed."

Silence reigned for several minutes as we continued more somberly through the countryside. Then, mindful of little ears, Jane smiled brightly and pointed ahead. "Look, Anne, darling! Sheep!"

As fluffy distractions diverted our young charge, I flicked the reins lightly across the pony's back. The images from the river played over behind my eyes... the overseer's angry countenance, his work-roughened hands clenching into fists. How keenly Mr. Darcy's original predictions of mill troubles had rung true in the voices raised and the stones hurled in defiance. What resentments stirred in other faces bent over the machinery that drove the great machines?

I thought with a pang of Mr. Darcy—two Mr. Darcys, rather. One, my dear friend and benefactor, who might now be with God. The other... My restless thoughts shied away from contemplating that stern-faced stranger in the Lambton cobbler shop. I would far rather think of George, with his sunny smile and his way of turning even a rainy day into sunshine.

Instead, I pictured a tall, grey-haired man leaning over a table scattered with plans and ledgers—George Darcy, Senior, explaining his vision for the mill to my uncle all those years ago. He had spoken of prosperity not just for landowners but also for laborers and their families. Of course, disputes still arose, but was there not a way forward guided by wisdom and compassion on both sides?

As I drove, I gazed out unseeingly across the patchwork of field and forest calm that had replaced the towers of brick. I had forced my mind back to happier thoughts—a laughing tow-headed boy racing across summer lawns without a care. Alongside him ran a skinny girl, one stocking sagging, tangled curls escaping their ribbon.

Perhaps Jane was right. I could go to Pemberley, could I not? Strangers were always touring the estate, so why not I? It was not as if I would have to intrude upon the family's notice.

But if I should *happen* to stumble across someone I knew from before, and if they should *happen* to recognize me... then perhaps I might, at last, have some answers to the questions that had rumbled in my heart for seven years.

However, I would have to do it without Uncle Gardiner's approval. He never told me why, but he always warned me against any overtures, and on this journey, he was watching me rather closely. Well... he would be going back to London in a few more days. With a deep sigh, I turned the pony's head toward home.

EIGHT

Darcy

I PACED THE LENGTH of my study, hands clasped behind my back. The image of that laughing woman in Watson's shop still plagued me. There was something so uncannily familiar in her dark eyes and the defiant angle of her chin when our gazes met. And yet, she had looked away without a word of greeting as though I was a stranger.

Was it Elizabeth Smith? It *had* to be.

My memory conjured an image from years past—three young children racing wildly across Pemberley's lawns, shrieking and laughing. A scrappy blond boy of ten, my own awkward frame at fourteen, trying to keep up though my lungs screamed for air. And a girl with tangled chestnut curls escaping her braid, throwing insults and dares over her shoulder.

Lizzy. The girl I'd once loved like a sister.

Could it have been the same girl grown into a woman these seven years later? But if so, why had she not made herself known? An uncomfortable thought pricked at me. Had my manner not been warm enough? I was not the easiest man to read—everyone always told me that. Had she mistaken my shocked silence for haughtiness or disregard? Should I have taken a risk and gone back to find her once I conjured her name?

With a sigh, I strode to the window overlooking the drive. Somewhere beyond that gently sloping hill lay the village of Lambton. And perhaps, in its winding streets, the mysterious woman who had blushed crimson and hidden her face at the sight of me.

Never in my life had a woman—well, a woman unrelated to me—seemed not to desire my notice. Granted, my awkwardness and reserve in female company often worked to my detriment, but outright avoidance was unheard of. What had made Elizabeth Smith, if it was her, refuse even to greet an old compatriot? Did she resent me somehow for her abrupt removal from Pemberley all those years ago?

I winced at the memory. Both George and I had beleaguered Father relentlessly for weeks after she left, demanding an explanation for her sudden banishment. We wept, we threatened, we fought and shouted, but his stony features and curt replies gave nothing away. Over time, I had nearly managed to block the hurt of abandonment from my heart, only to have it come crashing back upon seeing those dark, defiant eyes once more.

A knock at the door interrupted my musings. I tugged my waistcoat straight and willed the scowl from my face. "Enter."

Bingley walked in, an eager lightness in his step that made me instantly envious. If only my mind could know such untroubled thoughts.

"Good afternoon, Darcy," he greeted me. "I have just come from a meeting with your solicitor regarding those land surveys we discussed."

"And?" I prompted. "Did he have the reports you were hoping for?"

Bingley grinned and withdrew a sheaf of papers from his coat pocket with a flick of the wrist that would have done a magician proud. "He did, indeed. Bloody good luck, I say. He had heard of it the very day you sent word of my interest. A property in Hertfordshire called Netherfield Park. From the descriptions, it sounds ideal. Large manor house, good acreage, excellent hunting... Not too far distant from London, either."

My momentary, dark mood lifted as I ushered Bingley to a chair and poured two glasses of port. Engaging in dissecting surveys and maps always soothed my restless thoughts. As Bingley spread out the documents, my mind alighted on a name that stirred memories of another name, almost as lost to the mists of my memory as Elizabeth's.

"Hertfordshire, you said?" I glanced over the top of my glass as I took a slow sip. "I don't suppose the property bears any connection with Edward Gardiner, the financial advisor?"

Bingley's eyes snapped to mine. "You know Gardiner? Yes, it says right here, 'The neighboring estate of Longbourn, property of Thomas Bennet Esq., is entailed away from five daughters in favor of a cousin. However, the family is reputed to have the support of two uncles—a solicitor, Mr. Philips, and a wealthy merchant, Mr. Gardiner of London.'"

"Your report said all that?"

Bingley grinned. "Your solicitor is most thorough. I had asked him to get for me any information he could about the families in the area... particularly with respect to the... ah... social landscape."

I scoffed. "You are learning, Bingley."

"I have an apt tutor. So, what is this, then, about someone named Gardiner? Do you know him?"

"No, this is not my Gardiner," I said with a shake of my head, feeling more refreshed for the momentary distraction.

"'Your' Gardiner? How do you know the name?"

"My father once retained the services of a man by that name. He was here the day that..." My voice trailed as I was lost for a moment in boyhood memories. But no matter. My nostalgic turn of mind regarding Lambton was clearly infecting my mood. "Well, let us examine these other reports. How many acres is it?"

We passed a productive half hour reviewing the details of acreage, annual rents, and structural condition. In truth, it was rather unlike me to take such a personal interest or advise so intimately on a business matter that little impacted Pemberley. But Bingley's friendly camaraderie and perpetual optimism were a tonic to my dour mood. I quite enjoyed living vicariously through his search to set up his own household and launch into the social circles local to whatever estate he settled upon.

A smart rap at the study door brought Huxley, the butler, to announce that George and Lord Winston had just arrived from Matlock, and would Bingley and I be available for a turn round the grounds? I was more reluctant than Bingley, but we set aside the documents and agreed to meet him as soon as we had dressed for a ride. I only hoped that George and Lord Winston did not intend to drag us off to the latest spectacle in town or some other scheme equally unnecessary.

Striding toward the stables where the other three awaited me, I felt the lines around my mouth grow tight. What could be so urgent as to cut short my business with Bingley? But there George stood, flushed with vigor, a wide grin that looked oddly genuine, even... triumphant? I would almost have credited his disposition to a clandestine assignation with Lady Lucilla, save that her brother stood beside him looking equally cheerful.

Two stable hands held four saddled horses at the ready. George's smile deepened as I approached. "A magnificent day for a ride, brother!

I was telling Winston that we must show you those fields to the west. I was thinking they would be prime for barley next season. And Bingley, no time like the present to begin inspecting fields."

His words, echoing my own thoughts to the steward just the other day, gave me pause. Not typically his area of interest or expertise. Hesitantly, I glanced from him to Winston. But the young lord seemed unusually genial himself, lacking the mocking manner I disliked in many privileged youths of his station. I awkwardly returned their smiles. "Indeed... that would be most... instructive."

As soon as we set off on a brisk trot that prevented intimate discussion, Winston dropped back beside Bingley on some pretext of adjusting his stirrup leathers. George edged his mount closer, his expression almost comically expectant. I steeled myself for whatever folly he was about to announce. Had he purchased a menagerie lion or convinced a troop of gypsy performers to camp on our lawn?

"Fitzwilliam," he began, then hesitated. I arched a brow. George, at a loss for words? This must be truly momentous.

"Well? Speak up, what is it?"

He took a breath, his eyes refocusing on the road ahead with unwonted steadiness. "I spoke with Lord Belmont this morning regarding Lady Lucilla and me."

I shot him a sharp look. Had he broached the subject of his attachment? Surely not without my counsel, knowing what high stakes rode on Belmont's reaction.

"We were quite alone, and he received me with the utmost cordiality," George continued. "Naturally, the conversation turned to my admiration for his daughter. And—well, you will scarcely credit it, brother, but not only did he not seem displeased, but he gave what amounted to approval of my addresses to her!" He loosed a disbelieving laugh. "By heaven, what luck!"

I slowed my horse to better study his countenance. Had I misheard? "He... he gave you leave to pay your addresses to Lady Lucilla?" I repeated stupidly.

"Better than that! He hinted—well, more than hinted—that an offer from me would receive favorable consideration. What do you think of that!" His wide grin seemed in danger of cracking his face in two.

My head spun, and I forced my horse back into motion before he could detect any emotion beyond laden astonishment on my features. What could Belmont be playing at? Surely, no man in his right mind would consider George, penniless second son of minor Derbyshire gentry, as a serious suitor for the only daughter of one of the highest noblemen in the land. It made no sense. And yet...

"I confess I am... surprised," I finally ventured. "Pleasantly so, for your sake, but it seems rather against reason. Are you quite certain you correctly understood his intent?"

"Fitz! Such a damper you are determined to be upon my happiness," George exclaimed, though his jubilant smile never wavered. "But what does it matter? I am determined to settle it one way or another now I have such encouragement. Tomorrow at dinner, I intend to make it known to Lord and Lady Belmont both—and, of course, dear Lucilla—that I wish her hand in marriage, and I fully expect her father's blessing!"

I flinched at his brash determination to rush in, visions of a furious Lord Belmont rising before my mind's eye. And yet... who was I to crush such bright hopes if her father hinted approval? I could only nod and promise to stand by him, all the while hoping fortune continued to favor his reckless dreams.

Elizabeth

I WATCHED THE BUSTLE of preparations for Uncle Gardiner's departure with a knot in my stomach. He was to return to London while Aunt remained here with Jane to assist the Westings. I had avoided being alone with my uncle, unable to meet his too-perceptive eyes. But as I handed his small business case to the coachman, a gentle hand closed on my wrist.

"A moment please, Lizzy, dear. Take a turn in the garden with me?"

I swallowed hard but allowed him to tuck my hand in the crook of his arm and steer us down the path between the roses. Their delicate scent filled the summer air but did nothing to slow the rapid pounding of my heart.

"You have seemed quiet since arriving here," Uncle began. "Not quite yourself. Tell me, has it been agreeable for you to revisit childhood haunts?"

I forced a lightness to my voice that sounded strained even to me. "Oh yes! It is just as lovely as I remember. I've enjoyed rambling the countryside again with Jane."

His searching gaze did not waver. "And yet I've observed a kind of... wistful eagerness in your expression of late. As though anticipating something just out of sight around the next corner."

My face warmed. Was I such an open book? Still, evasion came naturally to my tongue. "Do not all wanderers long for the next vista, the next undiscovered delight over the rise?"

His frown told me the blithe metaphor did not satisfy. We walked on in silence until he halted suddenly and turned me to face him.

"Lizzy, I know that being so near to Pemberley again must stir old memories and unanswered questions. But promise me you will not seek out—"

"Why!" My simmering frustration suddenly boiled over, preventing him from completing the thought. I flung my hand up, forcing distance between us. "Why must I avoid people who were once closer than family to me? Why are they forbidden to me now?"

Uncle Gardiner waited patiently until my outburst faded. Then he captured my restless hand lightly in his own and led me gently to a stone bench in a sunny patch of garden. We sat without speaking. At length, he asked in a tender voice, "You still trust me, do you not, Lizzy?"

I dashed a betraying tear from my cheek, my heart aching at even the possibility that he could doubt it after seven years of unreserved affection. "Of course I do. You are as dear as if you were my own father."

He tilted my chin up until I met his warm brown eyes. "And do you also trust that Mr. Darcy had only your well-being at heart when he sent you to us?"

A lump formed in my throat at the unexpected question. But I could only nod. "I always used to."

He sighed. "Then, believe me when I say it is best you remain in ignorance about certain things for now." His fingers brushed my cheek with paternal tenderness. "I wish I could explain, for no one deserves answers more. But I am bound by a promise that I pray you never have cause to regret."

His solemn import struck an uneasy chord. But as I searched his face and saw only loving concern, the fight slowly drained from my defiant posture. My shoulders sagged under the resignation his cryptic words compelled. "Very well, Uncle. You have never guided me wrongly. I will respect your counsel in this, though my heart rails against it."

He drew me into a close embrace. "You have ever been as a daughter to me. I only want your happiness."

I hugged him tightly, his familiar scent of spice and leather enveloping me in safety once more. "I know. My true family is right here. What need have I to go digging up the past?" I attempted a teasing tone.

A glint of moisture shone in his eyes as he pulled back, hands braced on my shoulders. "That's my good girl." But his smile faded as quickly as it had come. "Still and all, I think perhaps I ought not to leave you and Jane here unprotected with the Darcys so near..."

I waved my hand airily. "Oh, think nothing of that! What opportunity shall I have to encounter any of them?"

His expression grew graver still. "Lizzy, when we were in Lambton, I was having a drink with Westing in the inn when Mr. Fitzwilliam Darcy came in to attend to his custom. He spoke some words of business with the innkeeper, and then I watched out the window as he walked toward the cobbler's shop. Where you and Jane were waiting."

I swallowed, my gaze low. "I see."

Uncle touched my chin to make me look at him. "Did he speak to you?"

I forced a light smile. "Fitzwilliam Darcy, speak to a lady in the boot shop? You must be thinking of George to imagine such impropriety. Why, I do not believe he even recognized me. Likely, he has long since forgotten that awkward girl who used to trail after him and George." The admission brought an unexpected twist of sadness I swiftly buried.

"All the same, you understand my concern. You see how easy it would be for you to stumble upon them if you are not prudent."

"You may leave with an easy heart. I shall keep my promise."

The creases lining Uncle's forehead relaxed at this assurance. He patted my hand warmly and escorted me back toward the bustling carriages, his natural cheerfulness returning. "Well, then! I will return for you all in September. Do remind your aunt and Jane daily of my fondest love. And Lizzy—" His momentarily sober eyes sought mine, "—take care, my dear."

I stood, blinking back hot tears as his coach rumbled down the drive. Whatever secrets and unanswered questions lingered in my past, I must find contentment in the present joys all around me. With Jane's sweet companionship and country rambles yet ahead, how could I repine? Smoothing my hair, I turned resolutely back toward the house. The future awaited somewhere up that sunlit garden path. No sense dwelling on faded dreams from long ago.

NINE

Darcy

T HE DINNER PARTY AT Matlock House sparked with a vigor I had seldom witnessed at my father's table. George commanded the conversational space before the fire, keeping Lord Belmont and even the reserved Lord Winston entertained with colorful tales and humorous anecdotes. Lady Lucilla's occasional trilling laughter wove silver threads through their rumbling tones like a sparrow's song lifting above the station clock's steady chime. I observed it all silently from the fringes, smiling when expected but seldom venturing to add my voice to the livelier discourse.

My uncle regarded me pensively over the rim of his wine glass during a brief lull when George paused to wet his throat. "You are quiet tonight, Fitzwilliam. I would have thought Lord Belmont's gracious manner would put you more at ease. He has been nothing but good-humored, has he not?"

I twitched a shoulder, eyes following Lady Lucilla as she drifted closer to murmur privately to George. "I find such easy conversation does not come naturally when I have weightier matters occupying my thoughts."

I regarded my uncle pensively over the rim of my wine glass. "Still no word from Richard's regiment?"

Matlock's gaze darkened, and he shook his head.

"I see." I swallowed the rest of my drink and stared at the carpet. Richard had been on the Continent for six months, but letters had been regular until just over a month ago.

My uncle laid a sympathetic hand on my arm. "Do not abandon hope. Communication around the Spanish conflict is slow and unreliable. And Richard was ever one to land on his feet."

Despite his consoling tone, shadows lingered in Matlock's eyes. My chest squeezed with the shared burden of concern. But my uncle promptly masked his anxiety and nodded toward the fireplace where George was now deep in amused conference with Lord Winston.

"Take a page from your brother's book tonight and try to relax. This gathering is a triumph—see how Lord Belmont includes him as one of the family!" He lowered his voice conspiratorially. "Why, at this rate, George could be announcing his betrothal by Michaelmas!"

My answering chuckle rang hollow, but I thanked my uncle for his tireless support and turned my attention back to the party. If even Richard's fate remained uncertain, how much more this improbable courtship balanced on a sword's edge? Yet I must not let idle misgivings spoil the promising camaraderie blossoming before us. With a concerted will, I joined the outer fringes of lively discussion, determined to play my part.

Some hours later, the last of the ladies had retired upstairs for the night. But George showed no inclination to abandon the comfortable gathering by the fire, which the replenished glasses of port had transformed into our own gentleman's club. His ease and status amongst our noble guests no longer surprised me—when had my gregarious brother ever failed to shine at the center of jovial society?

Feeling suddenly restless as the night grew long, I excused myself. George and Winston, and even Bingley, had descended into racing tales to which I had little to contribute. Though bedrooms had been prepared for our party, sleep did not tempt my wandering thoughts. I found myself pacing the corridor outside the drawing room instead, straining to decipher threads of conversation that floated up the stairs.

What devil had possessed George that he could not convince his companions to make their revelry elsewhere? I clenched my hands behind my back. If Belmont took offense or thought poorly of George's frivolous friends so close to receiving an offer for his daughter's ha nd... But a reprimand from me at this point would only undermine George.

A soft footstep sounded on the stair behind me. I whirled, then inclined my head politely to find Lady Lucilla slowly descending, her small hand skimming the banister.

"Pardon me, Lady Lucilla. I could not sleep and often pace when restless."

"Oh! Think nothing of it, sir." She halted two steps above, peering at me through golden lashes with an inquisitive smile. "I expect that I, too, will find slumber elusive tonight."

Her manner was all gentle grace and modesty. Such a contrast to George's exuberance. How complementary they could be. I studied her silently. Years of fostering harmony between my unrestrained brother and fastidious father had taught me to discern deeper motives and truths from what lay beneath the surface. Yet nothing but sincerity of affection shone from Lady Lucilla's candid eyes.

"Derbyshire is a lovely part of the country, Mr. Darcy. I do hope we shall have the pleasure of touring Pemberley soon. Particularly..."

Her cheeks bloomed rosy pink, and she dropped her gaze as delicate footsteps echoed down another corridor, followed by a maid's gentle call that Lady Lucilla was wanted below stairs. With a look from lowered lashes that I could only call giddy, she dipped her head as she passed by me to complete her descent. Watching until she disappeared, my earlier tension eased. There was true fondness kindling behind her coy manner. And though George's suit seemed mismatched and unlikely, who was I to oppose it?

Alone once more, I followed her down a few steps so that I could see some of the activity below. And there was George—no longer laughing over the billiards table in the far drawing room but standing in the hall outside Lord Matlock's study. His face was ashen, and he was tugging at his collar.

Lady Lucilla passed by him, her head turning slightly and her hand secretly slipping into his before she was summoned into the study. Only then did he look like he took a breath, but the instant she vanished again, he was back to blinking and gulping.

"George?" I called quietly.

He glanced up, giving me a wan smile. "Wish me luck, brother."

I inclined my head, and he nodded with a jerk.

I did wish him luck, but perhaps not in the way he hoped. I wished for whatever his best might be—be that with his fair lady or with a righteous blow to his pride that set his future on a more directed path. I straightened my waistcoat and addressed the looking glass across the hall without seeing. "Tonight, you seal your fate, George Darcy. For good or ill, may it be the making of you."

Hours later, Jefferson roused me from weary dreams with a summons to the study. En route through the darkened corridors, I espied George's valet sleeping upright against the wall like a sentry abandoned at his post. No doubt, standing ready for the order to help George prepare for celebration or commiseration. I edged past his lightly snoring form without disturbance. Some welcome, or warning awaited me—of what nature I was about to discover.

My brother sprawled in our uncle's old leather chair before the dying embers of a neglected fire—the only light in that shadowed room. Was this symbolic? His quest for true love already burnt through, leaving only ashes? Or perhaps carrying the last hope of reigniting a steady flame if properly tended? Such fanciful thoughts did not sit well in my usually practical mind. I shook off my imaginations and cleared my throat into the gloom.

George turned, spectacles glinting in the dim glow. Our father's reading glasses—an odd accoutrement for my fashion-conscious brother. Where the devil had he found those? Had he been reading books or poring over documents while awaiting my arrival? Even more peculiar. My skin prickled, sensing portents on the air beyond common comprehension.

"Well, George?" I took hesitant steps nearer. "Do not keep me in suspense. What did Lord Belmont say?"

Lifting the glass for a long swallow of amber liquid, George stared into the ether. Then his head lolled toward me on the chair back, and he loosed a gusting sigh that transitioned seamlessly into laughter.

"Oh, Fitzwilliam. You should have seen Belmont's face when I made my offer over the brandy. He very nearly choked. I made him repeat it twice to be perfectly clear I had not misunderstood." He took another generous gulp. "We are officially betrothed, Lucilla and I. Engaged to be married!"

The floorboards seemed unsteady beneath my boots. I sank into a facing chair, my mind grappling for rational words. "He... consented? So easily? I cannot believe it!"

George chuckled into his glass. "Nor I at first. But you were right—happy chance indeed smiled on my courtship. Lucilla is to be my bride, come Michaelmas."

I studied his profile, waiting for the crack that would betray this as an elaborate hoax. But his features remained curiously earnest despite the celebratory spirits. My pulse jumped erratically, and I rose to splash more whiskey into my glass.

Questions crowded my tongue. How ever would George support a highborn wife in the style to which she was accustomed? What prospects did a second son have of maintaining her interest once passion cooled? But not tonight—this night belonged to my brother and his improbable triumph against fate.

I raised my glass toward him. "To your felicity, brother. I wish you both lasting joy."

He grinned lopsidedly. "When shall I be able to return the favor?"

I shook my head and drained my glass. "With you out of my hair, perhaps I will give the matter some consideration. But let me see you settled first."

Elizabeth

"I SIMPLY DO NOT understand what has come over him," I muttered, securing the ribbon around Mrs. Westing's list of household needs. "All these years, Uncle Gardiner has supported my questions about the past. Why the sudden insistence on secrecy?"

Jane eyed me sideways, her gentle face creased in a thoughtful frown as we made our way into Lambton. "Perhaps there are private reasons it would distress him to share. Likely for your own protection."

I kicked a loose stone on the road, watching it skitter into the dusty grass. "But I am no helpless child in need of 'protecting' from the truth! What harm can simply knowing why I was sent away do?"

"Oh, Lizzy." Jane looped her arm through mine consolingly. "I am certain it is all meant kindly, even if the method frustrates. We must trust it is better to respect their wisdom. See how happy you have been as part of our family!"

I stared down the bustling high street, Halstead the butcher's familiar painted shingle just visible around a curve in the road. Jane's sweet placidity, however sincere, never fully aligned with my restless spirit that endlessly questioned and challenged and sought truth—even uncomfortable truth. But I swallowed back further argument for her sake. What point to keep battering at her unruffled calm?

"You may be right," I conceded with a rueful half-smile. "And here we are at our first stop already. Let us see if Mr. Halstead can furnish all Mrs. Westing requires to keep up her strength."

Soon, we were making our way back out, laden parcels filling our baskets—ham and sausages wrapped in brown paper, ready to grace the Westing's humble table. Lost in Mrs. Westing's list for the bakers, I did not notice why Jane stopped suddenly, and I did not look up when she stumbled on the uneven pavement until a dismayed voice cried, "Miss! Take care!"

I looked up, startled. Jane teetered unsteadily and then crashed to her hands and knees with a cry, her packages spilling across the dirty road. A handsome gentleman leapt down from a polished chestnut horse just in time to catch her elbow as she struggled back to her feet.

"Oh heavens, you are injured!"

Jane attempted to smooth her skirts with one hand while the other gingerly probed a ragged tear across her knee, already welling crimson. She looked fit to sink into the pavement under his solicitous attention even as she protested being perfectly well.

Dropping the packages, I stepped nearer, prepared to excuse us if the impetuous young man meant to take further liberties. But in my haste, I stumbled against the horse he had left untended in the road. The beast whinnied and shied, yanking the reins from my hand even as I grasped for them.

"No! Here, now!" My desperate grab missed. The last thing we needed was to be saddled with damages from a runaway nag. I hitched up my skirts, prepared to give chase into the busy street after the creature.

But quick as thought, a commanding voice rang out, "Jupiter! Stand, sir!" Large hands closed calmly over the dancing reins just before the horse bolted. My steps faltered as a tall gentleman turned toward me, touching the brim of his hat courteously. "Pardon me, Miss. Is your... friend...?"

I froze, words dying on my tongue. No verbal response was necessary—the instant our eyes connected held all the recognition needed. Fitzwilliam Darcy went still as stone before me. Seven years had only added definition to his angles and planes, lending gravity to features I knew better than my own.

A crease pinched his brow, and he opened his mouth. "Liz—"

"Fitz! There you are! Blast, I thought I would never catch you up." A second gentleman trotted up, pulling his steed alongside the first with a reckless grin I could never fail to recognize. Everything inside me turned to water as I beheld that beloved face once more. "Making the acquaintance of local beauties without me? For sha—"

George Darcy's teasing address slammed to a halt mid-word. He stared down at me for a single uncomprehending moment. Then, in the next breath, his stunned features transformed with dawning wonder. "Lizzy?"

Tears blurred my vision at the achingly poignant address. George slid carelessly from the saddle without breaking our locked gaze. I forgot Fitzwilliam, Jane, the bustling street—my very breath hung suspended as George moved one slow step nearer with a hand half outstretched...

TEN

Darcy

I STOOD AT THE window of the Lion's Head Inn, staring sightlessly out at the bustling street. Behind me, George paced with the restless energy of a caged tiger.

"Confound it, what can be keeping her so long up there? She disappears for seven years without a word of explanation, then treats us as strangers she cannot wait to escape!"

I flinched at his wounded tone, the echo of my own bewilderment and disquiet. When I stumbled upon Elizabeth in the cobbler's shop, I had not allowed myself to believe it could truly be her. Yet here she was, materialized as if from the past itself. Still, her averted eyes and hurried excuses to return upstairs to tend her injured "sister"—*Sister?*—maintained an impassable gulf between us. Was she still resentful over being sent away all those years ago? Surely, she did not blame George or myself? We had been mere boys—powerless over Father's implacable authority.

Well... I was a young man of twenty, but still, my father's will was not to be gainsaid. I cornered him in his study and thundered how he had wronged us all—as much as I dared—and even threatened to hire a private investigator on my own coin to search for her. All he had ever told me was that Elizabeth had found her rightful family, and it would be best for her if we let her carry on with the life she was meant to live.

I turned to offer my brother some word of comfort, but George had abandoned his restless prowl at last to fling himself into a chair. He now sat slouched, elbows braced on knees, his hair disheveled from raking hands. I had not seen him so agitated in years. My stomach twisted anew, seeing the feverish light rekindled in his gaze. This meeting had awakened more than simple curiosity in my brother regarding the playmate of his youth.

Before I could frame a suitable reply, feminine footsteps tripping lightly down the stairs heralded Elizabeth's return. George sprang up so hastily that his chair tottered backward. I caught it just before the legs gave way completely. When I lifted my eyes once more, Elizabeth had gone stock still three feet away. Her startled gaze flashed from George to me like a trapped doe calculating avenues of escape.

George appeared oblivious to her discomfiture. He started forward, hands extended beseechingly, his voice reproachful. "Lizzy, is something amiss? Do we really mean so little to you now?"

Elizabeth backed up a step, slim fingers worrying the edge of her worn pelisse. "No, I... That is... Forgive me, I am not quite myself." She attempted a tremulous smile that only amplified the confusion in her dark eyes. "I ought to return to my sister."

She made to dart past, but George moved quicker, intercepting her with a gentle hand hovering just shy of grasping her arm. "Sister? What sister? Lizzy, please. Must you keep fleeing us? After so long parted, have we nothing to ask one another?"

Her throat convulsed on a difficult swallow. The longing and uncertainty so naked on George's face seemed almost an imposition. Yet how could she fail to read the depth of warmth and affection he had evidently carried all these years? I shifted my weight, unsure whether to intervene on either's behalf—brothers and estranged friends make poor mediators.

Before the strained moment could drag further, a stout matron bustled from the kitchen, wiping her hands on a stained apron. She bobbed a brisk curtsey toward Elizabeth. "Just come to say we've almost got your sister put tidy again, Miss. Won't take but half a mo' more if you were of a mind to settle yourself a spell?" Her shrewd eyes took in our little tableau with deepening creases at the corners.

Some of the tension ebbed from Elizabeth's posture. She summoned a wan but grateful smile for the woman. "Yes, thank you, Mrs. Barnes. I suppose..." Her resigned gaze drifted back to George and me. "Might we speak freely here without notice?"

""George wheeled instantly, seizing the olive branch with undisguised eagerness. He ushered her to a corner table well distanced from the few other midday patrons" "Yes, yes! Please, Lizzy, join us." His concerned frown belied the cheerful tone. "You are so altered and quiet—has life been very hard since you left Derbyshire?"

The furrow above her brows smoothed away, and a sad sweetness touched her lips. "No, indeed! I could not ask for better than the family I have." I sensed volumes unspoken behind those careful words. But George nodded, appeased.

An awkward beat of silence fell. My mind churned with a thousand fruitless openers. Why had she been exiled? How did she come here? Why did she seem so ill at ease in our company when once we had been as close as siblings?

Fortunately, George rarely found himself at a loss for words. That was why they had always got on so well, after all. He leaned nearer with a mischievous smile, chasing the sobriety from his face. "Well, what a merry trick of fortune this is, Lizzy Smith! I still can hardly credit that it is truly you here before us—you must think me some dull-witted farmer gaping at an exotic bird flown into his barn."

"I am called Elizabeth Bennet now."

George's head ticked sideways. "Bennet? So... you're married, then?"

She shook her head and glanced tightly at me before her eyes found George again... and there was adoration in that look, just as there had been all those years ago. "The Bennets took me in, and Uncle... That is, Mr. Gardiner, who became my guardian... he thought it would sound better if... being a sort of foundling, you see... if I had a name people knew, like a distant cousin. Not... Smith." She swallowed, and her look flickered to me.

Wise advice. Was not Smith nearly the ubiquitous name for someone of illicit origins? At least now she had a real name, even if it was borrowed.

"So, it *was* Mr. Gardiner who carried you away," I mused softly.

"Not quite in the sense you seem to convey. He has seen to my care, and he is as good a man as ever drew breath. But I did not come to live with him and his wife. His sister is Mrs. Bennet, you see, and she had four daughters already... well, they became sisters to me, just as you both were..." Her mouth stopped moving, and her eyes fixed on George again, but my heart gave a thud when I realized that was not filial affection lighting her gaze.

George laughed and grasped her hand across the table. "Well, Lizzy Smith, Lizzy Bennet, however you are called, I say it is jolly good to see you again. Come, catch us up on lost years! What of your family now, and life in..." He broke off, brows knitting. "Dash it, where the devil have you been hiding all this time?"

A peal of delighted laughter escaped her. At that moment, the gulf of years and separation seemed to melt away. I watched a blaze of lively spirit flare up in her eyes, casting me seven years back in time, just as if the years had never parted us. "Oh! Forgive me. The Bennets have a small estate in Hertfordshire."

My heart kicked a little when I put the names together. *Hertfordshire... Gardiner... Bennet.* Why, Bingley was considering becoming her neighbor!

"Hertfordshire!" George threw up his hands dramatically. "Well, that is something at least. Small mercy you did not sail off to the Americas without a backward glance!" He clasped her hand, giving it an impulsive squeeze. "I cannot tell you what it does to me to see you again, Lizzy."

Pink blossomed in her cheeks, but she did not pull away. Only the briefest shadow in her downcast lashes betrayed deeper reactions at war within. I shifted in my seat, my pulse quickening. And despite my joy at learning Elizabeth was safe and had a good life, I feared the gleam in George's eye just now. Even worse because it was mirrored in hers.

This reunion was unwise. George had only just won the favor of Lady Lucilla and her father against all odds. And whatever my reservations might be, Lady Lucilla was good for him. I had seen more maturity in him since he first spoke her name than I had in his entire life. And that was to say nothing about my own ambitions regarding a connection with Lord Belmont.

To have Elizabeth return now, awakening old affections and associations in my brother, could only court disaster.

Elizabeth

I PERCHED ON THE edge of the hard oak chair, painfully aware of both sets of penetrating eyes fixed upon me from across the scarred table. Fitzwilliam's gaze reminded me of his father's—keen and assessing beneath a formidable stillness. His dark eyes held pools of feeling, mostly kept in vicious check. But George's... his vivid blue eyes still danced as of old, crinkling at the corners with irrepressible humor that seven years had not diminished.

My heart performed a complicated series of flips behind my ribs. To be with them again was rapture and torture mingled. I had yearned for this reunion, whispered imagined conversations to their phantom ears through endless lonely nights. And yet... the promises wrung from me by Uncle Gardiner curdled in my throat. I should not have come to town, where I could chance letting this happen. Should not shatter the fragile peace built over years of forced separation. Whatever mysteries and injustices carved the jagged rift that divided us, I owed too much to the Gardiners and the Bennets now to reopen old wounds.

George leaned nearer. "We asked about you for months. Waited for word. Why did you never write to us?"

Did he think I had deserted them voluntarily? Before the old ache could sharpen into fresh resentment, his hand covered mine. "We were wild to find you, Lizzy, once we knew you had gone."

I studied our joined hands, overcome with memories. "I wrote," I whispered finally, daring to meet his earnest gaze. "For two years, I wrote letters."

Fitzwilliam straightened abruptly. George's startled glance flashed to his brother's grim face. "You wrote... yet we never received..." Confusion creased his brow.

I nodded. "At first, your replies would come. Oh, how I cherished those brief notes in George's untidy scrawl!" The old wound bled as

I voiced it aloud. "But after six months... nothing. I kept writing but received only silence."

Utter incomprehension washed over George's features. "I never wrote a single line! Upon my honor, Lizzy, I've no notion what letters you refer to. Had I known your direction, wild horses could not have kept me from replying."

I swayed where I sat, the carpet seeming to shift under my feet. "But... the letters I received were signed by your hand. I would swear to it!" I glanced desperately between the two brothers, willing one of them to produce some rational explanation for this dizzying bewilderment.

Fitzwilliam's mouth had drawn into an implacable line, his eyes frozen shards of flint. "Father," he bit out. Such *weight* of accusation and injury in that single word!

My own chaotic emotions stilled abruptly at this pronouncement. Of course... what other answer could there be? "Do you mean that he not only copied George's..." I broke off with an apologetic smile. "...*meandering* thoughts, but his haphazard penmanship? Impossible!"

"I do not doubt it," Fitzwilliam sighed. "He might have felt it helped ease your transition to your new family. At first. Then, he probably discontinued for whatever that same purpose was that he sent you away."

I gaped at them. They truly did not know more than I? Well, where was Father? Could I not ask...? *Oh.*

Ice formed around my heart as the great unspoken words hung between us. And the way they were suddenly looking at the table, their hands—anything but me... "Then...your father... Is he...?" I could not force the words past stiff lips.

Fitzwilliam's severe expression softened. He reached across the table hesitantly to cover my spasming fingers with his own. "Yes. Our father has been gone these five years past." His tone held gentle regret at being the bearer of such news.

A cry tore from my throat as I clapped my hand over my mouth too late. Tears scalded my eyes. *Dead!* Now, there could be no chance of reconciliation or explanation from his own lips. I grieved the finality of doors closed and questions that must remain unspoken.

Dimly, I heard George's anxious queries about whether I was quite well and needed assistance. But Fitzwilliam's steady fingers lacing through mine kept me anchored as I mastered the storm inside. At length, I lifted my head from the handkerchief he had pressed into my hands to find his eyes waiting. Such compassion and solidarity of spirit shone behind the somber gravity of his features. He gave my hand a slight squeeze.

"He spoke of you at the end, Lizzy. His mind grew... confused, but he asked for forgiveness again and again. For what, I do not know. He never would say."

A fresh tear tracked down my cheek despite myself. Had even grim deathbed remorse not compelled Mr. Darcy to break his baffling silence regarding my lost connection to his family? What was so shameful about me? I would never know. Yet Fitzwilliam's steadying grip kept me tethered to firm ground, instead of permitting me to spiral. However little sense his vague words made, they reassured me I had not slipped wholly from the heart of the man I loved as dearly as any father.

Just then, a flash of blue through the window caught my eye as a gentleman crossed the street and reached the door—of average height, with pleasant features swiftly creasing into a smile as he glanced through the window. His searching gaze roved the occupied tables of the inn before alighting on our little tableau.

"Ah, Darcy, George—there you are!" He strode toward us, nodding affably to us as the taproom door swung wide. Then his eyes drifted to me. "And Miss...?"

"Bennet. Elizabeth Bennet," I supplied, noting with some perverse pleasure the way Fitzwilliam and George flinched at my new surname.

He removed his hat. "A pleasure. I trust your sister is..." His friendly address turned suddenly uncertain, brows lifting when footsteps on the stair gave us both pause.

Jane had just appeared on the steps, a noticeable flush rising prettily in her cheeks as she saw who awaited below. Even across the distance, the admiration kindled a telling glow in the gentleman's fixed stare that could not be mistaken as their gazes caught and held for a long moment.

Oh, this was too much Bad enough that I broke my promise to Uncle Gardiner—accidentally or not—and had my heart shattered with the intelligence of Mr. Darcy's passing. Now Jane had to go and fall in love with their friend at first glance.

I scrambled to my feet. "Jane. There you are. Are you ready, then? Aunt will be wondering where we've got to."

"Wait!" George cried, catching my hand. "You've not told us where you are staying. Why are you back in Derbyshire, and for how long?"

I felt the weight of Jane's stare, but I could not very well lie to them, could I? Now that they knew I was here, my presence could not be kept a secret. "At Farthingdale. Aunt Gardiner's sister is Mrs. Westing, and she... had need of some help for a few months. But now we must return, for Mrs. Westing is no doubt looking for her fresh cheeses and ham."

George took both my hands now. "You must come to Pemberley, Lizzy—soon as may be. Let us not lose each other again as soon as we have found you. Bring Miss Bennet and Mrs. Gardiner too! What joy to have you close once more!"

His unchecked enthusiasm wrenched my heart even as it warmed me. I opened my mouth, not knowing what promise or refusal lay ready.

But Fitzwilliam had gained his feet swiftly. "Come, George, we have imposed long enough on Miss Bennet and should return. Lord Belmont will be awaiting us."

The reminder shocked George to awareness. "Lord Belmont! Dash it all, I had forgot." He turned to me, the bright feeling in his eyes undimmed. "I will call on you at the first opportunity, Lizzy. We have years to catch up on."

His gaze held that special light reserved for me alone in days of old—still able to turn my bones to water all these years later. Yet as I curtsied my farewells, my eyes followed the elder Darcy's retreating figure. What inner secrets motivated such deep currents behind that inscrutable facade? My heart whispered I had only glimpsed the surface of hidden depths yet to be plumbed.

ELEVEN

Darcy

I PACED THE LENGTH of Pemberley's cavernous entrance hall, boots echoing sharply against marble tiles. At the mullioned window, George craned his neck, peering eagerly down the drive.

"I can see the dust from the carriages just there past the great oak!" He bobbed excitedly on his heels. "Darcy, did I brush all the horsehair from my coat this morning?"

I waved my hand, my pulse already quickening in response to his nerves. "For the third time, yes, you are perfectly presentable." Under normal circumstances, I would tease him for showing such uncharacteristic uncertainty before a country visitor. But today, tension thrummed through my frame. Soon, we would stand before George's formidable future father-in-law, tacitly presenting my scatterbrained brother as suitable enough to share guardianship of Lady Lucilla's future.

And the sizeable fortune she would bring to the marriage, I reminded myself grimly. Ever the pragmatist, Lord Belmont was unlikely to be swayed solely by the couple's mutual affection. No, George must prove himself a competent steward and guardian as well if he hoped to truly keep Belmont's approval as Lucilla's husband. I only prayed he was up to the challenge.

"Here they come," George muttered needlessly. I could already make out the two carriages rounding the curving lane, plumed horses tossing glossy heads, and George's curricle stood ready in the drive, harnessed to his fleet bays to greet them. No turning back now.

I straightened my shoulders and forced an attitude of calm assurance as the first vehicle pulled before us. Lord Matlock called the matched grays to a prancing halt and turned to hand Lady Belmont down. Lord and Lady Matlock would lend us much-needed gentility and refinement in place of the absent mistress at Pemberley. At least Lady Lucilla need not want for noble companionship.

Lord Belmont descended last, keen grey eyes sweeping his surroundings as if determining whether the reality matched prior reports. I stepped forward, schooling my features to impassivity beneath that penetrating assessment.

"Lord and Lady Belmont, welcome to Pemberley." I bowed correctly over her ladyship's deferentially extended hand. A faint smile hovered about Lord Belmont's mouth as if secretly amused by such a stilted ceremony between neighbors.

"Come now, we stand on no formality today," he pronounced, shaking my hand heartily. "I desired an intimate glimpse into my prospective new son's world." His sharp eyes glinted with private humor that did nothing to settle my nerves.

Before I could frame a coherent response, Lady Matlock bustled forward, graciously shepherding all within doors to take refreshment and allow the gentlemen time alone to discuss' business.' I breathed a silent prayer of thanks for her social deftness. Though what 'business' Lord Belmont anticipated discussing with a mere backcountry landowner and tradesman remained to be seen.

Barely half an hour later, the parties sorted themselves back into the readied carriages. I handed Lord Belmont up into my phaeton's rear seat, relieved when he made no demur. Whatever trial or assessment awaited, best to meet it head on.

I flicked the reins, and the high-stepping greys surged smoothly forward. Behind me, I heard George's voice lifted merrily as he handed Lady Lucilla into their private vehicle. At least one of us rode toward his heart's desire carefree.

"The prospect is everything Matlock claimed." Lord Belmont eyed the distant hills appreciatively. "Well situated, Darcy. Your family chose with care."

I could not prevent foolish pride kindling at his approbation. "Four generations have called Pemberley home. My great-grandfather built the current manor."

His lordship made an interested noise, still surveying the passing scenery. "He chose with an eye to prosperity. The mill below—also established by your family line?"

"My father erected that, yes." I hesitated. "Would it please you to take the road nearer the buildings, my lord?" If discussion was inevitable, best invite it on my terms.

Shrewd eyes glinted a silent salute at my transparent maneuver. "By all means. I am interested to see the workings of this woolen trade that featured so prominently in that letter of yours." He settled back as I redirected our course, hints of a smile still playing about his mouth.

I flicked the reins, guiding the carriage toward the distant mill. Its tall chimneys spewed thin trails of smoke that vanished into the clear summer sky. Beside me, Lord Belmont observed its approach through narrowed eyes.

"Impressive structures," he remarked. "Welsh steel beams unless miss my guess?"

"Just so." I allowed myself a glimmer of pride. "My father wished to build both to last and to allow ease of modernization when needed."

His lordship harrumphed, twitching his mustache. "Let us see if the reality matches your optimistic vision, then." He fixed me with an arch look. "I have heard you boast of maintaining high standards for workers within. Paying them fair wages and the like."

I bristled at his skeptical tone. "I make no boast, my lord. I hold the health and safety of my laborers as accountability before God."

We drew up before the formidable brick edifice, and Belmont eyed me askance. "Pretty ideals. Tell me, do you limit your workers' hours or employ children under the age of twelve? What of these controls you propose, to limit the smoke I see belching into the heavens?"

My grip tightened on the ribbons. "At present, only safety measures have been attended to—those which prevent exhaustion and injury, particularly to children. Other plans are yet to be implemented. But I aim to transition once feasible. I wish to lead by example. If more mill owners provided sanitary housing, fair wages—"

He cut me off with an abrupt slice of his hand. "Enough, you prove my point! What real experience have you to guide legislation? This is not how you earn your livelihood. You are a hobbyist, Darcy. You play at running mills and factories with none of the pressures of actual commerce."

My temper flashed. "I beg your pardon, my lord. But merely because I weigh concerns beyond profit does not make mine a 'game.' And if you would hear me out—"

"Oh, certainly! Regale me with more tales of your workers' paradise by the stream."

I mastered my irritation with effort. Losing my temper would only affirm his dismissal of my position as youthful ignorance. "That is not my objective," I replied levelly. "I agree laws should not choke businesses struggling to stay afloat. I only propose accountability that prevents the workers from being misused. It is a delicate balance." I held his skeptical gaze. "If you truly wish the good of the realm, ought you not seek wisdom wherever it may be found, Lord Belmont? Not just from privileged voices in London?"

Slowly, he sat back, eyes still piercing but less combative. "You have courage to challenge me so bluntly, Darcy. I begin to see why my headstrong daughter is enamored of your family's charms." He stroked his chin, musing now rather than mocking. "Very well, I shall consider these issues of regulation more carefully before I vote. Your insights may balance other biases." He eyed me for a long minute. "As for George, I can find no fault in either of you. Provided he proves deserving of Lucilla's regard in time."

I released a careful breath. There could be no better outcome from this first true test of George's position. If he continued thus... I inclined my head in return. "I am certain he will strive to do just that, my lord."

Belmont's eyes glinted. "See that he does."

I gathered my courage as the last chimney faded from view. "Forgive my boldness, my lord, but I struggle to comprehend your acceptance of George as Lady Lucilla's suitor. Their attachment appears genuine, yet surely you harbored... doubts regarding his suitability?"

Lord Belmont barked a laugh. "Doubts? Grave ones, I assure you! When Lucilla first wrote naming your brother as her beloved, I fully intended to nip this folly in the bud."

My breath caught. "What changed your mind, my lord?"

His gaze grew distant, lingering on the horizon. "My daughter can be willful, and she made an ardent case. It does carry some weight, with me, at least, that she recently attained her majority. She is no naive girl of sixteen. Still, I remained unmoved... until I recalled..." He shifted, suddenly awkward. "Well, let us just say I found cause to reconsider."

Puzzled, I waited for him to elaborate. But Lord Belmont offered nothing further. Whatever private grief or obligation had softened him towards George, he seemed disinclined to confide his reasons. I bobbed my head, accepting the unspoken boundary. "I see. Well, for George's sake, I thank providence for your change of heart."

We spoke little for the remainder of the drive. My mind churned fruitlessly, seeking any clue illuminating the mystery of Lady Lucilla's abruptly successful courtship. Had Winston pleaded his friend's case? Or had the countess's gentle influence swayed her husband?

I was shaken from my fruitless speculations as we passed through a pretty hamlet. With a small shock, I recognized Farthingdale's sloping fields and humble manor house nestled beyond. And there, framed clearly in an upstairs window, sat Elizabeth bent intently over a book.

My heart performed an odd stutter-step at the unexpected sight of her. Oblivious to my gaze, she turned a page, eyes dreamy and far away. Did she still think of our bizarre reunion yesterday? Before I could wrest my attention away, a second jolt of surprise struck. For there, peeking from the carriage house, stood a horse I would recognize any-where—Bingley's tall chestnut, Jupiter. Unexpected warmth rushed through me. So, while I guided noblemen about the countryside, wise Bingley had been making much cozier acquaintances. I was happy for him, truly, though an unfamiliar pang stirred, watching Elizabeth disappear from view as we drove on.

I risked a sidelong assessment of Lord Belmont, but he seemed absorbed in cataloging woodland acreage, with no indication he had marked Jupiter's presence. For propriety's sake, I held my tongue. But internally, I wished both my friend and the fair Miss Bennet happy progress in their... friendship.

Elizabeth

I LEANED AGAINST THE window frame, the open book in my lap long forgotten. My eyes followed a pair of sparrows flitting through the rambling back garden while my thoughts danced elsewhere. Namely, Pemberley. And two gentlemen currently under that venerable roof.

Since our surprise encounter yesterday, I had scarcely thought of anything else. The astonishment written on both Fitzwilliam and George's faces seemed etched into my vision. Nor could I escape the memory of George's impulsive grasp of my hands or the way his voice wrapped warmly around my childhood name. Things I had mourned as only echoes of the past for endless years.

My book slipped unheeded to the floor. How long I had ached for resolution with the Darcy family I was forced to abandon! And miraculously, here it was, delivered unexpectedly back within my orbit after seven years. Both Uncle Gardiner and harsh reality urged me to restrain my revived hopes. But neither could eclipse the glow kindled inside at regaining two figures who had filled my young world with affection and adventures untold.

I was roused from my reflections by approaching voices and a knock below. I straightened expectantly. Likely Aunt, come to remind me afternoon tea awaited. My confession yesterday of encountering the Darcys had set her predictably on edge. While sympathetic to past hurts, Aunt also took seriously Uncle Gardiner's cryptic reasons for discouraging contact with old acquaintances in Derbyshire. Reasons never fully explained, despite my most persistent demands over the years. Well, their protective secrecy mattered little now. The cat was out of the bag, so to speak, and Aunt would simply have to make peace with my resolution to reunite with George and Fitzwilliam.

To my surprise, it was Jane's gentle voice that responded below instead of Aunt's. And unless I was mistaken, a masculine rumble answered. My brows lifted. Callers at teatime? How singular. Unl ess... Surely not again! My lips twitched while traversing the stairs. It would seem Mr. Bingley had wasted no time finding an excuse to call, conveniently while I was occupied upstairs, and she had to receive him alone. My poor Jane's cheeks must resemble the roses in Mrs. George's Westing's garden.

Sure enough, I entered the parlor to find Jane posed gracefully by the window, studiously arranging late blooms with only the kitchen maid for a chaperone. And her admirer was none other than one Mr. Charles Bingley. I nearly laughed aloud at his celerity in calling.

But any teasing remark died swiftly. This was no transient flirtation, if one judged by his animation and undisguised admiration. Sudden certainty flared within that I beheld a man already halfway lost to my sister's unassuming charms. And possibly, one intended by providence to be found by her own quiet heart long accustomed to stand in others' shadows.

"Oh, Lizzy!" Jane looked up, her gentle features suffused in a glow no amount of sunshine could impart. "Mr. Bingley has been good enough to call and inquire after my health."

"The gentleman sprang to his feet, all solicitous concern.""Indeed, I could not be easy until fully satisfied there were no lingering effects from the unfortunate fall." His searching gaze lingered on Jane'ssson's face. "But I see Pemberley's fair roses cannot equal your bloom, Miss Bennet."

A tide of crimson confirmed my earlier suspicion of Jane's sentiments. But words failed her under such effusive compliments. Taking pity, I stepped smoothly into the gap.

"How thoughtful, Mr. Bingley! Jane is almost restored, apart from the occasional twinges she attempts to hide. I do believe it will be some days before the abrasion heals perfectly." My pointed look elicited a sisterly grimace. Turning apologetically to our guest, I continued, "Forgive me, I was meaning to have a word with our aunt. Unless Jane, you would like me to stay?"

Her wide eyes and faint headshake required no translation. Clearly, my presence would be more of a hindrance than help, and she did have a maid to sit with her. Laughing inwardly, I excused myself to the pianoforte room in search of Aunt. However, that lady was not indoors. Likely occupied with some matter in the still room that often stole hours without her notice. But no matter—returning to play the third wheel between Jane and her suitor held little appeal. Better grant them a few moments' privacy to nurture the delicate plant so full of hopeful promise.

Eventually, I discovered Aunt amid her herb pots, sighing over ailing plants that felt autumn's early chill. Brushing dirt from her apron, she straightened to greet me wryly. "Let me guess. Mr. Bingley is come inquiring after a certain maiden's health and requires no chaperoning?"

I grinned. "You know my sister too well. They are all propriety of course, but who am I to intrude on their tête-à-tête?"

Aunt pulled off her worn gloves with a pensive look between house and garden. "No doubt Jane has the situation well in hand. That girl was born with greater sense and poise than the rest of us mere mortals combined." Her keen gaze shifted to me then. "And you, Lizzy girl? I confess since speaking yesterday, I hardly know how to broach certain ... delicate topics." She shook the dirt from the gloves, fidgeting. "What are your thoughts now regarding chance reunions in Lambton?"

I drew breath to air my secret hopes, only to hesitate. Would she understand? Drawing nearer under the guise of admiring her herbs, I chose my words carefully. "Only that refusing to acknowledge past friends prevents nothing. The links exist, though stretched thin by years and silence." I permitted myself the pleasure of giving voice to my dream. "I find my heart much eased and revived by the prospect of restoring those severed ties." I risked meeting her studious gaze directly. "I intend to know them both again, whatever objections others may raise, Aunt."

Silence reigned while I held my breath. At long last, she bestowed a tremulous but bracing smile. Reaching to grasp my hand warmly, she spoke the words I hoped but hardly dared expect. "Then I am happy for you, my child. It seems Providence means your paths to cross again."

TWELVE

Darcy

I STOOD AT THE wide window overlooking Pemberley's rear lawns, hands clasped tightly behind my back. The fading light cast the empty expanse in melancholy hues that matched my pensive mood. I had readily agreed when Lord Matlock requested a private conference following the lengthy tour and al fresco luncheon for our noble guests. Too much weighed upon my mind after the morning's revelations. I required an attentive ear and thoughtful counsel. Hopefully, my uncle could supply both.

At length, the door clicked discreetly closed behind His Lordship. I turned to find his sharp gaze already fixed expectantly on me. "You seem out of sorts this evening, Darcy. I hope our guests found everything at Pemberley to their satisfaction?"

I attempted an easy denial, but it rang hollow even to myself. Sighing in defeat, I abandoned all pretense. "Forgive me, Uncle. I fear I am poor company just now. The honor of hosting Lord Belmont does not occupy my thoughts so much as... an unexpected encounter in Lambton yesterday."

Matlock raised one eloquent brow, matching my oblique manner. "An encounter, you say? Of what nature can it be to distract my most focused nephew so?"

I turned back to the darkening window. "Do you recall my father's ward, Elizabeth?" I finally voiced the name, instantly resurrecting a dozen memories. "She who used to follow George and me everywhere as children?"

Matlock stared. "Miss Elizabeth Smith? But surely not—she has not—?"

"Returned to Derbyshire after seven years? Indeed, though I can scarcely credit it myself." I grimaced at the glass, seeing my haunted expression reflected. "I stumbled upon her in the village the other day, but we did not speak. I thought it was her but did not confirm it. Then we happened upon her again yesterday, and we spoke at length. Can you conceive it? Just like that, without warning, she materialized as though seven years were merely seven days."

"Astounding!" Matlock crossed the room to stand beside me, keen features alight with interest. "I always was fond of the lass. Lively little whirlwind of a girl. Where has she been all these years?"

"Hertfordshire, but if you mean to ask why, I am afraid I cannot answer that."

"Well, how ever did she turn up here after all this time?"

I lifted a hopeless shoulder. "By the most improbable chance. Some errand called her into town just as I happened to enter the shop. Although..." I slanted a look sideways at my uncle. "...she gave no indication of pleasure at crossing paths. Indeed, she could scarcely meet my eye and fled with her friend at the first opportunity. I am quite at a loss to explain such a cool reception."

Matlock tugged at his chin, reflective. "How strange. She adored you boys. But perhaps bitterness has taken root after your father so abruptly sent her off without explanation."

I winced. The memory of Elizabeth's unconcealed anguish when she asked about Father still pricked my conscience. If anyone deserved answers for Father's inexplicable actions, surely it was Elizabeth herself.

"I cannot make sense of any of it," I admitted tiredly. "If only Father had shared his reasons before the end. He never said aught to you of it?"

"Not a word, though I asked him more than once. Asked him whence she had come when he first brought her here as a babe—you know, we all made assumptions—and asked why she had gone. He never uttered a syllable."

"The only thing I know... well, that I still believe... is that the 'assumptions' you speak of were not true. She is not my half-sister."

"How can you be so sure of that?"

I shrugged and paced to another window, avoiding his gaze. "Mother died giving birth to George, leaving Father a widower for two years before he brought Elizabeth here as an infant. If he had been her sire, he would have married her mother. There would have been no shame in it, and he was not the man to leave a woman in such a state. Why would a man who was free to marry again seek comfort in the arms of another woman, then refuse to wed her but raise her child? It makes no sense."

"Unless she was a doxy. A disgrace to him. Or married elsewhere, and her husband bade her to get rid of the child."

I scoffed. "I cannot credit it. You can believe me when I say that I wrestled with this notion for years, watching his character and conduct. He vowed to me that he was not Elizabeth's natural father, and that is sufficient for me. But in every other way that mattered, he *was* a father to her, and he left us all with unanswered questions. Without the truth, how are past wounds to mend?"

I yearned simply to call on Elizabeth and beg her confidence once more. Perhaps between the two of us, our shared memories might click together like so many pieces of a puzzle. But uneasy premonitions held me back. There was more at stake now than just childhood attachments. My wayward brother's future hung tenuously suspended, ripe to be shattered by one ill-placed gust from the past. I slanted another sideways look at my uncle.

"The only explanation I could ever conceive for why Father sent her away was that he saw the... attachment George and Lizzy used to share. Saw it, and disapproved."

"Well, that reinforces the theory that she could be..." He stopped and cleared his throat when he saw the dangerous look in my eye. "But as you say, that could not be the case. I do suppose he would desire better for his sons than marriage to some by-blow."

"Do you think... could renewed friendship tempt George to renew... other sentiments as well?"

Comprehension sparked at once in Matlock's keen gaze. "You mean might his betrothal to Lady Lucilla be threatened if that old affection reignites? Oh, surely not! He seems quite enamored with his lady."

I shifted restlessly. "So he appears. But you did not witness their reunion yesterday. I saw it—that old spark in George's eyes. He has never looked thus, not even in Lady Lucilla's presence." I exhaled heavily. "I fear he will not forget Elizabeth Smith easily a second time."

Matlock's brows snapped together. "Confound it, you may be right! We cannot risk George sacrificing this golden opportunity and Belmont's good graces on a whimsical fancy from the past, no matter how charming the lady." He gripped my shoulder urgently. "Darcy, you must keep them apart!"

I stared, consternation rising. My own longing to reconnect warred powerfully against the duty to guard George's prospects. I respected Elizabeth too much to simply cut her again with no explanation. Yet what alternative presented itself?

As if reading my thoughts, Matlock hastened to add, "At least until vows are exchanged and this match irrevocably settled. Once George marries Lady Lucilla, he will be safely anchored from lingering regrets over roads not taken." His mouth twisted ruefully. "We must both wish the course of true love could run smoothly for once in this family. But the world little considers the yearnings of the heart."

I studied the dark lawn sightlessly. The laughing girl with chestnut curls was now a whisper on the summer air—so near and yet as distant as those golden days of youth. Could I, in honor, forbid her the explanations my father denied? Or must practical considerations carry the day?

"You speak the truth, Uncle," I replied heavily at length. "I shall... consider carefully how to proceed."

Matlock nodded. "See that you do. Much depends on it." He moved toward the door, then paused to glance back with a glimmer of his usual humor. "Unless you fancy testing your diplomatic skills against Belmont's wrath, should this wedding disintegrate?"

The feeble jest barely stirred a flicker of wry response. My soul felt weighed beneath old regrets and present dilemmas as Matlock left me alone once more with the creeping autumn shadows. Past and present seemed fatefully intertwined across the years by three youthful players blindly dancing to melodies only time understood. Wherever this strange reel led, I sensed the coming movements must tread carefully indeed through a minefield of divided loyalties, dangerous secrets, and loves both old and new.

Perhaps I would write her a note. Yes, that would do. Something pleasant and intentionally vague, speaking of a desire to welcome her and her party for tea but failing to name a date. That way, I could take a day or two to see which way the wind blew with Belmont. He would not remain in Derbyshire forever, and once he and his family were safely returned to London, we could have that reunion with Elizabeth.

Elizabeth

I TURNED THE LETTER over in my hands, drinking in every graceful stroke of ink. Such bold, decisive penmanship compared to the haphazard scrawl I recalled as George's. My eyes lingered over the signature—Fitzwilliam Darcy. Just that bold black name sent a tremor of anticipation through me.

"Well, Lizzy? Do not keep us in suspense!" Aunt leaned nearer where we sat, circled around the morning table, forgotten tea growing cold. "What does Mr. Darcy have to say?"

I released a shuddering breath I had not realized I had held. "He writes that nothing could give him greater pleasure than to formally receive us all at Pemberley." My voice quavered with a surge of mingled excitement and trepidation. There! His own words, an irrefutable stamp marking seven years apart as mere illusion. I lifted my shining eyes to take in the answering delight dawning around the table.

Aunt pressed an anxious hand to her breast even as excitement pinked her cheeks. "Thank heaven! Perhaps your uncle's fears were for naught. Is he not still the kindest young man breathing?"

I bent again hungrily over the letter, tracing each slanted word. "Indeed! Although he offers no specific date yet, he only makes... vague mentions that they currently have important guests whose convenience must be considered. But once departed..." My voice trailed off, imagination leaping ahead to tender reunions beneath Pemberley's ancient oaks. I fairly tingled in anticipation.

Beside me, Jane cast a sympathetic look at my glowing cheeks. "It seems almost providential that you should chance to meet again. I am truly happy for you, dearest Lizzy. But you will not..." She leaned her head toward me. "You will not forget *us*, will you?"

I squeezed her slender fingers, my heart too full for speech. "Forget you, who have become my sister as surely as if you were flesh and blood? Never! The only greater felicity awaiting would be seeing you as happy as I am at present. And I *think* that happiness is not far around the corner for you."

Jane giggled and blushed behind her teacup. "Mr. Bingley is thinking of taking Netherfield. Can you fancy that? He would be our neighbor!"

"There, you see? Providential."

We finished breakfast amidst animated speculation about mysterious guests whose convenience must not be encroached upon. Aunt seemed inclined to take a poor view of anyone who dared stand in the way of our reception even a day longer than necessary. But I counseled patience. We had waited this long to regain what was lost—what harm in a short delay more?

Still, as soon as I was able, I slipped outdoors, suddenly restless as a caged bird. I must walk, and walk hard, until equanimity returned.

Some hours later, the summer sunshine had burned away the last shreds of mist clinging to hollows and copses. My rapid steps carried me unerringly through remembered woodland paths barely changed by intervening years. How easy here to slip back into that carefree young girl endlessly racing through Pemberley's leafy sanctuary. I had not intended this destination when I first fled the house. Yet somehow, my feet knew where my soul longed to wander this day.

A glimpse of Greek columns through the trees brought me up short. I lingered at the edge of the tree line, suddenly timid. It would be nothing to cross the lawn and proceed inside those soaring doors as though seven years had never passed. Surely no one could begrudge me simply drinking my fill of memories long denied? Brushing aside wisps of ivy, I ventured one step, then another, onto close-clipped grass. Soon, I was skimming the perimeter of Pemberley's rear lawns, pausing frequently to soak up half-forgotten vistas of stream and meadow limned in summer's verdant crown.

A fountain's cheerful splashing drew me irresistibly to circle a copse until the ornamental gardens lay open before me. There indeed stood the marble statue fount I recalled dotting cool jets of water into the air high enough that George could run through without a single drop striking his golden head. My feet carried me to its edge before I quite realized, eager fingers already trailing in the crystalline water.

Laughter rang out from a little distance, and I lifted my head. A bright grouping of ladies strolled just visible between sculpted hedges—elegant morning gowns marking them as gentlewomen of quality. Perhaps they were even those important guests Aunt endlessly speculated about over breakfast. And was that... *George* with them? It could be... The gentleman was about the right height. But he was using a walking stick and escorting one of the ladies on his arm. Well, that settled it. George always said walking sticks were pompous affectations.

From the opposite direction, striding across turf I knew led towards the Grecian gardens, came a more isolated figure. I knew that proud carriage and unfashionably tousled black hair that poked out from his hat immediately. Joy sparked through me, and I straightened, hand lifting in an eager wave.

"Mr. Darcy!" My cry rang clear as bells across the autumn air. His dark head jerked up, astonishment washing over his stern features. I watched him check mid-stride and turn toward my voice as if not quite trusting his senses. The two ladies in the rear of the group, wandering through the topiary, glanced around in mild curiosity. But I had eyes only for Fitzwilliam Darcy as he swiftly changed course toward me, a wondering look of doubt breaking like sunrise over his face that probably echoed my own delight.

"Miss Elizabeth?" Disbelief weighted his rich voice as he drew up hastily before me. "What... what brings you here today?" His wide eyes devoured every aspect like a drowning man sucking in air. Before I could reply, he seized my outstretched fingers, pressing them fervently between both palms. "By heaven, I had not thought to find you here!"

Confused pleasure surged through me at words I could only interpret as gladness despite his evidently shocked countenance. My face stretched wide in an irrepressible grin. "Pemberley was always open to visitors. Have I no right to presume to ramble this particular acreage uninvited? Unless you will set the dogs on me for old time's sake?"

The tease broke past his astonishment at last, wrenching a rusty chuckle forth. But all too swiftly, sobriety shuttered his features once more. He flicked an uneasy glance toward that merry party still meandering through garden paths, then abruptly offered me his arm.

"Come, let us walk this way." Bewildered, but willing as ever to match Darcy strides for adventure's sake, I consented. However, his manner remained strangely oppressed as we wandered silently through the yew maze. My unrest quickened.

"Mr. Darcy, is something amiss? You seem quite discomfited. Can it be as unwelcome as all that to chance upon me?" My light laugh could not quite conceal the genuine thread of uncertainty weaving beneath. He must have heard the wistful note, for he hastened to quell my doubts.

"No, indeed! I am only startled. In truth, I..." He paused as if listening to something. "I have been looking forward to having you here. Let me see... was it a left turn at this bend?" His long legs increased their pace, and I hurried to match them, bemused how a man could grow so unfamiliar in his own ancestral gardens.

"Oh, but you said you had guests just now. Truly, I did not intend to intrude..." My weak assurance trailed off at his instantly protesting squeeze of my hand on his coat sleeve.

"Nonsense. I cannot tell you how very felicitous this accidental meeting is. In fact..." Here, he paused to scan our surroundings in mounting bewilderment. "Good Lord, surely the path lay..." Another perturbed glance behind wrenched a laugh from me.

"Oh, Mr. Darcy, surely you cannot be lost? Why, you could tread this maze blindfolded since boyhood! Let me guess—too many hours poring over accounts and crops behind your father's old desk?"

His features softened, something like his old shy warmth creeping back. "You know me too well, Miss Elizabeth. Guilty as charged on all counts. I fear managing Pemberley these five years has not left me as much time as I would like to roam its grounds."

I gently detached my arm from his to wander toward a gap in the hedge, knowing it afforded a view downhill toward the lake. "What a shame. I always envied you such a paradise for rambles and exploring. You own all this, but you have no time to enjoy it." I half-turned back, arrested by the sight of his tall frame silhouetted against the vivid green foliage. "Do not let the weight of responsibility rob you of life's simpler pleasures, Fitzwilliam."

The Christian name slipped out unawares, hanging sweetly familiar between us. Something indefinable shifted in his hooded gaze though he stood very still. "Perhaps you are right... Elizabeth."

Thirteen

Darcy

I GLANCED OVER MY shoulder, oddly reluctant to end our ramble... and put an end to whatever that snap was, humming in the air between us. Had she sensed it, too? Surely, it was my imagination. But better draw this encounter to its necessary conclusion before uncomfortable explanations or injudicious meetings proved inescapable. Clearing my throat, I took a half step backward, gesturing awkwardly toward the distant house.

"You must think me a poor host, keeping you walking out here in the heat of the day." I attempted a convivial smile but feared it emerged wan at best. "Allow me to offer you some refreshment indoors as partial restitution."

Surprise and something I decided must be pleasant anticipation lit her expressive features. "Oh! Are you certain? I would not wish to take you from important affairs. Is George...?"

"He is occupied at present, but I am quite at my leisure." I waved away such conscientious demurs and offered my arm once more to guide us from the maze. "Please, it would be a very great pleasure." And so, it unquestionably would be, under any other circumstance not cursed with secrecy and subterfuge. Oh, how I hate disguise! I quickened our pace, praying George yet kept to the farthest edge of the garden, entertaining his own elevated company.

Once within Pemberley's soaring foyer, I detoured briskly past salons likely to invite casual visitors. George was to escort the ladies back to Matlock this afternoon, but I doubted he would let them go without inviting them in to refresh themselves before the drive. I did not need *that* complication.

The library's isolation and distance from certain occupants made it the safest choice for privacy. If questioned later by the servants, my reclusive tendencies provided a plausible excuse for sequestering Miss Elizabeth there. I ushered her through the towering oak doors with breathless haste, softly latching them closed against all intrusion.

Safely ensconced in hushed scholarly surroundings, some of the tension ebbed from my frame. I inhaled the familiar soothing scent of leather and beeswax. Nothing remained now but to ring for tea and play the genial host. Ignoring the prickling awareness of my companion wandering slowly, silently through rows of shelved books, I crossed to tug the bell pull. Soon, I would have Elizabeth smiling over tea and comfortable in a plush leather chair—which happened to look *away* from the window.

Shrugging out of my coat in the over-warm room, I turned to find her trailing one wistful fingertip along the intricate wood carvings fronting my father's section of legal archives. Something squeezed painfully in my chest at her unguarded profile. Before I quite intended, words slipped out softly. "It pleases me greatly to see you here again, Elizabeth."

She started slightly, eyes finding mine in the dim light, wide and luminous. "I can scarcely describe what it means to be here, where so many happy memories live." Her gaze drifted around the shadowed perimeter, seeing far more than solid walls and floors. "I can envision Father—Mr. Darcy—in that chair, you at the window bent over some weighty textbook, while George and I..." She faltered, her color rising.

I stared, lost for a reply. The tender note infusing her voice when she spoke of George played discordantly against my better judgment. I moved slowly to her side, cautious, as if I were approaching a skittish colt. "I apologize that I could not invite George to join us." At her surprised look, I rushed on, "But our guests still await him. Whereas you and he were always such particular friends..."

I left the observation suspended meaningfully. Elizabeth's gaze dropped to study the intricate Turkish carpet. A darker color rose in her cheeks at the implied question. When she did lift her eyes once more, something vulnerable and resigned had replaced her usual vibrant mien.

"I suppose you perceive more clearly than I the damage wrought by years and silence." Her slender shoulders lifted and fell helplessly. "I see now that resuming any special intimacy would be unwise. Likely impossible."

My breath stopped. Could she... did she still harbor deeper sentiments where George was concerned, then? Surely innocent fondness for a childhood companion had not unexpectedly transformed into genuine tenderness in the intervening years apart? I fumbled for a judicious reply. "That is... understandable. Such attachments often leave lasting impressions, however unwittingly formed."

Elizabeth bit her lip, shamefaced. "Oh, you must think me a fool pining after nursery rhymes and old affections."

She attempted a careless laugh, but it struck a jarring note. My heart clenched, cursing the necessity for discretion. How could I fault her candor when my conscience shuddered under the burden of truth withheld? I reached to lightly touch her hand, where it rested on the shelf edge.

"Indeed, I think no such thing. You forget how well I know that particular heart." I waited until she shyly met my gaze. "I remember too clearly how it was... *before*. Losing your place here must have wounded you deeply—too deeply for time alone to erase."

Her eyes glistened, and impulsively, she turned her palm to cling to my tentative fingers. "I wished a hundred times to hate you all. But that was impossible." Her whispered confession plucked at my soul. Gently, I folded both her hands between my own, allowing silent communion to speak what words could not adequately convey.

A discrete cough at the door broke the spell weaving around us. I dropped Elizabeth's hands swiftly as a maid entered, balancing an overladen tea tray. Burning with embarrassment at having been discovered in so intimate a posture, I stepped back stiffly and invited Elizabeth to make herself comfortable by the fire while I prepared her a plate.

The familiar rituals of stirring cream and sugar into tea allowed equilibrium to restore itself. By unspoken consent, we avoided further dangerous intimate conversation. And if regret tinged our silence throughout, we both wore our social masks with practiced skill.

Elizabeth

I CRADLED THE DELICATE China teacup, letting wisps of steam wreathe my face. The refreshing liquid seeped into my parched mouth and throat, still overheated from our lengthy walk outdoors earlier. I gladly drained my first cup, hoping the hot tea would revive me. Across from me, Mr. Darcy sat with one long leg casually crossed, his own replenished cup in hand. But his eyes seldom strayed to the refreshment. Instead, I sensed his pensive study drifting over and around me at regular intervals when he believed my attention fixed elsewhere.

Odd how a silence shared with George always brimmed with lively expectancy, both of us leaning in with quivering anticipation toward the next wild scheme or burst of infectious laughter. Quiet with Mr. Darcy felt akin to the hushed reverence of a cathedral nave—breaths measured and muted so as not to disturb some fragile sanctity held suspended in the vaulted air. When, at length, I lifted my eyes to meet my host's thoughtful regard, curiosity drove me to break up the heavy silence.

"Forgive me, have I disrupted important affairs by descending upon your hospitality unannounced?"

Fitzwilliam blinked as though shaking off deeper ponderings before mustering a genial smile. "No, indeed. As I said, my time today is entirely my own." He took a slow draught of tea. "And there are few friends whose company I should prefer."

I hoped the steam would disguise my gratified flush at such uncharacteristic effusion. But honesty compelled an uneasy reply. "Even so, with prior engagements commanding your attention..."

Darcy's expression shuttered subtly at the delicate allusion even as he waved it aside. "It is no matter. Their interests and... amusements differ from my own." His mouth compressed, and I sensed the topic held sensitivities not to be further encroached upon.

Casting about for safer ground, my regard fell upon various small changes marking my absence throughout the comfortably familiar room. I set down my cup and rose, wandering closer to examine the new base trim by the door and an unfamiliar landscape adorning the far wall. "You must think me impertinent, remarking on household arrangements like a nosy aunt, but I see many updates since the days when I would secrete myself here for rainy-day adventures."

My host unfolded himself from his chair to join me in surveying the redecorated corner that had once boasted shelves of legal archives. Faint melancholy tightened his eyes and the set of his mouth. "Yes, much necessarily shifts when leadership and authority exchange hands. Even had I wished it, preserving every detail precisely as my father left, it could not be."

I watched the play of emotions crossing his face as he gazed at the signposts marking the passage from one generation's administration to the next. On impulse, I touched a sympathetic hand to his wrist. "Will you tell me how it happened? His passing, I mean." I swallowed the fresh swell of sorrow. "I realize death often strikes unannounced, but still, I wish I might have seen him one last time, or at least heard his voice."

Darcy—for I suppose I must call him that now—turned his arm to clasp my tentative fingers loosely. The muted ache in his eyes echoed my own. "There is little extraordinary to tell. His health had been strained for some while—the demands of estate and mills constantly multiplying. Then that last winter, his heart..." His shoulders rose and fell heavily. "Well. He went peacefully, they tell me."

"You were not there? I thought..."

"Oh, yes. Every minute. But I had never witnessed death, and to me, it did not look 'peaceful' and 'natural' as the doctor tried to say." He shook his head. "It was dreadful in every measure. And worse so because George had not yet returned from school..." He cleared his throat and tried to offer a smile, but it only looked like a grimace. "I fear I did not prove as capable as he had hoped for me to be—at least, not at first."

My gaze searched the beloved lines of that face, so like and yet unlike the proud father I adored. "Surely the load need not fall solely onto your shoulders now. Even the most devoted son deserves his own life and purposes."

Darcy smiled gently down at our joined hands. With one final, friendly squeeze, he let mine drop. "You know me too well, Miss Elizabeth. I confess responsibility weighs heavily at times. And yet... I find myself unwilling to relinquish control. The estate—why, that is one matter. There are rules, traditions. Though it is work, it requires little innovation. But that mill... I wish to Heaven he had never built it, but since he did, I must see it through. If reforms and improvements are to take shape, the vision must carry through steadily from start to completion."

I considered him thoughtfully—this earnest, conscientious elder brother whose boyhood watchwords had been solitude and obligation rather than mischief and passion. "They do say the mill strains even its strictest overseers." At his raised brows, I rushed on. "Jane and I drove by it on an outing a few days ago, and we witnessed a troubling skirmish." I studied his eyes—the somber depths of them. I had not remembered them being so expressive when I knew him as a boy. "Do you never despair at effecting meaningful change in such a volatile environment?"

Darcy shifted his weight, features shuttering subtly. "I do my utmost to mitigate the worst conditions. But one must retain realistic expectations." He stepped nearer the window, looking out over sloping lawns, his chest rising and falling on a weighted exhale. "I am attempting negotiations to regulate wages and safety requirements with Parliament later this year."

"Parliament! Have you some leverage there?"

His wistful smile turned a little more confident. "Perhaps I have. Now. It is not for myself I make the effort, and Heaven only knows what will come of it, but I think perhaps Father would not be displeased with my intentions."

I listened intently, arrested by this unexpected strain of social advocacy emerging from such an intensely private source. Who else but I could appreciate how taxing such efforts must be for a man accustomed to private study and self-sufficiency? My heart stirred, seeing fresh facets of character Time had worked silently since our parting long ago. I moved to join him at the window, but a brisk scrabbling heralded a new arrival. We turned to behold an exquisitely proportioned brown and white pointer trotting through the open door straight toward us, tail waving proudly.

"Wellington! There you are, boy." Darcy bent as if to greet the dog, but the elegant pointer trotted right past his master's extended hand and made directly for me.

I went down to my knees, gratified when Wellington immediately padded over to thrust his elegant head beneath my hand, brown eyes eloquent with welcome. "He is magnificent. Yours?"

Darcy watched his pet accept several minutes of delighted stroking from me before responding with wry awe coloring his tone. "He is indeed mine in name, although now I wonder whether he comprehends that fact. He so rarely offers affection to anyone besides me that when he does, he has no dignity whatsoever. Consider yourself singularly esteemed, Miss Elizabeth. Woe betide the guest who presumes upon Wellington's dignity without invitation."

"Seeing you with another dog reminds me a little of dear old spaniel," I mused, stroking Wellington's velvety ears. "Well! Perhaps he was not entirely a spaniel. Do you recall that little mutt we had as children?"

Darcy's eyes softened with remembrance. "How could I forget? Father found him eating scraps in Lambton and brought him home. What was his name?" His brow clouded. "Oh, yes!"

We both voiced the fond name simultaneously then— "Piglet!"

Fitzwilliam smiled. "How you adored that dog. Do you remember insisting we call him that silly name because his spots resembled piglets?"

I chuckled. "As if either of you mighty young sirs would dare oppose my infallible logic."

Darcy shook his head wistfully. "Faithful Piglet. I regret to tell you he did not long survive your... your departure. Faded quickly as if he had lost life's savor."

I blinked back sudden tears, touched by this further evidence of the mysterious broken circle of loss my unexplained exile had marked. Darcy's hand closed briefly over mine, a silent acknowledgment of shared pain as we honored a loyal friend's memory.

I gazed up to share a smile that broadened into shared laughter. And in that moment, I perceived the boy I cherished, now matured into this quietly capable master striding confidently into his birthright. Somber he might still be, but not hardened or uncaring. Rather, his silent, steadfast spirit shone all the brighter amidst gathering shadows and uncertainties to guide those longing for light. I blinked back sudden foolish tears, filled with nameless happiness to see him so.

All too soon, I became aware that the shadows cast by our figures through the western window were growing longer. "Oh, dear," I sighed. "Likely Jane and Aunt will be wondering at my absence by now. I told them I was only going for some air, not walking three miles and taking tea at Pemberley." With sincere regret, I gathered my shawl and gloves to take a reluctant leave.

But Mr. Darcy appeared to share my hesitation, rising from petting his dog to standing at his full height with a sudden anxious mien. His gaze darted to the windows and then back to me.

"I have... enjoyed this immensely. But you must not leave just yet!" At my startled look, he amended swiftly. "That is to say, it would be my honor to send you home in the carriage when you do depart. But perhaps you might stay a little longer."

I shook my head with a chuckle. "Longer? But I have just said... unless you think George might be able to join us?"

His shy smile hit me squarely in the heart. "I had hoped we might take a little more refreshment together. Or even a game of chess, as in old times?" Uncertainty overwhelmed his awkward invitation, and he looked aside as if to mask whatever he was leaving unsaid.

I smiled tightly. "I think it best that I go now. Thank you, Fitz..." I frowned. "I apologize. I ought to be calling you 'Mr. Darcy.'"

His brow furrowed, and his gaze fell somewhere around my middle. "Yes... Yes, I suppose so. Well, let me call a carriage for you. I would not have you worrying your aunt further by taking the time to walk the entire distance back. Just one moment." He held up a finger and stepped to the door, closing it behind himself as he went to speak to his butler.

That was very odd. Why would he not have used the bell pull? I bit my lip and wandered the library, admiring those dear familiar shelves with Wellington following at my heels. A few minutes later, Mr. Darcy returned, closing the door softly behind himself.

"The carriage will be ready momentarily. Er... I thought you would prefer a more... scenic drive than the main road. If I may, I will order the carriage to take you out the west entrance and down the old stone road before returning to Farthingdale?"

I smiled and tilted my head. "How very thoughtful, Mr. Darcy, but I would not wish to impose."

"No imposition at all," he insisted. "The least I could do."

Fourteen

Darcy

I stood framed in the library's wide front window, one arm braced against the ancient, warped glass as I watched the last glimpse of the carriage disappear down Pemberley's winding drive. My imagination must be cursed, because I could almost swear the summer breeze carried faint drifting notes of Elizabeth's laughter.

My shoulders sagged as tension melted, a bone-deep exhale escaping my lips. She was safely away, and soon, the confusing echoes of her presence would fade, leaving only poignant memories behind.

Wellington padded over to thrust his sleek head comfortingly beneath my hand. I smiled down absently as he tilted his head to offer his left ear first and then his right. "There, now. No harm done, eh, boy?" The familiar soothing ritual failed to settle my disquiet tonight. Before coherent thought could take shape, a polite rap heralded the butler's entrance.

"Begging your pardon for the intrusion, Mr. Darcy. But I wanted to inform you that Master George and his guests departed by the front avenue not five minutes ago. Your own carriage bearing the young woman would not have encountered them."

I managed an approving nod, still distracted. "Thank you, Huxley. Please have a cold collation sent to my study. I expect Mr. Bingley to share the evening meal shortly." At his acquiescence, I added as an afterthought, "And kindly put Wellington's dinner out. He appears ready to settle in for the evening."

I crossed the darkening room, each step weighted by restless energy that had plagued me since parting with Elizabeth. Sinking into my desk chair, I roughly pushed both hands through my hair. What madness had possessed me, inviting her within these walls with Belmont's party still touring the grounds?

All common sense urged their paths must never publicly converge. Especially not with George still besotted by some foolish memories of the fae enchantress from his boyhood. Yet, there she had stood, smiling up at me in dappled sunlight, joyous and open-hearted as ever... and my reservations had melted away unheeded.

I grimaced, shame heating my cheeks in the empty room. Father would be appalled by such carelessness regarding propriety and family duty. At this rate, I would soon prove as capricious and undependable as George.

Wellington wandered back to flop with a contented sigh across my boot tops. I reached down to stroke his silken ears. "You seemed mightily taken with our wild-haired visitor today." His foot thumped the floor in rhythm with his tail. "Let us hope your master manages the association with equal aplomb."

Another discreet knock heralded Huxley's return to announce, "Mr. Bingley to see you, sir." I straightened from my tired slump, feeling every one of my seven-and-twenty years. Bingley's amiable companionship promised a welcome diversion from restless speculations. And any man whom fastidious Wellington tolerated could not fail to lift my spirits.

"Show him in, thank you, Huxley."

I stood to exchange greetings, appreciating anew Bingley's unaffected friendliness as he crossed the room. My gaze lingered a fraction longer than strictly required, arrested by his glowing coloring and open features. Had he been *only* to town on business? Or had he driven by Farthingdale on his way back to Pemberley? The fair Miss Jane Bennet seemed to have arrested his notice and put yet a higher spring in his step. Perhaps I would have to counsel him, as well, on the dangers of meditating on the face of a woman with no prospects.

But I was hardly any better after such an afternoon as I had passed. Had Elizabeth always boasted such arresting eyes and pleasing figure? I could conjure every varying hue and pattern of those dark irises with sudden, unsettling clarity. Chestnut locks had darkened to mahogany with time, and what was once a rat's nest of tangles and ringlets was now a crown of sumptuous curls that invited fascinated study of their whorls and depths. Her laughter that bid the world laugh with her...

"Been out riding as well, Darcy?" Bingley's cheerful hail jerked me forcibly back from disturbingly pleasant imaginings. I hastily schooled my features to calm interest, befitting one gentleman conversing with another as we moved to take places before the hearth. No need to burden Bingley's uncomplicated existence with unsettled reflections not fully understood myself.

"No, only attending to some business." I moved toward a chair, gesturing Bingley toward the one opposite. "Come in and make yourself comfortable. We've a cold collation on its way. I did not fancy a formal dinner after such a hot day. Brandy? You look as if you have been riding hard."

Bingley grinned. "Nothing too arduous for me today, I assure you! Although..." He gave his buckskin breeches an absentminded brushing after Wellington rubbed against his leg. "I did have a splendid gallop across some pretty countryside. But that was the extent of my adventures."

I nodded absently, more preoccupied with the vision of dark curls and laughing eyes that persisted in invading my concentration. With effort, I redirected my attention to where it belonged. "You mentioned yesterday that you were making progress in your search for a suitable estate?"

"I did, indeed!" Bingley leaned eagerly forward, reminding me oddly of that old spaniel we used to have as it begged for praise. "In fact, I took your advice to heart and made it a priority to investigate more thoroughly." His chest puffed up. "And I am happy to say I have just this morning signed a three-year lease on Netherfield Park, near Meryton in Hertfordshire."

I bolted upright so suddenly Wellington shot me an aggrieved look. "You did what?" Incredulity sharpened my tone. "Forgive me, Bingley, but last we spoke of it, you had only glimpsed a few papers detailing the place. You have not even seen it! Surely prudence urges more careful inquiry and numbers analysis before entering any binding commitment?"

Bingley's smile faltered slightly even as he waved a dismissive hand. "Oh, as to particulars of acreage and annual rents and so forth, naturally, I employed a man for just that purpose." At my pointed stare, he amended, "Well, *your* man, actually—thank you again for the introduction to Mr. Morris, capital fellow! His reports were what decided me."

I pressed my thumb and forefinger to the corners of my eyes, tension gathering. "I see. And these reports were verified as accurate?"

"Certainly! I have every faith in Morris' skills."

"Bingley, he cannot possibly have had sufficient time to gather all the information you require."

"Oh… Well, besides…" Pink tinged Bingley's open features. "I was fortunate to encounter a young lady familiar for many years with the property and environment who painted such a delightful picture of society and countryside that I could not demur."

I dropped my hand, eyes narrowing. "A young lady, you say?" Suspicion quickened my pulse. "Which young lady would that be?"

"Why, Miss Bennet, of course!" Bingley leaned back, a dreamy smile playing over his lips. "We have enjoyed several conversational rambles after our initial meeting. She described not just the charms of Netherfield itself, but the whole neighborhood." His look turned introspective. "In truth, I think I would find any locale pleasing that boasted her as an inhabitant."

I studied him silently. So much for my intentions to warn against sentiment's folly. That particular horse had undoubtedly quit the stable once Miss Jane Bennet entered Bingley's sights that day at the inn. One could only hope that the buildings did not boast leaking roofs and rotting timbers.

With an inner shrug of resignation, I merely said, "Well, if the property suits your purposes, I wish you very happy there. Although—" I held up one finger. "Take care not to neglect due diligence purely out of, shall we say, social motivations? One cannot live on the beauty of scenery and neighborhood alone."

Bingley's expression cleared. "Too right you are! Not to worry. Once settled, I assure you the estate's business affairs shall receive utmost meticulous care." His eyes drifted once more to the middle distance. "Provided, that is, I can prevail upon the fair creature who has utterly stolen my attention to allow me to wait upon her in detail."

I smiled despite myself. "So that is the way of it? Well, if Miss Bennet is an accurate representation of local young ladies, I dare say you shall do very well for yourself in Hertfordshire society."

We shared a rueful laugh before Bingley's musing look returned. "I confess, though, Darcy, to some concern on one account regarding my angel's connections." At my raised brows, he leaned nearer. "It shames me to admit noticing such mercenary details. But I have formed a rather less favorable impression of some members of her family."

"Oh? I was under the belief that her relations are generally well-regarded, given your glowing reports."

"Indeed, indeed!" He hastened to assert. "The uncle who escorted them here, Mr. Gardiner, seems most amiable by all accounts. And her sister... well, I suppose she is not a natural sister, but they have been raised together, nonetheless—Miss Elizabeth is gentleness personified. But..." He lowered his voice, shamefaced. "From certain reluctant confidences, I gather the younger Bennet sisters leave much to be desired as far as decorum and discretion."

My brow furrowed. "That is unfortunate. I presume the father neglects proper governance?"

Bingley shifted in patent discomfort. "I really could not say. Miss Bennet mentions very few details. Except..." His mouth turned down. "Perhaps it is only my impressions—a narrow looking glass, of course, but it almost sounds as if he cares more for his library than managing a gaggle of headstrong girls. And her mother sounds... excitable."

My heart sank pondering such an upbringing for Elizabeth. Where had Father sent her? And why under such circumstances, with so little inquiry made into the situation? It was miracle enough that she blossomed unspoiled, surrounded by apparent poor influences and questionable guardianship.

But what did that suggest about Elizabeth's sudden appearance? Surely, the family had not sent her for illicit means as a way of elevating their own circumstances. Suddenly, my earlier qualms about Elizabeth renewing old ties seemed founded on more than past loss. She merited closer scrutiny... particularly given her persistent fascination with my distractible brother.

As if reading my thoughts, Bingley offered consolingly, "But truly, Darcy, whatever their faults, Mr. Bennet must deserve some credit! His two eldest daughters surely stand as testaments to hidden merit. Can many fathers claim such superior blessings?"

I nodded silently. No father could ask for greater accolades than the conduct and virtues of honorable offspring. Yet uncertainty lingered. Were Elizabeth's substance and principles nourished by Bennet's influence? Or was her true nature more a reflection of former seeds planted in worthy soil transplanted long years before?

I watched Wellington doze before the cold hearth, chin propped on my fist. My mind churned with details still lacking that prevented charting any definitive course regarding Elizabeth. With her foster relations largely unknown quantities and George's future hanging precariously in the balance, nothing could be safely assumed or predicted.

I required wise counsel to unravel uncertainties from multiple quarters. My uncle must be consulted, of course, and discretionary letters must be dispatched to this Mr. Gardiner without delay. Between us, some reasonable path might be discerned that allowed me to uphold family duty while still establishing the true measure of Elizabeth's situation.

I set aside my empty glass with gathering resolution. For now, keeping her close yet separated remained paramount. But I would not leave her abandoned to uncertain tides without an anchor. And the only such anchor at hand... was myself.

Elizabeth

I HUMMED SOFTLY TO myself, secateurs in hand, as I moved
down the row of heavily scented roses lining Mrs. Westing's garden. Their luxurious fragrance perfumed the morning air, mingling
with the cherry tart I had baked just that dawn. Blight had affected
some outer stems that must be swiftly cut away to preserve the main
blooms.

Intent on my task, I failed to mark the approaching rider until a
horse's eager whicker preceded the creak of the picket gate. I glanced
up, shears arrested halfway through a diseased cane, to behold George
Darcy swinging down from a tall bay, grin flashing brighter than summer itself. My heart performed an instantaneous stutter-step, the years
between us blinking out of existence faster than I could draw breath
to hail him.

"George!" Secateurs and basket tumbled forgotten as I flew down
the gravel path, skirts hiked past decorous limits in a most unladylike
fashion. I cared not a whit, nearly flinging myself at him in unrestrained delight.

Laughing, he caught me in the air. "Lizzy Bennet! Still a wild creature, I see!" His vivid eyes roved my face hungrily. "How I have missed
that look daring me to match you step for scandalous step."

My heart almost exploded. To hear him speak my name just so,
to see joy and welcome so vividly painted on features my memory
had never quite captured accurately... I playfully swatted his shoulder,
finding my voice. "As if you ever could! Why, I was running circles
around you since infancy."

He pressed one hand theatrically to his heart. "You cut me to the quick! Never could I aspire to equal you, oh queen of tricks and troublemaking. Is this any way to greet your dearest friend?" His eyes sparkled as bright as ever, crinkling into merriment lines beside them. "Look how you have ambushed me! Where is your famous fair warning?"

"When did you ever wait for fair anything? Come now, confess! Did you not appear this morning expressly hoping to take me unawares?" Laughing, I grabbed his hand and towed his taller frame toward the garden bench, heart lighter than it had felt in years.

I settled onto the stone bench, patting the spot beside me. "Come, you must tell me everything. What wild schemes and escapades have you pursued since we parted? I still have no notion of how you have passed your time. Not squandered it, I hope."

George sprawled comfortably close beside me. "Let me guess what ridiculous notions that lively imagination has concocted. No doubt you picture me as..." He tapped one finger to his chin ponderously. "...a struggling barrister buried under mountains of legal manuscripts?"

I scoffed in mock affront. "As if you could apply yourself long enough to pass the examinations! No, I rather fancied you took holy orders and are even now a country parson scandalizing your parishioners."

George threw back his head with a crack of laughter. "Me! A man of the cloth! Why, Lizzy, have you accounted me a saint?" His eyes glinted wickedly. "I promise you the army would have ejected me faster than the bishop if I attempted preaching."

"The army, then. Doubtless, you were a cavalry officer leading glorious charges until some hilarious prank went astray?" My sideways glance brimmed with unspoken shared memories of youthful misadventures.

He shook his head, still chuckling. "You know me too well, m'dear. I confess, I briefly contemplated purchasing a commission, but the reality of army discipline quashed that fancy swiftly."

I angled to better study the face I had dreamed of so often. Traces remained of the reckless boy who was my partner in every youthful folly. But maturity had lent him an air of purpose that sat with easy confidence on his broad shoulders and animated features. Impulsively, I squeezed his arm.

"Well, come then, out with it. What has the inestimable George Darcy made of himself since we parted?"

He slanted me a sudden uncertain look from beneath lowered lashes. "You shall laugh, I fear. I confess most of my hours are spent at races and gaming hells." At my eloquent arch of brows, he rushed on. "Oh, not exclusively! Truly, Lizzy, credit me some decency."

I tilted my head, unwilling to dismiss him so easily. "I know well a good heart beats under such fine clothes. Surely you have some worthwhile pursuits?"

George smiled then, and the glimpse of the boy I loved so dearly shone through. "As it happens, I have lately turned my thoughts toward studying estate management." He gave an affected sigh. "And even investing—can you imagine!"

I pursed my lips, studying him. Some subtle shifting in his countenance hinted at more unspoken. "Those are rather domestic ambitions for an erstwhile liberty-taker. Any particular reason for such industry of late?"

He hesitated, something hopeful and vulnerable hovering on his mobile mouth. But at approaching voices from the house, he merely patted my hand with hasty cheer. "You shall know soon enough! But come, let us enjoy this all-too-brief interlude together without melancholy thoughts."

I surveyed his pensive features, the shadow of earlier playfulness fading. "Come now, something weighs on you. I know that look too well." Gently, I lifted his chin with one finger until he met my searching gaze. "We never kept secrets in days of old. Why can you not confide your hopes to me now?"

George grimaced. "I wish I could, Lizzy, truly!" He shifted restlessly, avoiding my eyes. "Suffice it to say prospects lie before me fairer than this wastrel son of a country squire deserves." His rueful laugh held a bitter note. "But I am pledged not to speak openly as yet. You must allow me some mystery."

My forehead creased, struggling to reconcile this newly grave George with the smiling suitor of minutes before. What changeable humor was this? "But why ever not share happy news? Unless..." I studied his averted features. "Can it be Fitzwilliam objects to your prospects?"

George's shoulders jerked slightly before he mustered a tolerable façade. "My brother, the eternal tutor, you mean? Well, he does ride me cursed hard about application and industry and a dozen other dull virtues." He flashed a grin that didn't reach his eyes. "You know I never could endure lectures."

I shook my head slowly, pondering what lay unspoken behind his thin veneer. This new inscrutable George unnerved me. We had ever been open books to one another. What altered him now?

"I am sure Fitzwilliam only desires your best interests," I offered gently. "But come, if we cannot speak of whatever mysterious future occupies you, at least entertain me with gossip of yesterday's visitors! Are they relations, come to assess Pemberley's new master?"

A queer look shuttered George's sunny features briefly. He studied me closely. "No family of ours. But pray, what makes you imagine guests yesterday?"

I waved one hand airily. "Oh, I happened upon your brother while out walking the grounds."

"Wait... 'grounds?' Tell me you did not *walk* all the way from Farthingdale to Pemberley!"

"On my honor, I did," I retorted stoutly. "Should you be surprised? I walk that distance back in Hertfordshire several times a week."

He blinked. "Indeed! You are quite right—I should not permit myself to be surprised. But go on. You said you encountered Fitzwilliam?"

"Oh, yes, I did, and he explained you were otherwise engaged. Though he welcomed me warmly once I braved intruding." I smiled impishly. "Does it surprise you Fitzwilliam has not forgotten our childhood friendship?"

George's stare sharpened. "He invited you inside? But when was this meeting, precisely?"

"Oh, perhaps the middle of the afternoon, but I believe I stayed above two hours, all together." I studied him, bewildered by his odd probing. "Fitzwilliam mentioned obligations to some important party prevented you from attending us. Though Wellington provided company in your absence."

George looked swiftly away with a muttered oath. Alarm spiked through me.

"George, what is amiss? You appear quite out of countenance all at once."

"Do I?" He rearranged his features swiftly back to nonchalance. "Forgive me. I merely regret having missed you. But I suppose..." Was that relief softening his taut mouth? "Well, no matter."

He captured my hand, former warmth suffusing his vivid gaze once more as he smiled. "I cannot linger today, but you must come again soon, Lizzy Bennet. Promise me?" He pressed a swift kiss to my knuckles that left me flushed and tongue-tied.

I managed a credible curtsy despite trembling limbs as he vaulted back atop his mount. "I shall hold you to that, George Darcy. It seems we have much to rediscover after too long apart."

His answering grin blazed bright as summer itself. "Indeed, we do! Until next we meet, m'dear!"

I watched him canter briskly down the lane, butterflies still fluttering wildly in my chest. However would I endure their absence now that both brothers had reentered my life so unexpectedly? The years ahead looked unaccountably brighter, with my two stalwart champions returning to stand shield and sword beside me once more. What did it matter why George hesitated over his mysterious hopes? Likely some triviality blown out of proportion as ever. Laughing softly, I turned my steps back toward the house, George's irrepressible smile warming me to the core.

One day soon, I would tell him that I loved him.

FIFTEEN

Darcy

"I FEAR THE NUMBERS offer little encouragement for the course you propose, Mr. Darcy."

I dropped the most recent ledger onto my desk with an audible thump. "I cannot limit the work week without cutting into the pay they say they cannot do without, and I cannot increase wages without stirring violence elsewhere or putting the mill's very survival at risk."

Across from me, my steward gathered the scattered ledgers and reports, peering at me over the top of his spectacles. "As you have observed before, there are issues with whichever course you choose."

I grimaced, leaning back in my chair to knead tired eyes. We had spent the better part of an hour dissecting profit margins, production targets, payroll—every detail of the Pemberley Mill operations. And still, a solution eluded me.

"Confound it all, there must be a way forward that serves all interests fairly, Daniels! The men deserve decent conditions and wages that provide for their families."

Daniels gave a noncommittal murmur, stacking his burden neatly atop a cabinet. "An admirable aim, to be sure. Yet, as you say, implementing reform risks sowing deeper unrest." He hesitated, then added delicately, "And without careful balance, declining profits may force cutting jobs further."

My jaw tightened. The workers' petition still lay squarely before me, the X's marked by the laborers offering nothing but reproach for my indecision. Daniels spoke the truth—reforms cost dearly. However, allowing unjust conditions also came at a price. I stared sightlessly at the darkening window. If only resolution to industrial quandaries proved as straightforward as a farmer plowing even furrows!

The door crashing open made both Daniels and I start violently. Before I could bark a reprimand, an all-too-familiar voice exclaimed, "Dash it all, Fitzwilliam, there you lurk! Trouble enough tracking you to earth. I should bloody well have known you would be here, darkening that cursed desk all day."

I closed my eyes briefly. "Forgive the intrusion, Daniels. We shall resume this tomorrow." With a bob of acquiescence, my steward hastily gathered his remaining ledgers and disappeared. I turned a glacial stare on my thoughtless brother. "Well? This had better be nothing less than a fire in the east wing."

George waved away my sarcasm, throwing himself into the vacant chair. "Never mind that. I suppose you think yourself devilish cunning! But you did not fool me yesterday."

I raised one sardonic brow. "I beg your pardon?"

He braced both hands on my desk, eyes stormy. "Do not play innocent! Did you truly think I would not learn of Miss Elizabeth's visit?" At my carefully neutral look, he burst out, "Dash it, man! Hiding her away from Lucilla's party was beyond the pale!"

Comprehension struck with the force of lightning. He had seen Elizabeth. Or worse, loose-lipped servants had evidently carried tales.

I regarded George's indignant countenance resignedly. No help for it now, but press through and hope to limit damages.

"Where did you learn of this?" I asked mildly. I could not believe any of Pemberley's servants would gossip to anyone outside the household, but a judicious word in the butler's and housekeeper's ears could forestall a disaster.

"From Lizzy herself! I went to see her this morning at Farthingdale."

I narrowed my eyes. "That was... ill-judged of you."

"Ill-judged! She was like a sister to us! Or have you already forgotten?"

"Calm yourself, George. The situation called for discretion regarding certain guests. Miss Elizabeth understands."

"The devil she does!" He surged from his chair to pace my study, his features thunderous. "Confound your stuffy secrecy! We ought to welcome Lizzy openly as family, not skulk about concealing her!"

I leaned back, schooled to patience. "Family she may be in spirit, but I hardly need remind you of appearances. Your betrothed has only just departed. Parading a pretty childhood playmate before Lady Lucilla could severely undermine recent progress."

George swung round, mouth agape. "Progress—you mean that stuffed-shirt Belmont's blessing? By God, *Lucilla* chose me, not Belmont!"

"So I understood it." I steepled thoughtful fingers. "Nevertheless, recall how slender her chances appeared. Lord Belmont was hardly predisposed to accept a second son lacking any real prospects. Your suit remains... unconventional."

George's hackles rose. "I'll have you know many ladies of quality find me perfectly eligible!"

I sighed. "Yes, fortune hunters and widows, perhaps. But for a marquess's sole heiress? You cannot deny the mismatch. Nor your own capricious reputation." I held up a hand to stall his angry retort. "However unfair, past frivolity leaves you on tenuous footing. One injudicious move could yet bring disaster."

My unvarnished candor gave him pause. He slumped into the chair with a gusty exhale, the fight departing from his countenance. "But to ignore Lizzy... Surely, we owe her better!" Raking both hands through his blond curls, he demanded in sudden suspicion, "Unless you, too, mean to deny her very existence henceforth?"

I looked away from the hurt accusation in his eyes. How could I answer truly when every path seemed fraught with thorns for someone beloved?

"I intend nothing of the kind. But until the mystery of her abrupt removal is solved, we remain hampered. Embracing renewed intimacy appears... premature."

George surged upright, fists clenched in frustration. "Damn Father's secrets to perdition! Am I to keep hazarding Lizzy's feelings to indulge his confounded eccentricities from the grave?"

"Of course not." I met his burning stare directly. "But we never did learn why Father was so eager to separate her from us... from *you*. It could be that there was a reason that is as much in the interests of her better good—egad, perhaps in the interests of *morality*—as anything you might have imagined."

"I say! You do not now accuse Father of siring her? You always swore he did not, and so did he. Have you changed your mind?"

I swallowed and let my gaze drift to the window. "No. And I do not deny your frustration, for you have every right to it. You have ever cared more deeply than most for her. I fully acknowledge those ties." I held his gaze meaningfully. "Ties likely best left... dormant with your present obligations."

George's throat convulsed. For an instant, pain and longing warred nakedly across his countenance. Then he whirled away, features shuttered. My own heart twisted. Cruel necessity that forced me to such ruthless amputation!

In the fraught silence, the clock's steady clicks marked the slow death of careless possibility. At length, George turned back, wearing once more the mask of careless nonchalance. "Well! A pretty problem you've left me, brother. But never fear—" He tugged his waistcoat straight with a determined smile. "I'm for the village on an errand with Bingley. No diverting to certain flower-strewn cottage gardens en route."

The tease held more plea for approval than confidence. I offered a wan answering smile. "See that you do not. Oh, and George?"

He glanced over his shoulder, poise still shadowed by banked yearning. I cleared my suddenly constricted throat. "You may not credit me in this. But I desire her happiness no less than you."

Cryptic shadows shifted behind his eyes. Then winked out as sunny charm resurfaced. "Never doubted it! Wish me luck choosing some bauble sparkly enough to make Lucilla swoon. Small chance of that in Lambton, but I remain valiant in the effort!" With his customary flourish, he departed, the merry tune floating back down the corridor belying all beneath.

I moved to stand once more at the window where our interview began, unsought words slipping free in the empty room. "Godspeed you in that quest, Brother."

But the indifferent glass swallowed up my futile wishes. The golden dream of halcyon childhood faded with it, reality's gray mists rolling back to claim long-awaited due. I straightened my shoulders beneath the familiar weight of duty and pragmatism. If providence denied my brother ease in reconciling past and present affections, the struggle at least was his alone to bear.

Whereas I... I would hold fast to higher principles that must supersede mere personal fancy. The gate on old hopes had clanged irreversibly shut the day I inherited leadership at Pemberley.

Elizabeth

"NO, ANNIE, WE MUSTN'T pull Flossie's tail so." I gently extracted the protesting kitten from my small charge's determined grip. "See how she cries when you hurt her?"

Two-year-old Anne Rose pouted up at me, protests forming on her cherub mouth. But quicker than thought, the threatened tears transformed into delighted giggles as the ruffled tabby leaned forward to butt her fuzzy head beneath the little girl's hand. Crisis averted. With a relieved sigh, I lifted my eyes to see Jane regarding us in amusement from the kitchen doorway.

"I begin to see the merits in your campaigns for either a cage or a string to follow these little wanderers outside," she remarked wryly, nodding to where Anne Rose had already tottered off after the cat into the hall. "How ever did you manage her so long this morning while I helped Aunt?"

I followed at a discreet distance as my charge discovered the furled roses hiding among Aunt's hats. "Never underestimate the appeal of feathers for distraction," I replied with a laugh, nodding to the currently abandoned avian plumes. "But come, you look done in. Shall I take over the marketing and menus today so you can rest?"

Jane smiled, one hand going absently to the pendant at her graceful throat. "Oh, I am quite refreshed, really. It was pleasant to enjoy some discourse with our caller earlier."

I raised one brow, crossing my arms meaningfully until she blushed. "A caller, you say? Anyone whose name rhymes with Mr. Tingley by chance?"

"Lizzy!" Despite her color heightening, Jane's eyes met mine directly. "As it happens, our visitor *did* express such decided admiration that I find myself... considering perhaps that my determination to wait for a truly amiable man has paid off. Only think if I had not the confidence of a respectable dowry when Mr. Collins wrote to Papa with his offer!"

My grin stretched wider, and I squeezed her hands. "No one deserves happiness more! And think nothing of Mr. Collins's disappointment. I say five thousand pounds surely earns the right to weigh such offers carefully." I kept my tone delicately teasing. "'Tis not a large fortune, but you needn't settle for the first gentleman to make doe eyes at you."

Jane tilted her head, hesitation entering her limpid gaze. "Do you believe I ought to delay, then? Wait to see if another more eligible prospect presents itself?"

I waved my hand, sobering. "Forgive me, dearest. I merely want you to know your worth. Although..." The memory of George Darcy's smiling countenance earlier that morning caused me to flush unaccountably. "Eligibility takes many forms. And genuine attachment must supersede other considerations, or what is the point?"

Jane opened her mouth to reply when a crash sounded down the passage. We turned to behold Anne Rose happily dismantling the hall table urn. As we rushed over amidst fluttering curtains of ostrich feathers, I firmly banished all thoughts of gentleman callers for now. My present charge demanded far too much focus for drifting into pleasant daydreams of golden hair and laughing blue eyes.

"Lizzy, might I ask you something?" Jane kept her voice low, glancing pointedly toward where Anne Rose sat, absorbed in scattering rose petals across the carpet.

I straightened from righting the luckily unbroken vase, intrigued. "Of course!"

Jane moved nearer, dropping her tone further. "When I was upstairs, changing into my work gown earlier, I looked outside. I—I could not help but observe you deep in discourse with Mr. George Darcy in the garden." At my startled look, she rushed on, "Please do not mistake me. I do not mean to pry! Only he seemed uncommonly... attentive in his manner." She bit her lip. "I merely wondered if you think his intentions bear scrutiny?"

I felt an unaccountable flush steal into my cheeks and busied myself, brushing off my apron. "Oh Jane, what fanciful notions! We were but renewing childhood ties after a long separation." Even to myself, the denial rang hollow. I forced a teasing smile. "Next, you shall have us clandestinely betrothed!"

My sister surveyed me silently for a long moment from beneath delicately arched brows. "And if that were the case... would his addresses be so thoroughly unwelcome?" she asked gently. "I see how he looks at you, Lizzy."

I twisted my hands together, pulse jumping erratically. "It would be the stuff of all my girlish dreams come true," I whispered finally. "But alas, some dreams linger as only that—lovely but insubstantial visions." I shook off the momentary melancholy, brightening even as a nameless pang caught in my chest. "Come now, we have had enough matchmaking for one morning! Let us tackle this menu plan while Miss Anne is so obligingly occupied."

T HAT AFTERNOON, AUNT GARDINER insisted that Jane and I each seek our leisure. Jane, dear girl, wanted nothing more than a good lie down. I, however, pulled on my boots and bonnet and took to the hills.

I wandered slowly through the gently rolling fields behind the manor house, my feet finding the path more by rote than conscious thought. My mind drifted, only vaguely aware of cows grazing placidly as I passed or swallows wheeling overhead in preparation for their long journey south. Try as I might to focus on my surroundings, my traitorous thoughts kept returning to dashing blue eyes and a devastating smile promising everything I had long dreamed of.

What was I to make of George's sudden attentiveness? The old camaraderie between us had ever possessed a special understanding. But dare I read the deeper meaning behind his pointed looks and warm clasp of my hands today? His mystifying hints of awaiting changes haunted me. My practical nature argued against investing in premature hopes where cold reality must eventually intrude. And yet...

Caught in restless reverie, I had wandered some way from home. I had been careful this time not to let my feet stray to the road that would carry me heedlessly to Pemberley. Nor was I going in the direction of Lambton. Glancing up, I found myself standing atop the gently sloping ridge that formed Farthingdale's western border. Pemberley's folly beckoned enticingly in the distance, framed between an embracing pair of ancient oaks. Unthinking, I moved to perch atop the worn boundary stone wall, drinking in the achingly familiar view.

How vividly I recalled that one particular time I was there with the Darcys. Early autumn had set the trees aflame with vivid color, and Fitzwilliam had gone away to school. In another year, George would be going as well, but not yet. Mr. Darcy had taken George and me for one last picnic before the weather turned foul, his mood uncharacteristically subdued during the long walk to the folly. Upon arrival, he had drawn out a much-annotated volume of poetry, leaving George and me to race unchecked through the fallen leaves.

When I paused eventually in my play, breathing hard beside the silent figure on his bench, Mr. Darcy had become so lost in melancholic reflection he scarce noticed my approach. Only after several repetitions of "Sir? Father?" had he glanced up wearily to meet my concerned gaze.

His face had cleared faintly, and for a few seconds, he came back from wherever he had been. "Yes, Poppet?"

"Are you sad, Father?"

His eyes had gentled instantly, large hand cupping my small one where it rested on his sleeve. "You are observant as ever. I confess that after ten years, I still mourn my dear Mrs. Darcy. The season reminds me of the day we met."

My small brow had furrowed. "Then you should not be sad to think of her today."

One silvered brow lifted. "Oh?"

I traced the intricate gold ring on his hand. "Remembering happy things helps them stay close." I leaned my tousled head confidingly against his broad shoulder. "Fitzwilliam said that when he went away last month. He gave me a ribbon. See?" I had tugged a soiled blue ribbon from a pocket in my dress. It had been Fitzwilliam's bookmark, but upon seeing my tears at his departure, he'd given it to me to remember him by.

Mr. Darcy regarded the rumpled ribbon, eyes crinkling gently. "What a thoughtful gift from your brother. He is growing into a fine young man." He folded his large hand tenderly over mine. "Keep your ribbon safe. I am certain whenever you look at it, you will find happy memories very near."

I smiled sadly, the intervening years between then and now feeling like an insurmountable chasm. I had kept Fitzwilliam's little gift for years until my sister Lydia one day snatched it, losing the precious memento almost instantly. I had cried for its loss, feeling as if more cherished pieces of those I loved slipped irrevocably away.

Remembering the echo of such loss now in the senior Mr. Darcy's resigned features, something in my heart whispered caution through longing joy. No matter the hurt he had once caused me, he had been the very best of men. And such a man could never have wished me harm.

So, what *had* been his purpose in sending me away? I turned back to Farthingale, more restless than when I had ventured forth.

SIXTEEN

Darcy

I DROPPED ANOTHER HANDFUL of fraying parchment onto my overflowing desk with a frustrated sigh. It seemed my father had been more fastidious regarding record keeping than maintaining useful correspondence. Three hours spent digging through an entire drawer of dated ledgers had yielded nothing but increased resentment over past secrets.

Restless, I abandoned the latest moth-eaten ledger and began pacing the Turkish rug instead. There must be some key, some trail overlooked, that would explain the missing history of the smiling, dark-eyed phantom haunting Pemberley's halls and my imagination these past days. Pausing near the window, my gaze wandered instinctively downhill toward Lambton as though half expecting a rider even now approaching with long-delayed elucidation.

"Your pardon, sir. Will there be anything further tonight?"

I started slightly. My usually unobtrusive butler awaited direction beside the quietly closed door, his deferential posture indicating curiosity despite neutral features. I raked a hand through my hair, my frustrated exhale stirring abandoned pages on the desk.

"No, thank you, Huxley. Doubtless, I am keeping everyone from their beds to no purpose." An apologetic glance took in the cold hearth, and the candle burnt nearly to its base. "You may retire. I fear answers lie not within my father's meticulous ledgers in any case."

The butler cleared his throat delicately. "One further possibility occurred to me. Will you permit me, sir?" At my bemused nod, Huxley moved to kneel stiffly beside a little-used shelf tucked beneath the side window. I watched curiously as he stretched to extract a slender, leather-bound volume tucked behind its dusty fellows.

"Your father often made temporary notes or scribblings in this before transcribing them into more official estate records." He extended it almost shyly toward me. "Perhaps within…"

I accepted the offering eagerly, moving nearer the guttering candle flame. "Let us hope you are inspired indeed! Though I shall be astonished if Father departed from lifelong habits of discretion even in an unofficial capacity."

I ran my fingers almost reverently down the worn brown leather, strangely reluctant to slip the leather binding from its keeper. But as I cautiously opened to the middle pages, hastily dashed lines arrested my attention, though ink and paper had moldered almost indecipherable together.

Heart suddenly stuttering, I grasped the corner under our lone flickering light, straining to interpret cramped script belying shaking fingers. "…regarding the property designated for…" I squinted fruitlessly, then snatched up the candle itself, heedless of hot wax now dribbling unnoticed over my wrist. "Miss Smith… Southgate Park… to be signed over on…"

I clenched my jaw, willing ink long deteriorated into muddy obscurity to render up precious secrets. But apart from place names, my rushlight could not resurrect; no further revelations emerged from the damaged journal entry. With a stifled oath, I slammed it back onto the shelf, knocking loose a cascade of dust.

"There was an inheritance meant for Elizabeth?" My stunned demand seemed to echo in the midnight stillness. "Here—in Lambton!" I resumed my restless prowling gaze, once more seeking futilely toward the distant village. "But why? By whom?" I spun back to face Huxley, struck by a sudden realization. "You clearly knew what this volume was. Has it been handled or disturbed lately? Could my father have extracted any pages before his death?"

The butler spread his hands regretfully. "I sincerely wish I had more to divulge, Master Fitzwilliam. Your father's affairs were ever his own."

I resumed my agitated pacing, pausing as a new thought struck. "But you recollect the day Miss Elizabeth departed all those years ago. George and I were out—by Father's design, I am certain. What do you recall of that day?"

Huxley's brow furrowed pensively. "The maids were all in a state, weeping copiously. When I inquired after the cause, they told me Miss Smith was being sent away. I remember..." He hesitated, then continued delicately, "I chanced to observe your father escorting the young miss outside. He held a large portfolio, and the footmen carried a small trunk to his carriage. And his face was very grave."

My heart sank like a stone. So, there had been documentation exchanged with Mr. Gardiner then. Likely the same mysterious estate arrangements disclosed here. Father would have given Gardiner everything, leaving no more for me to find. Defeated, I waved a hand toward the door.

"Thank you, Huxley, you have been most helpful. I apologize for keeping you so late over ancient history best left buried." I attempted a rueful quirk of my lips. "We must both look to the future now. Perhaps time will reveal whatever must be known."

He bowed acquiescence. But in the darkened doorway, Huxley paused, eyes glinting oddly. "If you will permit me, sir... have you spoken with Lord Matlock? Your father often confided in his brother-in-law about business affairs."

"I have already done so, but I will do so again, and soon. Good night, Huxley."

I MARCHED THROUGH MATLOCK Estate's wide front doors and asked a footman to announce me to my uncle. Scarcely five minutes passed before Lord Matlock himself emerged, looking vaguely perplexed.

"Darcy! We did not expect you this morning." He cast an experienced soldier's eye over my hastily donned riding attire. "Has something arisen needing my attention?"

I waved aside his solicitous inquiry. "Forgive the early call. I had a... well, it is probably not important, but I had a question for you, and I fancied a brisk ride this morning. But I see I have come at a bad time." Through the open front door, I noticed several carriages loaded for departure.

Lord Matlock followed my gaze. "Preparing for our excursion, yes. We are off to Dovedale for several days to permit Lord Belmont and the ladies to indulge in the area's beauty, and Lord DeWinter has agreed to host us." His smile faded swiftly. "I do not suppose your brother is with you? He promised to join us but seems to be lagging behind."

My stomach dropped, but I summoned a polite smile. "Knowing George, he shall come flying up the drive in hot pursuit any moment. Some unexpected entertainment likely waylaid him. But please, do not let me delay your trip! I am sure George will provide lively company whenever he makes his entrance over the next few days."

"Oh, do not go so quickly, Darcy! Why not join us? Your steward has everything in hand, and you could do with a bit of leisure."

"Some other time, but I thank you. Uncle, forgive me for being impertinent, but have you ever heard of a property called Southgate Park? My father might, perhaps, have mentioned it?"

A mystified look crossed his face. "Never. Should I have? Confound it, where is that brother of yours? Belmont is looking impatient to be off."

I grimaced, a leaden weight sinking through my stomach. If George could not make an appearance for a pleasure tour with Lady Lucilla's family, what the devil was keeping him? I had a terrible suspicion. What was there to stop him from acting on the disastrous impulses I both feared and anticipated?

"I am sure he will catch you up on the road, Uncle. But perhaps I had better go and... supervise matters." I took a hasty step backward even as Lord Matlock opened his mouth to inquire further. "Please convey my respects to Lord and Lady Belmont. I am eager to hear what they think of the land."

With a vague promise to call again soon, I spun on my heel toward the door. But my uncle's sharp command arrested me mid-stride.

"Darcy! I know well when trouble brews behind that façade of yours." He stepped nearer and gripped my shoulder firmly. "What has you rattled, Nephew? This unease seems more than absent brothers or vague mill troubles." His piercing stare demanded candor. "Has that chit Lizzy's reappearance caused the sort of trouble you feared?"

I held myself rigidly aloof despite an inward flinch. "The lady cannot be blamed for any trouble, sir. But I begin to think certain waking dreams might lead somewhere they ought not." I touched deferential fingers to my hat brim, subtly signaling the need for discretion. "Good day, Uncle. I shall... apprise you when I have clearer information."

Without waiting for dismissal, I slipped out the closing door. Wheeling my mount's head toward home, I touched spurs to his flanks. Never had negligent heart's impulses carried graver consequences if my foreboding proved accurate. All depended now on how fast I could forestall catastrophe.

I URGED MY LATHERED mount up Pemberley's last rise, anxious to assure myself of no family carriages missing from the drive. If George had already set off in stealth for Farthingdale, there was no telling what pretty nonsense he might whisper into susceptible ears.

The faint ring of shod hooves on gravel and a laugh I knew too well halted my progress. I reined up sharply to behold George swinging into Jupiter's saddle, blithely nodding to whatever comment Bingley had uttered beside him.

"Going somewhere, Brother?" I inquired pointedly. At George's guileless smile, my hand shot out to snatch the riding crop from his gloved fingers.

"Good God, man, what is amiss now?" His dancing eyes clouded, taking in my bedraggled appearance. "Has something happened?"

I drew breath to blast both thoughtless dawdlers from here to Wales. But Bingley's uneasy shift in his saddle recalled discretion's necessity in his presence.

"I have just come from Matlock where your absence was remarked upon," I bit out instead. "You do recall a prior engagement today? Lord and Lady Belmont and *your betrothed* await you even now for the intended excursion to Dovedale." My meaningful stare bore down until a faint color rose on his neck.

"Confound it, Fitz, cannot a fellow enjoy other friendships occasionally?" George blustered, kicking at Jupiter's oil-brushed hooves. He slanted an abashed glance toward Bingley. "Forgive me; it's only I have neglected you since our arrival. Seems my time is forever spoken for elsewhere of late."

The naked appeal for understanding twisted my conscience. I moderated my biting retort, attempting patience. "Far be it from me to discourage you from doing your duty as host. But best not keep your betrothed's family languishing further, hmm?" At his mulish look, I added grimly. "I shall instruct Hardwicke to drive you over directly in the barouche. Go and change, George."

He rolled his eyes skyward dramatically. "Heaven forfend Lucilla pines in my absence a quarter hour longer! You worry overly, Brother." But a speaking look from me set him grumbling toward the house, pride offended at receiving orders before Bingley.

I turned apologetically to my bemused guest the instant George was out of earshot. "Forgive that uncomfortable scene. Family obligations, you understand. I am afraid George will not be riding with you today." Glancing at the sun's climb, inspiration struck. "Perhaps you would care to join me on an errand nearby to pass the time until George returns?"

Bingley's face transformed instantly, his ready grin returning in full force. "Capital idea! I should be delighted to accompany you. And look, here is a fresh horse saddled for the occasion."

I shook my head. "I am afraid for this outing, a carriage is needed. Perhaps my phaeton?"

His brow crumpled, but he lifted his shoulders with a cheerful grin. "It seems I am at your disposal, Darcy."

Seventeen

Elizabeth

I POURED ANOTHER STEAMING cup, sighing inwardly at the uninspiring leaves before me. The morning room seemed lifeless and dull despite the golden morning light pooling around us. Or perhaps some deficiency lay in my own low spirits of late, out of tune with nature's unfolding splendor outside tall windows.

Across from me, Aunt Gardiner added a liberal splash of cream to her tea, glancing up with a smile. "This new blend is quite smooth. What do you think, Lizzy?"

I opened my mouth to reply when sharp hoofbeats and wheels crunching purposefully on the drive brought my head around. We so seldom received calls, with Mrs. Westing abed. Perhaps it was the parish priest and his wife, come to look in on her again. Before I could voice curiosity, Jane went to the window and gave a little gasp.

"Lizzy! Is not that Mr. Darcy and Mr. Bingley arrived outside?"

Hot tea sloshed over my suddenly trembling fingers. Darcy here? Which one? Surely, Jane must be mistaken in saying "*Mr.* Darcy." She must mean George, which meant...

I rushed to peer over her shoulder, pulse kicking into a canter. Sure enough, a highly polished carriage waited just outside, Pemberley's crested oval gleaming clearly on the door. My breath stopped, joy leaping irrationally. George had come! Every fiber of my being strained toward the door, body taut as bowstring vibrating for beloved fingers to pluck it into song once more.

As we watched, Mr. Bingley's hat tipped so we could see his face, laughing at some remark from his companion. He turned to offer a polite hand down to... But abruptly, my view was blocked by Jane whirling away from the window, dismay writ large on every feature.

"Oh heavens, my hair! And this old gown..." Frantically, she began attempting to pin stray blonde tendrils back into some semblance of order.

I might have smiled watching such unusual agitation in my serene sister if my knees had not unexpectedly liquefied. Aunt bustled over, straightening Jane's fichu as she cast a wondering look between our flushed faces.

"What possible reason could the gentlemen have for calling unannounced?" Her dark eyes narrowed, coming to rest assessingly on me. "You don't suppose... But no. That would be highly irregular."

A glimpse of flawlessly polished Hessians mounting the front step galvanized me from helpless speculation. "No matter now, they are already at our door! Come, let us greet them calmly. Oh, how glad I am that Lydia and Kitty are not here!"

Then the door swung wide, and my spirit plunged instantly down from dizzy heights. For there, haloed unexpectedly against mellow sunlight, stood Fitzwilliam Darcy, suddenly materialized when I had ardently expected another. Hot blood washed my cheeks, shock and dismay barely mastered behind a rigid smile. I could not even summon proper pleasure at this further evidence of the elder Darcy's restored goodwill, so violently had longing warred with reality in that instant.

Praying for the poise that still eluded me, I managed a passably cordial curtsy in answer to the gentlemen's bow. If Mr. Darcy marked my heightened color or the betraying quiver in my knees, his countenance gave little indication. But oh, I fancied his piercing eyes saw straight through to the sudden riotous beating beneath my breast as he regarded me somberly.

"Miss Elizabeth. Miss Bennet. Please forgive this intrusion." Darcy's rich voice sent an inexplicable shiver racing down my spine, even as bitter disappointment curdled in my heart. He had come in his brother's place—but where was George, who ought to have stood smiling down at me instead?

I found my voice, though it trembled faintly. "Of course, what a... surprise to see you just now, Mr. Darcy. To what do we owe the unexpected pleasure?" I faltered under his enigmatic stare, pulse skittering unevenly. *Where* was George?

Fortunately, Mr. Bingley stepped smoothly into the gap with an easy smile. "We happened to be riding nearby and could not resist stopping in when we caught sight of your delightful situation." His gaze lingered on Jane for several seconds, then took in Aunt Gardiner as well. "Seeing you all looking so cheerful through the windows, Darcy thought perhaps you ladies might care to join us for an open carriage tour of the area?"

I stirred, tamping down unreasonable pique. However disappointed, I could not ignore the sweet reminder of friendship restored in Mr. Darcy's unexpected call. "How perfectly delightful!" I summoned my most eloquent smile for the visitors. "Fresh air and fine prospects sound just the thing for such a summer day. What do you say, Aunt? Might we accept for just a brief turnout?"

I saw the hesitation writ clearly in my aunt's dark eyes, her quickly masked dismay at this probable overture she had vainly hoped to discourage. But true hospitality demanded a gracious concession now in the face of such unlooked-for attentions. Aunt Gardiner pressed her lips together, clearly wrestling etiquette against protective care. But at length, she offered a gracious nod. "Just briefly, mind. We have not a chaperone if you go far." Her glance at me entreated me not to misuse her fragile trust.

Darcy stirred, drawing himself up decisively. "I assure you, Madam, we shall not keep them past appropriate bounds." His steady gaze caught mine, flickering oddly. "Some ties cannot in honor be ignored whatever the passage of years. I... I would make amends for... past deficiencies."

My eyes pricked inexplicably at his solemn assurance. Yes! Surely, time would reveal all in due course. Until then, I must seize happiness where offered. I grasped Jane's hand and smiled sweetly up at Mr. Darcy's grave features. "Then please lead on, kind sirs! What fair prospects await discovery?"

I allowed Mr. Darcy's steady hand to assist me up into the phaeton's plush seat. I was to sit beside him in the front—naturally, I suppose, for that left Jane free to join Mr. Bingley in the rear. The phaeton's owner soon joined me and took the reins with easy confidence. I eased back against rich leather as we turned in a wide arc back down the drive, stealing occasional sidelong glances at my companion.

My few encounters with Fitzwilliam Darcy, the grown man, had taught me to think him still as serious and devoted to practicality and duty as he had ever been in his youth. But this, a leisurely jaunt through the countryside on a fine day in such a carriage and drawn by such a fine pair of grays? Surely, carriage rides in my childhood never boasted such style. He almost seemed as if he were trying to enjoy himself, or impress me. How very unlike the Fitzwilliam I once knew!

"You have quite the turn for speed, I see!" I laughed at last as the grays' gaits swung into a ground-eating stride that made the light phaeton sway thrillingly. "Do your horses set the pace, or their master?"

One dark brow quirked, though Mr. Darcy kept his eyes decisively forward. "I confess some eagerness to be off before second thoughts could arise. But have no fear. Your aunt's injunction against questionable jaunts shall be respected." His sober gaze cut briefly sideways. "I would not risk Mrs. Gardiner's displeasure, but I am glad fortune brought us by your door today."

My breath caught oddly at his oblique earnestness. Impulsively, I laid a light hand on his sleeve. "I rejoice no less in this happy accident, Sir. Truly."

Something eased subtly in the set of his shoulders, though he replied lightly. "An accident indeed, as I had thought to show Bingley some lesser-known local attractions nearby." His eyes glinted teasingly. "Unless the admirable Miss Bennet manages to monopolize his interest today?"

I laughed aloud, dizzy with this unexpected sunny humor. When had Fitzwilliam ever jested like that? "See how well you claim to know us after so little renewed acquaintance! I cannot answer for Mr. Bingley or Jane, but I am all curiosity. Which lesser-known sights do you intend to impress us with, then?"

"Ah, but you mistake me. The only impressions that interest me today are those you ladies convey." His smile turned abruptly introspective. "Although I did hear recently of a small estate called Southgate Park just beyond Lambton."

I shook my head. "Southgate? And it is an estate? What road is it on?"

He glanced at me with an oddly piercing look. "The name means nothing to you?"

I spread my guileless hands wide, chuckling. "Very little penetrated my juvenile consciousness, I fear. Derbyshire itself seems half a dream, save what fragments my memory nurtured all these years." I tilted my head, studying his pensive features. "Southgate, you say? It is quite close, then?"

His hooded eyes skated away across the wild heather. "Within easy reach when needs must. And I do not rightly know how large the house is, whether it is more an estate or a gentle farm. However..." His smile turned determinedly bright. "My steward advised me that there is a fair prospect from there for looking on the mountains, as well as a field and stream perfect for picnicking. We have a hamper of cook's best and the whole of the afternoon—or, as much of it as you dare, passing with two gentlemen while your aunt awaits you."

WE BOWLED ALONG SMOOTHLY for nearly half an hour, chattering about our favorite local haunts and childhood adventures beneath Derbyshire's brooding crags. Well, *I* was doing most of the "chattering" because I could not seem to settle my nerves under Fitzwilliam's steady gaze. I was in the midst of recounting a favorite secluded forest glen when he suddenly checked the grays, his attention fixed on something ahead.

"And here we have it—Southgate Park in all its modest glory." He slanted an inscrutable look my way. "The very place I mentioned earlier. I thought we might pause to admire it."

I leaned forward, eager for my first glimpse at this hitherto unknown neighborhood gem. What we beheld as the phaeton turned off the main road, however, was no breathtaking model of architecture and groundskeeping. Instead, a pleasant gentleman's residence of modest red brick sprawled comfortably beneath the sheltering wing of a fine old oak. Its sleepy air spoke more of unhurried country life than noble entertainments.

"What a perfectly charming house!" Jane offered politely behind us. "It looks so peaceful there."

"It does, indeed!" Mr. Bingley hastened to concur. "Although I wonder that such a handsome place does not seem to be occupied. Should we not see signs of servants at work?"

I glanced reflexively back at Mr. Darcy, arrested by the peculiar expression hovering over his usually inscrutable features. At Bingley's artless query, however, he rearranged himself back to polite interest.

"Just so. My own reaction upon first hearing of it. But these things do occur—properties changing hands or held in trust for distant relations yet to take possession." His casual tone convinced no one, but Bingley let the matter pass without further comment.

I resettled myself, glancing approvingly over the mellow golden stone aglow in the glaring afternoon light. Whoever eventually took up residence here would be blessed, indeed. My gaze caught on an arching footbridge just visible behind a stand of drooping willows.

"Oh! Is that not the prettiest little bridge over the stream?" I leaned my head playfully onto Fitzwilliam's shoulder, just as I used to do before he became all "Master of Pemberley." He didn't even flinch. "How ever would you tempt me from a book if I lay claim to that spot for my private refuge?" I asked.

He glanced down, something undefined flickering in his eyes at such unguarded familiarity. But no objection or offense marred his smile. "Who says I would try to tempt you away? Perhaps I might join you."

"And 'perhaps' I would steal your book until you promised to read it aloud to me. What of that, Fitzwilliam Darcy?"

"Then I would be undone. It is doubtful we would ever be discovered before it became too dark outside to see the pages. Wellington would have to bear messages to the house, leading concerned parties to our location before we were feared lost forever."

I laughed. "Just as I once tied an urgent message to Piglet's collar when I had been out in the garden and twisted my ankle! I sent him back into the house, and George came to rescue me."

"Far be it from me to cast doubt upon the reliability of your memory, but that was I who found you. Your stocking was muddied and shredded, and you were certain Nurse would punish you for ruining yet another one. I had to carry you indoors because you were hurt and crying."

I blinked. "Truly? How very strange! All these years, I remembered that as George, but yes, now that you mention it, I do recall being carried, and he would have been too young. Oh, dash it all, now I shall have to give you credit for every gallant deed of his!"

Fitzwilliam chuckled and set the brake on the carriage. "Never mind that. Come, will you not step down and tour the property more closely? We shall not trespass too intimately, but it does not appear as if we will trouble anyone, and we need not resume our drive just yet."

Laughing, I placed my hand in his to descend from the carriage, and Mr. Bingley was already gallantly handing Jane down behind us. Truly, this was paradise found! Everything in Derbyshire was, for that matter. I cast my face up to the sky and wandered the shade-dappled grass, turning about and reveling in the warmth of the afternoon.

While Jane and Mr. Bingley strolled quietly along the banks, Mr. Darcy set to unloading our ample picnic, shrugging off his coat to lay it beneath the swinging basket. Despite informal surroundings, not a single item lacked refinement, from crystal glasses to silver utensils carved with the Darcy crest.

"My word, such provisions!" I exclaimed, selecting a wrapped wedge of crumbling cheddar. "One might fancy themselves dining at Pemberley's own table."

Darcy's glance held quiet satisfaction as he uncorked a bottle of wine with practiced hands. "I instructed Cook to supply her very best in honor of the distinguished company I was expecting to host." He pushed the laden hamper invitingly nearer my perch on the blanket edge. "Do sample her cherry tarts—I believe they were always a favorite of yours."

I reached unthinking for the indicated delicacy, only to pause with my hand arrested halfway. Yes, these were my favorite childhood treats. But how should Pemberley's present master and cook retain such intimate culinary details from seven long years past? I lifted bemused eyes to Darcy's placid features as clarity dawned.

"You arranged this entire outing beforehand, did you not?" I laughed. "Was even this property's 'chance discovery' part of an elaborate stratagem?"

To his credit, Darcy met my unveiled assessment steadily, a rueful quirk touching his lips. "You have found me out. I cannot pretend happenstance alone guided us to this specific spot today." He extended the coveted plate gently toward me in wordless entreaty. "Can you forgive the benign deception?"

I accepted the proffered tarts slowly, eyes still holding his. Then, with deliberate pleasure, I bit into sticky sweetness, dancing instantly on my tongue with joyful sensations almost startling in their acute familiarity across the years. I savored the rush of memories conjured from Pemberley's kitchens, shaking my head in admiring censure toward my undeceived host.

"You are all consideration, Mr. Darcy, though your machinations hardly need begging pardon." I patted the seat beside me invitingly. "Come, we are long overdue for the thorough accounting only hours of conversation can supply"

Barely waiting for his acknowledgment, I leaned contentedly back against sun-warmed grass to resume my blissful repast. If Pemberley were a food, it would be a cherry tart, best consumed from a picnic basket.

Eighteen

Darcy

I lowered myself onto the plaid blanket, watching Bingley lead Miss Bennet toward the footbridge some yards distant. Doubtless, they meant to relish a bit of private discourse, out of earshot from even the most discreet chaperone. I hardly minded playing inadvertent guardian for such a modest, unaffected chap as Bingley. Far better than trying to chaperone George.

A throat gently cleared nearby and drew my attention back to my fair companion. I found Elizabeth regarding me, curiosity and veiled amusement dancing in her fine eyes. "I suppose such a pretty prospect invites a stroll, Mr. Darcy?" Mischief tilted the corner of her mouth. "Or ought we leave all examining to Mr. Bingley lest we 'trespass' too intimately?"

Heat stole up my neck at the thought of escorting her on my arm as if I were courting her. But better to let her be distracted by touring the grounds than permit her to study my face and learn more than she ought. She already saw through my thin excuses—I never had possessed the talent of disguise, as George had, and nor had I ever desired to cultivate it.

I rose and offered my arm in silent invitation to wander the garden and lawn about the house. To my relief, she consented with ready laughter, tucking her hand snugly into the crook of my elbow. And it didn't... well, *she* didn't feel like a sister when she took my arm like that.

We meandered some minutes in equable silence, her head turning to take in ornamental urns flanking steps leading up to the front door. Curiosity drew her attention back like a lodestone as we circled behind neat boxwood hedges surrounding the charming residence.

"Do you deny then that you possess mysterious insider knowledge about why this house lies so quiet?" She paused, glancing back meaningfully toward the door's dark mouth. "Are we truly at liberty to be strolling so freely, uninvited?"

I could not restrain the twitch of a wry smile. "You suspect me of bringing you intentionally to play house-breaker?" My free hand covered the slender fingers resting on my arm. "I promise most lawful permission, Madam. Though the particulars of ownership lie... temporarily vague."

She huffed softly, lips still curved teasingly up at me. "One day, I shall learn your whole shocking scheme, Sir!" But her eyes lifted upward, and I followed her rapt gaze to glimpse the age-darkened timbers of the house's interior framed through wide front windows. "Is it permissible to look inside?" She pressed closer to the dusty glass pane. "This darling place only wants a loving family within to make it a home."

She leaned nearer as if to pass straight through brick and wood by fervent wishing, so endearing and natural her reaction. On impulse, I moved to test the latch, startled when the door swung silently inward at my touch. Behind me, Elizabeth gasped in soft surprise. I turned, and her dark eyes searched mine, lips parted uncertainly. Her brows raised, and I nodded, gesturing silently forward into cool dimness.

Floorboards briefly protested our intrusion and then settled with a creak. We moved slowly, footsteps muffled across bare expanses once undoubtedly graced by fine carpets and furnishings. Now, empty rooms echoed only questions.

What family had once filled these vacant spaces with life and laughter? For whom did gray stone walls still stand sentinel until some unknown hand gave Elizabeth the key to her future? I trailed my fingertips along windowsills and wainscoting, irrationally hoping for some whisper or inspiration. Only dust met my inquiring touch, concealing rather than disclosing long-hidden truths.

Beside the parlor's carved mantlepiece, Elizabeth paused, slender neck craned back, inspecting the plaster ceiling centerpiece still boasting faint flecks of gold leaf. "Such loving detail lavished everywhere. As if it were built for someone who loved their home... these are not mere walls turned to dust by time."

Her fanciful musing wrenched me back from useless woolgathering. Clearing my throat, I turned my steps back toward the entrance hall, pulse oddly quickening for no clear cause. "Curiosity inspires poetic turns of phrase, I see. Although... Speaking of time's passage, remind me, please, when you mark your next birthday? You are presently twenty if memory serves?"

"Why yes, I shall be one and twenty next April. On the sixteenth."

"So, you have not yet reached your majority. I thought it was nearer to hand."

"Not until next spring. Just a few weeks after your own birthday, as I recall." Eyes glinting impishly, she added, "I do hope you noted the date this time, sir."

I moved slowly back toward the entrance, then turned back to her with solemn eyes.

"I remember everything of importance. Even the things that I wish I could forget."

She went very still, her cheek twitching faintly. "Such as?"

I forced words past my suddenly numb lips. "I recall too clearly the day Father brought you home."

I heard her soft, indrawn breath, but the floodgates had opened now. "I was but seven years, and you were a red and wailing scrap in his big arms. He let no one else hold you—not the nurses, not even Mrs. Reynolds. Just cradled you himself."

My glance was drawn back to her upturned face. "I asked your origins, and he said..." I hesitated, seeing a spasm of hurt cross her expression in anticipation of his crushing reply. I longed to erase every sorrowful line from her beloved countenance.

"What did he say?"

I swallowed. "He said you were a gift from Heaven to ease our sorrows after the loss of Mother."

She fell silent. I watched emotions chase across her features—wistfulness, grief, loss. With a choked cry, she turned aside, slight shoulders trembling violently as she struggled not to weep. My fingers twitched with the effort to remain motionless, warring instincts dividing me. Was I a gentleman or protective guardian now? The stranger or the one person on earth who could fully share her sorrow in this moment?

I crossed to her side before I could second guess my instinct. Gently, slowly as one would approach a wounded deer, I covered her shaking hand with mine where it rested on the mantel. At my touch, she hesitated, then turned into my arms all at once, quiet tears soaking into my coat. And there we stood in empty rooms once filled with life, silently sharing the grief of love lost and journeys interrupted too soon.

When, at last, she leaned back, I offered my handkerchief and brushed one final tear from her soft cheek. I stood mute, clenching my jaw against effusive apologies better left unsaid. Sympathetic silence must serve where paltry words stalled, inadequate to convey fellow feeling. At length, she drew a shaky breath, features still turned aside though heavy drops yet clung to her dark lashes. I yearned to brush away that mute evidence of past hurts, yet I was powerless to salve those wounds myself.

"Oh, do not stare so, Sir!" A fragile laugh escaped her, though she kept her glossy head bent. "You shall think me a watering pot indeed, dissolved into tears at the least provocation."

I moved slowly back into her orbit, hoarsely clearing my throat against inexplicable obstruction there. "Tears do you credit rather than shame. Only marble resists the deepest stirrings of humanity."

Another wan smile flickered. "Perhaps. However, I blush to be so undisciplined before you. Such childish clinging to old sorrows..."

"Elizabeth." I waited until she hesitantly lifted those wounded doe eyes to mine before continuing gently. "No one could expect you to feel nothing. Does the sorrow still haunt you frequently?"

Her lips twisted, though she blinked back any fresh tears. "Oh, by no means! Time and happy occupation have worn smooth my jagged recollections of that hour." She turned her shoulder, denial written in every line of slender frame. "I am content enough these seven years."

"Elizabeth." My low tone brooked no evasion, and she unwillingly pivoted back, features now shuttered to conceal what lay beneath. I risked feather-light touch beneath her lowered chin. "Even the most determined sufferer craves an outlet when too much is bound up inside. Will you not unburden yourself now, if only this once?" My hand fell away slowly as she searched my face. "Let me share the weight as a friend and... and confidant."

My pulse bounded unevenly. Whatever our past connection had been, it was no longer. She was not a relative I could comfort with impunity but a young lady. A single, attractive young lady, and I was alone in a vacant house with her. Had I overstepped discretion's bounds? But surely even the strictest etiquette code permitted me to comfort one in need?

When she offered no refusal, I curbed the urge to grasp her hands. But she read the unspoken wish in my eyes. With slumped shoulders, she turned toward an aged settee, settling onto the faded damask. She patted the space beside her in invitation.

As I settled cautiously beside her, she spoke haltingly. "I cried myself to exhaustion every night that first week. And the second. And the third! Poor Jane suffered the worst, attempting to cheer me up and soothe my wounded pride." A rueful smile ghosted her mouth, though eyes remained downcast. "I had been cast off without explanation or farewell by those I loved most and trusted utterly."

My throat closed. How thoughtlessly our father had denied her vulnerable spirit even that small comfort of an explanation! How could he? Struggling to keep my voice even, I managed a gruff murmur. "Your reception there was not... unkind, I hope?"

Elizabeth lifted her head swiftly, reading shadows in my averted face. She hastened to pat my wrist reassuringly. "Oh no, indeed! Aunt and Uncle Gardiner have ever treated me as their own. And dearest Jane's companionship proved just the balm to heal a bitter heart. I might have been truly lost without her tender championship those difficult weeks."

Wistfulness softened her features. Impulsively, she turned toward me, a fragile hope kindled in her look. "But tell me truly—did Mr. Darcy never disclose... anything? Any reasons?"

I shook my head. "He was ever close beyond measure. Even now, I grasp at straws, trying to think of an explanation." Frustration sharpened my tone before I caught myself. I was her sympathetic ear, not a victim. Softening my glance, I said, "Take heart. If we are patient, surely, we can uncover the truth." Silence fell between us—fragile as ice over a stream. When her hand slid hesitantly over mine, something lurched inside me. I had to know her mind.

"Does it comfort you—that he spoke your name those final days?" I searched her glistening eyes, willing her to unburden herself to me alone. "Whatever his reasons were, he did not undertake them lightly or without regret."

Her voice broke on a shuddering exhale. "I grieved never seeing him again to ask why he sent me away... or embrace him one last time as my father."

As tears spilled down her cheeks, fury surged inside me—at my father for wounding her so deeply, and at myself for stirring this pain now. I gripped her hand, desperate to restore her shattered smile. "He should not have denied you answers or solace." My voice rasped with emotion. "But I vow you will know joy again."

"You think I have not had joy?" She sniffed and smiled. "Do not give yourself airs, sir! It *is* possible to find happiness somewhere other than Pemberley." Her shadowed gaze turned cheerful again—she always had possessed that trick of turning even the gravest conversation into a jest, but not in the same way George did. Elizabeth might smile and laugh as merrily as he could, but while he turned his thoughts purposely to the most frivolous things, she was still grounded through it.

"In truth," she confessed, "Mr. Bennet took me in with open arms, raising me almost more like a son than a daughter. He guided my mind and understanding, and... dare I say it... he became Papa to me. As much as Father ever was... Father."

I could not decide if I was more pleased or dismayed to hear how swiftly Father had been replaced—all by his own doing, but still... "I am grateful such care was given in our stead." I hesitated. "And I hope my father... did something to forward the interests of the family?"

Elizabeth's wry chuckle held no resentment. "I am no simpleton. I recognized long ago that the dowries he settled on the Bennet daughters secured my place. They had very little before that, and now they can each afford to look for some affection in marriage." She eyed me askance. "Mama—that is, Mrs. Bennet—made her advantages plain when I first arrived. But truly, over time, she has accepted me as one of her own, as have my sisters. All in all, it has been a good life with the Bennets. But I confess, I never quite forgot dear George." She glanced up, a bashful flush staining her cheeks. "Silly, I suppose, after so many years."

I regarded her steadily. "George made quite an impression when you were younger, I see."

She gave a small shrug, not meeting my eyes. "He was always sweet and merry and ever the one to touch my heart where no one else could. And it is still so." She risked an upward glance. "You do not... disapprove, I hope?"

I hesitated, questions swirling. Had George's behavior during their recent reunion reignited tender hopes? Carefully, I asked, "Has he given you any reason to believe such admiration would now be returned?"

Elizabeth tilted her chin defiantly. "I should say that his words and manner convey deepest regard, I am sure of it. I know he would not trifle with me."

"Indeed." I mastered my outrage, fists clenching at my sides. That reprehensible flirt! I would not stand idly by while George dallied and raised expectations where he had no intentions. And it was not only his childhood playmate's heart he toyed with, but Lady Lucilla's as well! And, heaven strike me dead for saying it, but the consequences of breaking Lady Lucilla's heart were staggeringly worse than if he dallied with Elizabeth's.

But I dare not distress Elizabeth with accusations against her glowing assumptions. She would not even credit it, if I told her that he had already led her astray. The confession must come from George's own lips. So, I must deal with errant George in my own way.

I offered her my arm, rage tightly leashed. "Shall I return you safely home?" Escorting her outside, I vowed George would soon feel the sting of my unrestrained rebukes until he mended his careless ways.

Nineteen

Elizabeth

MY DEAR LIZZY,

I write to you from the refuge of my library, having escaped eight ladies in the drawing room, all aflutter over ribbons, officers, and neighborhood gossip. The usual mayhem, in other words. I suppose you have found more peaceful environs over there in Derbyshire just now? Or has your sister Jane infected even staid Aunt Gardiner with her smiles and good temper?

We are all eager for your return, most especially that black hairy creature who resides under this roof under the guise of being "my" dog. I believe Barker still awaits your whistled call from the garden gate each morning. Mrs. Hill trots him round the park daily, but he mopes without you.

As for the other creatures under my roof, I shall update you on their various fixations. Mrs. Bennet has taken to her room with lavender water and cold compresses after learning the militia may not be coming to Meryton this year after all. Had you been here, Lizzy, I've no doubt clever words from you could have prevented her descent into despair. Alas, she says our daughters are all doomed to spinsterhood and poverty *now. I wait in dread for each day's post, wondering what elaborate hat or gown she has ordered this week to assuage low spirits. At least this trend keeps her occupied upstairs and out of my library.*

With your mother thus indisposed, most management of household affairs falls to Mary and Kitty. I often find Mary gazing dreamily out the window when she is supposed to be totting up figures. Perhaps she composes sonnets in her mind for distant suitors attracted by her new musical prowess.

As for Kitty, I believe aspirations of flirting with officers have transferred seamlessly to hopes of attracting the wealthy gentleman interested in leasing Netherfield one day. Yes, your mother caught wind of that rumor and has spent the past week outfitting your sisters in hopes of favorable first impressions. But with Jane's informative letters keeping me apprised of recent developments nearer your current abode, I rather think Mr. Bingley's eye will not be caught by lesser local beauties. Not that I have enlightened your incorrigible mother on that point!

What news of your adventures amongst old haunts, I wonder? By now, you will have called at that great house after such an unceremonious reintroduction to the family. Are the present residents as amiable as you recall from tender youth? Have stately manners replaced the carefree days of chasing pups across lawns long ago? Or does some enduring merriment still reside there to welcome wandering sprites displaced by time? You must indulge your lonely second father with every detail!

I remain safely ensconced among my books here, emerging only when appetite drives me to sample whatever concoctions arise from Mrs. Hill's kitchen. I miss your company, and Jane's, as we would share many happy hours reading together in this very library. At least you both share my preference for books over your sisters' gossip. Now, with you gone, the silence here often reminds me of your absence... as does the renewed

chatter from downstairs each time I open my study door. So do take care
not to abandon your old father entirely!

Promise you will not allow former ties to permanently supplant our
humble claims upon your heart, Lizzy dear. These rooms stand ready
to receive you back, whenever wanderings release their siren call into
nostalgia's roots. Until then, I am ever,

Your Loving Papa

I PASSED FATHER'S LETTER to Jane and found her waiting to share her letter from him with me. I read his words to her, snickering my amusement at his wry commentary. But mirth faded swiftly as a new thought came to me. When had I last felt so universally welcomed among friends? So seen for myself beyond my usefulness to others?

"What bothers you, Lizzy? I know that look."

I flashed a smile. "Nothing. Just the startling realization that I seem to have two homes, where once, I might have said I hadn't even one." Unbidden, George's laughing visage swam before me. He had called again yesterday afternoon—a mere stop out in the garden, but he had teased memories from me that I had once tried so hard to forget. How well I recalled trailing after him, vying daily for his infectious attention and admiration. My staunchest childhood ally.

"He does seem to fancy you," Jane said softly.

"I think so! He makes no secret he hopes to revive our childhood attachment into something enduring." I felt girlish excitement bubble up. Did he truly still care for me as I had secretly cared for him all these years?

But contrary thoughts followed. However much George welcomed me, his elder brother confused me. "Only Mr. Darcy gives me pause,"

I confessed. "He seems at times to hold back... and then at others, he is so..." I bit my lip. What *was* he? "I suppose it is understandable that he would be reserved, given my background and connections... or lack thereof."

Jane arched one brow. "Believe me, Lizzy—propriety is not first in that gentleman's thoughts around you!" She leaned forward confidingly. "He watches you most attentively when he thinks none notice."

I flushed. "Fitzwilliam! You are imagining it. No, he never had a thought for me, nor I for him—not in *that* way, surely. But..."

"Yes?"

I hesitated, then offered a wicked grin. "I suppose if one were to be introduced to them for the first time—not knowing their personalities, you understand—Fitzwilliam does cut the more dashing figure, does he not? So tall and mysterious! And my goodness, have you seen his eyes? I never noticed before that they looked like melted chocolate."

"He is, indeed, rather a pleasure to look at." Jane eyed me quizzically. "So does this mean your heart is divided between the two brothers?"

"No!" I hastened to assert, ignoring her knowing look. I loved George. I always had. Since girlhood, his smiles and praise were my chief ambition and reward. Surely, renewed closeness would rekindle our understanding. "I only mean to say that he has... turned out well."

"Ah. Yes, I daresay they both did."

"Their father would have been proud," I asserted, getting to my feet and smoothing my skirts as I went to the window. "Fitzwilliam is so like his father, and George... why, I expect he must be like his mother, God rest her soul. He *is* ever so charming, is he not? Funny and handsome, and just... just like I always imagined he would be."

And yet... why did Fitzwilliam's dark, steady gaze suddenly intrude, full of banked feeling I had never noticed until our recent time together? Perhaps I was imagining it, but there seemed a... an intensity, I suppose... the sort of look a gentleman ought more properly to bestow on a lady he was courting rather than a long-lost family member.

I still favored George's bright, playful eyes and sunny temperament. But yesterday, something in Fitzwilliam's tender tones, as he recounted funny childhood misadventures, stirred bewildering reactions. Without conscious thought, I had nearly been tempted to lean closer to trace the emerging humor lines time had wrought in noble features once so serious...

Flustered by my wandering fancy, I took abrupt refuge in brisk certainty. "Well," I turned to face Jane with a wide smile! "Whatever burdens duty now lays on Mr. Darcy, I trust open enjoyment of our former friendship lingers still to hold us all happily together."

She smiled back. "I believe you will not be disappointed."

I stood decisively, linking Jane's arm through mine with a rallying laugh. "Now, enough idle mooning! Daylight wanes, and our fine hosts await! Dear Aunt must be thinking we forgot about evening tea."

But even as Jane and I sashayed to the door, arm in arm, Aunt entered my bedchamber, features clouded with uncharacteristic gravity. Wordlessly, she passed an opened letter, one section folded outwards in plain summons. My heart sank, guessing the sender even as I took it reluctantly.

Aunt's soft murmur confirmed my suspicion. "Your uncle felt you should see this page he addressed specifically to you, Lizzy. I will allow you to digest it in privacy." She pressed my hand ere exiting silently.

Apprehension mounting, I moved nearer the window's waning afternoon light and began to read.

M *Y Dear Lizzy,*

Ill news reached me yesterday that cast longer shadows than mere questionable conduct. Your aunt wrote of your accidental reunion with the Darcys, speaking highly of their renewed attentions. And yet, with every line, my disquiet deepened.

You, above all, must understand the precautions long necessary in your case. I speak not now of propriety or discretion—those ships have evidently sailed. Nay, hazards of more lasting impact may arise that I shudder to contemplate.

You know I have never denied you explanations without cause. I respect you too well to reject hard queries or dismiss righteous feelings. But neither can I break confidences sworn to one no longer here to release me from a sacred pledge. This you must also understand and forgive.

What I can reveal is it may no longer be safe or prudent to linger there, inviting further intimacy. I realize how harsh this must sound when your heart yearns for a restored connection. But consider, more lives than your own are narrowly bounded by choices made in innocence. If affection for family and friends cannot sway you, then I appeal to self-lessness rather than self-interest. Look beyond personal wishes to guard others now vulnerable through no fault of their own making.

My sympathies extend to you in this trial, yet prove I know you equal to difficult sacrifice when the welfare of beloved ones hangs in the balance. Do not fail them now through stubbornness or blind hope. The duty-bound path often proves hard and steep—but the summit view may surprise with unexpected prospects discovered.

I am returning to Derbyshire as soon as possible so we may speak face to face of what weighs so oppressively now in mystery. All shall be made clear with time, I solemnly vow.

Your Loving Uncle

I SLOWLY LOWERED THE letter as the door creaked open to admit Jane. One glance at my stricken expression brought her to my side in an instant. But before compassionate arms could enfold me, the reaction burst its numb confines. Blindly, I tore past her mute reach, clattering heedlessly down narrow stairs and through the kitchens 'til I burst into open air.

There were no more words just then—only raw, anguished gasps with nowhere for explosive pain to vent but skyward. I ran hard to outdistance specters of love and laughter turned ominous threat. But shadows leaped faster still, Uncle's reasoned arguments no match for protective familiar arms hungering to draw me back despite the unknown peril behind Pemberley's sheltering bulwarks.

Oh, how I ran—as if physical force could reroute unbearable destiny arriving by urgent post! But when at last streaming tears blurred each sight into indistinguishable gloom, I sank defeated upon an obliging oak root tangled near my feet. Truth would not evade me much longer. Light must replace this strangling shroud of mystery soon...or flickering hopes guttering in uncertainty's cold wind would expire beyond rekindling. Pierced by nameless dread, I wept as one already bereft.

TWENTY

Darcy

"**G**O ON, THEN, LAD!" I pointed my gelding Claudius over a tall hedge, and my heart soared in my chest as he took the leap. This, *this* was what it was to fly! To leave my troubles behind for but a moment and ground myself to both earth and sky. To indulge in the purest feeling of power and grace while staring my own mortality in the face. Here, I was free, unfettered, and untroubled.

But not today. Today, no matter how fiercely we raced, I could not outrun the fearsome specter of consequences awaiting my reckless-ly wayward brother. I learned that George had paid a short visit to Farthington again yesterday afternoon. Secret, brief, and, probably to his thinking, innocent. But where Elizabeth was concerned, George's attentions could never be innocent.

He had gone too far this time. I fumed as hooves thundered, a drumbeat echo to turmoil in my brain. Bad enough, he was toying with Elizabeth's renewed affections. But to be wooing Lady Lucilla in actual courtship while playing dishonorable games of deception and divided hearts? It turned my stomach. That guileless young woman deserved far better from one purporting ardent devotion.

Very well, the time had come for blunt speaking and ultimatums, however distasteful between siblings. George must swear off Elizabeth beyond propriety's bounds if he hoped to retain the prize Lord Belmont had inexplicably dropped into undeserving hands. And if he did not... well, perhaps it was time for me to lay certain uncomfortable facts before him.

My hands tightened almost brutally on the reins. George would chafe under any restraints, of course, but I held greater leverage now than erratic temper or fickle sensibilities. Let him scoff and froth—certain debts discreetly transferred into my name guaranteed compliance, if hints about scandal and reputation, failed to motivate reform. I cringed from stooping to mercenary blackmail. But neither could I stand idle while George inflicted lasting hurts through selfish pursuits. His days of dancing heedlessly away while others paid the reckoning ended here.

Gradually, the hot roil of plans and arguments battering fierce inside me eased as we entered gentler countryside. I guided my spent mount toward sun-dappled woods, a vision forming unbidden behind my eyes... elfin features alight with pleasure or animated in spirited debate... slender hands clasping mine tremulously as today's shadows fell... the trusting appeal unveiled for one fleeting moment unguarded...

My breath snarled in my chest, my pulse abruptly thundering for vastly different reasons. Fatefully, we had begun traversing uncertain terrain well off familiar paths. Each glimpse behind Elizabeth's resilient defenses revealed arresting new depths. And my traitorous soul mirrored each discovery, refusing to maintain seemly boundaries.

No. I jerked my head sharply, denying such dangerous reflections. The role I had adopted countenanced no questionable wanderings in that direction, however softly alluring green glades now tempting just within reach. To safeguard every threatened heart, mine must remain staunchly disciplined against delicate rosebuds strangled too soon by grasping thorns.

With a remorseless will, I turned my back on green hollows wooing me toward sparkling streams and silver laughter. My course lay instead toward flint-eyed duty and coming storms, which must be weathered before this blackest night yielded to frail dawn. Elizabeth and George both would cry out against the coming separation my harsh means required. But far kinder fleeting pain now than enduring devastation later. I steeled myself against the agony of delicate hopes crushed under inevitability's grinding heel... not all my own.

I wheeled my lathered mount round toward home, determined to outpace unwanted sentimentality clouding rational thought. But as the folly's distant outline crested the next hill, some restless impulse turned my hands toward the winding path instead. My horse needed a drink and a good blow, and perhaps I could use a moment of quiet reflection in my father's favorite haunt.

I had not visited the delicately carved stone gazebo overlooking Pemberley's granite cliffs since he passed. Yet suddenly, the peaceful vista's siren call drowned out stern self-lectures, promising a serene perspective unattainable in my cluttered study. Surely, an hour's reflection gazing out at timeless hills could only grant clearer sight to mark out prudence's difficult road ahead.

I touched impatient heels to sweated flanks, covering the last furlongs swiftly beneath overhanging oaks. But as the summerhouse came into view, my breath arrested as violently as if my careening steed had cast a shoe. For there, huddled wretchedly at the base of the steps curled into a shuddering ball of abject misery, lay a familiar slight figure.

"Elizabeth!" I threw myself from the saddle, my heart crashing wildly. She was huddled wretchedly at the folly's base—a shuddering ball of grief many miles from home.

At my hoarse cry, she slowly unfolded from her muddy skirts. My heart twisted to behold her ravaged face swimming into bewildered view. She swiped at streaked cheeks, clearly battling for composure.

"Mr. Darcy! Forgive me, I did not... hear you ride up."

I attempted a quavering smile. "Nor I any maiden in distress. Are you injured?" My glance took in her bedraggled state. She had stumbled repeatedly to end up here alone in such a manner. Alarm surged through me even as protectiveness flooded my veins. Gently, I grasped her chilled hands, willing warmth to flow between our entwined fingers. "Please, you are greatly overwrought. Will you not unburden yourself so I may offer comfort?"

She shook her head, covering her face with her hands.

"Please, I... has someone hurt you?"

Her hands fell away, and she stared at me with those eyes that made my insides turn to jelly. "No! Oh, no, nothing of the kind."

"But you are very distressed. Come, is there something I can do for your comfort?"

Elizabeth dipped her head and swallowed, and I thought she would say nothing at all. Then, her words spilled out in a sobbing rush. "My uncle insists I must leave Derbyshire immediately before harm comes through renewed ties. What is he talking about? *Why?*"

I blinked, flinching when her hand squeezed harder into my own. "I've no idea. He said that?"

"He said..." she gulped and bobbed her head in a ragged gasp. "He said I was being selfish if I stayed. As if my being here could bring you harm! What can he mean? And how can I abandon those I love now, after just finding them again?"

I stared helplessly as fresh tears carved trails in the dust on her cheeks. At my ongoing silence, she ventured unsteadily, "You wrote to my uncle yourself... did you not? You would have—I know you too well for you to deny it. You demanded answers, I am sure of it. What did he have to say?"

I nodded heavily. "You do, it seems, know me well. Yes, I wrote, asking the very questions plaguing you. But no reply has come yet."

She searched my face beseechingly. I hesitated before voicing the harsh truths that must temper fragile hope. "We should heed wisdom from those able to see farthest, however it wounds us."

Silence hung between us as Elizabeth searched my face. Her earlier anguish still simmered beneath the surface, along with my own churning helplessness. Devil take it, it was not as if *I* wanted to send her away again, too! But for George's good and her own... and apparently, Mr. Gardiner feared whatever my father had told him to fear. Perhaps it would be best if I used this as an opportunity to see all concerns answered, quickly and quietly.

But Elizabeth was still weeping, still clinging to my hand as if I were her only champion. I could not misuse that trust. Gentle comfort was needed, not harsh reality.

I drew in a deep breath, softening my tone. "We cannot know yet what wisdom prompts your uncle's warning. But clearly, he believes removing you from here shields someone from harm."

Elizabeth brushed hastily at wet cheeks. "But who? How could my presence hurt those I love best?"

I shook my head. "I cannot guess. But trust it does not speak ill of you." I hesitated. "Might continuing our acquaintance truly put others at risk?"

She gave a small shuddering sigh. "I cannot see how or why. But then little makes sense anymore."

My fingertips found her shoulder, squeezing in tender solidarity, though words still failed. We remained thus, unspeaking, while her heaving breaths slowed and a semblance of calm returned.

At length, Elizabeth sniffed and forced a smile. "I make quite the watering pot soaked in misery. That is twice now you have had to dry my tears." She gestured to her ruined gown and the flopping heel of her boot. "I even broke my heel again! Quite the picture of distress for a gallant hero encounter."

I snorted, relief loosening my tongue to match her shifting mood. "A laughable damsel indeed."

She attempted a broken laugh. "I suppose you need to return me safely now before my state undoes all reputation."

"Unless you mean to pass the night out here." I helped her to stand, keeping her hand warmly clasped in mine.

"I can think of worse places to sleep. Under the stars on a summer night? Far away from the demands of duty and the chagrined looks that inform me of what I 'ought' to do? It sounds like heaven to me."

"Yes, until I have Mr. Westing pounding on my door, asking what has become of the young lady currently living under his roof. Come along." Before she grasped my intention, I had swept her up securely against my chest and started striding for my horse.

Elizabeth yelped, wriggling in instinctive protest. "Mr. Darcy! Fitzwilliam! Put me down this instant!"

I merely tightened my hold, striding toward my grazing mount. "Not a chance. You will only do further damage trotting about on one heel. Had you no thought for ankles or reputation staggering this far alone?"

"And had you no thought I might object being hauled about like a sack of flour?" she shot back. But a smile tugged reluctantly at her lips even as she swatted ineffectually at my shoulder.

I laughed outright as I positioned her sideways on the saddle, then swung up behind, encircling her securely. "Admit it—you would object more if I left you limping all the long miles home." I felt her lean tentatively back against me. "Now, shall I play the gallant rescuer or unforgivable rogue stealing you away?"

She glanced sideways, eyes dancing. "Neither, if you remain determined to shock Aunt Gardiner into palpitations, arriving with me boasting both ruined boots and gown." Her brow arched challengingly. "But as long as you have compromised my reputation beyond salvaging, we may as well ride to Farthingdale with no further harm done."

I grinned at this incorrigible maiden nestled willingly in my embrace. I touched my heels lightly to Claudius's sides. "Hold tight, then. Stray neither left nor right, and trust me to keep you steady." Laughing softly, she obeyed, wrapping her arm around my shoulders.

We rode for some minutes in companionable silence, the evening air rushing sweetly past. My mount's smooth gait soon reassured any lingering tension from Elizabeth. I felt her gradually relax, weariness replacing rigid alarm. Careful not to encroach, I nonetheless shifted position, granting her slighter frame more support.

"Comfortable?" I murmured near her ear.

She startled slightly, shivering as she turned to look me in the face. "Oh! Forgive me, I must make a poor armrest flopping about—"

"Nonsense. You endure this journey quite valiantly." I meant to soothe, but she twisted again to survey me skeptically.

"Valiantly enduring would suggest some trial or hardship in progress." Humor danced in her eyes. "Do you imply discomfort in my present situation, Mr. Darcy?"

I cleared my throat, avoiding that arch look. "My meaning was only, I cannot imagine it is an easy seat for you, sitting sideways before me, almost on the horse's neck. And after such an emotional ordeal—"

"Ordeal!" She bubbled with laughter. "As though you rescuing me was a burdensome duty and not theatrical whimsy on your part. Confess, you mimic knight errant tales sweeping damsels onto noble steeds in desperate flight."

I chuckled, inclining my head in defeat. "Well, I cannot claim it is a chore, playing the gallant hero for once. Although..." I slanted her a sly look. "The role becomes less rewarding if certain damsels insist on puncturing illusion with mockery."

She nudged my shoulder reproachfully. "I do no such thing! Why, my gown is even dirtied already to better fit the part." Her grin held a silent challenge. "You take liberties, accusing me of ingratitude before I have even had time to tender my thanks."

I met her sparkling eyes, pulse quickening at this new facet emerging. Had Lizzy always possessed such readiness to parry and return teasing in kind? Strange that I had never noted it before. Strange, also, how delightful the discovery proved.

"Shall I furnish proof of my sincerest dedication as rescuer then?" Impulse seized me. Before she guessed my intent, I wrapped both arms snugly round her and touched heel to Claudius's sides, urging him into a long trot that made her grasp my neck with a startled stranglehold. "What think you? Shall you finish the ride bound captive as insurance against further mockery?" I held my breath, praying she read playfulness, not impropriety, in my daring gesture.

To my vast relief, she took a deep breath and relaxed. "I suppose that convinces me thoroughly." Her glance turned rueful. "You are a fearful tease, fancying yourself to be a Cassanova or some nonsense like that."

I blinked. "Cassanova? I should hope not. And I have never teased anyone in my life, Miss Elizabeth."

She waved her hand airily. "That I know for a perfect falsehood, for what was that little stunt you just did but a tease? You would like me to admit how terrified I was and how desperately I needed your help."

I raised a brow and met her gaze. "I was not aware any of that was up for a debate."

"Anything can be a subject for debate." She tipped her head yet closer to mine, her breath tickling my cheek as those speaking eyes locked with mine. "*Both* my fathers taught me well in that regard."

I cleared my throat because it seemed suddenly difficult to draw air. *Get off,* my better sense urged me. *Get off now and walk beside the horse the rest of the way to Farthingdale.* Instead, I ventured—hopefully neutrally, "Mr. Bennet encouraged the improvement of your mind, did he? And here I feared you had not known good society."

Her eyes glinted impishly. "Sir! I shall have you know 'society' nearly expired attempting to tame me before surrendering all hope." She tilted her head pensively. "But yes, Mr. Bennet did teach me chess and philosophy, thus tempering youthful fancies with wisdom."

I chuckled, intrigued. "Well, so long as you have not turned complete bluestocking on me."

"Shall we find out?" Elizabeth shifted slightly, and my breath caught as something... rather *soft* pressed against my arm.

I sought distraction and was mortified to hear my voice cracking like a fifteen-year-old when I spoke. "If you please. What think you of the Greek philosophers? As excessively dry and prosy as my old Cambridge texts?"

"On the contrary! Why, of all Western thought, the Athenians prove most insightful regarding human sentiment balanced with reason."

"Indeed?" I guided my horse around a rut, intrigued by her unconventional assertion. "Pray, enlighten this dull scholar on examples of sentiment's superiority to logic."

"Very well, prepare for a sound thrashing!" Laughing softly, Elizabeth launched into a spirited defense of emotions and moral intuition guiding conscience. And I found it...

Instructive.

Twenty-One

Darcy

I STRODE THROUGH PEMBERLEY'S echoing corridors, sunk in restless reflections that had plagued me since yesterday's encounter with Elizabeth at the folly. How blindly I had underestimated the depth of feeling renewing my acquaintance with Elizabeth might stir! Alternating fury at her uncle's mysterious interference and piercing remorse over enforcing another exile warred ceaselessly in my breast. I wanted to bring her back under Pemberley's roof, where she belonged, and never again let her go.

Foolish dreaming! With position and prospects worlds apart, harsh reality must govern us both. Neither character nor obligation permitted encouraging anything more than presently existed. I had sworn guardianship of George's future when I inherited my father's name, and thanks to him, I owed Elizabeth's future the same consideration.

And yet... Unbidden rose sensations of a lithe figure tucked trustingly against me, tangled hair tickling my chin with laughter on the summer wind... Unnerving flares of protectiveness and startling awareness awakened at each newly unveiled facet of the woman she had become... The odd kick in my pulse, watching her eyes light as we debated poets and philosophy... What powerful force was at work shifting my view of Elizabeth from childhood friend to compelling temptation no defenses could resist?

I halted to grip the sill, scowling fiercely out at the land—my heritage, the reason I had to act rationally. My feelings mattered not! With secrets still shadowing her birth and George's prospects at a delicate point, sober duty must steer every action. There lay safety as well as rightness. I had no time for tender folly, however tempting dreams whispered.

Sharp bootheels echoed down the corridor, sparing me from further eviscerating myself over things I could not control. I turned with relief, expecting the steward with the post. But my heart sank, realizing the approaching stride spelled nothing but trouble—the toes were dragging, and the heels still managing to stomp in a way I knew too well.

"George!" I moved to intercept him, my pulse quickening at the feverish look in his eyes. "I am glad to see you returned. How was—"

My brother burst past without stopping. "Yes, yes, you may all cease clucking over the prodigal's return! I am sure Belmont holds me vastly negligent, but it matters little now." He stormed on toward his chamber, coattails whipping violently round corners.

"George, enough!" Striding after him, I grasped his shoulder only to meet a threatening scowl. "For pity's sake, what is amiss? Did the party not find Dovedale's delights sufficient?"

He barked caustic laughter without slowing. "Oh, indeed! Rocks and dales proved fair enough when one could view them unobstructed."

I blinked in confusion, matching his rapid pace down the upper hall. "Your anger seems less directed at landscapes than companions. Did Belmont offer some criticism—"

"Belmont's was not the discourse proving most offensive, no!" George rounded abruptly, gold hair in wild disarray. "Must Lucilla drag half the countryside to act as her attendant when we made particular plans to talk privately? Every turn, I found some cursed officious elder ready to play audience!"

My throat tightened at this unprecedented outburst against his beloved. "Come, the size of the party was no mystery when you set out together..." Something in his look turned my stomach. He was *not* such a fool as to call it off now. Or was he? "What can have occurred to provoke this dramatic shift? Can you not... reconcile your differences discreetly?"

But George only snorted. "Reconcile, indeed! As though meek tolerance repairs wounds dealt so sweetly by a skilled hand!" His wild laugh turned mocking. "Oh, she anoints every cut with healing balm in case I faint from the shock." He made short work of neck cloth and cuffs, bitterness twisting each savage motion. "Thank heaven such exquisite courtesy arms us for married life. Hah! I can see myself already, kowtowing my obeisance to Lord Belmont's august bidding whenever he should choose!"

I pulled the decanter firmly from his reach as he lunged past toward it. "You are testing my patience, George. I urge you to think before acting or speaking in anger—"

"Think!" He rounded furiously, fists clenching at his sides. "A fine counselor you prove, delivering that prescription so liberally lately! Tell me, oh Wise One—if all thought of self lay chained below decks, would your heart sail smoothly on its virtuous course with no contrary wind ever tempting it to revolt?"

I fell back, stricken. How had George, the most careless of all men, managed to level this unexpected insight with such blistering accuracy? Before my voice returned, George had vanished down the hall, leaving accusing echoes in his wake.

I stared blankly after him for several minutes. A drink. I needed a drink.

I eventually found myself in my dim study—the room where my father had spent most of his days—seeking direction from his darkened portrait. What the devil was I to do? But his stern eyes offered no guidance.

A horrible suspicion jarred me upright. Father had sent Elizabeth away not in cruelty but clear-eyed calculation! He *had* seen it—the youthful affection that once ignited between his ward and second son, and he chose to stop it before it could grow into flames that threatened Pemberley's future stability. Choosing to defend family dignity over young hopes was precisely the pragmatic decision that would haunt him for the rest of his days. He never was right again after Mother died, and he was even worse when Elizabeth left. Because he blamed himself for the unhappiness he must have known she bore.

And here I was, prepared to do the same all over again.

I dropped my head into both hands. God forgive my ruthless designs, much as I had judged them needful! Were it not for George's commitment to Lady Lucilla—a fanciful attachment I still struggled to credit—I would have to let them have their way. But as it was...

Elizabeth

T HE MORNING LIGHT OFFERED little warmth—or promise—filtering through my bedchamber windows. Like the landscape, I felt suspended between the seasons, my heart pitching between budding hopes with old friends and my uncle's ominous warnings.

His most recent letter cut deepest of all, demanding I quit this place, however it wounded me. How could he justify wresting away the restored ties I had but tasted? Yet his words allowed no doubt. If I stayed, harm would surely follow. And so, I must go, marching off like an obedient soldier to shield those nameless "others" now deemed at risk.

I moved slowly through the fragrant lavender rows, secateurs limply dangling. I had beaten my pillow most of the night, but by dawn, I had reached some level of acceptance for what Uncle asked of me... along with some rather confused sentiments regarding the Darcy brothers. George would forever own youth's glowing memories and the first sweet awakenings of love. Yet something in Fitzwilliam's eyes yesterday... the strong arms that had held me against his chest in the saddle, the way he had debated with me... laughed with me... listened to me... The depths I could see in his character left my poor dear George looking terribly pitiful, indeed.

My wayward thoughts strayed too often to that strong, steady presence. Was I disloyal? Or was it just the natural appreciation any woman would have for a man such as Fitzwilliam Darcy had become? Oh, but surely, it was foolish. Why, Fitzwilliam was the heir! The Darcy, the one who carried the responsibility of continuing the family line by marrying an heiress worthy of his station. My sights must naturally rest... somewhere lower.

Sudden hoofbeats and a beloved voice shattered sweet reverie. My foolish heart lurched wildly even as pleasure surged seeing George leap the hedge on that shining chestnut of his. I drank in lively eyes and wind-tousled hair, golden as nostalgia itself.

"Lizzy!" In three eager strides, he had captured my nerveless hands, sending the gardening shears tumbling unheeded amidst blossoms. "Thank heaven I caught you unattended." He searched my bemused face intently. "Might we speak privately? There is much to say and scarce liberty to unburden myself fully."

This was not the George I knew. All pleasure at his arrival evaporated like the dawn mist as I searched his countenance with growing worry. My pulse skittered anxiously. "Of course. Shall we take refreshments near the beehives? Dare I hope this surprise call brings... glad tidings?"

His swift grimace suggested the opposite. "Would that my news proved so felicitous." He turned abruptly as if to master inconvenient feelings away from my notice. "In fact, I am quite overset by new arrangements chafing against my long-established habits." He flung a bitter glance skyward. "It seems Providence and the peerage conspire to prod me onto irrevocable paths before I am quite prepared..."

"Well..." I cleared my throat. "At times, Destiny does steer the carriage over unknown terrain." I moved to stand by his side, my toes nearly touching one mud-flecked Hessian boot. "Surely, dashing George Darcy never met an obstacle that failed to vanish at his whim eventually?"

He barked a sound halfway between laugh and scoff, finally pivoting to scan my gently smiling face. "You grant me far too much credit for charming my way through trials, Elizabeth." Humor faded as quickly as it surfaced. "If only innate diplomacy won me a reprieve from the world's endless impositions! Alas, the last weeks have crushed any fanciful pretensions utterly, until..."

"George... I have no idea to what you refer, but..." I winced. For all my affection for him, I was not blind. George did require a little... maturity. I swallowed. "Perhaps less emotiveness and more prudent thought might be a way of knowing how to respond to... whatever is troubling you."

George made an impatient noise. "You sound like Fitzwilliam and his mechanical notions of arranged outcomes. As if human hearts beat obedient to some great Accountant's tally sheet!" He turned a sudden penetrating look on me. "Would you have me committing all my living days to one who loves wealth and position more than the man himself?"

I faltered, caught off balance by such uncommon gravity. "What are you talking about?"

He stared hard at me for a moment, his chest heaving. Then he just shook his head. "Nothing."

He checked abruptly whatever lay poised to spill over, raking one hand roughly through golden curls. My conscience smote me unexpectedly. How selfishly I had wrestled romantic notions when last we met, with scarce consideration for whatever paths might already be before George's feet! I seized his hand. "George, I can see you are wrestling private burdens—do not feel obliged to air more than you ought." At his mute chin dip, I rushed onwards, cheeks warming. "Rather, allow me to cheer you with a harmless bit of Nonsense. We were always able to cheer each other, were we not? Even if your problems still await, I might—"

Sudden pressure cut off my air as he crushed me in his arms. What was I to do? I yielded to his anguished embrace, senses swimming dizzily. George Darcy was kissing me! I tried to suck in a breath, but his hold on me was too tight.

"Lizzy..." He broke off, his breath coming as ragged as mine as he stared into my eyes. "I know we always fancied ourselves the dearest of friends, but... oh, blast and damnation, I cannot even ask what I want, not with everyone breathing down my neck!"

I shook my head, still trying to catch my breath. "Are you asking for what I think?"

He dropped his hands from my shoulders and straightened. "Not yet. I'm sorry, Lizzy, I..." He started to back away.

I thinned my lips. "I think you should go home, George. Talk to Fitzwilliam. Surely, he can help—"

George laughed bitterly. 'Yes. Yes, that is just what I will do. Good-bye, Lizzy."

TWENTY-TWO

Darcy

I HAD NOT SLEPT all night. By seven the next morning, I was back in my study, but I was not working. No, I was pawing through every scrap, every hidden drawer and secret compartment of the furniture and the walls, searching for anything I might have missed before. Anything that would give me the answer I needed. Two hours, I searched, with no better results than before.

The door crashed abruptly open, loosing a blast of sulfurous language that almost stopped my heart mid-beat. I scarcely recognized the hellion barging into my study, golden hair disheveled and jaw stubbled like a dock worker after a fortnight's debauchery. Breathless disbelief held me mute as I took in the splattered mud on his boots and George's bare chest, exposed by missing buttons at his throat.

"Good heavens, are you mad?" One glance confirmed that his appearance was no less wild than his thoughts. Grasping both shoulders, I gave him a firm shake. "Have you been out drinking all night?"

He barked raw, mirthless laughter, breaking my hold on his sleeves. "Who needs a drink when he has a woman to drive him mad?"

"So, it is Lady Lucilla, is it? Have you been to Matlock already this morning?"

He snorted. "Heavens, no. No, I cannot imagine she would welcome me this morning."

I sighed. "Tell me you have not done something irrevocable. Did you offend her father, or has he decided to cast you off?"

"Cast me off! Yes, you would think it could be that easy, wouldn't you? Anguished eyes searched my face. "Do you want to know what goads me? I look upon you now—so grave, so resigned to nobly guard the gates as if Atlas' full load rests on your shoulders alone—and I cannot do the same! Am I now to turn into you?" He shook his head, sniffing as his features broke.

"George, come now. No one expects—"

"Ah, but they do! You should have heard Lady Belmont in the carriage, all the schemes that worthy lady has planned. And it occurred to me that she has been making these plans for twenty-one years. Twenty-one years, Fitz! Do you truly think *I* am the sort she envisioned hosting a wedding breakfast for? Giving her daughter to? And Lucilla, she..."

"She what? What is it between you two so suddenly? Did you think pledging yourself to a woman was going to be easy? That you would not have to change at least in some measure?"

"Well... Perhaps I was wrong. Perhaps..." He scowled and sniffed again as his eyes dropped to the floor. "Perhaps what I really ought to have been looking for has just come back into my life, just waiting for me to recall." He lifted his gaze to me slowly, and one eyebrow quirked.

My stomach plummeted through the floorboards as an appalling suspicion took form. Surely even besotted George would never risk... Blindly, I seized his collar, dragging us nose to nose. "Bloody bullocks, *that* is what you are about. The muddy boots, your hair torn by the wind. Tell me straight, George, are you arrived from Farthingdale just now?" At his mute glare, my fingers tightened to bite the fabric. "Damn your eyes, speak! Have you left Lady Lucilla at Matlock while you—"

"Why shouldn't I?" He wrenched my hand off his collar and jerked backward. "Lizzy understands me. She wouldn't ask me to become something I'm not."

"But you made a promise to Lady Lucilla! Good heavens, I cannot even begin to imagine the breach of promise lawsuit Belmont could bring to your door, if you disappoint his daughter."

"You said it yourself. Belmont is so far above me, the whole thing was laughable anyway. They're better off. I'll just... I'll go propose to Lizzy. That's what I'll do."

"You will do no such thing. Break both their hearts and disgrace yourself in the process? What will Elizabeth think when she learns the truth—that you only came to her because you were too much of a coward to face up to your previous commitments?"

He stiffened. "I am no coward. I just changed my mind."

"A man does not have the luxury of 'changing his mind,' George! You gave your word! I warrant you have said nothing to Elizabeth of Lady Lucilla. Does she know you are engaged?"

"Gads, no, unless you told her. Why would I say something like that?"

I wanted to punch him. "Because it's the truth! And it is not my place to tell her. It is yours. If you force me to, George, I will ride to Farthingdale right now and tell her all, but it will be *me* she despises, not the man who fooled her!"

"Ah, and so you would have her despise *me* instead?

I clenched my fists. I was going to do it, God help me... "I want you to tell her the truth. Both of them! Have you even spoken to your betrothed about your change of heart?"

He ground his teeth and stared at the window. "Look, I said she'd be better off without me. I never said I did not... Oh, buggar off!"

"Would that I could! Tell me the truth, George. Have you already compromised Elizabeth? Have you seduced her?"

He glared at me. "Like anyone *could* seduce Lizzy. She was always two steps ahead of either of us. I say 'tis the other way round, you know. She has been trying to seduce *me* since that day in Lambton!"

I rolled my eyes. "She has hardly played the temptress."

"That is because she does not have to. All she has to do is *look* at a man, and... egad, if I thought she was enchanting at thirteen, I was a bloody fool. Have you even *looked* at the woman now?"

I crossed my arms as my stomach turned an odd flip. "I have eyes, you know."

"Eh? Then you know what I am on about. *Nobody* has eyes like Lizzy, and when she laughs, it is like my own heart is singing. But that is nothing to her tears, and when I think..."

"Enough, George!" I spun him around and marched him toward the door of my study. "Go upstairs and let your valet have a go at you. And as soon as you are decent, you are going to ride directly to Matlock and make yourself agreeable to the woman you proposed to."

He turned around slightly, a morose look now overtaking his countenance. "Will you come, Fitz?"

"No," I growled. "You must face this as the man you claimed to be." Besides, I had just got an idea.

If Elizabeth's sweet smiles and sparkling eyes had been leveled at George to smite him with all the efficacy of one of Bonaparte's canons, perhaps... Perhaps I could give her a different target. At least until her uncle had carried her away from Derbyshire, and George had safely overcome whatever this nonsense was.

Heaven help me.

Elizabeth

S UNBEAMS FILTERING THROUGH MRS. Westing's cheerful kitchen seemed to mock my chaotic emotions. I attacked dough for the third batch of rolls with vigor directly proportional to turmoil since George's abrupt appearance that morning.

Kissing, his arms around me, that impassioned plea... all taunted my focus away from the mundane tasks occupying my hands. Never in seven long years had I permitted such unchecked romantic fancy about first love blossoming anew. And that was saying a great deal, indeed!

But something had not felt... right. After years of pining for George, knowing—or thinking I knew—what my heart wanted most, all I could say now was... it was not as satisfying as I had hoped.

"Lizzy? There you are!"

I jerked guiltily upright as Jane entered, her keen gaze missing no detail from my flushed cheeks to the neglected dough on the board. Briskly, she crossed the warm kitchen, laying one slender hand gently atop mine, clenching the worn pine surface. "Let Martha finish here. I have been searching you out above this half hour at least. I thought you disappeared in the hills again."

I attempted a dismissive laugh, avoiding her eyes. "Nonsense! I am trying to make myself useful That was the condition of our invitation, if you recall."

"Yes, I do. And Martha has just arrived to tend to the cooking, as she does every day, so why are you hiding in the kitchen?

Avoidance was impossible with one who read my heart as her own. I straightened slowly, brushing loosened curls wearily back off heated cheeks. "What are you really asking, Jane?"

Jane bit her lips together and sighed, her eyes darting to the window. Wordlessly, she drew me toward the back stair where none would chance overhearing us. "You have been out of sorts all day, Lizzy. Is it that letter from Uncle?"

I glanced up at her, then dropped my eyes and shook my head.

"You are going to force me to ask, then?" Jane's voice was soft, and she tucked a lock of hair behind my ear. "Very well, then. I saw you in the garden with George."

I groaned. "Don't you have anything to do but stare out the window? First, you see Fitzwilliam calling, then George!"

She lifted a shoulder. "He came galloping up at such a pace, I think Mrs. Westing even heard him from her bedroom. I ran to the window to see if it was an express rider from Uncle. But when I saw him..."

I rolled my neck, gazing at the top of the staircase. "Kissing me?"

"Yes, that. Has he... did he declare himself?"

"Not as such."

Jane shook her head. I suppose her poor, pure heart could not fathom a man passionate enough to kiss a girl without either intending to propose or intending to ruin her. "But why would he do such a thing?"

I laughed. "Why? Because he is George! He doesn't know what he is about half the time until he finds himself halfway down the road."

"And today, you were sitting in his path?"

"I like to think I was a planned detour, at least. Come, Jane, I just reappeared in the man's life after seven years. Surely, he has made other plans, perhaps even..." My brow crumpled. "Other attachments. The way he was talking today, I..."

"Lizzy, is it possible that you might have misjudged him? Do you not see how vulnerable you would be to any sentiment he expresses, even if he himself cannot be sure of it?" As I remained wordless, she ventured delicately nearer. "Unless... you find your feelings have already begun to shift?"

I snapped a sharp glance upward. "What do you mean?"

Jane hesitated, then asked baldly, "Did George... behave improperly this morning? I saw him take your hands, then suddenly disappear down the lane with you..."

I sucked in a swift breath. Of course, Jane saw it all, and whatever she did not see, she could guess easily enough. My jittery laugh sounded pathetic even to me. "Oh, Jane! I thought his kiss was all I'd ever hoped for. But feelings that were once so vivid seem oddly faded and... confused." My cheek pressed into her shoulder shamefully. "Kissing George should have felt wonderful. I should have begged him to stay, to hold me in his arms until evening. Instead, I... I scolded him and sent him home. Am I fickle, Jane? Or a shrew?"

Jane's gentle arms came round me, bless her eternally steadfast heart. "Oh, Lizzy. I do not believe you fickle or unjustified. It has been a long time, and things are not as they once were. George may be just learning that, too, and I daresay he has some matters to settle in his heart. Perhaps you will even find that your own heart lies elsewhere."

I straightened slowly. How deftly Jane untangled my prickly emotions! Fresh resolve budded as I took a deep breath. "Fitzwilliam warned me against reckless choices too often. Perhaps schooling sentiment more carefully holds greater merit than I credited once."

Slim comfort yet, but baby steps turned the obedient heart, not passionate abandon—however alluring. Arms around each other, we descended the stairs together, and she said no more on the matter.

Twenty-Three

Darcy

MY GELDING SEEMED TO share my restless energy this morning, hooves peppering the ground as I guided him toward Farthingdale's back lane. A dazzling morning sun failed to penetrate the restless fog shrouding my mood despite having turned myself and my horse out to look our very best. I glanced down at my new hunt coat, cut a little broader for my shoulders than the last one. I'd donned a waistcoat to match—one I hoped Elizabeth would like. She had always admired green, and blast if I would not do everything in my power to attract her eye.

Did I even have a prayer of turning her head? She had fancied George for too long, perhaps. A child of thirteen may set her heart on whichever rascal she chooses, and it may come to nothing. But a woman such as Elizabeth had become... why, she deserved somewhere better to place her hopes because, quite frankly, George was not good enough for her.

Not that I felt myself to be the better choice! But at least I understood constancy and devotion, just as well as I did duty. She deserved a man who could match her intellect and character, and if all I achieved today was to show her that there were other men in the world... men worthy of her... well, hang it all, I would do my duty by her, even if that meant making her fall for me.

Just a little.

But how? I had little enough experience with this. I had never had to try to gain female notice. They just... found me. Even when I did not wish to be found. How did a man set about pleasing a lady he admired when she barely noticed him?

I could ask her to take a turn in the garden. Or sit in the drawing room and see if she would debate Byron or Milton with me. That might do. I had no designs of seducing her or falling for her myself. This was just... a diversion.

But all my schemes shattered abruptly at the sound of a loud crack ahead, followed by some rather indecorous language. I forgot contrived obligations, cantering urgently round the house toward the odd disturbance. But the figure struggling to raise an axe as tall as herself was no angry cook. My heart clutched as my mouth dropped open. "Miss Elizabeth?"

"Mr. Darcy!" Elizabeth cried in dismayed surprise, color rising swiftly. She scrambled to tug her skirts over her ankles, where they peeked from beneath her hem as the abandoned tool crashed down just shy of her slippered foot. "I did not hear your approach."

I swung down from the saddle. "I do not wonder. You probably could not hear anything at all over the epithets I heard just before I rode up."

She picked up the axe and tucked it behind herself, ducking her head in a guilty snicker. "And you are too much the gentleman to accuse a lady of such language."

"I fear it would not be the first time I have heard such from you. Let me see your hand."

She swallowed, hesitated, and cautiously offered her left hand. It looked as if she had tried to mash her thumb along with the wood, because the flesh around the nail was bruised and split, dripping blood. How ever had she managed that? I glanced at her eyes, then wordlessly, I pulled a clean handkerchief from my pocket to wrap it over the offended appendage. And I was alarmed to notice blood soaking through it almost immediately.

"We must get you inside at once! You may need stitches."

"Please, it is nothing!" She recoiled slightly, hiding her hand again. "Just a scratch from attempting tasks beyond my skills."

"Why would you try to split kindling in the first place?"

She shrugged. "I was craving a cherry tart."

"Sorry?" I gently circled her wrist with my fingers and tugged her hand back into view. "How does craving a cherry tart lead to a mangled thumb?"

"Mr. Westing is out inspecting the fields, and Joseph was supposed to split the wood, but I do not know where he went. As Martha disappeared about the same time, I..." she cleared her throat. "Well, suffice to say I thought it might be better if I brought in wood for the kitchen fire myself. And now I shan't be able to roll the dough." She held up her bleeding thumb and inspected it with a sigh.

I mastered my amusement, bending swiftly under the pretense of collecting scattered logs. "Perhaps you will permit me?" I handed her my hat, then stripped my coat and waistcoat off, preparing to take up her abandoned post.

Soon, I had split enough kindling to fuel a small forest fire. Elizabeth gathered what she needed, but once I plunged the axe head into a stump, I took the load from her. "After you," I insisted.

Elizabeth let me take her load, but she didn't turn to lead me into the kitchen. Instead, she just stood there, cocking a strange look up to me from under the brim of her bonnet.

"Something amiss?"

She shook her head. "Only my gratitude. Thank you... Fitzwilliam."

I paused, permitting myself just a moment to drown in those chocolate depths. *Delicious..* why, I believe my heart puddled into my boots and my mouth filled with drool like a dog.

Perhaps I had overestimated my fortitude.

Elizabeth

M Y HAND THROBBED DESPITE Fitzwilliam's makeshift bandage as we entered the kitchen. I winced as I went to inspect my dough, clutching my thumb to my chest. Meanwhile, my unlikely rescuer deposited the kindling and bent to start the kitchen fire. Flecks of bark and woodchips still clung to his shirt. His tousled hair and bare forearms revived long-buried memories of the awkward boy who used to trail at Father's heels. But there was nothing awkward about Fitzwilliam Darcy now... unless one counted that bashful look in his eye or the hesitant quality about his smile every time he glanced at me.

Clearing my throat, I tried distracting my wayward thoughts. "Do take care with your cuffs. Wood sap leaves the very devil of a stain."

He blinked then grimaced, brushing ineffectually at soiled linen. "You must think me the veriest clod mucking about your kitchen so."

His glance held such chagrin that I relented instantly, waving off his apology.

"On the contrary! Why, you assumed the role of knight errant perfectly. What lady could be so churlish when thus rescued? Truly, no olde worlde gallant or mythical hero ever made a grander entrance, I daresay. And besides, I warrant you have never tried to light a kitchen fire before."

Fitzwilliam chuckled, his features easing as he located and struck the flint box. I leaned against the table, watching flames slowly kindle in the grate. How many more intriguing facets remained to discover about this man fate had so unexpectedly restored to me? As rewarding as probing that mystery promised, it would surely prove as foolhardy as sticking my hand in that fire would be.

He shifted, scattering my wayward reflection. "There now. Rest that poor hand while I fetch linens to bind it properly." I obeyed meekly, sinking onto a stool as discomfort throbbed anew. Pensive still, I endured his gentle ministrations. With the care of a mother for her child, Fitzwilliam Darcy, master of Pemberley, bent over my damaged thumb and cleaned away the blood, pausing to look at me in alarm every time I hissed in pain.

"How badly does that hurt?"

I grimaced and forced a smile. "I believe the injury is survivable. But your handkerchief is beyond all hope."

"And I am so very concerned about a bit of cloth." He dabbed his rag in the warm water, then eased it over my bruised thumb once more. "Once we have this cleaned, keep it elevated above your heart so it does not throb as much. And you ought to bring in a bit of ice from the icehouse to help with the bruising."

I gave him a quizzical look. "Farthingdale does not have an ice-house."

He paused, his brow crumpled, and looked up. "So, it does not. But Pemberley does. I will have some sent for you."

I laughed. "Thank you, kind sir. But I would not wish for you to... ooh." I closed my eyes and sank my teeth into my lower lip. "I must have done a good job there."

"You certainly did. Can you bear up a little longer? Nearly finished."

I nodded, but every proprietary brush of cloth against my torn skin made me flinch at a visceral level. Who knew a simple bruised thumb could hurt so badly? And so, I found something to distract myself. It was not difficult—Fitzwilliam had removed his hat. I am sure his valet sent him off into the day with perfectly groomed locks, but they were so no longer, and the effect of his mussed hair falling over that thoughtful brow... the broad shoulders hunched over my hand... Well, who was George Darcy, anyway?

As if sensing my sudden confusion, Fitzwilliam abruptly stepped back, features shuttering swiftly. "There, not too brutishly done, I hope? Not that I've had overmuch practice, past battlefield scrapes."

"What battlefield?" I scoffed. "Unless you mean your sticks and slingshots with George and Richard."

A wry smile twisted his lips. "Quite so. It fell to me to stay home and endure peaceful years while others must away to the battlefield." He grimaced down at the water and rag he had used to clean my thumb, then offered a tight smile. "Apologies if my clumsy efforts pained you overmuch."

"You have not told me where Richard is," I accused softly.

He blinked, and his eyes focused on my face. "I suppose I have not. The truth is that I do not know. He was in Spain with Wellington when last we had word, but letters have been... delayed. I know it distresses the earl greatly, but he says little of it."

"I am sorry."

He had begun to roll the ruined handkerchief up around his finger but looked back up in surprise. "It is not your fault."

"But I can see it worries you. You hide it well, but you forget how long I have known you."

He smiled a little and finished the task of putting the damaged handkerchief in his pocket. Why he bothered, I did not know—perhaps he thought it could be saved. "Just as you think you are playing a game with me, Miss Elizabeth?"

My stomach dropped. "What game?" Oh, blast, he had come to warn me off of George. I knew it.

He leaned closer. "Pretending all is well. Acting as if you haven't a care in the world. When did you say Mr. Gardiner was coming to carry you back to Hertfordshire?"

Well... perhaps this was not about George, after all. "It... it could be any day. His letter to Aunt said he had a matter to tend to before he could leave London, and then he would be arriving. He wrote that letter on Wednesday last, so..." I shrugged. "We might see him as soon as tomorrow."

Fitzwilliam studied me carefully, then backed away. He seemed not to know what to do with himself—his hands flexing, glancing about the kitchen. Finally, he moved to the bowl of cherries I had pitted and inspected them. "You cannot cook these with your hand injured. Come, tell me what we must do."

I laughed. "You cannot be serious."

"Indeed, I am. If it is cherry tarts you are craving, then cherry tarts you must have. Before they are out of season."

"Very well. I would not turn away help. We need to boil them in sugar."

I watched Mr. Darcy set gingerly to work on the bowl of cherries, entirely too conscious of how dashing his forearms appeared with sleeves rolled up. Had they always looked so... sturdy? No, no they had not, for I would have remembered that. And the way his dark hair fell boyishly over one eye as he concentrated on spearing the stubborn fruits ought not to incite such unaccountable reactions within me! I blinked rapidly, showing him how to stir the boiling cherries with burning cheeks. Heavens, was I truly admiring the precise elegance of Mr. Darcy's fingers? This would not do! How the deuce had demure thoughts unraveled to such mad fancies?

I peeked sideways through my lashes, careful not to betray the way my insides were slowly melting and turning to jelly like those cherries. Yet my wayward gaze lingered too long, drinking in his proximity. Was that a dimple flickering at one corner of his mouth? How had I never noticed that arresting indent lending his features such unexpected charm? *Look away, look away!*

A cloud of his scent enveloped me unexpectedly, clean linen and soap mingled with leather and open sky. Why did my knees suddenly require gripping the table edge? This was surely just the lingering effects of earlier distress. Mr. Darcy remained the same steady anchor, providing comfort in chaos. Only somehow stronger and more compelling than in my childhood memories... *No!* I sternly smothered such wayward musings.

Some minutes later, he proclaimed victory over the cherries with such endearing awkwardness that laughter bubbled up unbidden. Was he trying to set me at ease? How kind. And yet, such tantalizing glimpses of playful humor lurking beyond that serious visage only amplified everything virile and masculine surrounding me. *Oh mercy,* I hardly recognized myself! Since when did Mr. Darcy, of all men, incite such unruly awareness within me? Perhaps the oven's warmth was merely too stifling for rational thought. Yes, of course.

"Capital," I praised him. "Let them cool a bit while I roll out the dough." I moved to the worktable and dusted it with flour so I could begin.

"And how, exactly, do you mean to do that?" Fitzwilliam took the bowl of flour from me and continued tossing such a liberal coating of flour that it looked more like a pillow than a worktable. "Is that enough?"

It was all I could do not to snicker at the flour now rising in the air and settling in his hair. "I should hope. If you insist on helping, fetch that bowl of dough over there and turn it over on the table."

"Like this?" He plopped the dough in the middle of the white cloud, causing more of it to dust upward. He turned to look at me, and I had to bite my lip to stifle a loud laugh.

"What?"

"You have..." I winced and came close, reaching for his face with my uninjured hand. "Flour on your cheek."

I'm not sure if either of us were breathing. And when did his eyes suddenly turn black? His Adam's apple bobbed as I swiped his face clean with the tips of my fingers. Uhm... now what?

"Thank you," he whispered.

I stepped back, clearing my throat and reaching for the cook's tools. "Here. You will need a rolling pin."

"I will need instruction in how to use it, as well."

"Oh, nothing to it. You just..." I braced both hands on the rolling pin and tried to move it, but my wretched thumb was throbbing like the devil every time I let it drop below my heart.

"This will not do." Fitzwilliam shook his head and stepped in behind me, pulling my left hand back and substituting his. "Like this?"

he asked, giving the left side of the rolling pin a shove into the lump of dough.

All I could do was stare at his cheek—the faint stubble already growing after his morning shave, the way his pulse thumped just below the line of his jaw .. Oh, good heavens, I was even admiring the shape of his ear and the way a lock of his hair curled around it.

"Ah... something like that."

"Then let us coordinate our efforts until we have a rhythm. One... two..."

I let him set the pace, which was not difficult because his chest framing me set my arm into motion. I could not breathe, but somehow, I managed to talk, prattling unnecessarily about flaky crust and the Pemberley cook's inimitable recipe to disguise my flustered state.

With his body pressed so distractingly close, I prayed he could not detect riotous thudding beneath my ribs. What woman could retain her senses enveloped thus? *Just keep rolling dough*, I commanded my trembling fingers. Good gracious, did my wayward thoughts conjure his woodsy scent intensifying? Impossible! *Ignore the tingling nearness down your back. You are NOT leaning faintly nearer, seeking more contact...*

But sanity's shift never came. Heaven help me, I could not wrench free of this unexpected spell weaving round us. Mr. Darcy ought not prove so utterly irresistible with sleeves carelessly shoved back and hair endearingly disheveled! Yet here I stood wrestling wholly unfamiliar yearnings never roused by another soul.

As I fumbled to finally slide the tarts into the oven, the fresh warmth blooming over my cheekbones had little connection with baking. Because undeniably, as I floated like one enchanted through the most ordinary of tasks, every fiber of my being spoke a singular truth. This man's intoxicating nearness was awakening and shifting irrevocably my entire perception of dear, steady Fitzwilliam Darcy.

The only thing I understood was that I was wholly lost without ever knowing where I went astray.

Twenty-Four

Darcy

T HE BREEZE SLIPPING OVER my flushed cheeks failed to temper the simmering chaos within. What madness had possessed me back there, offering to assist as a makeshift cook? My hapless fumbling with the sugared fruit and dough had not produced even the faintest hint of the beguiling laughter and adoring smiles from Elizabeth that George unfailingly coaxed forth. Could she not discern my own sorry efforts at playfulness and good humor? Had she even perceived my effort? Likely not, for to a young lady taught from childhood to admire George's easy, artless charm, what could I hope to do with my bumbling efforts?

I shifted irritably in the saddle. Confound it all, I had intended to show her that other varieties of gentleman existed besides devil-may-care scapegraces. Steadier companions perhaps less prone to careless impropriety. Someone who might appreciate more subtly her resilience and fiery spirit. Egad, instead, my traitorous body reacted as though it would expire the moment I wrapped it about her delicate but deuced distracting frame!

I raked a hand roughly through my hair, scattering the last crumbs of flour. How had even the mundanity of baking conjured forth wanton imaginings of cinnamon-dusted lips and buttery caresses? Had I become one of those overeager youths requiring a bracing cold plunge to regain mastery over untimely reactions? I groaned, ducking beneath low-hanging branches as Claudius bore me onward. At least no evidence of my discomfort had betrayed me to her innocent eyes.... hopefully.

Almost against my will, one hand moved to loosen my suddenly snug collar. Mercy, but those smoked cherry tarts had been delectable—not quite to the standards of Pemberley's cook, but exceeding respectable, indeed. Of course, such treats might merely have tasted ambrosial due to the beguiling company, elevating the experience to sensory intoxication. I blinked hard, sternly directing wandering thoughts back from soft, dangerous curves to more proper channels. Such madness must not repeat itself, no matter the temptations! Set firmer boundaries and cling tenaciously to them for everyone's protection and good.

And yet... might not a trifle more harm await if walls rose impassibly high around my battered heart? Those merry dark eyes still smiled into mine, a teasing invitation echoing to test defenses erected perhaps overhastily. Elizabeth's laughter filled my ears, mingling with Claudius's rhythmic hoofbeats. I groaned aloud. Sweet torture indeed if she made a habit of conjuring herself at my side, even across six long empty miles and a half-eaten batch of tarts!

I HAD SCARCELY ENTERED the house, boots still dusted from the ride... and the flour... when my butler presented me an urgent summons from Harris at Pemberly Mills. One look at Huxley's sober features banished any lingering fanciful reflections from my encounter with Elizabeth. Trouble was brewing, and not of the sort cherry tarts and coy smiles could sweeten.

"Thank you, Huxley. Send word to the stables to have Apollo saddled and waiting for me. I will go as soon as I have changed." I was swiftly mounting the stairs when Bingley's voice rang out, halting my hurried progress. "Ah, Darcy! Thank goodness, there you are!" His normally cheerful features looked uncharacteristically grave as he emerged from the drawing room.

I paused reluctantly, impatience rising. "Forgive me, Bingley, but some urgent business calls me away. Might we speak later?"

"But I have been waiting to apprise you of a worrisome matter these last two hours!" He hurried to catch me up before I could continue on. "I rode past one of your tenant farms this morning and happened to overhear talk of gathering trouble at the mills. I wondered if perhaps I might be of help."

My focus sharpened. Few better understood the delicate balance required between owners and laborers. If he lent firsthand experience... Decision made, I beckoned him onward. "Come, then. Your insights may prove invaluable should cooler heads not yet prevail there."

We hastened upstairs, where I swiftly stripped out of flour-dusted garments into fresh attire. My mind churned with uneasy speculation about what exactly awaited as we rode for the mill. Apollo's nervous energy matched my own foreboding that the summons indicated exactly what hard experience suggested.

I had just implemented improved safety mechanisms in the carding and fulling areas, straining budgets dangerously near margins. Surely recent concessions regarding children's hours eased some disgruntlement? From his office window, Harris' anxious face confirmed gathering storms even before his words did.

"They mean to strike, sir, if recent petitions go unanswered!" His bass rumbled above the churning mill race. "I've tried every method short of fisticuffs, but they won't be satisfied."

My boots rang sharply against iron stairs leading down to the factory floor, Bingley and Harris on my heels. Sullen faces and hunched shoulders greeted my entrance. The throbbing machines seemed to slow infinitesimally, though no hands left their posts.

I moved to stand central upon the platform, forcing all eyes upward. "Men, I come in good faith seeking conciliation..."

Uneasy glances bounced between me and Bingley as I pled my case. The men's stony silence unnerved me more than angry shouts. At last, one bold voice shouted, "We want nowt of your prattling committees! Justice demands fair wages if t'master won't curb this cursed machinery stealing honest men's work!"

Incensed grumbles swelled dangerously. I lifted placating hands, my pulse racing. "The automation cannot be uninvented! We must have faith to find appropriate balance as times change. Now, as to wages..."

"Aye, balance indeed whilst you play king, and we brave the daily risk of life and limb to line your pockets!" came the embittered cry.

I insisted calmly, "I keep not one penny aside from maintenance and wages here!" But uproar drowned all reason.

"Lies! We'll not be pacified by stale promises. We want bread!"

The ominous din swelled. Harris's anxious face was enough for me—danger brewed potent as gunpowder, and we were not going to succeed here today with words. We ought to withdraw before violence erupted.

Just then, someone flung something... was it a rock? I ducked, pushing Bingley out of the way, but the object struck me on the ear...

mercifully not a rock, or I might have been laid out unconscious. Shocked gasps and nervous titters erupted, seeing my face dripping an egg that had started to turn foul. I glared out at them, swiping the worst of it off my jaw before it dripped down my collar.

Then pandemonium erupted with guttural force. With undignified haste, I plunged down the stairs before the mob's fury claimed more than my pride and a good beaver hat. The office door provided sole sanctuary from the screaming maelstrom. Heart pounding, I slammed it closed.

Safely ensconced in Harris's office, I sagged against the barred door as angry shouts still penetrated the battered wood. Bingley mopped his brow, eyes wide.

"By Jove, Darcy! I've seen men riled, but never a spectacle like that."

I swiped ineffectually at my slimy cravat, my pulse still hammering. "Demonstrations grow more defiant by the month. This cannot go on." I frowned at Harris. "You should have alerted me sooner!"

The overseer threw up aggrieved hands. "And have you ride in sooner to receive the same abuse? Your fancy London guest got off lightly." He stabbed an accusing finger toward the window where howls still echoed. "Mark me, sir, that rabble understands one thing only—the back of a hand! Meet insolence with strength if you want obedience."

I bristled, jaw tightening. "I'll not rule Pemberley or the mill through force. There must be some reasonable compromise to ease strains."

"Begging your pardon, sir, but reason holds little sway when men work fourteen hours without respite." Bingley settled carefully on the corner of a rickety table. "My father contended that better value arises from treating men humanely than driving them like animals. Within reason," he amended hastily.

"Then shorten their hours! I'll have no truck with men dropping from exhaustion."

"Aye, and then they claim they can't get enough work. There's no pleasing them, sir."

"We've had it the same," Bingley put in. "But we enforced a somewhat shorter day because of safety concerns. A steel mill is a rather dangerous place."

The ominous cacophony outside seemed to crescendo before the mob's rage spent itself. I pinched my temple wearily. "You both speak the truth. But what remedies exist, not merely temporary and palliative?" My glance shifted between their contrasting faces. "If grievances arise from desperation, how best to answer their needs? What can I supply to alleviate hardship beyond wages that are controlled by far larger markets than our little mill?"

Bingley brightened. "At our Sheffield mills, we provide meals for those traveling distances that prevent returning home to sup. It was my mother's idea, God rest her soul," he confessed. "Might something similar ease the strain here?"

I considered this, turning to Harris. "What do you think? Do long hours leave men scarce opportunity for proper meals?"

He shifted uncomfortably. "Cannot speak to their habits, only to skill keeping machines running. Not my place to nose into private affairs, Sir."

"Please, Harris, any insight helps. Might the provision of regular hot meals help keep the peace? I can find the money to fund such an enterprise." At his continued reticence, I leaned intently forward. "I beg you to speak freely. As a youth, I watched my own father wrestle with similar problems, with the hope of doing right by all men. I aim to continue his legacy, but your experienced guidance is what will make a success of my naïve good intentions."

The craggy face twitched. Harris sighed gustily before mumbling, "Some do confess heading straight to their machines come dawn with nowt but tea sloshing an empty belly. But you'll not hear me repeat it." He slashed one knotted hand across his mouth as if locking away the confidence.

"Thank you, Harris. Both your counsel and discretion become you." I straightened determinedly. "If hunger fuels desperation, the remedy seems clear, however much it strains resources. If the factory reform legislation I proposed in my letter is enacted, perhaps other mills will find similar remedies, and our local concessions need not threaten the peace elsewhere."

The last defiant shouts had faded outside, so I deemed it safe enough for us to emerge. Nothing remained of the seething mob save a lingering sulfurous miasma. Dark looks smoldered from the watchful stragglers, but rage's fever had broken.

I wiped down my hat the best I could and swung astride Apollo, knuckles white on the reins. Bingley and I left the mill at a canter, anxious to distance ourselves from the lessening chaos. Perhaps it was only my imagination, but I could feel Harris's skeptical eyes following our departure, no doubt unconvinced that hot meals could make any difference to the rising tide of discontent at the mill. Still, I meant to enact the change without delay.

"You've something brewing behind that frown, Darcy," Bingley ventured once the hammering hooves put a comfortable distance between us and the mill. "Have you any other ideas to appease the workers?"

I shot him a sidelong glance, noting genuine interest rather than merely polite inquiry. "Too many notions clash just now for a single worthy resolution," I replied ruefully. "But your mother's strategy seems a reasonable start."

Bingley nodded thoughtfully. "It made a difference at the steel mill." His modest smile turned self-deprecating. "I only wish I had half her talent for household economy and moral governance. One bachelor on his own is unlikely to establish such niceties, but I suppose one must start somewhere."

Something in his diffident address gave me pause. I studied my friend more closely. His normally open features seemed uncharacteristically pensive. "Speaking of domestic affairs, I had wondered if you mean to pursue your interest in Miss Bennet?"

Bingley started slightly in his saddle, color creeping over his neck above an already disheveled collar. "Er, yes, of course. Am I that obvious?"

"I am afraid so."

He cleared his throat. "Why, yes, I fancy Miss Bennet is the finest lady I have ever met. But I had not realized my attentions were already so well-known."

"It is nothing to fret about. I was only speaking to Miss Elizabeth earlier today, and it put me in mind... well... forgive me, Bingley, it is no business of mine."

"No, truly, Darcy, I would value your advice. That is, I mean to establish myself, and it seems that I can trust your experience and..." He tugged at his cuff before visibly collecting himself. "Forgive me, Darcy. I did not seek a connection with you merely to lean on your counsel."

I glanced at him. "Quite all right, Bingley. Perhaps your example will be instructive for my brother. He has had an... eventful week, it seems. I daresay he could use a friend who has his head put on right."

Bingley chuckled. "Do you know, it quite slipped my mind earlier to inquire after your own obviously eventful day." His puzzled glance took in my bespattered coat. "Dare I ask what you were about to find yourself so, er... bedraggled when you first returned to Pemberley?"

A chuckle escaped before I curbed it. Poor Bingley had attempted manfully not to gawk at my disheveled state earlier. "Think nothing of it. I was out riding earlier today, and I had chanced upon Miss Elizabeth. The dust you saw on my coat was flour."

He blinked. "Darcy, you needn't explain yourself to me, but if that is your way of 'explaining' something... well, perhaps I might do you a turn by a bit of instruction in the art of conversation."

"I might have need of it Although," I mused, grinning reminiscently, "Miss Elizabeth could probably deduce clever methods to manage me a bit more smoothly." Sobering, I recollected myself. These flights of fancy must cease altogether! I had no intention of winning her affections for myself—I could not possibly. And besides, even if I desired it, her guardian had something else to say on the matter. My thoughts and opinions weighed little when her absence loomed decidedly nearer.

With an effort, I shelved further reflective commentary to eye Bingley directly. "And what of yourself? Were you not planning some call at Farthingdale today?"

If I thought the color staining his collar earlier betrayed diffidence, it was nothing to the sudden effusion turning even his ears scarlet. "I, well... yes, I did have some hopes of enjoying the afternoon with the charming Miss Bennet," he confessed. "Although I had not worked out how best to subtly inquire if..." Here, he broke off awkwardly. "That is... I was hoping you might accompany me, but you have already called once today. I certainly understand if your own affairs must naturally take precedence..."

I took pity on my friend's obvious discomfiture. "No need to abandon hopes of calling, in my view. In fact, given their imminent departure, I applaud your eagerness to enjoy what society you may while both ladies grace our neighborhood."

At this, Bingley jerked round to gape openly at me. "Departure? Whatever can you mean? Has some development arisen I am ignorant of?"

"I regret to say yes. I have it on some authority that Mr. Gardiner is expected shortly to convey both ladies home." Seeing his fallen countenance, I added candidly, "Although I confess facts could as easily prove otherwise. In truth, it is only Miss Elizabeth's departure that is decided. Perhaps Miss Bennet shall remain with her aunt." I shifted in the saddle under Bingley's measuring look.

"You seem uncommonly well-informed on Miss Elizabeth's affairs," he ventured carefully.

I shrugged, feigning casualness to mask the hollow opening under my ribs. "We share some long acquaintance. But you are right—in light of this intelligence, we ought to make such opportunities count." I clapped him bracingly on one shoulder. "Well, then! I insist you waste no more time on my account. Ride for Farthingdale and take shameless advantage of a pretty young lady's conversation whilst you still may."

Bingley laughed, then straightened determinedly. "I believe I shall! And do not think I shall forget *your* sage advice either, Sir. If your Miss Elizabeth's hours amongst us are dwindling, I suggest you seize the present." Grasping my hand impulsively, he nodded a brisk farewell before wheeling his mount off in energetic pursuit of—hopefully—his heart's fondest desire.

I gazed after his retreating figure, still lingering long after the merry chestnut passed from view. Yes, here was wisdom I could ill afford to ignore. Too many opportunities had already slipped heedlessly through my fingers where Elizabeth was concerned. I had thought duty's grim obligations must stand inviolate. But perhaps matters of the heart refused to submit meekly to such stark governing? Bingley's eager devotion shone a mirror to my own restless longing, though I fought acknowledging it.

Well, fight no more. Resolution hardened within. If Elizabeth yet tarried briefly within my sphere, I would meet her gladly at every turn Fate allowed. Let us bask in joyful hours too long denied by past misunderstandings. For Bingley spoke true—whatever my intentions regarding Elizabeth Bennet, I could not bear to lose another second.

TWENTY-FIVE

Elizabeth

"J ANE, WHAT DO YOU think of this rosebud shade? Dare I pair it with my favorite bonnet when we tour Lambton market later?" I bent closer to the patterned muslin Aunt had brought downstairs for us that afternoon. The pastel shade of the ribbon looked well next to Jane's flaxen curls but might clash dreadfully with my own darker complexion.

Before Jane could reply, Aunt burst abruptly into the morning room, cheeks flushed and auburn hair in disarray. "Girls! Thank heaven I found you straightaway. Helen has taken ill—quite suddenly, severe pains have come upon her!"

Jane and I shot concerned looks toward one another, then instantly rose to our feet. "But surely it is too early?" Jane questioned anxiously. "The baby was not due for two months yet, at least!"

Aunt wrung her hands, a helpless look belying her usual serene confidence. "Aye, by her reckonings, she still had many weeks ahead. She is terribly afraid she might be miscarrying." She made a visible effort to collect herself. "I need to stay with her, but we must find Robert directly and send for the midwife and doctor without delay!"

"Then allow me to convey word, Aunt!" Jane swiftly gathered her bonnet and shawl. "I know Robert was out surveying his western fields this morning. I'll go at once to inform him Helen has been taken ill."

"Bless you, Jane, dear!" Aunt turned beseeching eyes my way. "And Lizzy, you recollect the doctor's house in Lambton still, I trust?" At my swift nod, she continued, "Could you fetch round the phaeton or mount the plow horse—I cannot recall which is still here—and beard the man himself in his den?"

"Consider it done!" I assured her, stopping only long enough to squeeze her shoulder comfortingly before hastening out the opposite door toward the carriage yard. Saddle the sturdy plow mare or venture out in the noisy contraption? Deciding on expediency over style, I opted for the latter and endeavored not to run full tilt toward the grubby building at the side of the house. My hands only trembled faintly, tugging Mrs. Westing's worn driving gloves into place as I swiftly negotiated the narrow phaeton back up the lane.

Truth be told, my pedestrian driving skills saw little opportunity for practice, my independent rambles requiring only sturdy boots and a tolerance for a bit of dirt. But needs must! I set my jaw, gathering reins determinedly. Propriety never condoned ladies careening unchaperoned on urgent errands, outside emergencies notwithstanding, but what was independence for if not seizing control when crisis demanded action?

Lambton's modest streets seemed eerily deserted under scudding grey clouds when I finally threaded through its outskirts. But no matter—the doctor's shingle still hung over a shabby green door near the draper's shop, close by the inn. I drew rein and vaulted down, rapping the shining brass lion head knocker imperiously. Muffled cursing preceded reluctant shuffling steps and the emergence of a silver-haired housekeeper blinking at my unexpected appearance.

"Is the doctor in?" I pleaded.

"Gone to Smithfield's," the housekeeper replied shortly. "Young Browning lad broke 'is arm."

"Pray inform him that Mrs. Westing of Farthingdale is in urgent need. She fears a miscarriage! Is there a midwife in town?"

"Aye, but she's off with Hattie Durham, blessed thing. Twins! 'Tis a bad business."

I sagged. "Will you please send the doctor as swiftly as you can? I am going back to Farthingdale now."

The housekeeper's promise that she would send him the moment she saw him brought scant relief as I raced the final dusty mile back to Farthingdale. Hoofbeats and shouts to clear the path went unheeded, my frantic speed unchecked until a familiar tall figure burst from a copse directly in my path. I yanked violently on the reins as Darcy reined his mount alongside, features creased in concern.

"Elizabeth! I have just come from Farthingdale, and your aunt said I would likely intercept you. Were you able to rouse Lambton's physician?"

My heart still rabbiting from my abrupt halt, I shoved tangled curls off my damp face. "I got word to his housekeeper, but the doctor was out. I asked for a midwife, but there was none to hand! Oh, Mr. Darcy, Mrs. Westing might be in a very bad way, indeed. Is there anyone else?"

"Peace." Darcy's steady tone calmed my resurging agitation. "Your aunt has things well in hand. I sent a farm boy at once to get word to Mrs. MacGregor from Pemberley without delay." At my puzzled look, he explained. "The estate has long retained a capable midwife ready to attend to tenants in their need. Pemberley's coachman will drive her, so she will arrive swiftly. She will help Mrs. Westing until the doctor arrives."

I loosed a shuddering breath, sagging against leather squabs. Of course, Fitzwilliam Darcy had already implemented his legendary competence to our aid. I ought never to have doubted. How did he always know just when to show up to save me? "Bless you for quick thinking." Impulsively, I reached for his hand, and he shifted his reins to give it. "How ever can I thank you for rushing to our help this way, Fitzwilliam?"

His glance gentled, thumb brushing lightly over my knuckles. "No need for gratitude between friends. Although..." He checked his horse beside me, features softening unguardedly. "Perhaps when the crisis passes, you might speak with me privately? There is something I must tell you."

I blinked hard, groping with a confusing swirl of emotions. "Yes, of course. I would always make time to speak to you."

S HADOWS LENGTHENED IN FARTHINGDALE'S drawing room as our small party maintained its anxious vigil. Mr. Westing alternately paced and sank into chairs as Mr. Bingley murmured a steady stream of encouraging words. The master's drawn features softened fractionally under such tireless sympathy. I marveled anew at Fitzwilliam and Bingley's quiet solidarity bolstering our worried host without being asked.

Jane was patiently amusing little Annie Rose upon the carpet, her graceful form concealing weariness from long hours of waiting. My poor darling sister deserved respite from restless toddler wrangling.

Impulsively, I crossed the room and touched Jane's shoulder. "I will take a turn entertaining Miss Anne if you wish to stretch your limbs."

Jane turned gratefully up to me, though still hesitating to shift her charge. "Are you certain, Lizzy? That hand cannot have improved, despite Aunt changing the bandages."

I waved off her solicitous concern with my good hand. "A little discomfort hardly signifies. Go, refresh yourself while Annie and I play a game."

Laughing softly, Jane yielded the child into my hold before excusing herself upstairs. I shifted the solid little body more comfortably on my lap, wincing slightly as my bandaged thumb throbbed warning. But Annie's openly adoring gaze raised my spirits far above trifling physical complaint.

Soon I was wholly absorbed entertaining the little girl. Seeing me struggle somewhat one-handed, Mr. Westing considerately fetched playthings from the nursery to tempt Annie Rose's restless energy. The toddler was gleefully sending wooden animals skittering over lately polished tables when Jane slipped quietly back within doors.

Wan but composed, she rescued an ornamental shepherdess just before pudgy fingers sent it toppling. "Come, Annie darling. Lizzy, I rather think we ought to look to supper preparations. Would you prefer to help Martha, or should I?"

"I will. Just take Annie, please."

Jane held out inviting arms that I willingly released my small charge into before standing to assist. Once Mr. Bingley and Mr. Westing politely averted their eyes, I bent stiffly to brush crumbs from my skirts, my thumb giving an unpleasant throb. I straightened wearily and moved toward the kitchen.

My step faltered just over the threshold, as an unexpected sight met my eyes. For there stood Mr. Darcy, shirtsleeves rolled back as he industriously chopped potatoes. Martha was nowhere to be seen, and I had lost track of Fitzwilliam while I was entertaining Annie. I had just assumed he had other business and went away.

My lips curved helplessly upward even as I pressed my fingertips to them. When had such a domestic tableau touched me so profoundly? There was just something viscerally affecting seeing evidence of those strong hands working at something other than pen and ink.

As if sensing my scrutiny, Fitzwilliam glanced up. Something in my undisguised turmoil seemed to pull him swiftly around the table, concern etching his brow. My smile faltered under such piercing perception.

"Forgive this intrusion. Has no one warned you not to stray into kitchens during a crisis for fear of conscription into menial labor?"

Fitzwilliam's solemn features remained unmoving, save the muscle flexing along his lean jaw. Gently ignoring my deflections, he searched my face with those fathomless dark eyes that seemed to see straight through to my soul. I sucked in a swift breath, my pulse skittering under such sudden scrutiny. Had he always affected me so profoundly without my conscious realization?

"You ought not to shoulder every burden without relief." His gravelly voice wrapped warmly around me, hinting at unplumbed depths beneath that stoic reserve. This was not the Fitzwilliam I once knew. Or had the awkward boy of memory merely ripened into this compelling man without my noticing?

I shook my head, trying unsuccessfully to ignore his nearness. "I am not the one laboring and in need of care. Truly, I am perfectly well..."

But words faltered as I noted the smudges of dirt on his shirt and sleeves. Before my better judgment could intervene, I yielded to the impulse. Stepping nearer, I wrapped my arms about his solid form.

Unthinking, I nestled close, softly burrowing my face into his shirt and feeding on the strength I could feel pulsing through his chest.

Fitzwilliam stilled briefly, surprise palpable beneath my cheek. New awareness arced hotly between us. Then his hands slid slowly upward, tentative yet undeniably intimate, as he cupped my shoulders. My senses swam dizzily. Surely, he must feel the wild stutter of my heart where my breast pressed to his?

We remained thus for a moment, just... being near each other. And I could not think of a safer place to be in the whole world. At length, I eased slightly away, abashed by my behavior, yet finding no judgment in the tender eyes searching mine.

"What was that for?" he asked in a husky voice.

"Just... thank you for always knowing precisely when you are needed most."

But Fitzwilliam Darcy was not so easily fooled. He sensed it—he *must* have—the hunger in the way I had thrown myself at him like the veriest wanton! But if I had acted on feeling, he had scarcely done less. His darkened gaze held more longing than censure for my forwardness. Casting about through the pleasurable disarray of my wits, I seized upon the trifling evidence of fresh mishaps on his shirt.

"Just how did you come to be so very decorated again?" I reached, unthinking, to flick a bit of dried yellow muck from his shirt before my fingers froze midair. Our eyes locked and held, simmering tension suddenly pulsing the space between us. I could not tear my gaze from his lips. What mad impulse had me poised mere inches from embracing potential disaster?

"I..." His throat bobbed. "I confess, I had a small run-in with some rebellious poultry..."

His rough admission broke the charged moment at last. I sputtered a surprised laugh, then gulped a breath that seemed suddenly difficult to draw as I took a careful step back, clasping nervous hands tightly behind my skirts. What was happening here between us? Forces beyond understanding threatened to break every prudent vow. Uncle Gardiner had made me promise!

I gulped. "Well!" False vivacity trembled only slightly through my attempted smile. "Egg yolk, is it? That puts me in mind of why I came into the kitchen. Are you hungry? My stomach is rumbling like an earthquake."

I turned hastily back to the waiting tea things, grappling to compose reactions Fitzwilliam's nearness provoked. I could scarcely meet his eyes now without heat flooding my cheeks. When had his presence begun undressing my very spirit? This new air flickering between us defied understanding.

Fitzwilliam lifted the tray, his warm looks speaking beyond platitudes. "Now come, lead on before this band of desperate wanderers forfeit all sustenance."

A breathless laugh escaped me. Whatever had changed between us, his caring support remained a steadfast foundation beneath my feet. "Well, sir, thus the student surpasses his teacher, for I never aspired to such a lofty turn of phrase! But heaven forbid you spoil me for other men's attentions now."

His smile turned boyish and familiar once more. "Perhaps I shall make it my chief ambition henceforth."

Impetuously, my hand sought his where it rested upon the silver tray. No matter uncertain outcomes or goodbyes looming, just now, Fitzwilliam Darcy was the only friend I wanted in the world. "Then I consider myself in very best care before whatever future brings."

H OURS LATER, THE DOCTOR had come at last to pronounce Mrs. Westing beyond immediate danger. I bid Fitzwilliam and Mr. Bingley farewell at the door, scarcely trusting my voice to remain steady facing fresh parting with Pemberley's master. No matter that necessity rather than caprice dictated our separation. Gazing into those fathomless eyes, still scintillating with banked warmth from tender moments past, my restless heart cried out against the dictate of reason. What new sorcery had this man unwittingly woven to bind me thus helplessly to his side though miles and duty must shortly intervene?

I watched long after the gentlemen turned their mounts toward distant Pemberley, clinging still to precious final glimpses. Had ever parting smiles held such wealth of unvoiced yearning? What bitter twist of providence or malice tore beloved faces from my reach no sooner than found again?

But silent rebellion mattered little when time and authority conspired as they would regardless of individual wishes. The bills soon must be paid for golden hours stolen out of keeping with prosaic reality's demands. Head high, I turned resolutely back toward candlelit halls and companions awaiting, endeavoring to steel my own wavering poise.

TWENTY-SIX

Darcy

B INGLEY WAS SINGING. BLAST the man. Singing like an intoxicated swain, his head tipped back and his laugh merry as we
rode back to Pemberley that evening. I watched him in envy as misery
clawed at my throat. His golden dreams mocked my dread-filled heart.

I had never planned for love's cruel trap when I first pursued
Elizabeth. This was supposed to be about *her* courage and sense of
self-worth, and fortifying her against whatever charms George might
level at her! Yet her smiles intoxicated my starved senses beyond reason.
Now, terror mounted with every hoofbeat, taking me farther from
her.

Damn fool! My traitorous heart refused to shield itself from fresh
wounds as wisdom had urged. Those bewitching eyes had snared me
in mere moments. And she was not even eligible for me!

Hot fury simmered—what new separation would Mr. Gardiner
enforce? Would he forbid all contact? Even an occasional letter, as a... a
brother would write to his sister? And why, in heaven's name? I vowed
I would have answers this time. I knew how to find her now, and even

if I could not make her mine in the way my soul longed for, I could at least know that she was well.

But railing changed nothing. Soon, her angelic smiles must fade from memory. What right had I to demand she remain? Yet my spirit screamed in protest, unwilling to surrender her again. Could fate not relent this one time? Had not duty already consumed enough of my life without demanding this ultimate sacrifice?

I passed a haunted glance toward carefree Bingley. Would that I could share such untroubled certainty in new love conquering all sorrow. But providence had granted me no such mercy. The brief hours of joy were already bleeding away into the night.

Old grief merged with new anguish. I couldn't lose Elizabeth again. Yet, how could I alter fate's design? Even baring my soul gave no power to bid her stay when I offered no certainty. Better solitude than dragging innocent hearts down in my wake. My duty was to swallow that bitter draught alone.

With stoic resignation, I turned toward Pemberley's lights, barely piercing the darkness. Cold comfort, yet some bulwark against storms without. I must bar my longing's doors and steel myself to silence desire's cries. Such was my solitary destiny, no matter how fiercely longing now protested. No sweet song could break this isolation.

MORNING LIGHT DID LITTLE to penetrate the restless fog shrouding my mood. I paced Pemberley's halls, thoughts churning. I dared not venture to Farthingdale again. Ought I dispatch an errand boy to check on Mrs. Westing's recovery? But no, too impersonal. This dilemma would not resolve itself merely by avoiding the site of disruption. Perhaps if I rode to Matlock first, I might fortify myself before...

"Darcy!"

I turned, startled from my absorption as Bingley strode buoyantly forth. "You're awake early. No lingering abed to dream on tender hopes today?"

Humor glinted in his eyes. "And pass the chance to glimpse fair visions made flesh? I am for Farthingdale as soon as I break fast. Will you not join me?"

I hesitated. "I ought to look in on George first." At Bingley's questioning look, I elaborated. "He was strangely overwrought yesterday. I would not have his prospects jeopardized."

Comprehension lit Bingley's face. "Well, then! I shall convey glad tidings on my own and give your regards. And..." Inspiration sparked. "I will bring your midwife back if she is ready to depart. If you will lend me your carriage."

The tension eased fractionally from my neck. Bless Bingley for intuitively grasping my constraints without demanding an explanation. "That would be helpful. I will send word to the stables."

He waved my stilted gratitude aside. "It is nothing! I confess ulterior motives exist besides sporting your livery." His infectious grin invited shared amusement if I were so inclined. "We shall hope I return with a good report on all quarters, eh?"

I managed a weak smile in return. "Let us hope George's affairs fare as smoothly as yours appear to at present."

If life's orchard granted Bingley a bit of windfall fruit, would a merciful Providence not spare me a sole blighted tree? But resenting Bingley's unclouded delight served no purpose. I simply could not risk endangering George's prospects now, no matter how Elizabeth's absence grieved me. I left Bingley to his lively anticipations, a heaviness settling round my heart. There are burdens, once assumed, that even closest comrades cannot share or allay.

T HE RIDE TO MATLOCK strained my already taut nerves beyond limit. A dozen dire scenarios played through my mind regarding what awaited there. Would I find George packed off in disgrace for his temper yesterday, his prospects in ruins? Or worse yet, would he be gone entirely, having abandoned Lady Lucilla to renew tantalizing dreams with Elizabeth after his shocking display of passion when I stopped him riding for Farthingdale?

Thus preoccupied, the great house appeared around a bend in the drive sooner than I anticipated. I rounded the corner to the courtyard with trepidation mounting. But instead of shattered hopes, a charming domestic tableau greeted my entrance.

There stood George, sunny smile restored, assisting Lady Lucilla and her mother in mounting a matched pair of elegant chestnut mares, caparisoned for riding side-saddle. At my abrupt appearance, he turned with his usual unaffected welcome.

"Brother! Well met this fine day. You find me readying to play guide for the ladies through Matlock's picturesque splendors."

I could only stare stupidly, pulse resuming irregular beat. At length, I managed to dismount and murmur appropriate greetings to Lady Belmont and Lady Lucilla as they expertly gathered their reins.

Before I could quite determine how to voice the questions simmering in my mind, Lady Lucilla smiled down at me gently. "Will you not join our party, Mr. Darcy? With two such amiable escorts, I shall be the envy of all Derbyshire."

"We should be glad for your company, Fitz, if you have time to spare?" George's expression hovered between contrition and entreaty.

"Please excuse me a moment." Touching my hat brim politely, I drew George several paces away and pitched my voice low. "Forgive my astonishment, but you seem remarkably restored to good humor today. Can all be well after yesterday's... trials?"

Chagrin crossed his handsome features. "About that... Let us just say I have profited from salutary counsel against hasty words blurted in passion." His glance strayed toward Lady Lucilla, adjusting her hat. "And a gentle heart ready to pardon thoughtless folly."

I studied my brother closely but could glean little beyond surface impressions. Time enough later to parse puzzling details, when the lady was not awaiting with all eagerness for the ride ahead. I clapped George bracingly on one shoulder. "Well! I shall expect a bit more intelligence on the matter later. Shall I wish you a happy journey, then?"

George's lingering gloom evaporated instantly. "I should be wounded indeed if you abandon us now! Come, Fitz, you must ride with us. I see that gloomy look about you again. What better things do you have to do? Back to your study?" His ready smile flashed enticingly. "Come, Brother! Surely affairs of the estate can spare you briefly for a breath of air to clear the senses."

I wavered, temptation proving potent as curiosity regarding this astonishing reversal. But hesitation yet held me fast. A backward glance showed Lady Lucilla watching us, hope writ clearly in her open countenance. Squaring my shoulders, I summoned formal tones of deep regret. "I must speak to the earl just now, but I wish you all a pleasant ride."

George's crestfallen look stabbed my conscience briefly. But he rallied swiftly, bowing over my hand in a florid farewell. "We shall meet at dinner and take fuller measure of each other then!"

I stood watching their forms diminish down the drive, wondering anew if volatile George could ever settle fully to domestic harness. But for now, discord rested, as his heart apparently turned back to bask in Lady Lucilla's warmth. I could only hope it would last, however improbable that appeared.

With a pensive sigh, I handed my horse to a groom and mounted the steps to the house.

I PAUSED OUTSIDE THE drawing-room door, bracing myself before entering the arena. Would I discover yesterday's tensions still simmering regarding George's explosive loss of temper? Or had my mercurial brother managed to reconcile and repair damaged bonds? With a muttered prayer for diplomacy swaying in my favor today, I straightened my waistcoat and presented myself.

Lord Matlock was comfortably ensconced amidst leather-bound comfort and cigar smoke, while Lord Winston stood at polite attention nearby. My muscles unclenched slightly when neither of them leveled accusing eyes at me the moment I entered the room.

But my relief was short-lived. Cool grey eyes above an impeccably groomed mustache arrested my survey. Ah yes, there waited the true test, pitting shaky nerves against steely mettle—time to face Lord Belmont.

Matlock greeted me first. "Darcy! Your brother said we should not look for you until the dinner gong. To what do we owe the honor?"

His hearty welcome bolstered me a fraction as I advanced to shake Winston's proffered hand.

"Forgive me for arriving early. I wished to... look in on George." I cleared my throat discreetly. No need to expose awkward details, but perhaps key parties could enlighten recent puzzles surrounding my mercurial sibling? "He was riding out with Lady Lucilla when I encountered them earlier."

Had I only imagined Belmont's piercing stare boring into me? "Just so. My daughter and your brother seemed eager to explore local landscapes after yesterday's... confinement keeping company indoors." His sharp glance betrayed little beyond polished nonchalance. Winston appeared more ill at ease—perhaps fearing for his friend? Or his sister?

"I see." I turned the cut crystal glass Matlock offered between restless fingers. "Then you passed a... peaceful afternoon yesterday?" At Belmont's urbane nod, I pressed on delicately. "Forgive my curiosity, but George is a man of deep feeling regarding affairs of the heart." I hesitated. "As his brother, I worry sudden squalls may capsize happy prospects without warning."

"Let the young folks weather their seasons of storm and shine." Lord Matlock interjected breezily, seeming at pains to dismiss my concerns. "We scarcely navigated our own courtships without some buffeting, eh, Belmont?"

His lordship merely elevated one sardonic brow, shaking his head slightly. "Fits of passion oft attend new love." Still, that discomfiting stare probed as if discerning my very soul.

I mastered my irrational nerves under such piercing regard, adopting a tone of reasoned logic. "Most true, my lord. But not all lovers possess temperaments equally adaptable to wedded choreography. My own inclinations tend to be overly sober, while George never met an impulse he would not race recklessly after. His heart, I am convinced, is true, beneath any storms that might bluster."

Why did justifying George suddenly seem akin to the labors of Hercules? I persevered on, pulse kicking faster. "But I am certain it is only due to the depth of his regard, such a thing being unknown to him before." There! I had framed a diplomatic query without overtly naming my brother's intrinsic flaws.

Winston shuffled papers nervously as silence expanded. At length, Lord Belmont drained his glass and leaned back. "Philosophers argue action springs more from inner virtue than external deed. If your brother and my daughter follow our examples, respect may yet temper passion's excesses, however unlikely the pairing appears." He regarded me with inscrutable intensity. "I begin to think your brother's metal rings truer than the mere surface glitter suggested."

I blinked, stunned by this oblique praise. But ere coherent response took shape, a knock heralded the butler, requesting Lord Matlock's attention on some household matter. With smooth apologies, Lord Matlock exited, nodding me toward the sideboard hospitality as he went. Gratefully, I splashed a bit of amber liquid fortification into a glass before braving Lord Belmont alone.

Lord Belmont crossed one elegant leg casually over the other and regarded me through shrewd half-lidded eyes. "Come sit, Mr. Darcy. We have some matters to discuss."

I perched warily, entirely off balance. To what did His Lordship refer? Surely, no residue from yesterday's dust-up with George? I took a small bolstering sip, choosing discretion as the safest course. "I am at your leisure, my lord."

Amusement lurked somewhere behind the keen nobility of his visage. "Indeed. I trust you had business at Pemberley yesterday? Word reached us of unrest at the mill."

I froze. Blast! So, he had heard. I shifted uneasily. "Some... agitation did arise. But no harm done, and I daresay the men are even today seeing proof that I mean to attend their complaints. And I am reflecting on other means to—"

One greying brow lifted. "Reflecting, you say? These are not parlor debates but actual livelihoods hanging on such 'reflections'." Faded blue eyes held mine unerringly. "What qualifications justify your tinkering thus with other men's survival?"

I bristled, my temper flaring. How dare he condescend to me, after I was the one soothing maddened workers whose complaints were anything but academic! I leaned intently forward, my pulse elevated. "The men who walked out yesterday were no theorists. And they are not the last to air legitimate grievances with industrial advancements and practices outpacing prudent reform!"

Belmont waved this aside negligently. "Every age imagines itself at a violent cusp of history never glimpsed before. But humanity adapts, and society progresses. Your generation will manage somehow, I daresay."

I surged to my feet, indignation momentarily eclipsing discretion. "And if 'society's' onward march tramples too many who are unable to withstand the relentless drumbeat of 'progress' in its wake? How can we reconcile the suffering such change creates?"

I paced, my frame tingling with the conviction that here was a man capable of comprehending complexity beyond rote defense of status quo, if only I could induce his complacent intellect to *care*. "Forgive my bluntness. But how loud must the complaints become before they are heeded? Must humble men wait mute and passive for so-called 'betters' to acknowledge their cry?"

Silence greeted me. Lord Belmont merely stroked his moustache pensively, thunderous gaze unreadable.

"So." His rumbling voice echoed suddenly loud in that still room. He gestured brusquely with his glass toward me. "Enlighten me, then, regarding what brilliant 'reforms' you propose for these downtrodden sheep flocking your mill?"

I hesitated before plunging headlong over the precipice. If speaking truth to power here brought mockery or rejection, at least I could say I had made the effort and not quailed in shame. I moved to stand squarely before my unwavering judge and jury of one. Then, in the simplest eloquence at my command, I pled the humble case of those whose hopes and lives hung now in the balance. And miracle beyond reason! Instead of derision, something almost akin to gruff admiration kindled behind those flinty eyes.

When I had finished, I stood awkward and exposed, awaiting Lord Belmont's pronouncement. Would he crush clumsy enterprise with an arch word? Or might he discern in my awkward mixture of zeal and inexperience some grain worthy developing? I held my breath and waited.

Then, that imposing noble personage slowly unfolded from his chair. With lumbering dignity, he extended a large hand that I hastened to clasp in bewilderment. And to my shock, he favored me with a brief but undeniable smile.

"Very well, Darcy. I shall put your letter before the committee."

TWENTY-SEVEN

Elizabeth

I CRACKED OPEN HELEN Westing's bedchamber door, relieved to find Aunt Gardiner in bright spirits tending her sister. Helen looked vastly improved from yesterday's pallor and distress, calmly sipping some restorative beef broth.

She greeted me with a welcoming smile. "Come sit by me, Lizzy dear. My sister vows I must keep entirely abed until the child is born, but it will prove less tedious with such fine company."

I arranged myself carefully on the coverlet edge, clasping Helen's hand lightly. "You seem much better today! We have Pemberley's capable midwife to thank, I daresay." I studied her hopefully. "Was last evening comfortable after we left you?"

"Oh, indeed! Mrs. MacGregor's very presence was a comfort." Helen squeezed my fingers gratefully. "Will you kindly convey my thanks to Mr. Darcy for so promptly sending her? Please tell that excellent gentleman that his foresight may well have saved my baby's life, and perhaps even my own."

"Indeed, I shall, at the first opportunity! Mr. Darcy's instincts do him much credit." I felt a telltale blush rise under Aunt's suddenly sharp glance but ignored it breezily. "Perhaps you will feel equal to receiving visitors later today? I will go below and see that refreshments are prepared."

Rising to withdraw, I turned back at the door to favor both ladies with an arch smile. "And do ring if any little wants present themselves. Your devoted allies await any summons below!"

Laughing softly at Helen's promises, I descended with a lighter heart than yesterday's uncertainties warranted. Truly, fate had showered unexpected blessings on our humble little circle. And it was all thanks to Fitzwilliam. Fitzwilliam Darcy, the brother I had always ignored because I never understood him. But wherever his quiet strength abided, peace and comfort also prevailed.

Voices below announced Mr. Bingley's arrival. It seemed he had come in Pemberley's carriage to convey Mrs. MacGregor home, which meant he was probably not alone. I hurried my step, eager to greet the man who had orchestrated it all. But upon reaching the front sitting room, no tall figure presented itself. My hopeful smile faltered only slightly, beholding merely Mr. Bingley handing Jane a small nosegay with boyish ardor.

I curtsied brightly in greeting, nonetheless. "Good afternoon, Mr. Bingley! How fares the road between here and Pemberley? Not overly hot or dusty this morning, I hope?" At his assurance of a very pleasant ride, I went to stand opposite Jane, where I could face our guest. "Will you not sit awhile after your drive? Perhaps there is news of how Mr. Darcy and George are passing their day?" I could not help glancing out of the window again, but neither Darcy brother met my eye.

Bingley shifted his weight awkwardly. "Er... that is... Darcy sends his felicitations regarding Mrs. Westing's improving condition, of course! But he was engaged on various estate matters, so he could not accompany me on this trip. And George..." He cleared his throat, unease flickering over usually genial features. "... George felt it best also to remain behind some days rather than risk, er, overtaxing your hospitality with excessive guests under the circumstances."

I nodded politely over the awkward pause following this halting explanation. So... both brothers found an excuse to avoid further contact? But surely not even shy Darcy would stand on ceremony so soon after the way we had left things yesterday! There was a moment there, when he was leaving, that I had actually fancied he would have liked to kiss me. And I? I would have sunk my hands into his coat and kissed him back.

Well, that was that, I supposed. I firmly ignored the sharp pang of disillusionment. Clearly, other responsibilities commanded the Darcys' time, which could not revolve exclusively around the whims of inconsequential neighbors! With murmured excuses, I turned to leave Mr. Bingley and Jane to their cozy exchange, reflecting rather sadly how little real claim I possessed on either Pemberley's master or my girlhood beau, no matter what tender moments we might have shared lately.

But perhaps... perhaps I was overreacting. Just because neither Darcy had come with Mr. Bingley today did not mean they would not come tomorrow. Yes, that was possible.

I aimlessly wandered the back lawns after Bingley left, brooding over Darcy's absence. Had yesterday meant nothing? Was it silly to imagine those sweet moments were a prelude to something more lasting? With a rueful sigh, I determined to put girlish fancies firmly from my mind. A woman grown could not indulge romantic imaginings over passing attentions from charming gentlemen.

My cogitations halted at the approaching clatter of hooves. A scruffy boy drew up on a farm nag, saying he had a letter for me from one Mr. George Darcy. Surprised, I thanked him for the delivery.

Nearly stumbling in my haste inside, I rushed to the desk in the sitting room and broke the seal with trembling fingers.

But my eager smile froze, taking in the careless phrases marching across the fine paper.

*D*EAREST *LIZZY* (HIS HANDWRITING had not improved since the age of fifteen),

I trust you will rejoice to learn your old friend is happily pledged to be married! Lovely Lady Lucilla of Berkwell, daughter of Lord Belmont, captured my fancy last spring at Ascot, and I have been courting her these three months past. And would you credit it, neither Fitzwilliam's ambitions to see me leg-shackled early, nor my own roaming eye have wavered since beholding her angelic golden beauty!

Oh, I will confess to a brief temptation when fate so unexpectedly restored your winsome company to mine these past weeks. What red-blooded man could remain unmoved, finding your fine dark eyes once more alight with pleasure in my presence? For a fleeting moment, I fancied renouncing my sweet Lucilla (and her family's wealth—it pains me to confess it, but second sons must have something to live on, as Fitzwilliam so often reminds me) just to taste past enchantments long mourned as lost.

But my too-astute elder brother wisely intervened, sternly counseling against impulsive folly that could wreck shining prospects so carefully built. And he was right, of course. For truly, no lady yet has stirred me as my gentle darling does with but a glance from those twin emerald stars in her lovely face. Were there in this world a woman capable of tempting me from her arms, it would be you, my dear Lizzy. Patience, my dear, for I am certain that in time, you shall be similarly smitten with some worthy fellow.

So, whilst you sheltered blithely in your country cottage amidst rustic charms this summer, Cupid's arrow winged straight and true at last to pin this wild heart securely. Forgive me, Lizzy. Lucilla and I will deal extremely well together, I am certain, for all our contrasts in temperament. We shall enjoy the deep contentment only true minds perfectly fitted to one another can confer. My admiration for her person will undoubtedly increase as years augment familiarity with inner excellence if such outward brilliance finds any equal...

I COULDN'T READ THE rest. My knuckles whitened, crumpling the parchment cruelly. I stared numbly at the letter's careless phrases. George was engaged? While he flirted and toyed with my heart, he was pledged to another all along?

The page blurred as fury and anguish tore through me. How could he betray me so cruelly after all we had suffered?

And Fitzwilliam! He engineered this mercenary match while urging me to open my heart to him, instead of George. Did he dispassionately calculate pros and cons while holding my hand? Measure estates instead of feelings?

I crumpled the vile letter, chest heaving. The men I had trusted most had used me ill, yet now preached patience and forgiveness! Where was the justice? By heaven, I would not meekly comply to further insult! Deception layered upon deception!

Without a backward glance, I fled upstairs, nearly crashing into poor Jane emerging from the room we shared. I barged straight past her outstretched hands and cry of concern, choking back fresh anguish until I gained my chamber. Fumbling fingers shot home the bolt before rage and humiliation shattered the last vestiges of tattered pride.

Oh, what abominable treatment! Bandied about as a mere plaything between both brothers, then dismissed without a second thought once I had entertained them! How could I have deluded myself into believing either gentleman possessed a shred of integrity or cared for me beyond selfish convenience?

The years I had dreamed of George Darcy—nay, even the days of late when I had come to adore Fitzwilliam!—playing gentle words over in memory, imagining foolish, impossible dreams... now each recollection mocked and taunted me for being such a witless fool.

For Fitzwilliam knew—he knew George's circumstance and kept me blissfully ignorant so he could step into George's place! Likely, they had laughed together over dinner, congratulating each other on their supreme cunning.

What was I to do but have a good cry? And when I had done, I read that letter again and worked myself into fresh rage and tears all over again.

Some while later, as wretched weeping finally ran dry, a carriage's approach caught my dazed attention. I moved swiftly to peer out the window. Fresh pain lanced through me to behold Uncle Gardiner himself stepping down below!

New purpose erupted from simmering outrage and anguish as I stared in the direction of that dear place I had once called home. None should vanquish me so easily again! No longer would I linger abject in others' power, allowing mystery and injustice to reign unchecked around me.

Chin high, I turned from faithless Pemberley and started packing my trunk to return to Longbourn.

TWENTY-EIGHT

Darcy

I ROSE BEFORE DAWN, restless energy denying further sleep. George might appear to be settling once more, but that left the problem of Elizabeth to stir in my head. Saddling Caesar, I rode vigorously toward the folly, demons driving relentlessly on. Elizabeth's absence echoed through Pemberley's empty halls now with haunting finality. What insidious secrets compelled Gardiner's abrupt removal of her against all appeals?

Frustration goaded me on through abandoned copses and meadows, just kissing sunrise gold. No explanation had come, only implacable duty presented as justification for demanding my word not to interfere again. But Elizabeth's stricken eyes tortured my dreams. How was I to abandon her to a desolation not of her own making?

My throat clenched as trailing fingers brushed familiar worn stone where only days ago joy seemed reborn. But time erases naught while yearning hollows only deepen. Futile railing against unquestionable authority changed nothing. Unless...

Sharply, I acknowledged these snarling emotions owed naught to boyhood camaraderie. No familial affection kindled such unreasoning jealousy of callous George, nor inspired my tortured longing through the long watches of the night. No brotherly concern now hammered relentlessly through my breast, feeling empty days bleed inexorably ahead without Elizabeth's smiling presence brightening all.

I was in love with her.

I probably had been for years—at least, the memory of her spark and joy—but before, I had been able to pass it off as something less. No longer.

But what claim supported my raging protests against her loss? Only the staggering recognition, dawning like a relentless tide that somehow, despite denial, this woman had become the vital air I craved beyond discretion or damnable proud restraint! Before heaven, I confessed it now—no casual fondness lived and died within these wounded walls, but ardent timeless love blazed forth at last from smothering chains. My wounded heart stood naked and exposed, trembling vulnerably in her gentle hold, whether given consciously or not.

Hoofbeats pounded suddenly loud on the morning air. Frowning, I peered through dappling leaves—it was George, galloping as if the very devil were on his heels, curls in wild disarray, his loose shirt flung open to the breeze. My belly tightened grimly. What now?

"Has there been an earthquake?" I asked when he drew rein. To my surprise, he simply offered a silent greeting before awkwardly dismounting. No lively quip, no panicked declaration of catastrophe somewhere. I shifted, inviting him to sit. Wordlessly, George moved to accept, solemn and uncharacteristically withdrawn.

"What, nothing to say?"

He released a ragged sigh, roughly raking both hands through his disordered curls. "I'm poor company for jesting, Fitz. I have been doing some thinking." He shook his head sharply at my pointed look. "And before you mock me—"

"I was not going to mock you."

"And do not interrupt, either. I've made a wretched botch of everything." His hand sliced angrily through the air. "What madness makes me spurn Fortune's gifts the moment they land at my feet?"

I considered cautious responses as silence spun out. Before I formulated a reply, his attention drifted near Farthingdale's distant grey rooftops.

Finally, he spoke contemplatively. "It seems I lacked some crucial balance to maintain a steady course." His regretful gaze held only self-reproach. "Remember Father coming here whenever he wished a quiet moment to think?"

"Indeed. I thought today I might do the same."

"Hmm." He surveyed enduring granite walls with fond nostalgia. "I remember how, after an hour of just sitting here, looking at the mountains, he would quietly step back on his horse and ride home in a better humor. More peaceable."

I nodded, the memories returning vividly. George chuckled then, momentarily brightening. "And when we were old enough to ride with him, he would permit us to play in the creek down there while he watched. Hah! Do you recall Cook's indignation when we slipped frogs into her best soup pot? Poor things—we meant them no real harm, only fun. But discovery during that fine dinner brought stern lecture and a sound beating once Father forced a confession!"

I could not restrain answering laughter, the kitchen uproar caused by his youthful prank crystal clear still. "Do not try to share the blame for that with me. That was all you."

George shook his head self-consciously. "My antics often threw whole households into turmoil with scarce thought for others' distress. Yet Father stayed ever patient, soothing ruffled feelings once penitent culprits were cornered."

I acknowledged this truth ruefully. "His discipline relied more on weighty sighs and dreadful silence than bluster, as I recall."

George nodded. "Ten minutes pinned under that thunderous gaze had me tearfully vowing full reform!" Then, his brief cheer faded. "But no matter what trouble I stirred, somehow, I found forgiveness here. Father always pointed me on the pathway to rectitude when I thought surely, I was lost."

I nodded with a gentle hum as my eyes wandered to Farthingdale's rooftops once more. Yes, Father was like that.

George turned abruptly toward me, features etched with uncharacteristic gravity. "I must confess an ugly truth from yesterday. I was ready to abandon every vow made to Lucilla in a wild, heated impulse." He dropped his gaze, color rising. "Your timely scolding set me straight before irreversible damage resulted. But you should know how close my folly was to bringing it all crashing down."

I stared, pulse quickening as I pieced together likely events. Choosing my words with care, I asked, "What changed?"

George kept his eyes downcast, shamefaced. "When I confronted the family, prepared to cast Lucilla off regardless of the disgrace, something in me crumbled under the crushing weight of her reliance." One hand raked his hair until it stuck up wildly. "No one has ever had to depend on wayward, faulty George before! But the way she looked at me, Fitz! As if I were the only one in the world she trusted! And I cannot dream of letting her down. But with a formidable mother ever circling and a caustic brother commanding every move—though he is my friend, he is Lucilla's brother first— I felt myself unequal, undeserving." At last, he lifted pleading eyes to mine. "The full reality that her entire prospects in life now solely depended on my mercurial constancy nearly unmanned me completely!"

My breath halted, sudden insight piercing me. So, this had been the hidden goad driving George's increasing desperation before catastrophe loomed? Wordlessly, I grasped his shoulder, hope warring with compassion in my chest. Might iron truly temper undisciplined clay if fires now burned hot enough? Quietly, I asked, "What restored your courage?"

Incredulous laughter burst forth. "You'll scarce credit the miracle, Darcy! Just when craven retreat beckoned most tempting, who should stride forward but Belmont himself!"

I gaped outright as George vividly mimed the improbable scene. "There I cringed, liverish and stammering, pinned by Winston's dagger glare while serpents and daggers practically shot from her ladyship's stare." His wide eyes implored belief. "When without hint or warning, Lord High and Mighty Marquess of Stony-faced Snobbery drew me aside and spoke private words of approbation and encouragement!"

My jaw likely clattered to our feet in undignified disbelief. Before a coherent response formed, he rushed on earnestly. "I swear on Mother's gravestone, that granite pillar informed me in lucid detail how thoughtless ignorance had nearly shipwrecked his own brightest hopes. But Providence grants an opportunity for a wiser course if I would embrace it!" George shook his head in wondering disbelief. "I stood dumbstruck, unable even to choke forth gratitude before Belmont brusquely dismissed me to make apologies."

My mind spun dizzily, struggling to reconcile such astonishing revelation with long-held assumptions. At length, I found my voice to rasp, "But what brought about such an astonishing turnaround from the one with the greatest cause for objection?"

George slowly shook his head. "Dash me if I comprehend, Darcy! Unless..." Sudden thought arrested him. "When I spoke initially of childhood attachment to a lass of interesting background but irregular status, Belmont's reaction gripped me oddly." He searched my face intently. "Do you suppose some unwed indiscretion long past left him inclined toward sympathy in such sticky circumstances?"

I shifted uneasily, my pulse quickening at an unwelcome speculation. But before I formed the hasty words, George abruptly waved aside the notion with fresh sobriety. "No matter! Do you remember what Lizzy always used to say? Something like 'think on the past only as it gives pleasure' or something like that? I aim to do the same." He extended his hand, and I clasped it firmly in relieved solidarity. Whatever weaknesses once jeopardized my mercurial brother's happiness, perhaps metal indeed now annealed to stand fast when fires roared hot and unrelenting. And who was I to scorn Heaven's unorthodox methods of instruction or Redemption's call to the least likely, however late in the hour?

"I am proud you faced down your demons," I told him. "Lesser men would have fled without a backward glance. I had hoped this engagement would be the making of you, and so it has."

George's whole countenance brightened, years falling away. "Beyond my fears of not being good enough, nothing equals Lucilla's smile... to say nothing for her kisses. Oh, Fitz!" He sighed, and drat if he did not place his hand over his heart like a solemn pledge. "She is my angel, Fitz. Whatever sacrifice I must make, it proves cheap when I see heaven's own smile bestowed."

My throat tightened unexpectedly with bittersweet longing. How piercing sweet to be deemed worthy of such devotion! But I tamped the wayward envy down. "Then I wish you both lasting delight ahead."

But shadows crept back, dulling his cheerful visage. "I do have one regret—how I grieved dear Lizzy! Thoughtless ingratitude poorly repaid her ready championship." He grimaced. "I posted an apology and farewell yesterday, before emotions lured me astray from rightful vows. I know she could have had no real expectations of me. Still, tender heart must feel some pang, however transient regard proved."

My breath seized as premonition screamed ice through every vein. I grated through frozen lips, "What have you done?"

Bewildered, he hastened to explain. "I wrote kindly, wishing her well! Admitting attraction dangerously flared too fierce and must be banked. Of course, I credited your wise intervention steering my resolve back true."

Horror slammed my gut like a sledgehammer. I could scarcely rasp incredulous denial "Please, tell me your momentary madness did not—"

Realization slowly drained his features of all color. "I... perhaps hinted she posed a temptation from Lucilla's side I narrowly overc ame..."

"You said *what*? And you had not even the decency to tell her the truth to her face, but to write her a letter accusing her of being a temptress?"

Sickly green stained his cheeks. "Oh Lord, you cautioned expressly not to stir things up further over this! I told her you said—"

I gripped my fists to resist shaking sense back into his vacant skull. "And you blamed *me* for the faithless way you no doubt broke her heart?"

"Well, it was you who said.. " He sighed. "Oh, damn."

"Exactly what did you tell her?"

George scrubbed his palms nervously on the buckskin of his breeches, then miserably recounted damning phrases that painted me as a ruthless puppet master, deliberately angling to keep star-crossed lovers apart. Nausea and outrage churned acidic in my throat, hearing irreparable damage so callously inflicted upon a gentle spirit. Never had I imagined even reckless George capable of such brutal carelessness cloaked in brotherly concern.

"George, your thoughtless idiocy has wildly overreached this time! You wounded her more than Father ever did, and you made *me* look like the one at fault!

He winced, cowering under my blistering attack. "Surely any fancied attachment she had for me cannot cut so deep—"

"You are a fool," I hissed. I leaped from the bench and flung myself into the saddle. For too many years, I had stood passive witness to Elizabeth's bewilderment and distress without intervening. No more! Come heaven or hell's full wrath, this time, I would stand by her side. And woe betide any who dared obstruct my course now!

Twenty-Nine

Elizabeth

T HAT BREAKFAST COULD HAVE curdled fresh cream with bitterness. Seated elbow-to-elbow round the Westing's little table,
not one of us seemed able to lift eyes from our plates. Cutlery clinked
sharply amidst smothering silence until one could hear their teeth
grinding.

Jane made the first gallant foray with determined brightness. "The
ham seems quite nicely roasted! The maid added touches of honey, I
think."

Uncle Gardiner only raised his brows as he finished the last bite
from his plate. He swallowed and gravely set down his napkin. "Jane,
I see no reason for you to return with us today. Lizzy must go, but
perhaps your aunt and Mrs. Westing would still value your help. If you
are willing to render it."

"Indeed!" Aunt agreed. "Just until she regains her strength. I cannot know how I will sit constantly with Helen and still find the time
to manage that lively toddler!"

But Jane's tender features creased in compassion toward me. I swallowed and shook my head. No need for her to come away so soon... not

when Mr. Bingley was making daily pilgrimages to Farthingdale, and she could entertain him with our aunt as a chaperone and not... well, it was so much more peaceful for them to get to know one another here than it would be back in Hertfordshire.

Jane drew a slow breath and shook her head. "I believe Lizzy needs me more." Her resigned smile met mine. "I will go back today."

Dear Jane! Of course, she would not turn her back on me. She would not permit me to ride home alone in disgrace. It *was* sweet of her, but it only twisted the knives embedded deep inside. Before scalding tears broke free, I mumbled excuses and fled the table.

Because no matter the companionship offered, brutal truth remained——every anchor and guiding star orienting me towards home had been forever extinguished. No lighthouse beckoned this small, drifting vessel safely back to harbor. And every time I had felt sure that I belonged somewhere at last, that magic carpet had been yanked from under my feet. How long until Longbourn, too, tired of me as Pemberley had?

An hour later, I watched numbly as Uncle Gardiner and his coachman secured our luggage on the back of the carriage for our departure. Every thud of trunk meeting boot was like the scraping of my heart against my ribs. What few wounds had started mending this glorious summer lay ruthlessly torn wide again. I blinked fiercely, taking one last look around the beloved landscape through stinging eyes.

Footsteps crunched the gravel behind me, and then Aunt Gardiner's comforting arms enfolded me, her gentle hand smoothing my hair and retying my bonnet. Neither of us trusted our voices just then. At length, she pressed her cheek to mine in silent farewell before holding me at arm's length, eyes brimming with equal parts compassion and purpose.

"Courage, child. This is not the ending your true heart seeks. A time shall come to claim the answers and understand."

I managed a wobbly nod. "Thank you, Aunt. Thank you for bringing me." I forced a quaking smile. "At least I got to see the Peaks again."

When Uncle Gardiner handed us in, Jane wrapped me fast to her side, all tender solace. My sodden handkerchief twisted unmercifully in my fingers as the beloved hills and distant crenelated towers whipped past the window. Sweet anguish clawed my throat raw. *Farewell, Pemberley.*

Farewell to the friend once sheltering joyful girlhood within gentle halls. Farewell to the man awakening poignant longings too piercing to examine closely. Whatever bitter providence tore me away again, I would never forget the treasured hours restoring fleeting peace to a battered heart.

Nor could I forgive the callous schemes consigning me back to desolation's empty wilderness. Fate may compel us to live as strangers, but no force could erase the luminous hours fate granted, however brief... or the staggering discovery of love anchoring me beyond all power to forget.

Mercifully, no one demanded idle chatter as the carriage bumped over the road toward Lambton. I kept a rigid gaze fixed outside, the passing landscape blurred by scalding tears none must witness. Silent sympathy hovered oppressive as thunderclouds across our little party while emotion threatened to shatter my tenuous composure.

At length came Uncle Gardiner's weighted sigh. He rapped the roof once without speaking further. But my pulse lurched strangely when the crossroad to Lambton approached, yet we turned off toward the east. Had I misremembered our route? But no—this road led deeper into Derbyshire's snug heart, away from the borders I knew so well.

Ten mystifying minutes passed before wheels ground unexpectedly to a halt before wrought iron gates I knew all too well. There stood the cozy brick manor that had harbored such unexpectedly sweet stolen hours with Fitzwilliam Darcy! Shock paralyzed my muscles and tongue alike while I gaped in recognition.

Uncle Gardiner's eyes glinted purposefully down at me, his smile holding secrets and relief commingled. "Well, Lizzy girl. I judge it high time you learned certain truths I have been obliged to keep from you for too long." He gestured to the house. "Shall we go inside?"

I TRAILED UNCLE GARDINER through the empty house, my pulse racing wildly. Jane had stopped at the door and just looked around the sitting room, uncomfortable with entering, but Uncle and I toured every corner. Our footsteps echoed eerily loud in these unfamiliar rooms I had only visited once with... *Him*. My skin prickled as we passed the parlor mantelpiece, phantoms of tender confidences hovering ghostlike still upon the air.

At last, Uncle Gardiner turned, features somber beneath silvering hair. "It is time you understood truths too long hidden, child." He doffed his hat and spectacles slowly. "Have you any memory of this place?"

As it happened, I had a great deal too many memories, but none that I cared to confess. I swallowed and said nothing.

"Well, that ought not to surprise me. You were probably very young when you left. You were born here."

I narrowed my eyes. "What?"

"At least, that is what I was told. I believe you went to live with the Darcys almost that very day. But this house is yours, Elizabeth. Your inheritance from the mother you never knew."

My heart seized as the world tilted dizzily. Stunned words tumbled out. "Mine? How...? Why the secrecy until now?"

Uncle held up a staying hand. "Old Mr. Darcy hoped obscuring your legacy might persuade you to build a life elsewhere by independent choice. Somewhere... far from Pemberley. But you were never intended to be dispossessed of your family legacy."

My head spun in chaos, emotions clashing hotly through my reeling senses. Uncle Gardiner pressed on firmly before erupting demands won free. "A significant trust—thirty thousand pounds, in fact—was also established for your welfare by an anonymous party. It is still managed through a London solicitor's office." He met my wide-eyed shock unflinchingly. "Mr. Darcy specifically requested that I not reveal this to you until you had either married or attained your majority. But I suppose... I believe I have waited too long. It pained me, Elizabeth, to honor the oath I made. But you are mistress here, and you may come to live here whenever you wish."

My heart was hammering in my ears. This was mine? To do with as I pleased? A home of my own? "And... this faceless benefactor..." I rasped tightly, "...might he still live?"

Uncle shook his head helplessly. "I know not, though my duties continue unchanged. But the late Mr. Darcy bound me to ensure your name and circumstances go no further while the chance remains." His weathered hand covered mine, eyes filled with regretful empathy. "I am sorry, Lizzy girl. Pemberley must remain forbidden to you, despite old ties."

The polished floor seemed to sway under my slippered feet. The offended longing that had swarmed my heart since yesterday battled with shock at such earth-shattering revelations. My breath shuddered out. "So, you are saying that I... I have a father out there somewhere, who knows of me, but refuses to let me know him?"

Uncle Gardiner's steadying hand gripped firmer though compassion yet softened his resolute features. "I am sure he did what he thought was best. As did Mr. Darcy. They prepared every provision out of deepest care. You must hold to what is right. However it grieves me also, we cannot restore what is gone."

"And... what of the others? Did neither George nor Fitzwilliam know anything about this place or my inheritance?"

He shook his head wearily. "So Mr. Darcy claimed when entrusting his ward's welfare and future to my hands instead."

Suspicion niggled at me. "Yet Fitzwilliam himself brought me here recently. He walked me through the household like he belonged here. I imagined that *he* owned it, though he refused to confess it. What aren't you telling me?"

Uncle Gardiner opened his mouth, questions in his eyes. But his indignant response was cut short by wild shouts and frantic hoofbeats outside. We both ran to the open window. My heart cracked to see Fitzwilliam fling himself off his winded horse, worry etched on every harsh line of his handsome face. He stormed toward the door like a man possessed.

Every chaotic emotion warred through my overwhelmed spirit. Fitzwilliam clearly knew more than he had confessed regarding this place. Which meant his maneuvers at shielding me from George likely hid darker motives than merely rekindling old affections safely. My gut churned, fresh hurt bleeding through anger's fragile scab. I trusted him! Believed, despite all evidence, that this man stood apart from manipulation. Oh, what a blind, naive fool!

Fury rolled off Uncle Gardiner in waves as he moved to block the entrance. "It seems opportunity knocks for long-overdue honesty! We shall drag the truth out now, whatever scheme brought this reckoning."

I braced myself as boots pounded urgently nearer. Very well! If answers must be wrenched out by bare force of will, then I would claim them no matter the devastation. Eyes blazing through hot tears, I stepped up beside my uncle. The time had come to unmask whatever betrayals had defined my life to this point.

Thirty

Darcy

I SCARCELY FELT CAESAR's laboring flanks pounding beneath me, urgency lending wings toward Farthingdale. George's thoughtlessness had shattered my numb paralysis to blistering purpose. I must intercept Elizabeth before George's disastrous letter shattered her heart all over again! Explanations could come later—first, I must shield her from fresh wounds no matter the personal cost.

The estate finally crested the rise, and my chest was near to bursting. But at my frantic knock, I received only a curious stare from the kitchen maid who said I had missed Mr. Gardiner's carriage not ten minutes earlier. She had already left for Hertfordshire! Surely, I could not be too late. When did George say he posted that letter to her? Or had he sent it by an errand boy? Perhaps she had not yet been treated to its callous words.

Onward we plunged, though poor Caesar was nearly spent. But we needn't travel with all possible speed. Surely, on this remote road, I must eventually overtake a gentle landau's ambling pace. I leaned low over Caesar's neck and asked him for a little more heart. And if he had little left to spare, I had enough for both of us. My eyes raked the winding path ahead for some evidence, some cloud of dust heralding doom or redemption ahead.

At last, the road opened into a small valley, winding benignly toward distant Lambton. And there! In the shimmering heat-haze danced the promise of a crawling coach just entering a copse of wind-break trees. My heart seized mid-beat, a cracked cry of desperate hope half-strangled behind my raw throat. It could be anyone, of course, yet my instincts shouted with certainty that it *must* be her.

I eased Caesar's headlong plunge by necessity, letting him blow a little. But what was this? The distant carriage unexpectedly swerved eastward at the crossroads onto a little-traveled sidetrack. Alarm surged anew at this ominous sign. For that road led not toward Lambton as anticipated, but directly on to... Southgate Park!

Sudden conviction struck, chilling my very marrow. Gardiner was taking Elizabeth there for a reason. Perhaps we would at last have some answers! With a savage oath, I slammed my heels to Caesar's straining flanks, launching us up the next slope. I tossed prayers to the fickle wind and rode desperately on.

I LEAPT RECKLESSLY FROM the saddle the instant Caesar's hooves hit the drive. My legs eating up the flagstones four at a time, I took the front steps still at a near run, heart ricocheting wildly about my ribs. Just within the entry, I stumbled to an abrupt halt.

There stood Elizabeth, wrapped in icy dignity behind sparks of fury promising scalding retribution. Jane Bennet hovered uncertainly beyond one shoulder. Hastily reading the atmosphere, she sketched a brief curtsy before slipping noiselessly past me to the safety of her uncle's carriage outside.

Apparently, Elizabeth had read George's letter.

I stood awkward and exposed to a blistering inspection beneath Elizabeth's crackling gaze. Half-formed greetings went shriveled and useless on my tongue. Leadened feet refused cooperation as I reluctantly advanced deeper into the lion's den I had blithely manufactured. Finally, I stopped right before the blazing goddess of wrath, and my courage failed utterly. Lamely, I executed a humiliating bow, tongue cleaving uselessly to the roof of my mouth.

"Miss Elizabeth, I do not believe I have yet had the pleasure..." I croaked hoarsely, my shamed gaze sliding sideways to her bristling escort. Furious color darkened her cheeks, making the lightning in her eyes flash brighter still. Mortified by such bungling disservice my ingrained manners had been reduced to, I could only remain frozen at attention beneath her scorching scrutiny.

For an endless tense moment, Mr. Gardiner and I faced off. At last, Elizabeth took a visible hold of her composure, drawing a long, steadying breath likely audible even back at Pemberley. Haltingly, she made formal introductions, clipped tones cutting with arctic chill. An ocean voyage would prove less daunting than casting myself upon those unwelcoming shoals.

Mutely I endured her merciless regard, contrition and yearning's tempest raging futilely unvoiced. Explanations would emerge all in due course. For now, I deserved no consideration beyond the chance to voice amends before the axe fell irrevocably and forever.

"Mr. Darcy," Mr. Gardiner greeted me. His jaw was flexing in displeasure, and well did I know why. Perhaps Elizabeth had told him of George's careless brush-off, but more likely, he perceived me to be shattering the understanding he had with his ward, merely by my presence. If my father had charged him to keep her from me... from us... well, I was forcing him to betray that oath, was I not?

I cleared my throat. Perhaps I ought to appeal to my father's memory. "Mr. Gardiner, we have met before, back when you advised my father... although, I confess the precise details escape me after so long."

Unexpectedly, he smiled, craggy features softening. "Ah yes, I thought you might forget—it was years ago, and you were still a gangly youth." His reminiscent chuckle perplexed Elizabeth somewhat. "But your father often mentioned what a serious, dutiful son he had. I see time has not changed that overmuch."

I flushed, sensing a potential advantage with this amenable guardian. "You flatter me too highly, sir. In truth, I still struggle to uphold the lessons learned from my father." My glance brushed Elizabeth's rigid profile, yearning to caress the proud cheek averted coldly from me.

With an explosive sigh, Mr. Gardiner appeared to deflate before my eyes. "Well, I suppose it was inevitable that the past and present should collide after recent events..." He eyed me heavily. "No doubt you are wondering why I did not reply to your letter seeking truths about Elizabeth's past?"

I met his gaze unflinching. "You guessed rightly, sir. Now more than ever, the need for full honesty has gained new urgency."

"As I told Elizabeth, her late mother held a clear claim to this property. And by all indications, numerous assets from wealthy lineage accompany it."

My head spun, grappling with it all. "But my family safeguarded her future through childhood—" Doubt darkened my protest. "Surely you cannot mean her true parents simply abandoned a helpless babe to the mercy of strangers? Signed away her inheritance and her future?"

His grizzled head shook sadly. "Your own honored father undertook that sacred charge, and I suspect he did so as a personal favor—hardly the act of a stranger, though he took most of the truth to his grave." Piercing eyes met mine. "And now I invite you, Sir—speak freely any questions haunting your peace regarding the past. It has been plaguing you for many years, I can see."

I stared dumbfounded, my pulse thundering. At long last, an opportunity to demand answers regarding cryptic actions blighting two households over seven shadowed years. Wild chaos careened through my brain, questions rioting into incoherence. Blindly, I grasped at scattered wits, praying scattered words might form a rational plea.

"If such care was taken securing Miss Elizabeth's future, why the veiled demand that she vanish completely from our lives?"

Mr. Gardiner regarded me somberly. "Your father commanded her removal to save others' prospects." At my baffled look, he elaborated. "Were she presented to Society, members of her true family would assuredly recognize her features. Her eyes, I was told, and her smile would proclaim her as her mother's child in an instant to anyone who would have known her. And the ensuing scandal would cast damaging aspersions upon others, their prospects ruined by her discovery."

"What do you mean she would be recognized as her mother's child? What matters that, unless..." I swallowed hard. "Surely you cannot mean she was actually Father's by-blow? For he swore emphatically otherwise on his very deathbed!"

"Of course not!" he disclaimed, clearly startled. "No, by her significant bequeathments, it is plain that Elizabeth descends from a wealthy lineage. Yet what names or faces belong to that past I was never enlightened." He offered helpless palms upward. "I have obeyed my directive to the very letter through the years, though not without remorse."

A muffled sound twisted me back sharply toward Elizabeth, just withdrawing a damp handkerchief from her face. Tenderness overcame outrage's paralysis at last. Confound this miserable estrangement! Must not compassion cry louder? I moved swiftly, hand out-stretched, offering a useless square of linen, though my heart's depths yearned instead to enfold her wholly in my arms, where she belonged.

But Mr. Gardiner's swift frown checked my impulse comfort before I could do anything so rash. And Elizabeth evaded my small stingy bid, pain carving deeper lines beside her trembling mouth. "No, indeed! You need not attend me, Sir. I am quite myself again, I assure you."

Shame burned through me as Elizabeth rejected even a handkerchief's comfort. I had no right to presume anything while she clearly saw me as someone who had cast her off yet again. But her obvious distress tortured my conscience.

I paced in agitation, painfully aware of her blistering eyes tracking my futile circuits. Facing her wary uncle, I rasped a hoarse truth learned from years of gnawing silence. "After Elizabeth was taken, George and I were anguished beyond comprehension. My brother soon found diversion elsewhere, but long after his loss dulled, I still lay awake at night for years, grappling with the injustice of it all. I harassed my father those first wretched weeks, demanding some shred of explanation."

I risked a brief sideways glance, desperate for any softening. "Time faded the wounds, however fiercely buried beneath stern obligations." My eyes crawled back to Elizabeth's, my purgatory or paradise sentence hanging on her next words alone. I stood flayed open, awaiting release or a final crushing blow.

Elizabeth fingered her handkerchief, those glorious eyes cast low as she swallowed. "These past few weeks, I thought I had recovered everything I ever lost and then some. What do you think it was? To learn that I *had* been missed and not forgotten! I felt treasured again by my dear friends, especially sweet, careless George." I winced inwardly, hearing her confess renewed longings there. Oblivious, she pressed on earnestly.

"Ridiculous, I know, but with him, I felt as if we had picked up where we left off, as if not a day had passed. And I knew that I still cared for him as much as I ever did." Her brave tone faltered mournfully. "For a glorious moment, I even felt such affection returned... until reality crashed swift and merciless later."

Desperate to shield her from escalating distress, I blurted thoughtless interruption. "Forgive my interference, but—"

She cut me off sharply, eyes blazing with outrage. "Why *did* you interfere, Fitzwilliam? Why not just inform me plainly before the damage was irreparable? Why did you have to make me fall in love with you, instead?"

She... she loved me? Despite everything? I froze under her glare. No humble gesture could salve these wounds. I broke eye contact, my throat choked on my own festering regrets. But she demanded an accounting I was bound to render despite the gouging cost.

I sucked in a ragged breath, then forced myself to meet her scorching recrimination. "You speak justly, scorning such deception. If unwise souls presumed to grasp at heaven, then indeed, a harsh payment comes due."

"You made a fool of me," she whispered as her throat trembled.

"If I have, then I am doubly so. I love you, Elizabeth, as I will no other, beyond life itself, God help me."

THIRTY-ONE

I WAVERED, ANGER AND anguish rioting wildly as Fitzwilliam's shocking words echoed through chaotic thoughts. He loved me? Truly, beyond any casual boyhood fancy or calculated ambition? My mind recoiled from such a sudden reversal.

But he would not dare! Not after knowing his father's will. Fitzwilliam Darcy was ever the one to follow the rules, bend to the demands of duty. How could he let himself love me?

Yet, what other explanation could there be for such naked remorse writ plainly across his weary features? No velvet artifice masked the hoarse cry wrenched from somewhere deep in his soul. Still, I wavered. So often had I been shaken and misled astray by vows made with deep feeling and little fortitude.

Eyes narrowed, I searched tense lines betraying Fitzwilliam Darcy's struggle, as if dissecting a stranger suddenly laid vulnerable within familiar skin. The grave boy I knew long past never bandied words lightly or pledged hollow devotion. Guarded and reserved, he still was, but there was something there I had never witnessed in our youth. Something I had begun to glimpse only this summer.

I felt Uncle Gardiner's gaze heavy on me. He was not best pleased by any of this, but bless him, he was not interrupting. I could have asked for no more forbidding champion if I had wished to send Fitzwilliam

Darcy packing off to Pemberley with his tail between his legs. Curse me, however, for that was the last thing I wanted.

Finally, I stirred, offering a small, sad smile. "Well, sir! It seems an apt time indeed for full confessions since disguises are all around. Come then, let us test this startling notion together that icy Fitzwilliam somehow toppled helpless before my feeble charms. My, what would your father say?"

He shook his head faintly. "Do not mock me, Elizabeth. You know too well I am not your equal in that regard."

I stepped closer, my head tilted deliberately to press my advantage. "What magic could transform a noble guardian to an abject slave? No! I do not believe that you, of all people, could truly claim to be conquered by a silly girl who never aimed her arrows in your direction."

Fitzwilliam shuddered visibly as I stepped closer, a hunger lighting his eyes that I had only seen there the day he rescued me at the folly, and again in the kitchen. "You most certainly did, madam. And your aim is as unerring as ever. Eliz..." He closed his eyes and swallowed. "Miss Elizabeth, please forgive me. I care nothing for eligibility or the mischances of others. I do not know whose mistake or misfortune decreed that you must leave my sphere. All I know is that I cannot lose you again." His throat bobbed, and I daresay, there was a swift sheen over his eyes as his voice broke. "Not again," he whispered.

Oh, I should hold firm! I crossed my arms and choked down a little cry of my own. Dash it all, but if my uncle had not been there, I would have flung myself into Fitzwilliam's arms and devil take the rest!

For so much of my life, I had been told that the Darcy brothers were not for me. Even before I understood what such love was as a tender girl, long before Fitzwilliam kindled my heart, I remember Father's gentle reminders that one day, I would be seeking a life and a future abroad. But I was out of arguments. So, I looked to Uncle Gardiner with all the beseeching I could pour into a single glance.

"Right, then," Uncle said, at last stirring from his watchful position across the room. "I think that is enough. Come, Lizzy."

"Wait!" Fitzwilliam cried, stepping toward me. "Please, at least permit me to investigate... to speak..."

"I think you and George have both said enough," I whispered.

"George is a fool," Fitzwilliam almost spat. "Heaven knows I love him. He is my brother, my responsibility, my blood. But had he even a shadow of a spine, he never would have let you go. Or, being committed elsewhere, he would have protected your heart from the first moment."

I laughed. "And that is what you did?"

Fitzwilliam's eyes shifted to my uncle, who was already closing in, his arm beckoning me, and he stiffened. "I wanted you to know your worth. To believe from the very core of your being that others, besides faithless George, would see you for the treasure you are. You need not depend on a childish infatuation—not when you dazzle and sparkle as you do. As you always have." His throat worked, and he closed his eyes. "But God help me, all I managed to accomplish was to lose my own heart. Forgive me, Elizabeth."

I had no words for that. I could hardly tear my eyes from the anguish in his face, but when I did, it was to plead wordlessly with my uncle. I *had* to hear the end of this!

"Lizzy, the carriage..." Uncle Gardiner urged. "We should go."

"Please!" Fitzwilliam erupted, risking a step closer with hand outstretched. "One day! Two, if you feel generous. I beg of you, let me search... find the truth. There must be a way we can protect all concerned, and yet—"

"Yet what?" I challenged softly. "Would you make a foundling, a woman with no name of her own, mistress of Pemberley?" I scoffed. "With George poised to marry into nobility, and your own prospects no less rosy?" I shook my head and crossed my arms over my chest. "Uncle is right. It would be better if I left Derbyshire this minute and never looked back. I will sell this property, if it is mine to sell, and I will go back to Hertfordshire, where I belong."

"Eliz—"

"Do not address me so informal, sir, I beg you." I cupped a hand over my mouth and let Uncle wrap an arm around my shoulders. "Take me home, Uncle."

Uncle Gardiner guided me outside to where Jane awaited. I caught her gaze through the windows of the carriage and saw the compassion shining in her eyes. I ached to unburden the secrets churning inside. But then, a dark plume caught my attention—smoke boiling from over the hills. *Pemberley!* My heart seized with panicked denial... until I swung back toward Fitzwilliam.

He was staring at his feet as he followed me out, his jaw working and his cheeks crimson with shame. But when I stopped, his head came up, and his eyes followed where I was pointing. And then I saw bleak devastation, draining all color from his face.

"The mill!"

I looked back at the plume of smoke. He was right—it was not Pemberley's house rising into flames over that hill. The smoke came from farther to the west. George Darcy, Senior's dream, his hope for a better future for his workers, now engulfed in rolling black smoke.

Fitzwilliam bolted for his lathered horse, wild to respond. But Uncle Gardiner barked and cut him short. "Your horse is done in, Darcy! Turn him in the field there and send someone to fetch him later. We shall take you by carriage, and Johnson can drive like the very devil. There is more at stake than property!"

Fitzwilliam wavered at war with himself, rage and helplessness fighting for control. But finally, he stripped his saddle off his horse and turned him loose in a pasture behind the house. An instant later, he flung himself inside to join us, hardness settling over defeated features as he took the bench beside my uncle, opposite me. My hand found Jane's, clenched tight in voiceless hope.

"How many workers?" Uncle Gardiner asked tightly.

"Sixty-seven," Fitzwilliam rasped. "And over half of them are women."

"Good God." Uncle Gardiner put his head out the carriage window. "Hurry, Johnson!"

OUR CARRIAGE CAREENED AROUND the final bend, granting Mr. Darcy at the window—and me, seated across from him—a sickening vantage directly into the hellish inferno. Pemberley Mill raged, engulfed amidst smoke and human figures scurrying ant-like whilst flames roared malicious victory.

Even as the wheels slowed, Fitzwilliam sprang free with single-minded focus, shrugging off our protests for caution and barking orders. "Where is Harris? Report!"

I could not help wandering closer, despite shouts from my uncle to stay clear. I had to know that all was well... and I had to be near Fitzwilliam. My eyes roved about the scene in awe. Where the proud mill had once stood was a blackening inferno. I could still see steel beams where the flames had gnawed ragged holes in the walls, and no doubt it was due to these that the main roof had not yet collapsed. But walls had crashed in, whole floors buckling to the flames. I think my heart stopped.

Younger workers milled about in confusion 'til the overseer elbowed through, his features shining with sweat and streaked with soot. "The whole east wing's gone already, and my men are hauling buckets from the river. But no doubt how this evil started!" He sent a venomous glare toward a sullen knot amidst the frantic crowd.

Fitzwilliam cut him off. "Later! Are all hands accounted for? What casualties thus far?"

Harris shook his head even as another section crashed inward with a fountain of sparks. "No telling yet, sir! We scrambled free as the alarm went up, but that lot are vultures to disaster, raiding supplies and making free of the place!" He jabbed an accusing finger toward the workers.

Fitzwilliam barked at the overseer. "Forget their plundering! They can have the whole bloody lot for all I care. Direct the firefighters! Ensure every soul is safe first!" A terrific crash from within sent flaming planks belching outward. I flinched, but before I could cover my eyes, Fitzwilliam had turned and shielded my face with his body as fiery shrapnel raced past. I had no idea he even knew I was there, but now I gripped his arm, unwilling to let him go.

Harris waved an arm. "Bah! Let the devils reap what's sown! I warned you they meant trouble by those racketing committees!"

Uncle Gardiner strode past me, tossing his coat and hat aside to take his place in a line of men passing buckets up from the river. "Less assigning blame, more quenching flame if you please!" Water splashed on the nearest outbuildings amidst choking smoke. "Lizzy, Jane, see to the injured while we douse this blaze!"

Fitzwilliam slid his hands up my arms and held my gaze steady. I swallowed as I looked up to his dear face—grim and frightened. I had never seen Fitzwilliam afraid of anything in my life. He swallowed and gave me a single nod, and I squeezed his hands as they slipped away from me. "He's right," he said. "Be careful, please, Elizabeth. Go!"

I could only nod and swirl away, eager for a purpose. Jane and I flew toward a cluster of wounded sprawled on the grass. A young washerwoman held her blistered hand aloft, stumbling blindly whilst tears streaked her sooty face. Jane rushed to her side. "Here, some cool water! This way, you're safe now." Jane gently urged the sobbing girl toward the stream.

But more staggering figures emerged from the swirling haze, and my hands flew swiftly to a boy's head that was gushing crimson. I ripped part of my petticoat for a bandage to try to stop the bleeding, but the larger struggle was keeping him still. "My Molly!" he kept sobbing. "Did she get out? I've got to go back!"

"The only place you are going is to the bucket brigade," I said through clenched teeth as I tied a knot around his head. "You can help save her by putting out the flames."

I knew the words were hollow, though. What was it Father always said? A mill fire is the most dangerous of all things. Kiln-dried wood construction, several floors vulnerable to collapse. It was a miracle so many had already got out safely, and that, no doubt, only because Father had used those steel beams.

I kept on, moving through the thick of injured workers and stopping up blood, cleaning wounds as I could. There was almost nothing left of my petticoat, but what did that matter when so many were burned? Gradually, the trickle of bleeding millhands and bystanders steadied to waiting ranks of less critical injuries. I straightened from binding yet another weeping mother's slashed arm when terrified screams cut through dense smoke. "He's trapped! Lord save, Joey's still inside!"

My horrified glance met Uncle Gardiner's. One distraught woman was pounding anguished fists against Fitzwilliam's broad chest. Far from being offended for his person, he was trying to comfort her, and asking where the lad was. The woman said something, and then...

And then my whole world collapsed when Fitzwilliam turned and ran into the smoking mill. *Why*, in Heaven's name? My heart shattered into ash when another section of the upper floor caved, sending embers flying. Oh, where was he? He could not have been under that section when it fell! Providence could not be so cruel as to rob me of him again!

I ran blindly for the fiery doorway. What if he was trapped? A beam collapsed on his leg, or something knocking him unconscious? But iron bands fastened around my waist, holding me back. I fought wildly against Uncle Gardiner's unyielding clasp.

"He's still inside!" Raw, anguished screams tore from my throat. "I must reach Fitzwilliam!"

Uncle's gruff voice rasped in my ear, firm as the unmoving arms holding me. "Rushing heedless to your doom helps no one!" He grunted against my frenzied struggles. "Keep hope, child! Darcy is no fool. He knows how that mill was constructed."

I slumped, quivering into Uncle's grip, the truth of his words striking home. Grotesque shadows danced as my imagination conjured Fitzwilliam's beloved form already lost, sprawled, and lifeless where boards collapsed to consume all. "Please, heaven's mercy..." Prayers mingled with Jane's muffled weeping nearby.

Each agonized moment passed with excruciating slowness as human chains passed buckets unceasing—though with a rapidly fading effect against the hellish flames. But then Harris' shout heralded three ghostly figures emerging. One was a youth, his face so black with soot that I could not guess at his age. He was dragging his leg, but others ran to help him at once.

Another was a woman—at first, I thought her unconscious, but her head rolled, and she spasmed into a cough as the man carrying her eased her onto the grass. He checked her breathing, summoned someone to tend her, and then he looked up... directly at me.

Fitzwilliam!

I screamed wild joy, wrenching free and running desperately toward that blessedly familiar, battered form. His coat was gone, his shirt so black with smoke, he could have been anyone, but it was *him*. I flung myself into Fitzwilliam's arms just as he staggered clear, my legs giving way to sink us both earthward. Pressing fiercely close, I felt him suppress racking spasms even while cradling me gently. My overflowing tears mingled joy and relief.

Smoke-reddened eyes found mine, dirty fingers tracing my cheek tenderly. "Never fear, my love." His voice was raspy and broken by coughs, but his heart beat strong against my chest.

What else was I to do? My gown was already ruined, my face already smeared with soot. What did it matter if I wrapped my arms around his neck and kissed him breathless? Fortunately, he did not seem to mind.

Thirty-Two

Darcy

R ELIEF DROWNED OUT EVEN the crackling flames as I clung to Elizabeth, uncaring of prying eyes. Her blistering kisses against my scorched lips lit my battered spirit aflame, distilling us to vibrant essence impervious now to mortal trials. I cared not who was offended, who was disadvantaged. For once, I was going to do what was right, and what was right was holding Elizabeth. For the rest of my life.

A subtle cough interrupted us. My cheeks flamed as we sprang apart, and I saw Gardiner waiting.

"Pardon…" I rasped, mortified at my wanton recklessness before her guardian.

Gardiner slowly shook his head, his sharp gaze moving between us. "Love makes great fools of wiser men before now." His eyes pierced me through. "And I'll not pretend blindness to its formidable power."

My breath caught, hesitant longing dawning. "Then… might some chance remain? Surely, there must be a way!"

He held up a hand. "I have told you all I know. But I'll not force asunder what Providence itself has so obviously brought together." His rough smile turned tender toward Elizabeth. "I suppose I could just advise the trustee that she has received an offer she is inclined to accept. What can he say?"

What could be said, indeed? Perhaps Elizabeth's removal to Hertfordshire and her coming of age with the name Bennet could prove the difference. I could only hope. For a future with Elizabeth, anything was worth a chance. But for now, we could spare little thought for ourselves.

I clung protectively to Elizabeth's hand as we peered anxiously around for any other wounded amidst the chaos. Thank Providence, no lives had been lost, though the mill was utterly destroyed. I turned my soot-blackened face upward with exhausted relief. My father's dream was turned to ash, but... well, I never wanted this bother, anyway! Perhaps now, something new could take its place.

Just then, wild shouting heralded new riders approaching at a gallop. And in the lead, of course, was George, on that ridiculously expensive former racehorse of his. He flung himself recklessly from the saddle almost before his mount fully halted—hat gone again, fair hair flying wildly. Would he ever be able to ride without losing his hat? The man could keep every haberdasher from here to London gainfully employed.

"Fitz! Thank God we spotted the flames and came straightaway!"

"Spotted them from where? I thought you were at Matlock. Impossible to come so quickly from that distance."

"Oh, well, you see, we were out hunting, and... oh, good day, Lizzy! Anyway, we were out in the southern fields you see just there, and—"

"Hunting?" I interrupted. "Rather the wrong season for grouse, do you not think?"

"It is only a euphemism, and you know that very well. Any excuse to test our horses over the highest fences. I thrashed Winston rather soundly, but you are not letting me finish. We saw the flames and... egad, were you *inside* that thing when it burned?"

"I helped a couple of people escape," I muttered, wiping my hand unconsciously on what was left of my breeches as Lord Belmont and Lord Matlock trotted up.

"What the devil were you thinking?" George grasped my shoulders with a searching look. "Are you quite well? Is anyone else trapped?"

I shook my head wearily. "The last workers are now accounted for. My overseer believes some manner of sabotage sparked these voracious flames, but the investigation must wait. I rather wonder if it was an accident."

"Accident! Like as not, it was Luddites among your workers. I say, you look a fright. Are you sure you are well? I cannot afford for you to be injured, you know."

I arched a brow. "I expect I will keep, but why this sudden concern for my welfare?"

"Well, you do not think I want to take over all that desk work you do? The very idea!" George laughed and slapped my shoulder just as Lord Matlock and Lord Belmont dismounted. They were wearing identical looks of stern appraisal at smoking wreckage surrounding millworkers still salvaging tools and wagons. Lord Winston was slower, for he was circling his mount around at the stream, inspecting the ruin of the mill.

Belmont addressed me briskly. "No need to elaborate on how this new catastrophe arose, Mr. Darcy. Evidence proclaims itself plainly before all." His incisive glance took in various small clots of workers sporting resentful scowls and folded arms. I prickled under an accusatory look, implying blame cast too swiftly toward underprivileged masses over a smoldering disaster.

Before an indignant retort took shape, however, Belmont continued neutrally. "But perhaps now is not the time. What are the injuries?
Have you summoned a doctor?"

"No, we've not had time. There are a number with burns and
lacerations from falling debris. And everyone is coughing." I glanced
around and caught Bingley's eye, for he had ridden up just on George's
heels. "I will go, Darcy!" An instant later, he was gone, his mount's
hooves churning up the earth.

Matlock grunted, eyeing the naked ironwork that once held up the
roof. "Aye, it seems that costly experiment of your father's proved its
worth. The roof held long enough for everyone to get out, at least.
Recall how I told your father they were a waste of good coin when a
stout oaken beam would serve?" He shook his head. "George Darcy,
still schooling me from beyond the grave."

Amidst shifting rubble and dazed wounded, one small figure
caught Lord Belmont's suddenly riveted gaze. I tensed as Elizabeth
dropped a self-conscious curtsy under such intense noble scrutiny,
trying vainly to shake the worst of the soot from her gown and tangled hair. Instinctively, I shifted nearer, shielding her from his prying
examination. But swift movement drew the Marquess's intense stare
from the bemused maiden onto where I stood, dusty and hollow-eyed,
my arm still wrapped about her slender form.

Belmont's ruddy skin blanched deathly white, features contorting
as shock rapidly evolved to impossible recognition. "It cannot be!"
A shaking hand passed across his eyes like one beholding a fearful
apparition. Then wonder eclipsed incredulity before overflowing eyes,
and he spoke in a broken whisper. "E... Elizabeth!"

Elizabeth merely blinked in bewilderment while I stiffened to stone
beside her. "I beg your pardon, my lord. Have we been introduced?"

Belmont straightened, some of his color returning as he jerked his lapels and shot self-conscious glances between Lord Matlock and me. "No. But... heaven help me." He set his hands on his hips and cast a look to the sky... and perhaps it was the smoke, perhaps my imagination, but I thought I detected a tear in the nobleman's eye. He blinked and swallowed and said something that sounded very like a prayer. Then, he shook his head and smiled at Elizabeth.

"My dear girl," he offered in a cracked voice, "I thought never to see your face in this lifetime."

Elizabeth was still tilting her head in confusion, but my stomach felt like I had swallowed a rock. My mouth fell open, and I could not help the instinct that compelled me to tug her a little closer. "*You?*" I murmured.

Belmont smiled weakly and removed his hat. "Indeed." He shuddered a sigh, staring at his hat. Then, with a tremulous smile, he laughed quietly and gazed fondly at Elizabeth. "I would know you anywhere, my child. George Darcy was right. You look so much like your mother."

I swallowed and glanced at all the assembled faces, every one of them registering varying levels of shock. *Belmont!* But how?

I tightened my hand in Elizabeth's, and found hers trembling as mine was. For here stood the only man besides Gardiner capable of unveiling long-buried secrets. Belmont had the power to spring Elizabeth from her cage... or lock her behind it forever, barring her from my reach.

"If I may, Darcy," he suggested, "Perhaps we may discuss this at length in a more amenable setting. I believe you have more pressing matters before you."

I came back to some semblance of awareness. "Quite right. I must see to the wounded." But then, I paused. He would not think... he could not insist that Elizabeth leave me now. For now, I could not know of whom to be more wary—Mr. Gardiner, who had only been trying to keep a promise he made to my father, or Lord Belmont... who might insist that she leave my sight forever. Stubbornly, I whirled to stare back at Belmont as I reached for Elizabeth's hand once more.

He chuckled and replaced his hat. "Is that how the matter lies, eh, Darcy?" He shook his head. "Very well. I will present myself at Pemberley this evening. I fear a number of explanations are in order. Please, finish your business here, and I will speak with you later."

Elizabeth

B ONE-WEARY AND ACHING FROM the ordeal, despite now being freshly bathed and dressed, I straightened my gown nervously as a squadron of unfamiliar nobles entered Pemberley's impressive drawing room. Lady Belmont's piercing eyes instantly found and assessed me when she posed artfully upon the divan. My courage melted swiftly under such daunting inspection. *Flee!* some instinct screamed, before Fitzwilliam's comforting clasp bolstered me upright again.

Lord Matlock's face, I remembered. Dimly, but he granted me a curt nod—not unfriendly—and a look that seemed to wonder what had become of the adolescent he had last seen. I dipped him a curtsey as he passed by me.

By order of precedence, Lord Belmont and his lady had entered the room first, and they stood somewhat apart—he staring at me in wonder, and she as if I were mud on her shoes. Fitzwilliam invited everyone to make themselves comfortable, giving Lady Belmont the preferred seat by the fire.

A handsome young man, whom Fitzwilliam whispered to my ear was Belmont's son, Lord Winston, took up post behind his father's chair and regarded me with shadowed curiosity. Lady Lucilla hovered slim and pale beside her brooding brother until George made his way to her side and led her to a seat. My heart fluttered wildly, lungs fighting my suffocating corset for air. Was that lady truly my own flesh and blood sister, by some unfathomable twist of providence?

Perhaps if I strained my imagination, I could trace a resemblance. There was a wrinkle around the edge of her mouth, perhaps etched there by many smiles... or frowns. I really could not be sure which, but the clear, direct way she was regarding me was quite obviously inherited from her father. Did I do the same? I would have to look at my glass to decide.

I peeked sideways where George hovered, an irrepressible grin suggesting he thoroughly enjoyed this drama's latest sensational twist, with himself squarely at center stage. Insufferable scamp! Small consolation that Lady Lucilla now played chief lady in that theatrical repertoire. I permitted one discreet but indelicate inner snort. They say leopards cannot change their spots, and neither could George.

Another small astonishment made me gasp, for I had not realized until that moment that I did not envy her in the least. She was perfectly welcome to winsome George Darcy. I, for one, had altered materially in seven years, for I preferred steady, sincere Fitzwilliam. Fitzwilliam Darcy, who could steal my breath with a mere glance.

I stood facing Lord Belmont, sensing Jane and Mr. Bingley hovering just behind me. Across the room, Uncle Gardiner observed silently. Squaring my shoulders, I turned my attention fully to the imposing nobleman studying me intently.

Lord Belmont chuckled when I met his eye and refused to flinch. "You are very like her," he murmured.

I stirred, glancing uncomfortably toward Lady Belmont. She would surely object to my presence if I were indeed the by-blow of her husband's former mistress! But I could not alter my parentage, so I lifted my chin, grateful for Fitzwilliam's steady presence beside me.

"Please, my lord, say plainly what you came here to reveal," I invited.

Lord Belmont grew solemn, gesturing to where Fitzwilliam stood staunchly at my side. "I see you are not without some... imprudent attachments of your own. You believe, then, in the power of love?" he asked gravely.

I narrowed my eyes in confusion. "I do not take your meaning, sir."

Lord Belmont exchanged a speaking look with his wife. She lowered her gaze and gave a slight nod. Drawing breath as if steeling himself, he continued.

"I married hastily in my youth—rashly, some would say, for she was far beneath my station. Her family were mere gentleman farmers. Mine threatened disinheritance." He gave a rueful laugh. "But I loved her beyond reason or denial, and she loved me not for my station but for myself. That proves a heady wine for any young man to intoxicate himself on." He gave a short chuckle, his eyes flicking to Fitzwilliam first and then George. They both stiffened, but then Lord Belmont fixed his gaze again on me.

"But Society is not so forgiving. Nor is a family whose heads have been swelled by too much consequence." He shook his head. "Fortune made me the sole heir to carry on the title, helping reconcile them eventually. If it was to be she, by law and by God, to serve that office, then they had to accept her." He paused to touch his eye, fighting a wistful smile. "I thought no man could be happier than I. I had everything. Fortune, circumstances, and the sort of wife every man dreams of calling his own. Beautiful, merry, clever... she made my days joyful and carefree. She was called Elizabeth Walton."

Thirty-Three

Elizabeth

I BLINKED RAPIDLY, STRUGGLING to connect astonishing revelations to myself. My lips parted, but no words emerged.

"Aye, you have her look about you!" Belmont's throat worked, and he bit his lip to draw a sharp breath. "Indeed, I was a blessed man. But my joy dimmed when Elizabeth lost our son at birth. For two days, she struggled to bring him forth, and when she was delivered of him, the doctors said he had died only hours before. She nearly perished, too. I had the best surgeon in the country to attend her, and a host of midwives, but it was not enough to save..." His voice broke, and he fought to still his quivering mouth. "They said she could never bear children at all after that."

He passed a hand over his eyes at painful memories. "As my father's sole heir, an earl at my birth and a marquess in waiting, siring a child was paramount. But Lizzy loved me—foolishly and unreasonably so. And for my good, not her own, she begged me to put her away quietly, rather than have society scorn her barrenness and decry me as the last of my line."

I blinked rapidly, struggling to reconcile such astonishing disclosures. Surely, he could not mean...?

Lord Belmont grimaced. "I refused at first. We even plotted to pass off an orphan babe as our own. But word of the unsuccessful birth and her supposed 'delicate health' had already reached my family. No one would credit a 'miracle' child after that."

He searched my face intently. "For Lizzy's sake, and after holding her in my arms as she wept and pleaded with me to release her, I reluctantly announced her 'passing of fever' shortly after. In truth, I secured her the estate called South Gate, where she could live peacefully, far away from me, in Berkshire, and the scornful eyes of the *ton*. We wrote to each other often, but I did not see her dear face again... for five years."

I swayed slightly. The room blurred as revelations took shape. South Gate was mine... which meant...

Lord Belmont regarded me sorrowfully. "After a decent mourning, I made the more prudent match my family dictated. But it broke my soul to leave my heart buried here with my Lizzy."

I trembled, scarce able to draw breath. The impossible had found voice at last. As I struggled for a coherent response, a polite cough interrupted us. We both turned to behold Lady Belmont regarding us steadily through inscrutable eyes.

Lord Belmont managed a tremulous smile, extending his hand to Lady Belmont. "I confess, I was not kind to you early on, still outraged at losing my heart's delight." Their eyes met, his softening fondly. "But you slowly taught this stubborn fool to love again, my dear." His face clouded. "Yet not before I committed a grave wrong I shall ever regret."

I hesitated, but he seemed to be inviting me to make some comment, so I did. "And that was?" I asked softly.

He regarded his son and daughter somberly. "Though the Almighty granted me the children I craved, resentment long festered that fate denied their rightful mother. In a rage of injustice, I rode to Derbyshire, seeking solace from the only one who shared my loss."

Lady Belmont patted his hand comfortingly as he continued hoarsely. "I never dreamed my Lizzy could again conceive. We were wrong. When she perished birthing our daughter, my world shattered anew under the weight of bitter remorse." He passed a shaking hand over his eyes. "Her death lies on my head alone."

I stared, horrified comprehension taking shape as I read dawning distress in Fitzwilliam's taut features. I was the living proof of Lord Belmont's criminal betrayal!

"Then you admit to bigamy!" I burst out. "Your children were born before your lawful wife was deceased. By law, my very birth condemns and disinherits your legitimate heirs!"

Lord Winston and Lady Lucilla exchanged stricken looks while Fitzwilliam grasped my hand tightly.

Lord Belmont attempted a conciliatory smile. "You speak justly. I could not openly claim you without condemning my legitimate heirs. So, I entrusted you to the Darcys' care, never dreaming what risks loomed ahead."

"Why?" Fitzwilliam broke in. "Why my father?"

"That is a fair question." Belmont met his wife's sympathetic eyes before continuing heavily. "Lady Anne showed my Lizzy much kindness. She learned of Lizzy's residence in the area, believing her a widow, and visited her often. And Elizabeth had nothing but glowing things to say about the goodness of Mr. George Darcy, as well as their son. They would invite her to picnics with other neighbors, and their young son—you, Darcy—delighted her, touching her heart for the dear little son she had lost. But before I had the pleasure of meeting Lady Anne, she perished much in the same way as my Lizzy."

He tried to smile at me but failed. "I must say, I thought at first to take you with me and try to raise you as my own 'ward.' I can name but a few noblemen who do not have them. Everyone winks at the practice, claiming the gentleman must have done so out of the goodness of his heart. Poppycock! Everyone knows the truth. I would have claimed you in such a way, merely so I could keep some part of my dear Lizzy with me. But the risk of discovery was too much, and so, I sent a message to Mr. Darcy, who was similarly grieving the loss of his own wife."

Here, he hesitated, shamefaced. "I believed you would have everything I could never give you. A loving home, the company of a family, a place in the world where you would be cherished. But when Mr. Darcy wrote, warning that your marked resemblance to your mother invited unwelcome notice, I compelled your removal, to guard my children from scandal." He released a trembling sigh. "It was my fault that you were forced from the only home you ever knew to live with strangers."

I felt Fitzwilliam's hand slide reassuringly into mine. Through blurred tears, I took in Lady Lucilla and Lord Winston regarding me with dawning awareness. Strange pity kindled in Winston's eyes, but Lucilla's glistened with unshed tears. Joy and anguish warred wildly. The roots anchoring my existence now lay exposed, yet still beyond my grasp.

I rasped hoarsely, "Then I suppose I must vanish fully to shield them."

"Never!" Fitzwilliam's earnest objection warmed me even amidst despair. "I'll not lose you again!"

Lord Belmont weighed us solemnly. "Perhaps some solution may be crafted. Few are left alive who recall Elizabeth Walton. Even her family line has died out." He chewed a trembling lower lip. "Would that I could have given you the dignity of your own name! Even calling you a Walton..."

I stiffened, rallying wavering pride. "I already have a name. I am Elizabeth Bennet. And I have a family." I met Jane's tender eyes before facing Belmont resolutely. "All I ask is leave to live the life chance allotted me."

He smiled gently through sheening eyes. "Then Elizabeth Bennet, you are. Daughter of Longbourn in Hertfordshire, and I will fight to the death any man who denies it. Spoken like Lizzy's own brave daughter. I pray fate grants the happiness long denied you, child."

Darcy

I STOOD UNEASILY BEFORE Lord Belmont, scarcely crediting that I was seeking permission to wed his natural daughter just as George had petitioned previously for Lady Lucilla's hand. At least Mr. Gardiner stood solidly as the joint arbiter of Elizabeth's future, rather than some formidable marchioness.

Several hours had passed since the astonishing disclosures. The meal I ordered afterward was a simple affair, as no one seemed inclined to depart swiftly, given turbulent emotions still simmering. Now, the ladies had withdrawn, leaving the gentlemen to discuss practical ramifications in greater privacy.

I was still reeling over revelations explaining Elizabeth's obscure past. Lord Belmont's sentimental sensibilities clearly influenced accepting George's unlikely courtship of Lady Lucilla from a sense of honor—he felt unable to deny us after my family shielded his terrible secret. And His Lordship had seen perhaps enough of himself in my sentimental and spontaneous brother that, against all reason, he seemed to like him.

And now, it was my turn to try to earn his regard. Steeling myself, I addressed my own hopes to make Elizabeth mine. I cleared my throat and made my formal request.

Lord Belmont raised an eyebrow. "You believe yourself ready to take a wife, do you, Darcy?"

"I do," I answered firmly. "Recent events have shown me that Elizabeth is foremost in my heart. I love her and wish to build a life together."

Both men regarded me somberly. Lord Belmont glanced at Mr. Gardiner—and I wondered how often that pleasant tradesman could say that nobility had deferred to him. It was Gardiner who challenged gravely, "Are you certain this is more than youthful fancy rekindled?"

I drew a bracing breath, willing my voice to steady. "Since our recent reacquaintance, I have come to know and admire the woman Elizabeth has grown into. My feelings have only deepened beyond boyhood's memory. I love and desire her with my whole heart, undeterred by past mysteries or perilous prospects ahead."

"Love is all very well," Mr. Gardiner replied. "And blessed is the man who finds it. But have you considered the practicalities? As far as the world knows, she is the ward of a modest country gentleman. Hardly the sort of woman the master of Pemberley ought to pledge himself to."

I flicked a gaze at the marquess. "Other men have married without regard to station. I cannot see why I ought to be any different, as my heart is settled on one woman alone."

Lord Belmont finally smiled. "Well said, lad." He turned to Mr. Gardiner. "Surely, we can have no objections now? The man's clearly besotted."

But Mr. Gardiner looked dubious. "Even so, what of the risk she may still be recognized and your prospects endangered?"

Belmont steepled his fingers and pursed his lips, then raised his eyebrows to me in question. Indeed, what was I going to do about that?

I shifted slightly, fighting the urge to tug at my cravat. "I spend almost no time in London. And when I do, my circles are limited. Besides, it has been twenty years, after all. Memories fade."

"Some do," Belmont agreed. "And others are more stubborn, particularly in London circles."

"I care nothing for London circles, and neither ought you. Does there exist public proof that Elizabeth is the daughter of your first wife? Beyond mere resemblance, anyone wishing to accuse you of siring a child with a woman who was supposed to be deceased would also have to furnish evidence. I have looked for years and learned almost nothing, and I believe Mr. Gardiner knows as much as any soul alive... apart from this trustee."

Belmont's lips turned faintly. "And you will find no one more loyal or secretive."

"Just so," I agreed. "So, anyone who did try to cause trouble would find himself at a dead end. Should awkward queries arise, we need only confirm her longstanding identity as Elizabeth Bennet, 'cousin' to the Hertfordshire family who raised her. Any marked resemblance to your late wife could plausibly be passed off as mere coincidence. She is a daughter of Longbourn, as far as anyone need know."

Lord Belmont stared at me pensively before chuckling. "Well then, it seems you had better make haste to Hertfordshire, young man. For Mr. Bennet's consent, you must petition, not mine!"

My stomach swooped with mingled hope and trepidation. My fate now turned upon a country gentleman unknown whose singular blessing alone could secure my heart's desire.

"There you have it," Gardiner chuckled. "Proof positive that the man is smitten. He just turned positively green at having to ask yet another man for his blessing!"

Lord Belmont laughed loudly and slapped my shoulder. "Too right, Gardiner! Well then, Darcy? Shall we send you off to plead your case?"

"**D**O NOT FRET OVER Bennet's consent," Gardiner reassured me in a low voice as we walked together down the corridor toward the drawing room. "He may heckle and poke fun purely for his own amusement, but he hasn't half the stubbornness required to withstand Elizabeth's formidable will, let alone you both united."

I breathed a deep sigh of relief. "Thank you, Gardiner." I paused my steps and waited for him to stop and turn toward me. "And thank you, most sincerely, for guarding Elizabeth's welfare all these years. My father's faith in you was well placed."

Gardiner smiled and clasped my hand. "'Twas an honor seeing her thrive. She has been one of the joys of my life these seven years." His glance turned thoughtful. "But I ought to return soon to my own bride with these glad tidings. I hate to break up the happy party, but propriety suggests I not abandon Elizabeth and Jane here unchaperoned tonight."

Just then, the footman opened the door to the drawing-room, and I beheld my aunt, Lady Matlock, conversing vivaciously with the ladies, holding court as though she reigned mistress at Pemberley. She must have received word from my uncle that there was intrigue afoot and arrived post haste to sample it for herself. She looked up at my entry and inclined her head graciously before turning to address Lady Belmont once more.

I chuckled at the spectacle and assured Gardiner, "I believe Lady Matlock would object rather strongly to their removal at this juncture. She will ensure the ladies' every comfort and see that all propriety is observed. Travel arrangements to Hertfordshire can be finalized on the morrow."

"Very good, then. I will take my leave." Gardiner rested a hand on my shoulder as he smiled, watching Elizabeth across the room. "Your father would be proud of you, Mr. Darcy."

I warmed a little. "That is one of my fondest hopes."

Gardiner nodded with a light chuckle, then he moved to the door and let a footman help him with his coat.

My gaze sought out Elizabeth. She was nestled happily on the divan between Jane and Lady Lucilla as she regaled them with tales of boyhood antics with George. Animated and lively as ever, she was describing youthful adventures like sling-shooting grapes into George's mouth for stakes while he hovered nearby, denying every word. "George here always fancied himself a skilled marksman," she said. "But it was I who always claimed the forfeit."

"Not so, Lizzy!" George cried. "I swear, Lucilla, she is making half of this up."

Lady Lucilla looked up at my brother and shook her head, a faint arch to her brow that... egad, it looked just like one of Elizabeth's expressions. "I fear, my love, that I must believe Elizabeth and not you in this case."

"Indeed, it is the truth," Elizabeth vowed. Miss Bennet giggled as she continued. "Why, we used to wager on whether he could catch grapes in his mouth from across the lawn. I had quite a mean slingshot arm, if I do say so myself!"

"Only because you would cheat and move closer halfway through!" George protested with an exaggerated grimace.

"How dare you!" Elizabeth gasped in mock indignation between spurts of laughter. "You know very well I won fair and square at least three-quarters of the time. Isn't that right, Fitzwilliam? Oh! But if you want the juiciest tales, they are not about George, but that one, right there. The 'stoic' older brother."

At this, the merry trio of ladies dissolved into fresh peals of laughter behind their palms. As I moved to join them with a bemused smile, Elizabeth turned aside to whisper theatrically to her avid listeners. This sent Lady Lucilla and even gentle Jane into renewed gales of giggles they tried vainly to muffle.

Intrigued, I arched a teasing brow. "Come now, what amusing tales are being told at my expense?"

Elizabeth glanced up, eyes dancing impishly. "Ah, but that must remain a mystery until we can speak privately."

"Hardly fair, do you not think? At least George has a chance to defend himself if he knows what accusations are leveled at him."

Elizabeth smiled and reached up to let me take her hand. "The only 'accusation' I point at you, if you wish to call it that, is being far too irresistible for your own good. But I am afraid the details of that must await a more... discreet setting."

I raised a brow. "I am all anticipation, my love."

Just then, a footman entered behind me and beckoned my attention. I turned and took him aside so he could ask in a low voice, "Pardon me, Mr. Darcy. A gentleman has just arrived asking to see you."

"Indeed? Of course." It was probably an investigator, come to speak to me about the mill fire. They certainly wasted no time. Curious, I followed him into the hall.

There stood a travel-stained man, his hat already removed. He had turned away and was divesting himself of a greatcoat to reveal... a red military uniform beneath. My heart stuttered. "Richard?"

Colonel Fitzwilliam turned, a broad smile breaking over his face. "Darcy, old man! I finally tracked down the family."

"Richard!" I rushed to embrace him, thoughts churning in confusion. "When your letters stopped, we were worried sick about you. How ever did you arrive with no forewarning?" Then I noted his arm bound in a sling. "Good God, you are injured!"

"Took a bullet then was struck by fever," Richard explained matter-of-factly. "Packed me off home once I could stand. Came straight to Derbyshire without even stopping in London."

"You must be exhausted. Why would you not repair to your bed? Good heavens, you are hardly standing."

He grimaced ruefully. "Found the house abandoned at Matlock, so I made haste here instead, when they told me the family had decamped to Pemberley." His sharp eyes assessed me. "But enough of me—you look wearied, Cousin. What momentous events have I stumbled into?"

Laughing, I waved him toward the drawing room. "More than can be summarized briefly."

The moment we entered the drawing room, George yelped in surprise and bounded over to pump Richard's uninjured hand. "Bully, Cousin! You are arrived just in time for all the fun!"

Richard laughed and disentangled himself from George so he could kiss his mother on the cheek and greet his father. Hasty reunions followed with my stunned aunt and uncle before Richard recollected himself.

Turning back to the rest of the room, he removed his hat apologetically. "Forgive my lapse, ladies. I have not been introduced to everyone. I fear my manners..." His words died as he froze, arrested by one figure slowly rising to her feet. "Impossible!" he rasped, his jaw hanging open. "Can it be little Lizzy Smith?"

I moved swiftly to offer Elizabeth my arm. Facing my astonished cousin squarely, I announced, "I believe you are confused, Richard. May I present Miss Elizabeth Bennet of Longbourn in Hertfordshire, and my bride-to-be. Miss Bennet, this is my cousin, Colonel Fitzwilliam."

Richard stared hard, emotions visibly warring across his battered features. At long last, he loosed a crack of laughter and surged forward to press Elizabeth's hand warmly. "Well, bless me for a muddle-head! Forgive an old campaigner his exhausted eyes playing tricks from too long staring at foreign landscapes. Nothing but joy to you both!"

Elizabeth rested a hand on Richard's chest and stood on her toes to kiss his cheek. "I have missed you, too, Richard."

EPILOGUE

Elizabeth
Pemberley, 1814

I ADJUSTED THE HEAVY picnic basket on my arm, one hand instinctively supporting my cumbersome belly as I surveyed the happy chaos unfolding on Pemberley's back lawns. Our third annual summer picnic had drawn a merry party to enjoy idyllic weather and congenial company. I smiled to myself, drinking in joyful sights and sounds all around.

"Come now, Lizzy, you must rest yourself!" Aunt Gardiner hastened over, whisking away the overladen hamper. "No lifting anything heavy for my girl now in your condition."

I chuckled, patting my rounded stomach ruefully. "If only it were as simple to divest myself of other burdens of preparation!" My eyes tracked to where Mama held court amidst our noble guests, voice carrying effusively on the balmy air. "I may have escaped the most strenuous tasks, but preventing embarrassment remains a Herculean labor when Mama is determined on display!"

Aunt Gardiner followed my grimace toward where Mama was loudly expounding on my elevated connections to Lady Belmont.

That poor woman! "Ah well, what is one more inflated tale added to her repertoire? Although perhaps the gentlemen may benefit from a bit of distraction." She nodded meaningfully to where Mr. Darcy stood, politely trapped, manfully enduring a recitation of various Bennet family ailments.

With a smothered laugh, I squeezed Aunt's capable hand and moved briskly to intervene. "If you will play hostess, I will attempt a rescue mission." I wound my way between various clusters of family and friends toward poor Mr. Darcy's pained smile. But suddenly, Jane and Mr. Bingley were at my side, providing timely salvation.

"Lizzy! I was just telling Mr. Darcy he must come see what the little ones are up to," Jane gestured fondly to where her toddling son frolicked on a blanket, golden curls glinting in the sunlight. Ellie, who was George and Lady Lucilla's little daughter, was tugging on his toes and making him giggle. Beside them was my own firstborn, Bennet, sitting up and gravely regarding his cousins. What a delight it had given us to introduce them all, now that they were old enough to notice one another!

"Yes, Fitzwilliam will not want to miss this. How typically solemn Bennet is! Perhaps Edward or Ellie will teach him to laugh."

"He will learn that from his mother, I've no doubt." Giving me a speaking look, she added gently, "Just as his father did. I am looking forward to hearing him when he sees them playing, so we must call him over. Oh, but here comes Mama! Perhaps first, Mr. Darcy simply must come with me to admire how you have arranged the refreshments so beautifully." Smoothly, she stepped away and guided a grateful Fitzwilliam out of Mama's orbit toward safer pastures.

I bestowed a loving smile after her. Dearest Jane! Of all life's joys these past years, watching her blossom into bliss as Mrs. Bingley outshone almost every other blessing. I gazed contentedly around our idyllic gathering, warmed by the growing connections between loved ones present. Even Mama's effusions sparked more amusement than embarrassment when offset by the delight of seeing those I cherished most surrounded by happiness.

My tender musings were interrupted by a firm touch at my elbow. I turned to behold Fitzwilliam's smiling features beside me, his deep brown eyes alight with irrepressible joy. He had never looked *that* happy when we were children. I think I will claim the credit for it. Wordlessly, he drew me close, one large hand cradling the infant in my belly as his lips grazed my forehead. Secure in that tender clasp, I sighed contentedly. Moments like this never lost their blissful magic!

All too soon, duty reasserted its claim as various friends moved expectantly to speak to one another about this or that. Our little reunion in the summer was always too brief. I wandered slowly amidst colorful groups dotting the lawn like gay flower clusters. The sight of Miss Westing and little James and Anne Rose about stirred wistful yearnings for our own second child, soon to join in such play. Beaming benevolently over all stood Lord and Lady Belmont, conversing amicably with Uncle Gardiner and Aunt Madeline. Now, who would have ever conceived *that* as possible?

I made my way toward them when Uncle beckoned me eagerly over. "Lizzy, my dear! I was just telling Lord Belmont how the new mill construction progresses apace. He fears Darcy is overly ambitious with expanded worker housing, but I predict it shall prove just the innovative model ahead of its time."

Lord Belmont harrumphed good-naturedly. "You may crow if proven right, Gardiner. I call it a financial sinkhole, but young idealists will have their follies." His sharp eyes belied gruff words as they rested approvingly on my husband, deep in discussion with Lord Matlock as he crossed the lawn toward us.

"And how fares my future god-daughter today? And her mother?" Uncle smiled fondly, glancing at my swelling belly. I assured him of steady, vigorous health, then turned as Fitzwilliam and Lord Matlock strode up.

"I say, Darcy," Matlock was asking, "what new precautions are underway to prevent another conflagration at this elaborate new mill?" He gestured to the serenely flowing river wending through the prospering valley below. "Not merely relying on that stream should catastrophe strike, I hope? Those Luddites are not like to let you save the next one."

Fitzwilliam touched my elbow lightly. "It was not Luddites who torched the last one, Uncle. A simple accident with a lantern is all. The investigation was quite conclusive. And to answer your question, I have implemented numerous measures safeguarding against fire since the tragedy that claimed the last one. We now better understand how to balance productive innovation and judicious oversight." His glance met Lord Belmont's approvingly. "And I continue working with Parliament on wider labor regulations promoting both compassion and commerce."

I leaned contentedly into his sturdy frame, soul overflowing with gratitude at the man Providence gifted to share loving guardianship. And not merely over Pemberley's fair prospects, but a new generation poised to inherit a legacy of compassionate and just stewardship. Sweet anticipation swelled my maternal heart, contemplating little lives that were soon to unfold.

I SANK GRATEFULLY ONTO the bed's soft expanse, weary to my bones after our estate had spilled over with guests. My hands cradled the heavy mound of our unborn child as I slowly swung my legs up and reclined against the pillows with a soft moan. Moments later, strong hands gently cupped my belly's weight from behind, lifting the burden off my ribs in tender support.

"Allow me, my love." Fitzwilliam's whisper mingled relief and desire as he tucked me securely against him, my frame bolstered by sturdy strength.

I sighed blissfully, cradled in cherished arms. "Mmm, you take such good care of me."

His lips grazed my ear, tone turning playful. "I can think of other ways to please you even better."

Laughing, I swatted in mock reproach. "Roguish man! Is a woman's condition never safe from her husband's advances?"

Humor laced his voice. "Never, if she be my captivating wife." He settled me comfortably within his loose embrace before adding casually. "Speaking of irresistible allure, will you not satisfy a question plaguing me these three long years?"

Lulled by his soothing nearness, I murmured drowsily, "Mm, what puzzle besets you so persistently, husband mine?"

His breath was hot against my neck as he dropped scattered kisses, then murmured into my ear. "I have never forgotten how you set Lady Lucilla and Mrs. Bingley giggling over some naughty secret regarding myself on our whirlwind betrothal day." His fingers spidered warningly.

I grunted, pillowing my face in the feather down and closing my eyes. "What a pity that still torments you. You cannot believe I would tell you now, after eluding you for three years, can you?"

"On the contrary, I cannot believe you would *not* tell me. Nor have I abandoned extracting an answer, whatever the cost!"

Without warning, his hand had slipped down my knee to cup my foot and tickle it mercilessly. I jerked, breathless laughter escaping as those talented fingers found tender soles. "Please, sir, the babe!" I gasped weakly. "You may get more than just a confession out of me if you do not desist!"

He relented, all contrition instantly. "Forgive me, love, I forgot myself."

I rolled onto my back, eyes glinting upward roguishly. "Oh, very well. Prepare yourself for something terribly shocking."

"Come now, out with it! What exactly did you witness to send polite ladies into such transports of laughter?"

I bit my lip, holding back renewed mirth at the memory. "Oh, very well, if you must know... Do you recall the season I turned eight, when Nurse Barstow finally permitted me more liberty to play unattended?"

Fitzwilliam groaned theatrically. "How could I forget? You quite ran us both ragged, trailing after every boyish escapade once off your leading strings."

I swatted his chest lightly. "You make me sound such a hoyden! I merely grew tired of feminine arts and longed for adventure." I shifted to better meet his amused gaze. "One particular afternoon, I slipped away to seek your company. I searched for you both for hours... or perhaps at least a quarter of an hour, for I am sure it seemed much longer than it was. I looked in the stables, the yew maze, the woods to the north of the house. Finally, I discovered you at last down by the lake."

Fitzwilliam tensed, features arrested. "The lake? But Father expressly forbade..."

"Exactly!" I grinned impishly. "What better lure to a restless girl eager to emulate her dashing playmates?" My eyes danced at his rueful head shake. "Imagine my delight discovering both Darcy lads, already frolicking in the water, escaped from their stuffy schoolrooms."

"Your capacity for mischief outpaced George, even then," Fitzwilliam marveled. "Pray continue. I burn with curiosity now."

I traced idle circles on his chest. "I found a little hollow screened by bushes to watch you both unseen. Such freedom you enjoyed away from adult censure! Of course, I had to linger, not only so I might have some blackmail against you if I ever needed it, but because you were so very interesting to watch. I was never permitted to swim, you know, and it was fascinating."

Wry understanding lit Fitzwilliam's hooded eyes. "And did we provide an entertaining spectacle for one small defiant spy?"

I nodded, barely smothering fresh giggles. "Indeed! George kept diving below the surface, slick as an otter. While you..." Here, I lost my battle, collapsing into mirth once more. "...you paraded about bare as the day you were born, oblivious to observing eyes!"

Fitzwilliam groaned aloud as comprehension dawned. "And *that* was what you confessed to Lady Lucilla? No wonder I was deemed a figure of fun that day!"

I dabbed tears of laughter from my eyes. "Forgive me, but you were no doubt fearful of ruining your breeches, and I was but an impulsive girl with too much curiosity!"

He tugged me close with a mock growl. "That curiosity always spelt trouble! Well, Madam, our own young imps shall be guarded better than we were, I vow it!" I willingly melted into his kiss, all shadowed past buried now in present joy too full for words.

"And how many of those do you expect, Mr. Darcy?"

"As many or as few as my love decrees." He drew me into his arms, and I felt his chest heave, then soften as he mellowed beneath my cheek. "I care not for such things as heirs and family dignity and names. I am content, only having you."

I smiled as my eyes drifted closed. "*Only you,*" he had said.

And that was enough. What need had I of loftier acclaim or wealthier names when bounteous blessings daily enriched my world? No title nor treasure could replace the sacred trust I had found in this home, with this man.

Indeed, I had a family. Three of them, as it turned out. And every expectation of felicity in wholesome soil, as joy's quiet seeds unfolded before my eyes each day, binding each to all in love without end.

KEEP READING FOR A sneak preview of The Measure of Love!

FROM ALIX

T HANK YOU FOR INDULGING with me and spending a little time with Darcy and Elizabeth.

I hope you've had a delightful escape to Pemberley. I'd love it if you would share this family with your friends so they can experience a love to last for the ages. As with all my books, I have enabled lending to make it easier to share. If you leave a review for Mr. Darcy and the Girl Next Door on Amazon, Goodreads, Book Bub, or your own blog, I would love to read it! Email me the link at **Author@AlixJames.com.**

Would you like to read more of Darcy and Elizabeth's romance? I have one to tug your heartstrings and make you believe in the power of love! Reserve your copy of The Measure of Love now! and fall in love with Darcy and Elizabeth all over again!

And if you're hungry for more, including a free ebook of satisfying short tales, stay up to date on upcoming releases and sales by joining my newsletter: https://dashboard.mailerlite.com/forms/249660/7 3866370936211000/share

PREVIEW: THE MEASURE OF LOVE

One

DARCY POUNDED HIS FIST furiously on the weathered door, rattling the nearby shutters. This ramshackle "rooming house" in London's East End was no better than a brothel—exactly the vile sort of place Wickham would frequent. Desperation had chased Darcy to the city's filthy underbelly once before, but the viper had slipped his grasp. Not this time, though. The street lad who had taken Darcy's coin said that George Wickham was back, and he was not alone.

The door creaked open, and a pinch-faced woman in garish rouge peered out. "You, sir! State your business or be off!"

"I am here to see George Wickham." Darcy shouldered past her into the dim, smoky foyer, hand drifting toward the pistol holstered under his coat "Where is he?"

The Madame crossed her arms indignantly "Don't know any George. Now, see here, I run a reputable—"

"Silence." Darcy grasped her arm, pressing several coins into her palm and curling her trembling fingers over them. "Wickham is upstairs, is he not?"

The Madame licked her thin lips, eyeing the money. After a moment, she jerked her head at the stair. Darcy took them three at a time, his boots pounding up the rickety steps, his breath coming in heated puffs. The Madame's shrill cries echoed after him, demanding he behave "civil-like", but he heeded her not. His fury would not be contained a moment longer.

Wickham was here. After weeks of relentless searching, justice would be served. No more innocent lives ruined by that blackguard's selfish whims. Darcy ground his teeth, an image of his dear sister Georgiana's anguished face flashing before his eyes. *Never again*.

He took the last few steps in a single leap, the old wood groaning under his weight. This was the room—he could hear a feminine voice whimpering softly from within. Gathering himself, he kicked the door with an echoing crack. The lock splintered apart, opening on a dingy room wreathed in opium smoke and illuminated by one rusted oil lamp.

Wickham lounged on the bed like a sultan, shock melting into his trademark wolfish grin. But it was the girl who drew Darcy's blazing eyes—for all her buxom déshabillé, hers was the face of a child—a child with tumbling golden curls who couldn't be more than fifteen years old. She tugged the thin chemise up around her shoulders, her mouth opened in protest... but it was Darcy's voice that thundered first.

"Wickham!" he roared.

With nostrils flared like an enraged bull, Darcy seized the front of Wickham's shirt and slammed him against the wall hard enough to make the mirror rattle dangerously. Out of the corner of his eye, he glimpsed the girl fleeing from the room but paid her no further mind. His full fury was reserved for the wretch before him, now twisting and writhing in his tight grasp.

"Well, well, if it isn't Mr. High and Mighty," Wickham choked out. "Wasn't expecting to see you in a den of iniquity. Don't tell me you've finally come to your senses and sampled the wares for—"

Darcy cut him off with a swift right hook to Wickham's sharp jaw, sending him sprawling to the warped floor boards. "That was for Georgiana, you bastard," he spat. As quick as a jungle cat, he pounced, hauling Wickham up once more by the shirtfront. "Now, you dog, you are going to pay for what you've done!"

Wickham coughed wetly as Darcy threw him against the stained mattress. Yet as he swiped blood from his mouth, his cracked lips twisted in a jeering grin.

"Come now, what's all this about? Can't blame a fellow for enjoying a willing girl's company. Why, your delightful sister was the one who threw herself into my arms. Begged me to run away with her, she did! How is dear Georgiana?"

With a roar of outrage, Darcy seized Wickham by the shirtfront once more, hauling him up and slamming him into the headboard so hard his teeth clacked together.

"You will not speak her name!" he thundered, cocking his fist back again with murder in his eyes.

Wickham held up his hands, still grinning his infuriating, insolent grin even as twin trails of blood leaked from his flared nostrils. "Very well, very well. But tell me, Darcy, how ever do you propose I 'pay' for my indiscretion, as you call it? Will you take a cheque? For I dare say the entertainment was well worth more than you'd get from flogging a dead horse." His grin turned positively vulpine. "Why, I imagine your dear sister still misses my affections!"

Darcy trembled with rage as he gripped Wickham by the shirtfront, his fist raised and ready to explode against that foul, sneering face once more. How easy it would be to beat this blackguard within an inch of his life, to feel the satisfying crunch of bone and flesh yielding to his revenge. Blood for blood.

With Herculean effort, Darcy regained a shred of control. He was no street ruffian, and Wickham hardly worth dirtying his hands over further. Breathing hard through flared nostrils, Darcy released his foe and stepped back. Wickham collapsed against the mattress, face swelling grotesquely from Darcy's fury. "I have better plans for you."

Wickham spit crimson through his ruined grin. "What's this? The high and mighty Darcy gone squeamish at the sight of blood? You ought to have sent your attack dog cousin if you didn't have the stomach to see this through. Fitzwilliam would have happily finished the job."

Curling his lip in disgust, Darcy replied in a deadly soft tone, "Be grateful Colonel Fitzwilliam is not here. For your brutality against innocents, he would tear you limb from limb without hesitation." He flexed his aching, blood-stained knuckles. "Fortunately for you, some semblance of reason still governs my actions. But test that fraying thread further at your own peril."

Wickham leered up at Darcy through swollen lips. "Come now, old boy, no need for this unpleasantness. Why not relax and sample the wares? I've a tasty little tart just downstairs, ripe for the picking. Pretty as a picture, with fire in her blood—just how you nobles like them. Still innocent in all the ways that matter, too."

He licked the blood from his teeth, eyes fever-bright. "How about it, Darcy? Care to take her off my hands and school her in the ways of men?"

Revulsion churned Darcy's stomach. He hauled Wickham up by the throat, shoving him brutally against the stained wall. "Have you no shred of decency or conscience left? She is but a child! Ruining innocents for sport—you disgust me."

Wickham just chuckled. "Innocent? That one was born wild. Why, Miss Lydia is a gentlewoman in name only. She makes most London whores look saintly."

At this casual besmirching of yet another young lady's reputation, Darcy slammed Wickham back again, arm pressing viciously across his windpipe. "I'll see you rot."

Wickham just leered, undaunted. "Oh, I hardly spoiled anything. But sweet Georgiana, now there was a tender lamb ripe for the plucking. So softly yielding, so deliciously willing to be taught and shown and taken..."

With a savage roar, Darcy seized Wickham about the neck and began raining blow after brutal blow upon his fiendish, grinning face. In the distance, he was dimly aware of violent shouts and pounding footsteps on the stairs over the roaring in his ears, but all his world had narrowed to crushing the life out of the blackguard who had hurt Georgiana.

They grappled violently, crashing into the furniture and shattering some sort of bottle. Darcy deftly avoided a knife-handed strike at his throat but missed the knee rocketing upwards into his groin. He staggered, and Wickham slammed into him full force. They tumbled out of the shattered doorway, teetering together on the landing's edge with flailing arms.

Wickham managed to grab the splintered railing, steadying himself. But Darcy was already overbalanced—he felt nothing but sick terror as the stairs rushed up to meet him. His head cracked against the wooden floorboards, and pain exploded through his back like a gunshot. Still he tumbled limply down, every edge and nail of the crude staircase gashed his flesh until all went black.

Far off, a familiar voice cried out. "Good God... Darcy!" Strong hands rolled him onto his back. Darcy struggled toward consciousness, and pain—blinding pain—returned in nauseating darkness. Colonel Fitzwilliam's familiar face hovered above him, creased in horror. "Darcy! Can you hear me?"

He tried to stand, but there was... nothing. No response or sensation where his legs should have been. Fighting panic, he gasped, "My legs... oh God, I cannot feel my legs!"

E LIZABETH PACED THE WORN carpet of Longbourn's sitting room, twisting a handkerchief between anxious fingers. The family had gathered here each evening for the past fortnight—waiting, praying, as her father searched London's seedy underbelly for their lost Lydia. Thus far, his letters have been told of naught but failure. Yet when the creak of carriage wheels echoed outside in the twilight, Elizabeth's heart seized in her chest. Father had returned, and his journey ended. She steeled herself against a surge of hope as Jane gripped her wrist, eyes round with shared trepidation.

They hurried to the entrance hall as Mr. Bennet entered, travel-stained hat in hand. One look at his haggard face, the grim set of his jaw, and Elizabeth's fragile hope guttered out. The news would not be good. They had not found Lydia.

At this confirmation of her deepest fears, Mrs. Bennet collapsed into the same hysterics that had fueled her since that express came from Colonel Forster. "Ruined... my poor girls are ruined!" she wailed, dampening her handkerchief with tears. "And my sweet Lydia gone who knows where with what sort of man?"

Mary crossed her arms, rage smoldering beneath her sullen expression. "What does it matter whether she comes home at this point?

Papa not finding her changes nothing. The loss of reputation in a sister is a stain upon us all."

"Oh, how could you, Mary?" Kitty wailed.

"Yes, yes, how could you, Mary?" Papa asked tiredly. "You ought to rejoice, at least, that I did *not* find her with the constable or bring her home in a box. Jane, have some tea sent to my study." He braced his hand on the door leading out of the drawing room, hesitating slightly as his eyes found Elizabeth and Jane. Then he quit the room.

Kitty clung to Mama, weeping and hiccuping. "It's all so h—horrid! I cannot endure it. I wish I had gone to Brighton too! I could have stopped her... or at least gone so that we might be together—"

"Oh, such a state I am in. Oh, where is Hill?" Mama demanded. "My salts, I need my salts!"

Jane rolled her eyes to Elizabeth as Mama's lamentations rose to near ear-splitting volumes. "We should speak with Papa," Jane urged softly.

Elizabeth nodded. Their father's drooping shoulders and faded eyes terrified her like nothing ever had. With a fortifying breath, she followed Jane to the study. Pausing at the door, Elizabeth steeled herself, then knocked.

There was no answer for a moment, but at Elizabeth's second knock, they heard, "You may as well come in and hear the worst of it." Elizabeth spared Jane a glance. Then, biting her lip, she pushed the door open.

Mr. Bennet raised his head from weary hands, his eyes bloodshot and posture stooped. "Lizzy.. Jane." He attempted and failed at an encouraging smile for his eldest daughters. "I am relieved to see your compassionate faces, at least amidst the turmoil out there. Please sit, though I fear I have little to offer besides empty hands."

Elizabeth took the chair opposite her father as Jane perched beside her. The silver scattering his temples seemed so much more pronounced after even a fortnight away. Guilt and regret lined his face as deeply as grief.

He ran a trembling hand down his jaw. "Forgive me, girls—I've failed you all..."

"No, Papa." Elizabeth reached across the desk to grasp her father's other hand. "We must hope. Tell us, what did you learn in London?"

With a shuddering sigh, Mr. Bennet related the scant crumbs of intelligence gathered. Tracking the carriage bearing Lydia and this Mr. Wickham she had met in Brighton through several coaching inns... Hiring Gardiner's private investigator to navigate London's less savory districts without success... Long days pounding grimy streets and haunted nights plagued by visions of his youngest daughter's peril and ruin...

Jane's eyes shone with tears as he haltingly relayed it all. Even Elizabeth harbored little hope left untainted by dread after learning how thoroughly this man had disappeared into the urban labyrinth with her sister.

"...I confess my imagination torments me, supplying endless possibilities for why a scoundrel like Forster claims Wickham to be would run off with a gentleman's fifteen-year-old daughter," Mr. Bennet eventually finished in a bleak voice. "Would that I had been a better father..."

Elizabeth squeezed his hand. "The fault lies with the man's wicked intentions... and Lydia's own recklessness. We must not abandon hope."

"Had I but put something by for you all! Then my most deserving daughters need not be without all hope of a respectable future!" He dropped his head into his hands, his fists tugging at the tufts of hair above his ears.

"Papa!" Elizabeth cried. "There must be something to be done. You said Uncle hired a private investigator. Surely, there is hope! Why..." she tugged her lower lip to the side of her teeth. "No one could hide Lydia for long. She is too loud."

Her papa snorted, shaking his head. "Aye, and what I would give to hear her carrying on about her bonnet just now. Leave me, girls. Let me soak in my shame alone—I surely deserve it."

Elizabeth sighed as she nodded. "Hill ought to have your tea ready soon, and then you must rest, Papa. Surely, we will have some word tomorrow."

Yet despite her steadfast words, sick fear slithered in Elizabeth's heart. What horrors could Lydia be facing now at this strange man's mercy?

Two

FIRE LANCED THROUGH DARCY's body, dragging him cruelly back to wakefulness. He suppressed a pained groan as the ornate ceiling of his London townhome swam into focus over him. Panicked memories filtered back—Wickham's sneering face... a desperate struggle... plunging down the stairs... then sickening blackness.

Low voices filtered through, muffled by the pounding ache in Darcy's skull. He struggled to focus on the hushed exchange between a grim-faced stranger and his cousin Richard hovering behind.

"...spinal damage may be catastrophic... too early to determine full severity..."

Anxiety prickled sharply as Darcy stirred.

"What... what has happened?" He rasped weakly.

The colonel grasped Darcy's hand. "Thank God you're awake. Lie still—there, breathe easily."

Darcy's throat went dry as he struggled to order swirling memories. Why could he not will his legs to move?

Sensing Darcy's rising panic, the doctor leaned over him. "We have kept you sedated for two days. You suffered spinal damage in the fall, Mr. Darcy."

"Why can I not feel my legs?" he barked.

The doctor traded a significant glance with Richard. Darcy stared at his cousin, but Richard shook his head and covered his mouth with his hand. Then he turned away, leaving the doctor to answer.

"There has been a great deal of damage, Mr. Darcy. We... we cannot yet determine if... if you shall walk again."

"Cannot determine?" Darcy erupted hoarsely. "Blast it, when can I move my legs? I've matters to attend. Are you a doctor or not?"

The doctor held up a placating hand. "Please try to calm yourself, Mr. Darcy. It is still very early. The swelling may yet—"

"Calm myself and wait helplessly abed? When will you be able to answer me?" Darcy thundered.

"Now, surely, Mr. Darcy, you must know that these things take time."

"My back cannot be broken. It cannot be! I can..." He grunted, trying to sit up, but was only able to crunch his stomach muscles, and that, not without pain.

"I cannot say for sure, Mr. Darcy, but I am not entirely without hope for—"

He tried forcing himself upright, face purpling, but found his chest fettered and bound against such efforts. "I'll have no platitudes or false hope! Summon more doctors, if you must, until one gives me honesty!"

"See here, Darcy, be reasonable!" Richard grasped his shoulders as Darcy struggled. "Dr. James is already the third physician we have brought in."

"And what did the others say?"

Richard dropped his eyes.

"Blast and damn you. They inspect me while I am knocked unconscious with laudanum and are shocked when I do not respond? Find one who can repair my legs!"

Richard clasped the hand Darcy was waving around and anchored it to the bed. "Now see here, raving like a lunatic will not aid your recovery."

Chest heaving, Darcy's head collapsed against the pillows as his wrecked body betrayed his swirling, impotent fury. As enraged denial slowly spiraled into panic, the doctor tried urging more laudanum on him to dull the pain.

"Pain, what pain? That is precisely the problem, is it not? I cannot feel anything!"

"Sir, your head... the shock of it all—"

Darcy swept out a quaking hand, sending the glass vial flying. "Get out!"

The doctor sighed regretfully. "As you wish But I must insist you take the draught for your recovery if you refuse to rest."

He hesitated before withdrawing, but Darcy speared him with a molten glare. "I said get out. Now!"

Only when they were alone did Colonel Fitzwilliam cautiously approach the bedside chair. "The doctor only means to help ease your torment, Darcy."

Darcy turned his face away, shame burning his cheeks at this helpless, invalid state laid bare even to his cousin. As panic's cold talons sank deeper, his breath came in ragged gasps. "Richard... you must help me. I cannot bear this! I cannot be... Tell that doctor he is a fool. I shall walk!"

He grasped Richard's sleeve with fervent desperation, all traces of his customary stoic strength vanished. "Help me... in God's name, find someone who can make me whole again!"

Pity shone brightly in the Colonel's eyes as he grasped Darcy's trembling hand. "Here, now... peace. You must rest and gather your strength."

He gently pressed the discarded vial of laudanum back into Darcy's palm, closing his fingers over it. Darcy eyed him with a scalding glare, then sloshed the bitter liquid down his throat.

"Let this draught soothe your mind so your body may heal. I will do everything under heaven, cousin. And one or two things under hell, if I must."

"PERHAPS TODAY WILL FINALLY bring word from Lydia," Elizabeth mused as her slippers whispered through the quiet garden. Dapples of afternoon sunlight shifted over the path where she walked arm in arm with Jane, both their faces etched with worry.

"Or Uncle's investigator will have new information after pounding London's streets another day," Jane murmured back. "I know the chances seem slimmer each day, but we must keep faith."

Elizabeth sighed uneasily, eyes following a butterfly flitting among the roses. "I cannot bear imagining where that thoughtless girl is now. You do not suppose that Mr. Wickham might have abandoned her, do you? Anything might have... wait, do you hear hoofbeats?"

Both sisters turned sharply as the unmistakable thunder of a galloping horse echoed from beyond the garden hedge. Exchanging an anxious glance, they gathered their skirts and hastened through the rustic gate onto the lawn. An unfamiliar rider drew rein just before them, his horse lathered and heaving breathlessly.

"Excuse me, ladies!" The rider pulled off his cap, wiping sweat from his brow with a grubby hanckerchief "I've an express letter for a Mr. Bennet!"

Hope and foreboding warred in Elizabeth's breast as she turned to the house. "I shall fetch him at once!"

Jane led the rider round while Elizabeth rushed inside, gathering her startled sisters. Soon, Mr. Bennet stood scanning the mysterious letter, brow furrowed. His daughters crowded anxiously behind him, breaths bated for whatever revelation lay inside.

The rider touched his cap "I'll be off then, sir."

Mr. Bennet looked up bemusedly from the unfolded pages. "Oh yes... of course, your payment."

"Already rendered, sir." With that, the rider wheeled his mount, galloping down the drive as Mr. Bennet's outstretched payment faltered.

"Well, Papa? Oh, what does it say?" Elizabeth pressed tremulously.

Mr. Bennet turned the pages over once more before his shoulders slumped. "Thank God." He exhaled something unintelligible, then refolded the letter and handed it to Elizabeth, and went inside without another word.

Kitty craned her neck to see while Mary strained impatiently beside her. Jane nodded, and, hands trembling, Elizabeth unfolded the missive. She drew a sharp breath as her eyes scanned the first lines.

"It... it says here that Lydia is safe." She clutched Jane's hand, joyful tears pricking both sisters' eyes at this first glimmer of hope.

Elizabeth read on haltingly, "The letter writer, a Colonel Fitzwilliam, says he... no, his cousin... how very strange, they almost share a name. He discovered her still in the company of... of Mr. Wickham." Shocked gasps met this revelation. Kitty's hands flew to her mouth while Mary pursed her lips disapprovingly.

Collecting herself, Elizabeth continued, "...she is now returning home in this gentleman's carriage, with a maid sent to keep her company and the colonel riding alongside to act as her escort."

"Thank the Lord!" breathed Jane

"A colonel!" Kitty pressed her hand to her chest in a near-swoon. "Do you suppose he is handsome?"

Haltingly, Elizabeth finished, "It says here... she is expected on the morrow."

"Tomorrow!" Kitty trilled. "Oh, but what shall she tell us? Perhaps they were secretly married this whole while!"

Mary cut her off. "Foolish girl! If Colonel Whoever-he-is went through such efforts, likely there is shame yet to be unveiled." She shook her head ominously. "Mark my words."

But Elizabeth was too suffused with glad relief to heed Mary's cynicism just now. She squeezed Jane's hands, both sisters' eyes shining with gratitude. Against all hope, their dear, wayward Lydia was returning home.

—— *ele* ——

S UNLIGHT FILTERING THROUGH THE window stirred Darcy to wakefulness. For one merciful moment, as the chirping of sparrows filled his ears, he forgot. Then, full memory crashed down with all its bleak despair.

He was still numb below the waist. Even the slight shift of his head ignited fresh waves of agony from the stitches crossing his scalp. Darcy explored them with tentative fingers, then hesitantly slid a hand under the blankets. He focused every fiber of his being on willing his toes to move, tears pricking fiercely as only lifeless numbness answered.

There was a quiet knock, and then his valet, Giles, entered. "Thank the Lord you are awake at last, sir. Can I fetch you anything?"

"I am not hungry."

"Of course, sir. I beg your pardon, but I ought to..." Giles cleared his throat and dipped his head toward Darcy's bed.

Confused, Darcy searched the man's carefully schooled features. Then, with dawning horror, it struck him. Mortified heat flooded Darcy's cheeks.

"I... my person... I fear I cannot..." he stammered haltingly, desperation choking his strained voice.

Giles flushed but nodded in understanding. "Of course, sir. Allow me to assist you."

Mute with shame, Darcy stared blindly out the window as his faithful valet's gentle hands tended to his most private needs. He was now fully at the mercy of his traitorous body and the kindness of others! Like a helpless babe... or a cripple. Was this to be Darcy's life now under others' care?

The ignominy threatened to crush what fleeting dignity remained until Giles finished. Darcy rasped into the laden silence, "Where is Colonel Fitzwilliam?"

Giles tidied discarded linens, his gaze averted. "He set out before dawn, sir, escorting the young miss back to her family."

"Who?" Darcy's brow furrowed. "What young lady?"

"The girl found with Mr. Wickham. You rescued her, I believe?"

"I... I cannot recall her face," Darcy admitted after a frustrated pause. His memories of those frenzied moments were but shards of visceral panic and pain.

Giles nodded. "Well, sir, I am happy to see you returned to us, against all odds, by God's grace. Shall I fetch some tea? A book, perhaps?"

"No! Leave me be."

Giles thinned his lips and dipped his head. "As you wish, sir."

Once alone, Darcy indulged in a torrent of frustrated tears. Even victory over Wickham tasted as bitter ashes while he lay imprisoned in useless limbs. And he hardly spared a thought for the nameless damsel now making her happy return to her family under Fitzwilliam's protective wing.

A NERVOUS KIND OF busyness filled the drawing room where all Bennet sisters waited in tense silence. Though breakfast was long past, each daughter wore her finest dress as if expecting fashionable morning callers. Not that they had been troubled by *that* sort of business lately. No one was calling, save Charlotte Lucas, and no one was likely to receive them, either.

While the daughters of Longbourn waited in the drawing room, Mrs. Bennet, however, had not yet left her bedchamber, claiming she felt faint and dizzy every time she thought of stirring. She would not feel well again until her dear Lydia was back under her roof, and until then, she would nurse her nerves in the quiet of her room.

Every stray whinny from the barnyard or clatter of wheels from the farm wagon set their hearts pounding anew... until the clock crept past eleven and restlessness replaced fraught anticipation.

"It is very fine of this Colonel What's-his-name to return Lydia, I grant." Kitty smoothed her skirts for the dozenth time. "But the least he could do is be punctual about it!"

"Hush now, be grateful if they arrive at all." Jane laid a calming hand on Elizabeth's, where she clenched her handkerchief into a tense knot with her skirts. "The roads are still muddy, and surely..."

Jane's gentle chidings broke off as an unfamiliar carriage swept grandly up the drive, framed by a liveried rider.

"La! So, that is a colonel's carriage!" exclaimed wide-eyed Kitty. "It is positively enormous!"

"Kitty, the letter said the carriage belonged to the colonel's cousin, a Mr. Darcy," Elizabeth reminded her. Not that Kitty was listening.

"Why, it has gilded trim and scarlet wool upholstery! Oh look, is that Lydia?"

Elizabeth pressed herself against the glass, wondering what sort of shattered shell remained of her fifteen-year-old sister. Would she be frightened? Ashamed? Repentant? Bruised and misused?

All gazes fixed eagerly as a familiar giggling figure stepped down, assisted by the stone-faced maid. Even at a distance, Lydia looked thrilled, casting admiring glances back at the elegant equipage and saying something to the maid behind her.

Turning back to the house, Lydia paused only to adjust her jaunty bonnet before sailing toward the front door, chin raised as though returning from a grand tour rather than narrowly escaping ruination.

Jane and Elizabeth traded doubting glances. "Well! At least she appears unharmed," murmured Elizabeth with more optimism than confidence.

RESERVE YOUR COPY OF ***The Measure of Love*** now!

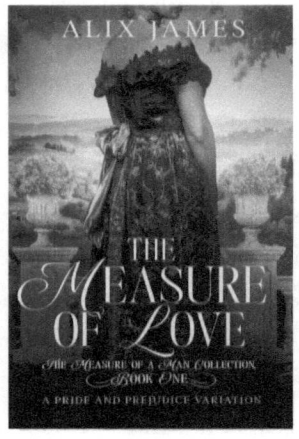

ALSO BY ALIX JAMES

A Good Memory is Unpardonable

Along for the Ride

Elizabeth Bennet: Frolic & Romance Box Set

––––––––––––––

The Short and Sassy Series:

Unintended

Spirited Away

Indisposed

Love and Other Machines

Elizabeth Bennet: Short and Sassy Compilation

––––––––––––––

The Mr. Darcy Series:

Mr. Darcy Steals a Kiss

Mr. Darcy and the Governess

Mr. Darcy and the Girl Next Door

––––––––––––––

The Measure of a Man Series:

The Measure of Love

The Measure of Trust

The Measure of Honor

––––––––––––––

Christmas With Darcy and Elizabeth

How to Get Caught Under the Mistletoe: A Lady's Guide

––––––––––––––

North and South Variations

Nowhere but North

Northern Rain

No Such Thing as Luck

John and Margaret: Coming Home Collection

––––––––––––––

Anthologies
Rational Creatures
Falling for Mr Thornton

Spanish Translations
Rumores e Imprudencias
Vacaciones en Londres
Nefasto
Un Compromiso Accidental
Reina del Invierno
Una Mente Noble
Cuando el Sol se Duerm
A lo largo del Camino
Reina del Invierno
Una Mente Noble
El señor Darcy se roba un beso

Italian Translations
Una Vacanza a Londra

About Alix James

Short and satisfying romance for busy readers.

Alix James is an alternate pen name for best-selling Regency author Nicole Clarkston.

Always on the go as a wife, mom, and small business owner, she rarely has time to read a whole novel. She loves coffee with the sunrise and being outdoors. When she does get free time, she likes to read, camp, dream up romantic adventures, and tries to avoid housework.

Each Alix James story is a clean Regency Variation of Darcy and Elizabeth's romance.

Visit her website and sign up for her newsletter at AlixJames.com